She's Not There

Marla Madison

She's Not There

Copyright © 2011 by Marla Madison

Published by Marla Madison.

Copyright 2011 Marla Madison

Cover art by Aric Zabel.

Edited by Red Pen Proofreading and Editing

ISBN 13: 978-1-4681-9595-8
ISBN 10: 1-4681-9595-6

This novel in no way attempts to duplicate the police procedures or actual police departments in the cities of Milwaukee, Brookfield, Oconomowoc, Pewaukee and Waukesha. Any discrepancies in procedure, locations, or fact, may be attributed to the author's creativity.

Acknowledgments

I would like to thank the members of my writer's group for taking this journey with me and encouraging me to keep writing even when I believed an outcome would be impossible; their support and instruction have been invaluable. Donna Glaser, Helen Block, Marjorie Doering, April Solberg, Gail Francis, Darren Kirby, and the dearly departed Bob Stokes you've each helped me in your own individual way.

Thanks to Terry Lee, my significant other, and my dear pets, Skygge and Poncho, for staying away when I was in the middle of an important chapter and encouraging me when I wasn't.

She's Not There

No one told me about her, the way she lied.
Well, no one told me about her, how many people cried.
But it's too late to say you're sorry.
How would I know, why should I care?
Please, don't bother tryin' to find her,
she's not there.

Ooh, nobody told me about her. What could I do?
Well, no one told me about her though they all knew.
But it's too late to say you're sorry.
How would I know, why should I care?
Please, don't bother tryin' to find her,
she's not there.

Well, let me tell you 'bout the way she looks,
the way she acts and the color of her hair.
Her voice was soft and cool,
her eyes were clear and bright but she's no there.
But it's too late to say you're sorry.
How would I know, why should I care?
Please, don't bother tryin' to find her,
she's not there.

Well, let me tell you 'bout the way she looks,
the way she acted, the color of her hair.
Her voice was soft and cool,
her eyes were clear and bright, but she's not there.

Words and music by Rod Argent
(c) 1965 Marquis Songs USA BMI (Marquis Music LTD PRS)

Prologue

A black pickup raced along a narrow road that twisted sharply left, crossing a bridge over a deep ravine. The river below marked the division between adjoining counties. Lit by the oncoming headlights, four pine crosses stood out in the ground fog shrouding the opposite riverbank. Faded to weather-beaten gray, they served as a reminder of young lives foolishly lost.

Years back, four varsity football players from a nearby high school were killed when the car they rode in left the road at an impossibly high speed in a mad attempt to cross the narrow river without traveling the bridge. The vehicle didn't make it over the river. Airborne, the car wedged into the opposite bank, leaving no survivors. It was rumored that the same car successfully completed the daredevil crossing many times before the deadly impact.

Imagining the impact of his vehicle against the riverbank, the driver of the pickup pressed hard on the accelerator as the truck approached the bridge. After tonight there would be five crosses on the riverbank. It was unlikely anyone would cover the fifth with sentimental memorabilia.

The driver's last thoughts—and he was certain in the split second before the truck sailed over the river they would be his last—were not of his life flashing before him. Instead, gratitude for a life ended.

1

Lisa Rayburn had hardly been able to focus on her class. She and Tyler didn't get together often, but when they did, the magic she found in his arms kept her smiling for days. Knowing she'd be with him soon, her senses tingled as she stuffed the leftover handouts into her briefcase. She'd had one eye on the clock since she'd walked into the room.

The annual Autumn Leaves event for women offered classes on everything from money management to how to handle a divorce. For the third year running, Lisa Rayburn's class on *How To Prevent Domestic Abuse* was well received by her audience. The class, one of many things Lisa did in an effort to get her message out to women, warned women not to stay in an abusive relationship. Better yet, avoid beginning one. The early signs weren't difficult to spot. The hard part came in walking away.

Lisa looked up to see a young woman standing in front of her. A brown dress covered her thin body to the ankles. She held a manila file-folder against her chest as if afraid someone would snatch it from her.

In a voice barely above a whisper, she said, "My name is Jennifer Hansen. I'm gathering statistics for my thesis on abused women. I need to talk to you."

Lisa motioned her to the student desks. The girl appeared upset, frightened even, her pale hands tightly clenching the folder. Once seated, Jennifer handed Lisa a sheet of paper. "I wanted you to see this."

Lisa scanned the page, her gaze stopping on a line highlighted in fluorescent yellow. It revealed a dramatic rise in the percentage of abused women who'd gone missing in Milwaukee and its neighboring counties.

The line practically levitated toward her from the paper—the number far too high to be a statistical aberration. If accurate, what could explain it? A predator—targeting abused women? There had to be another explanation.

She kept staring at the number. Lisa whispered, "Abused women were the topic of my dissertation too."

"I know. I read it. I thought you'd know what I should do." Jennifer's honey-brown eyes looked to Lisa for guidance. "What's happening to them?"

Lisa reviewed the testing method for accuracy. Everything appeared to be in order. "There has to be a mistake somewhere. I'd recommend you recount your data and run the numbers again."

When she looked up, the girl had vanished from the room as silently as she'd arrived. Lisa squirmed in her seat. She'd dressed in anticipation of meeting Tyler. The new, yellow lace lingerie she wore under her sedate, gray pantsuit wasn't meant for sitting in plastic classroom chairs. What she'd just learned had her heart racing but no longer with anticipatory lust. Jennifer Hansen had just dumped the matter into Lisa's hands.

Pewaukee Lake
10:00 p.m.

A Dodge Magnum purred into a dark parking lot, its lowered chassis and tinted windows giving it a hearse-like appearance. A few yards downhill, Pewaukee Lake shimmered in the rays from the moon.

Across the parking lot, Jamie Denison eased out of her sleek, red sports car, trying not to disturb a painful broken rib. She moved toward the door of the Sombrero Club, a popular bar and restaurant on the southwestern shore of Pewaukee Lake. Circled with expensive homes, it was the largest lake in Waukesha County. The few remaining businesses clung to the edges of the small town of Pewaukee, located about twenty miles west of Milwaukee.

Jamie entered a large, noisy room with a country rock band playing behind a crowded dance floor. Squeezing between a couple seated at the bar, Jamie ordered a glass of wine. While she sipped at the tart, yet fruity liquid, she watched the couples on the dance floor, remembering a time when she would have rejected every dance offer before she managed to entice the most attractive man in the place to her side.

The lights went down as the raspy-voiced lead singer began a slow, mournful version of "House of the Rising Sun," a song she loved, but its soulful sounds stoked her unease. Part of her wanted to bolt.

Her thoughts were interrupted by the sensation of her stomach growling; maybe that nagging feeling in the pit of her stomach had been hunger. She'd skipped supper to feel trim in her smallest jeans.

When a waitress passed near the bar hefting a huge tray piled with orders of quesadillas, burritos and nacho chips, the scent of the spicy food convinced Jamie she wanted to eat. She walked into the adjoining restaurant, and after placing a takeout order, took a seat in the waiting area.

Through a set of glass doors opening to a deck surrounding the building, she saw a sliver of moon sending a beam of light down to the lake, breaking into tiny, sparkling crescents dancing on its surface. Lured by the beauty of the scene, Jamie stepped out onto the deck. She felt the unseasonably, warm night air caress her skin like a lover's touch. Wineglass in hand, she lowered herself into one of the Adirondack chairs facing the water. A couple sitting on the far side of the deck held hands and talked softly. A few young children, bored with the dining process, ran back and forth, giggling.

Jamie didn't notice the man approaching her until he stood in front of her chair. In a warm, intimate voice, he asked, "Do you mind if I join you?"

She motioned to the chair beside her.

"You looked deep in thought. Problems?"

When she didn't reply, he added, "I'm a good listener."

At three the next morning, long after closing, a lone busboy rolled a squeaky cart out onto the deck. He picked up empty glassware and trash, giving no thought to the two unopened containers of food he tossed into the plastic bag lining his cart.

Or to the red sports car sitting deserted in the dark parking lot.

2

As a volunteer counselor on Monday afternoons, Lisa Rayburn had a schedule typically full, downtime a rare occurrence. She stared at the clock, wondering why her 5:00 appointment hadn't arrived. During the five weeks she'd been seeing Jamie Denison at the Oconomowoc Women's Center, she'd never known her to be late. She'd liked Jamie, a lovely young woman unsure whether to stay in a marriage no longer fulfilling.

Filled with a plethora of emotions, her mind wandered. She hadn't had an opportunity to talk to the director of the center about the statistics on the missing women. And Tyler's face, with its wide smile and rakish features, kept intruding in her thoughts. Their night together had been wondrously passionate. But over coffee the next morning, he'd broken the news he'd gotten engaged, finishing with, "I'm sorry. But we can still get together sometimes."

Lisa had wanted to throw something at him. She wondered what the fiancé would say if she knew about her. Lisa had never expected their relationship to be exclusive, but the engagement had taken her by surprise. One of these days she'd have to do something about the cycle of self-destruction she tolerated in her relationships.

At 5:30 she picked up the phone and dialed Jamie's cell number. When she got no answer, she tried calling her work number—Jamie hadn't been in. Worried, Lisa's last resort was her home phone.

A male voice picked up. "Jamie? Jamie?"

Now she had a problem; confidentiality rules prevented her from revealing Jamie Denison as a client. "I'm sorry. I must have dialed the wrong number."

Something had to be wrong if Jamie wasn't at work and her husband, assuming that was who'd answered the phone, sounded that worried.

Lisa gathered her things and checked out at the front desk before heading to her car for the short trip home.

The next morning Lisa rolled over in bed, intending to sleep in. Her first client wasn't scheduled to come in until eleven, giving her the luxury of a morning at home. A part-time insomniac, Lisa treasured nights she got a full seven or eight hours sleep. This morning sleep eluded her. Maybe it had something to do with the phone call she'd gotten when she came in the night before. It had been after ten because she had group therapy in her office on Monday nights. Tyler's words kept playing back in her brain.

"Hey. I didn't like the way we left things. You okay?"

Tired, she hadn't felt like hashing over the abrupt demise of their affair, and dating a man fifteen years her junior had to be considered an affair, not a serious relationship. "It's late. I really don't want to talk about it."

"I never wanted to hurt you."

"Did I say I'm hurt?" She heard him exhale.

"We agreed to keep things casual."

Lisa broke the connection.

There'd been nothing remotely stable about their relationship. Exciting, yes. Predictable, no. She had to put him out of her mind. His pathetic attempt to smooth things over angered her. No wonder she hadn't slept well.

She saw Phanny, her mixed-breed dog, sitting patiently next to the bed, her dark eyes hopeful. She looked at the pet fondly, reached over and stroked her silky head. Lisa couldn't imagine life without her.

Last autumn, on a day much like today, Lisa had stopped to sit on a bench during one of her walks along the lake. She'd been nervous when a black dog appeared in front of her out of nowhere. But the animal had simply sat and stared at her sadly. After a minute it came closer and leaned against her leg.

Concerned about the animal, she'd taken time out of her schedule to drop it off at the county animal shelter. A day later, Lisa bought a crate, dog bed, food, and a leash. By the end of the next day, the dog, which Lisa's daughter Paige named Phantom because of her shiny black coat, became a happy resident in Lisa's home. Her name quickly evolved to Phanny and she became Lisa's best friend.

Through the window, she saw pink rays of sun seeping out from behind a low stretch of steel-blue clouds, promising a pleasant morning. She had time to walk into town with Phanny and pick up a cup of steamy, hazelnut coffee.

When she arrived back home an hour later, Lisa showered, dressed for the office, and settled in at her desk to answer calls and go over her schedule. A message from Amanda Hawkins, director of the Women's Center, had been tagged as urgent.

Amanda picked up her phone on the first ring. "Lisa, have you seen yesterday's paper?"

"No, why?"

"It's in a small column in the 'surrounding counties' section of the Journal. A client has gone missing. Jamie Denison."

Lisa's nerves coiled. "Are you aware she didn't show up for her appointment yesterday?"

"Yes. Donna said you filed a Missed Appointment notice."

Lisa leaned back in her chair, attempting calm as a sense of foreboding overcame her. "Jamie's always been reliable. When she didn't show up, I tried her cell, but she didn't pick up. She wasn't at her job, either. When I tried her home phone, someone answered and asked if I was Jamie. I couldn't say who I was, of course, and apologized for dialing a wrong number. I've been worried about her."

"I wasn't sure if you knew, and I wanted you to hear it from me in case you hadn't."

"I appreciate that, Amanda. Did the article say what happened?"

"No. It was only a small piece. It did say her car hasn't been found, so I would imagine they think she left of her own volition."

"Hopefully, Jamie just needed to get away by herself to do some serious thinking. On another subject, someone informed me there's been a dramatic increase in the number of abused women who've gone missing. The numbers were based on figures accumulated by the women's centers."

Lisa heard a sharp intake of breath on the other end of the line. They made an appointment to talk and Lisa hung up the phone, noticing the clouds she'd seen dispersing earlier had regrouped, taking over the sky. A chill traveled through her as the two events, the missing women and Jamie's disappearance, merged in her mind like a bad omen.

3

A coworker advised Jeff Denison to hire an attorney. A disturbing suggestion, but Jeff knew without being told if it turned out his wife's disappearance was not of her own design, he would be the prime suspect. But this wasn't about him. Where the hell was Jamie?

He'd left the police station in the morning with no more knowledge of what had happened to her than when he arrived. And he didn't have to be a detective himself to see what they were thinking—she'd left him.

He arrived back at their townhouse at noon to meet Jamie's parents. They'd been in constant touch since Saturday morning when he'd gotten home after being in Appleton for three days and found his wife gone.

Sitting at a table with an untouched plate of sandwiches in its center, Jeff and Jamie's parents faced each other's panic.

Jamie's mother wiped her eyes. "Are they even looking for her?"

Jeff had already laid out every word of his meeting with the Brookfield Police Department. He felt his patience with them dwindling. It killed him to be sitting here doing nothing but talking about it. "Yes, of course they are. There's a statewide notice out for her car, and they're questioning all her friends. I imagine they'll talk to you soon."

He couldn't help but wonder what they'd have to say. Her parents shared his frantic concern about their daughter, but their eyes looked glazed with suspicion. Or maybe it was just his imagination, lack of sleep, and too much coffee making him paranoid.

They admitted having an appointment with the police after lunch. Jeff felt a twinge of guilt at his relief that they would be leaving soon. He had to *do* something. Drive around and look for her car? Anything but sit here and endlessly discuss her absence, while the 911 call, with its subtle accusations, lay huddled in the corner like an evil presence.

He said, "They seem to think she's just gone somewhere to be alone." He didn't add, "to get away from me," but the thought crossed his mind.

Her mother sniffled. "She would never go away without letting us know."

Jeff didn't think so either, but he had to keep hoping that's what she'd done. Struggling not to think about the alternative, he told himself any moment now she'd come walking through the door.

After Jamie's parents left, Jeff drove around the area, searching for Jamie's car. A senseless pursuit, he returned home to spend the evening searching through Jamie's things, looking for any clue to where she might have gone. At first surprised to find her checkbook mixed in with the clutter in one of the drawers, he recalled Jamie as an avid credit card user, and only wrote checks if she had to. Flipping through the duplicates of the checks she'd written in the last few months, a name caught his eye. Each week for the five weeks before her disappearance, she'd made out a check to the Women's Center of Oconomowoc.

Jeff knew what that meant. She'd tried to get him to go to counseling with her, but he'd put her off more than once. Jamie must have decided to go by herself; the fact she hadn't told him about it added to his torment.

He lost himself in his work the next day, grateful the others left him alone. When he'd arrived, they had been supportive and sympathetic. He hadn't seen anything in their eyes like he had in Jamie's parents. Not yet anyway.

Jeff, an electrical engineer, worked as a chip and circuit designer. Jobs in the field were rare, and when he'd gotten the offer to work at Durand Systems, a company manufacturing state-of-the-art defense equipment, he'd been thrilled to find work in his desired field and still be able to stay in the Milwaukee area.

Later that morning, thoughts of Jamie overwhelmed him. Trying to force his thoughts back to the project he was working on, the piped-in music caught his attention. Someone had put on an oldies station. His stomach knotted as he recalled the lyrics from a haunting song he'd never given any thought to. But now . . .

"Her voice was soft and cool, her eyes were clear and bright—but she's not there . . ."

He put his work aside and took out the slip of paper with the phone number he'd written down the night before. In the stark light of day, the numbers stood out as if they had something to tell him. Picking up the phone, he dialed the number of the Women's Center.

4

Seven years earlier

The Grotto, one of the newer nightspots in the Third Ward, a tony area south of downtown Milwaukee, had a waiting line in front of its door by 10:00 any night of the week.

After waiting in line an hour for the privilege, a man sat at the bar ordering a drink and thought it had better be worth it. Reflected in the mirror behind a bar running the length of the room, a face looked back at him—a face he'd yet to accept as his own. Sometimes it morphed into the old face— repulsively ugly.

He'd barely taken a sip of his drink when a red-haired woman leaned in and asked if he would call the bartender over for her. With no encouragement, she stayed glued to his side, boring him with idle chatter. Nauseated by the floral scent of her overpowering perfume, he had a mental flash of the bouncer tossing her out into the street where she'd land in front of a speeding truck. They should kick people out for being boring—or wearing tacky cologne.

Then he spotted her. At the far end of the bar, clutching a martini and swaying to the beat of the music, stood a woman he'd known in graduate school. And despised. The bitch had been one of the reasons for his intended life-ending plunge across the riverbank in the truck.

Nicole—hot, curvaceous and leggy in a shimmery blue dress. The dress and her long auburn hair lit up in flashes of color from the lightshow accompanying the band. He remembered the small bouquet of freckles adorning the bridge of her nose, delightful when she laughed. But she'd never laughed with him. Always at him.

Suddenly, she looked his way, smiling. He realized she had no way of knowing who she flirted with—would never recognize the man he'd become. An image flicked through his mind—a picture of her lying in the street next to the redhead—both of their bodies crushed, their lovely faces obliterated.

An urge to get her alone crept through him. He wanted to tell her things, show her things, do things to her. He wanted to fuck her so hard she'd scream for mercy. He watched as she went out on the dance floor, merging with the steamy mass of writhing bodies.

He ditched the redhead. And waited. He didn't have to wait long before she approached. It had been so easy. Before he had time to buy her another martini she suggested they go to her place, only a short distance from the club.

Inside her apartment she put on music and poured them a glass of wine. As soon as he set down his wine glass, she was all over him. Within seconds, he'd grown hard, his breathing rapid. When she rose from the couch, leading him to her bedroom, he followed, practically panting. They had their clothes off in an instant. With none of the niceties of foreplay, they fell onto the bed and he pushed inside of her, thrusting with a frenzy of pent-up sexuality.

When he rolled off of her, he knew she hadn't been satisfied. But before he'd caught his breath, she climbed on top of him, her breath hot on his chest as she nibbled downward. He gasped with exquisite pleasure when she reached her target. In the dim rays from a tiny nightlight, he saw her wild tresses drifting across his abdomen, her full lips making love to his cock.

Without warning, a hot, bubbling hatred invaded his ecstasy, curiously spiking his enjoyment. This woman would never have even spoken to his former, hideously ugly self, much less sucked his dick. She was a bitch who'd laughed at him behind his back—how could he have ignored that?

He reached down as if to caress her face. His increasing wrath nearly took on a life of its own as he pulled her off of him. She rolled onto her back, smiling wantonly as he pinned her to the bed. His hands reached for her throat, encircled it and began to tighten while her beautiful features became a mask of wild terror. She struggled against him, gasping for air as his fingers continued their vise-like grasp on her slender neck. His hands wrung her tender flesh until she no longer struggled beneath him.

He studied her as she laid there: a picture of serenity, hair a sunburst of curls on the pillow, her makeup worn off, the tiny freckles on her nose exposed. Death suited her; her beauty displayed in front of him like an opened rose.

He savored the memory of his hands on her throat, the feeling of ultimate power over her, and became aware of the huge erection jutting from his groin. Still gasping for breath, he took it in his hand.

5

Wednesday morning after Lisa finished with her early clients, she listened to a message from a troubled Jeff Denison. How had he managed to find her? The center wouldn't have given out that information. Unsure how she wanted to handle his call, she left the office, confident that a noon-hour walk would give her direction. She'd enjoy the beautiful fall day, the trees brilliant in a full palette of gorgeous colors.

The mystery of the statistical increase in missing women and Jamie Denison's disappearance weighed heavily in Lisa's thoughts. She'd been trying to decide what to do about it. Amanda Hawkins, though alarmed, had only been able to tell Lisa she'd check into the numbers and get back to her.

The dilemma, though, had given her a welcome diversion from the breakup with Tyler. She'd arranged to talk with Richard Conlin, a homicide detective in Milwaukee. Maybe talking to the police would stir things up.

Her walk ended at a small deli, where she picked up a turkey sandwich and carried it back to the office. She decided to return Denison's call. However he'd managed to get it, he had her name; she couldn't un-ring that bell.

When he answered, Lisa introduced herself, and without giving him time to interrupt, launched into a speech about confidentiality, explaining to him she couldn't discuss anything Jamie had told her in therapy.

As soon as she'd finished, he said, "I'd like to make an appointment with you—as a client."

Before she could protest, he added, "I'm not asking you to tell me anything Jamie said to you. I know you can't. I think therapy might make it easier for me to deal with this, especially if I can talk to someone who understands our situation. Whenever you have an opening, I'll make time."

Lisa, sympathetic to his anguish, knew seeing him wouldn't be an ideal circumstance for counseling. But the man's pain had come through during the obviously memorized speech he'd recited.

She wanted to help him. "How about tonight?"

Jeff Denison arrived at Lisa's office promptly at seven. "Thank you for seeing me."

He looked exactly how she'd pictured him—a serious young man in his late twenties, wearing wire-rimmed glasses, dressed in a well-pressed denim shirt and khakis. If it were possible for someone to look like an engineer, Jeff Denison represented the profession perfectly.

"Mr. Denison, after I talked to you this afternoon I double-checked your wife's paperwork. Because Jamie felt confident you'd eventually be joining her in therapy, she signed a waiver giving me permission to talk to you. Without it, I wouldn't be able to discuss anything she told me."

Seeing his eager look she quickly added, "But I'm afraid I'm not going to be any help in finding her. She never told me she planned on leaving. I'm sorry."

Jeff paled. "If she didn't leave, what happened to her?"

"It's possible she made an impulsive decision to leave, and didn't plan it out at all." She knew if she were to be of any help to him, it would be to ease him through his pain. His wife may or may not have met with foul play, but Lisa's function would be to guide him through the aftermath of Jamie's disappearance.

6

Enjoying a rare morning at his desk, Richard Conlin worked on an overdue accumulation of paperwork, although as a Milwaukee homicide detective he preferred action to sitting in the office. He'd been sipping coffee while he worked, and regretting his promise to meet with some shrink coming in to talk to him. Maybe he could finesse her over to someone else.

Lisa Rayburn worked as a psychologist and part-time counselor at the Women's Center in Oconomowoc. *Probably writing a freaking book.* Two days ago he'd gotten a call from Patty Barkley asking him to talk to Rayburn. Patty, from special crimes, acted as liaison between the department and the Women's Center. Refusing to see Rayburn would have made him seem unsympathetic to women's issues.

He looked up to see a woman with dark blonde hair standing in front of his desk. She held out her hand. "Hi, my name is Lisa Rayburn. Sorry to interrupt, but the woman at the desk told me I could come back."

Richard rose, accepting her proffered hand. "No problem. I've been expecting you. Have a seat."

He took in her dark blue pantsuit—he hated pantsuits on women. A legman, they hid his favorite part of a woman's anatomy. Attractive, about forty, give or take, she wore her hair pulled back on her neck and used little, if any, makeup. Everything about her looked conservative; she reminded him of the female attorneys he saw in the courthouse—unapproachable. He preferred his women colorful, flashy even. Good thing his partner wasn't around, she was definitely his type. With her even features and generous figure she'd be right up Justin's alley–not fat, but voluptuous by today's bony standards.

Lisa felt Conlin appraising her. She got right to the point of her visit.

"I'm sorry to take up your time, but I've come across something I believe you should look at. I'll try to outline it as simply as possible. Then you can tell me whether it's something that needs your attention."

"That works for me. Would you like some coffee? It's not Starbucks, but it's always strong and hot."

"No, thanks, I'm fine.

"Okay, give me the crux of it."

"I'm a clinical psychologist. I have an office in Pewaukee and volunteer one afternoon a week at the Women's Center of Oconomowoc. I'm writing a textbook for clinicians on the treatment of abused women. Most of the prep work for this kind of book deals with finding appropriate case studies and then gathering statistics relevant to them."

Lisa had decided he didn't need to know she hadn't gotten that far with her book yet—or that the statistic in question had come from a graduate student. He'd winced when she mentioned the book, so she'd have to be brief.

"About a week ago, I received the results of the current stats on abused women in Milwaukee and the surrounding counties."

When he said nothing, she continued. "What I found alarming, and the reason I'm here today, is to show you this." She opened a folder and pulled out a sheaf of papers, clipped together except for a top page on which several lines were highlighted.

"One of the statistics is way beyond the norm." She passed him the top sheet. "The highlighted section shows the number of women who have gone missing following the reporting of one or more instances of domestic violence. The percentage is at least seventeen percent above the norm and is based on numbers for the last three years. Statistical variation has been taken into account. You'll see references on that sheet explaining how the data was handled and the number arrived at. It is definitely too high to be put off as a statistical aberration."

Conlin looked at the sheet she'd handed him, his brow furrowed.

She said, "I find this very disturbing. That's why I'm here."

"Ms. Rayburn—"

"Please. Call me Lisa," she interrupted.

"Okay. Lisa. Isn't this something that should be taken up by the women's centers? Why homicide?"

Lisa had expected his reaction, but it didn't make his attitude any less irritating.

"Let me guess," he said with a wry half-smile, "you think there is a serial killer out there murdering abused women."

"You know, Detective, I'm not sure what is behind this increase, but I find it alarming. I was hoping you'd share my concern."

Lisa, regretting that she'd volunteered to come here, began to put her papers back in the folder, preparing to leave.

Conlin handed her the sheet of paper she'd given him. "Give me a minute to explain the realities of this situation."

Lisa took a deep breath, her ire rising. "The realities?" She fought for patience. "All right, tell me what you think is responsible for this number."

"The thing is, there could be more than one reason for this statistic to be so high." He sat back in his chair, offering no additional information.

Lisa, recognizing she would get nowhere with the boor, stood to leave. "Detective, I'm extremely troubled by these disappearances, and have no intention of letting this go. Since I haven't succeeded in capturing your interest, you leave me no choice but to meet with the heads of all the women's centers. I'm sure once all of them get behind the issue, your department may have a different opinion."

His eyes narrowed. "Well, Ms. Rayburn, let me see if I can put you in touch with someone who can explain our position to you."

Lisa followed Conlin into an elevator, taking a moment to admire his athletic build. She guessed him to be in his mid-forties and thought he might be attractive to a certain segment of women—a segment that did not include her. He wasn't really handsome, but detectives always had a certain appeal. Must be the shoulder holsters they wore. Lisa liked men softer, a little less worn than the hardened detective—and younger.

She asked, "Who is this mystery person we're going to see?"

"No mystery—there's just someone you need to talk to."

"Someone who will set me straight, you mean."

"That isn't what I meant at all. I'm taking you to see James Wilson. He likes to be called a consultant, but he's actually a full-time employee here. He doesn't have a formal job title."

"Then what exactly does he do here?" she asked as they stepped out of the elevator.

"Wilson is the unspoken head of the Computer Crimes department, but officially it's run by Lt. Marian Bergman. Wilson's a technical genius and also our stats person. He coordinates computer crime investigations and oversees computerized forensics."

"Impressive."

They entered an office sparsely equipped with basic office furniture. No photos, plants, diplomas, awards, or other personal items offered visitors any hint of the person the office belonged to. A man sat with his back to them, concentrating on a large monitor, quietly typing. He looked tall and broad-shouldered, his hair an unusual shade of silvery brown that, seen from a distance, made him appear to be in his forties.

He turned to face them. James Wilson looked nothing like the stereotypical computer nerd and appeared to be in his early thirties. Casually well dressed, he could be described as ruggedly handsome.

Conlin made the necessary introductions.

Wilson rose from his chair, extending his hand. She took his hand, warmed by his firm touch. He had the long slender fingers of a piano player.

"What can I do for you, Ms. Rayburn?"

He had eyes the same silvery brown as his hair—or were they gray? She doubted the faint growth of stubble on his face was a fashion statement. He probably had a thick beard and been at the job since early morning. Before she could respond, Conlin suggested they use the conference room.

Once they'd settled at a long table in the adjoining room, the detective began, "James, Lisa was referred to me by Patty Barkley. She's writing a book and came across some information she felt we should look at."

As soon as he mentioned writing a book, Lisa's experienced radar detected a barely perceptible shift in Wilson's features. Clearly, police perceived writers as an irritating distraction. Lisa repeated her story as she told it earlier, once more abbreviating it as much as possible. Somewhere in the middle of her narrative, Conlin excused himself and left the room, stating he'd be at his desk if she needed him for anything. He'd pawned her off.

Alone with James Wilson, she made her point, concluding, "Detective Conlin said you could explain why this figure is so high."

Wilson looked thoughtful. Before he could answer, a woman wearing a stern expression pushed into the conference room.

"James, as soon as you are done here I need to go over something with you," she announced, with no acknowledgement of Lisa's presence.

Lisa took an immediate dislike to the woman whose photo on a badge read, Lt. Marian Bergman. It hung from a cord around her neck, centered on the front of a double-breasted gray dress with two rows of metallic buttons down the front. She wore her black hair in a braided knot, polished and slick as a cue ball.

Remembering how Conlin had described the unusual pecking order in the department, Lisa wondered how Wilson would respond to the rude attitude of the woman supposedly his superior.

Unflustered, he looked at his watch. "When I finish up here I'm meeting Pettretti from the FBI. I won't be back until about 3:00, but I can meet with you then if that works."

Bergman didn't argue, her body language speaking for her as she turned on a spiky heel and left the room. "I suppose it will have to." Her mannerisms, clipped speech and rigid posture—like her appearance—contributed to her air of military composure.

Wilson studied the sheet Lisa had handed him as if there'd been no interruption. "I see your figures come from records kept by the Women's Center. Our statistics on missing persons don't break people down into defined categories. And abused women going missing? Our detectives would deal with those on a case-by-case basis.

"If you're only looking at abused women, I don't see how you could expect to gather accurate data. Many of these women leave of their own volition and come back just as readily.

"Assuming the figure is accurate, there could be multiple causes for the rise in numbers."

Lisa couldn't speak for the accuracy of the figures. She'd talked to Amanda but had yet to discuss them in detail with the centers, hoping to have feedback from the police when she did. Certain with this short discourse, James Wilson thought she'd go back to suburbia and forget all about it, she asked, "Do you mind sharing some of these multiple causes with me?"

He reached over to a table next to the wall and yanked over a wireless keyboard. As his fingers started tapping on it, a large computer screen hummed down from the ceiling at the end of the conference table.

He said, "I'm bringing up a website we were watching about a year ago."

A colorful website with a black background popped onto the screen. "This is the home page of something called 'The Vanishing Wife,' subtitled, 'How It Could Be Done.'" As he scrolled through the site, Lisa realized it was a how-to for anyone wanting to get rid of a spouse, the pictures explicit.

"Our Computer Crimes Division tried to locate the origin of the site and its operator. While not exactly illegal, we felt it worth our time to track down the source, and discovered it had already been dismantled—still there but no longer functional. After a while it popped up again at a different web address with a new look but in a watered-down format, and again, by the time we located it, it was defunct. On the third go-round, they wrote it in a way that would almost convince the viewer it was satirical."

Lisa, sickened, remained silent.

He brought up another website, again with a black background, titled, "The Men's Club."

The paragraph below the title described it as a place for *The gathering of men who find it difficult to control errant and disobedient women.* Connections on the site sold various tools used for punishment and bondage. Lisa flinched at the long list of handcuffs, whips, poisons, lightweight aluminum clubs and chains. One page gave a blueprint and instructions for installing an escape-proof room.

"We've checked into many of these websites. Some of these investigations led to the person or persons behind them and some didn't. Again, even when we had a real person to interview, their sites were cause for suspicion, not arrest. Without a link to a crime, there is little we can do to stop this kind of thing." The screen went dark, and Lisa watched as it disappeared back into its housing.

"My personal opinion? Since no bodies have turned up, the most likely explanation is an underground organization assisting women in changing their identities and leaving the area."

Lisa rebutted, "But in all my years of working with abused women, I've heard no hint of any secret organization of the kind in Milwaukee. I've heard about them in general, but it seems to me there would at least be rumors floating around if there was one here."

"We have a credible source claiming it does exist but no real leads as far as where or how it operates."

He tossed the keyboard back to the side table and faced her, crossing his arms. Annoying as he was, Lisa couldn't help admiring him; the man reeked of masculinity. God, she missed Tyler.

Wilson said, "It is very possible this statistical increase may be innocuous. With the advent of the Internet, it is becoming easier for these women to disappear on their own."

Before he could dismiss her, Lisa said, "A woman, a patient of mine, went missing recently. So my concern isn't based on statistics alone. I don't believe this woman left of her own accord or that her husband had anything to do with her disappearance. My concern for her safety, coupled with these statistics, has me very worried about her and others like her."

He stood. "While I understand your interest, I have to tell you I see no reason to believe these disappearances are related. As I said earlier, missing person reports are handled on a case-by-case basis, and that's how your client's disappearance will be investigated." He took a step toward the door.

Lisa rose from her chair, fighting her annoyance. "Well, I thank you for your time and the information you've given me, frightening though it may be. Maybe the women's centers should be giving these women warning pamphlets. They seem to be an endangered species, for more reasons than one."

Wilson smiled for the first time since she arrived in his office, a fleeting smile bearing no pleasantries. "We appreciate your coming in with your concerns. If anything more conclusive develops, please contact us." He handed her a card with his name and phone number. No title.

On the drive home, Lisa stewed about her visit to MPD. It had turned out to be a dead end. She had to do *something*. If there were someone or some group preying on abused women, it had to end. They'd be easy prey, vulnerable to assault from another front. As if abused women didn't have enough problems.

Lisa was all too familiar with it. She'd left her obsessively controlling husband when he'd begun to terrorize their daughter Paige, who at eighteen months couldn't get the hang of potty training. Lisa had put up with his rigid dominance when applied to her, but once he moved on to their daughter, she left him. He'd never been violent, but she'd been sure it would only have been a matter of time.

7

Lisa's office in downtown Pewaukee occupied the back half of an old storefront building, owned by a real estate attorney whose offices took up the front half of the first floor. He rented the upper floor out for storage. Earl Albright was seldom around unless he had a meeting in his conference room.

The view of the marshy, south end of Pewaukee Lake, adorned by ancient oak trees, had sold Lisa on the space. Taking advantage of it, she added a large bay window across the back of her office.

Shortly after Lisa's last client left, Shannon, Albright's assistant, tapped on the door and hurried through, closing it behind her. A tall, rather heavy-set woman in her late twenties, she had gleaming, long, black hair. Her face wore a mischievous look complementing her engaging grin. "Sorry to barge in, but I saw your client leave a few minutes ago. I thought you'd finished for the night, but there's a woman here to see you."

"I'm not expecting anyone. Did she give you her name?"

"Nope."

"What aren't you telling me?"

"I'm just surprised to have someone come in so late, unscheduled. If you want I'll send her in and hang around until you're finished talking to her. It'll take me another thirty minutes to finish up anyway, and I thought maybe we could grab some Thai food."

"All right, send her in."

A moment later, the woman made an entrance into Lisa's office. Wearing leather boots with stiletto heels, she stood nearly as tall as

Shannon. Built like a runway model, the woman wore slim black jeans snug across her hipbones, topped by a leopard print camisole. A short, chestnut-brown leather jacket completed the outfit.

Lisa asked, "Can I help you?"

She stepped closer to the desk. Her gold filigree earrings dangled nearly to her shoulders and shone brightly in the soft light from the green-shaded, antique desk lamp. Her face, graced with high cheekbones, a perfectly shaped nose, and incredible blue eyes, visible in spite of the tinted lenses of her gold-rimmed eyeglasses, turned to face Lisa.

Her voice when she replied sounded vaguely musical. Maybe a touch of Jamaica? "If we talk, will it be confidential? I mean, you being a psychologist and all."

Lisa speculated on the woman's ethnicity; her complexion was a shade of soft caramel and her hair a closely cropped Afro, the short curls defined and lustrous.

Perplexed, Lisa responded, "It would be if you were a client."

She reached into a hidden pocket in the small leather jacket, pulled out the tiniest wallet Lisa had ever seen and offered her a hundred dollar bill.

"How 'bout I put you on a retainer? This be enough to cover it?"

"That's not how it usually works. Do you plan on coming in for therapy?"

"Can't say I don't need it. May take you up on it sometime, but right now I need to have a talk with you and it has to be jus' between us."

Lisa accepted the bill. "I'll take this as a 'retainer' with the understanding you'll come to see me for therapy at some point in time. And, to make it official, I'll give you a receipt, so I'll need your name."

The woman reached into her wallet, this time pulling out a business card, which she offered Lisa. Printed on it was Teal J. Peacock, Security Consultant, and a phone number. A tiny peacock decorated the lower corner of the card.

Apparently expecting a comment on her name, she quickly offered, "Mostly, I go by TJ."

"TJ, is there someone in particular you don't want me to discuss our conversation with?"

She grinned, nodding her head. "You figured that out! Guess that's why you're the shrink."

Lisa fumbled under the desk for the pumps she'd kicked off, then gave up and came out from behind her desk in stocking feet. She led TJ to a matching set of green leather chairs, fronted with footstools. The chairs sat on either side of a round, beveled-glass topped coffee table in front of the bay window, the seating arrangement softly lit by a Tiffany-style floor lamp in shades of blue and green. TJ took a seat, slipping off her jacket to reveal a pair of well-toned arms, one of which boasted a hammered-gold snake bracelet wound around her bicep.

Lisa began, "Can you tell me who you want this conversation kept from?"

Her gaze met Lisa's, her chin up, defiant. "Detective Richard Conlin."

"Conlin? Are you with the police department?"

"Was once, but that's a long story for another time."

"Then what *is* your connection to him and why can't he know about your being here?"

"He and I kinda have a relationship." She paused, and put her feet up on the footstool. "He told me about your visit to the department. That's why I'm here. And he can't know about it, 'cause I been telling him for years somethin's goin' on. You got to see firsthand how helpful it was to tell him about it. Better if he doesn't know I'm still lookin' for answers."

Lisa's heart rate picked up. "Wouldn't my conversation with him have been in confidence?"

"Nothing confidential 'bout it, if there's no case."

"True enough. You're aware then of the statistics I brought to the police, and you probably also know they ran their own a while back. So why do you want to discuss this with me? "

TJ lifted her legs off the ottoman and leaned forward. "Have to go back in time a little to explain. Left the force 'bout six years ago and tried working as a PI. Got a license and hung out my shingle, so to speak. Didn't do real well, but things picked up when I finally got a few referrals from contacts in the department.

"Few years back, a doctor from Waukesha was arrested and convicted of killing his wife. Attorney who took up his appeal recommended me as an investigator. Thought my ties with the force would give me an edge in finding somethin' new to use for his appeal. The Doc got off on the appeal because I found out the search that turned up his wife's blood in his car was illegal. Great thing for him but pissed off the department and about put an end to my PI career.

"The Doc was real grateful and got me a part-time job doing security for a big bank near Brookfield Square."

"How long were you part of the police force?"

"'Bout eight years. Like I said, why I quit is the long story part."

Lisa said nothing, opting to let the other woman continue her story.

"Since then I've done real well doin' the bank gig and freelancing in security. Got to know the Doc well enough to know he was no killer or abuser. Loved his wife, but the woman drank. A lot. One night he came home from the hospital late. She was drunk and started accusing him of cheating. She lost it, started throwin' things around, smashing good china and glass, that kinda thing. When he tried to stop her she started screaming and dialed 911. So he ended up with an incident on record."

Lisa absorbed it all for a minute. "I'm still wondering why you're coming to me with this?"

TJ chuckled. "Forgot to mention I also hang with Patty Barkley from time to time. She told me all about you."

"Seems like quite a small world around that police department."

"Also need to let you know the good detective pawned you off on the department's biggest tight ass. I gave him hell about it."

"You mean James Wilson. He was actually rather informative, but I agree he isn't what you'd describe as warm and fuzzy." Lisa smiled, remembering the man's brusque demeanor. She neglected to add Conlin hadn't treated her much better.

"Yeah, nothin' warm about the guy. If he wasn't engaged to the chief's daughter, he'd a' been out on his ass a long time ago."

Lisa's eyebrows shot up. "That explains a lot. I wondered how he managed to be such a maverick and get away with it."

TJ stood, pacing. "Anyway, like I said, I been tellin' Richard—he hates bein' called Dick—that something's going on. Didn't need any fancy statistics to tell me. The Doc didn't kill his wife. An' that woman never woulda left him; she was way too crazy about all the goodies that came with bein' married to a rich doctor. She loved him in her own weird way—an' there wasn't any boyfriend. I never told him this, but after all my diggin', I'd have to say she wasn't the sharpest knife in the block. That woman never woulda figured out how to disappear without leaving tracks."

Drawn into TJ's tale, Lisa still had no idea why she happened to be its recipient.

TJ sat back down, her small butt balanced on the edge of the chair. "I know there's another wife missing an' there're rumors she was seeing you. That true?"

"You know I can't reveal that."

"An' you know with a little pokin' around I can find it out for myself."

"TJ, although we have the same concern, I don't understand what you want from me. James Wilson did make some good points. No bodies have turned up, and the police believe there is an organization in Milwaukee helping abused women to relocate." Lisa didn't add that she, too, was desperate to find answers to why women kept disappearing.

"Miz Rayburn, the police ain't gonna do nothin' about this unless they get some solid info. I figure together, we do some snoopin' around, get them something to go on, then they'll have to open an investigation."

Lisa nearly slid off the leather chair. "Together? I'm a clinical psychologist, not a detective. And even if I was willing to help, I really don't see how I could. And you can call me Lisa." Her feet getting cold in more ways than one, Lisa got up to retrieve her discarded shoes. She wanted to find out what was happening to the women, but this was way out of her league.

TJ followed, still talking. "What if I told you I know something the police don't? This secret group Wilson's so proud of finding out about is only one person, and I'm pretty sure there's only been about two women in the past two years who went that route."

Lisa stopped where she stood. "Have you told Detective Conlin about this?"

"Can't. Technically, it's illegal 'cause most of the women take their kids with them against child custody mandates. He'd feel obligated to report it. Wouldn't put Richard on the spot or risk giving these ladies one less chance to get out."

"I still don't see what you or I can possibly find that would change the minds of the police."

TJ grinned. "I have a plan. Can't do it alone, though; I'm gonna need your help."

Lisa paused, intrigued but unsure of the wisdom of getting involved. "Let's say I am willing to help. What do you think I can do?"

"Most important part of the plan is to get a list of names from the Women's Center. Names of abused women who've gone missing in the last few years. Then we start crossin' off names. Exclude any helped by this 'source,' any who've shown up, any who've contacted someone, and most important—any who we're pretty sure weren't offed by their abuser. Once we narrow the list, we look at what the rest have in common."

Lisa frowned, thinking of all the time it would require to gather so much information.

"Can also throw into the mix the Doc's wife and your gal that's gone missin.' Maybe this gets us something, maybe it doesn't. It's a place to start. Be a lot of people to interview, that's where you come in. Not trying to suck up here, but you must have damn good skills at siphoning through B.S."

As concerned as she was—and Lisa had been even more so since talking to Jeff Denison—part of her felt like she'd done what she could with her less-than-fulfilling trip to the MPD and agreeing to take Denison on as a patient. And Amanda was meeting with the heads of the area centers this week to go over the statistics in question.

"Wouldn't the police object to outside interference?"

TJ started pacing again, gesturing wildly with her hands. "Interference with what? They ain't investigating anything! If we piss someone off with our questions, the police can't do a freakin' thing about it. We aren't police. And don't forget, lots of folks will be real glad to see some interest in their missin' women." TJ took a deep breath, appearing to rein in her emotions.

Lisa realized TJ's initial coolness had been a cover-up. She wondered if the woman had told her everything. Maybe she had more personal reasons for wanting to get an investigation started.

For years Lisa's entire focus had been on raising Paige and building her practice. The textbook she'd begun writing had been her first outside interest in a long time other than fixing up her house. Her fleeting affairs didn't take up much time. Her head shouted at her not to do this, but her heart remembered her own troubled marriage, and begged her to do everything she possibly could for these women. Pandora's Box creaked open. "All right. What do we do first?"

TJ looked triumphant, her smile radiant. "There's someone I want you to meet."

"And that person is?"

"The guy who helps women disappear."

Finally slipping into her shoes, Lisa stopped, dumbfounded. Balanced on one heel, she asked, "You really know this person?"

"Yep. What are you doin' Saturday?"

Lisa managed to get both shoes on her feet. "I'm . . . not sure yet."

TJ moved toward the door. "I'll meet you in town on Sixty-Second and North Avenue at the Coffee Cup Café. Four o'clock, Saturday. An' don't wear what you're wearin' now. Turn it down a notch; don't look so shrinkish, you know?"

8

Saturday afternoon Lisa drove into Milwaukee to meet TJ Peacock. A crisp autumn day, the trees proudly displayed their vivid, warm hues. Giant white and steel blue clouds moved lazily across the sky.

Lisa, feeling good, but with reservations about the meeting, arrived on North Avenue and found a parking spot a few doors down from the coffee shop. The neighborhood, caught between the inner city and Wauwatosa, bustled with a diverse blend of people, interesting shops and every kind of ethnic restaurant.

Lisa didn't see TJ when walked into the coffee shop, so she slid into a booth near the back to watch for her. Two Asian women, who looked like mother and daughter, were the only patrons, sitting by the window sipping coffee and having a serious conversation in their native tongue. The lone waitress, decked out in a black smock embroidered with brightly colored coffee cups, wore multiple earrings, including one through her right nostril.

An adolescent boy entered the store wearing a blue, logo cap sideways, making most of his face invisible. Pants with legs wider than his shoulders and a sweatshirt hanging nearly to his knees completed the look. He crossed the room and sat down in the booth across from her.

Startled, Lisa asked, "Are you looking for someone?"

His face crinkled up with laughter. "Yeah, you!"

"TJ? Is it really you in there?"

"Great disguise, huh? Still do some security work for an outfit downtown on weekends. Thought I'd try to fit in with the crowd. See you dressed down, too, but I still recognize you."

Lisa had worn her Saturday uniform of jeans, sweatshirt, and walking shoes, her hair tied back in a hasty ponytail. "Do you wear disguises often?"

"Sometimes, when I wanna blend in. Like when I went to Pewaukee to see you the other night."

"You thought that outfit made you blend in?"

"Yeah, guess it was a little overkill. All them rich soccer moms out there wear snooty casual stuff from L.L. Bean and Eddie Bauer."

"They do. People don't dress up much anymore."

"Bring your wallet?" TJ asked.

"My wallet?"

"You're gettin' your hair done. Made an appointment for you next door."

"What are you talking about?"

"Person you need to talk to works there. If he's gonna give us what we need, he'll need to trust you, too. Get to know you."

So the mysterious person who could help women disappear was a hairdresser. Lisa did her own hair, even the highlights, because she hated to spend her precious off time sitting in a salon. "Well, I suppose my hair could use some attention."

A young receptionist with hair gelled to defy gravity and colored to challenge a rainbow, told them to have a seat, Roland would be ready for Lisa, "in a wink."

Roland, one of the handsomest men Lisa had ever seen, looked a little under six feet tall and wore slim pants with a silk T-shirt that exposed every bit of his buff body. His hair looked like a natural dark blond, the top frozen into hundreds of tiny, platinum-hued, one-inch spikes. Golden brown eyes lit up when he talked, and his bright, wide smile belonged in toothpaste commercial.

As he hot-ironed the long, nut-brown tresses of a teenager, she beamed as he appeared to be complimenting her on her look.

When she left, he invited Lisa to sit in his chair with a "Hello, lovely lady," that didn't sound like empty flattery.

He ran his fingers through her hair. "Looks like you aren't ready for color yet, but come back to see me in a few weeks. I think the new multi-tones would soften your look. For today, I'd suggest a shaping and texture cut. This length flatters you so I won't take much off. And a ten-minute honey and aloe conditioner would make your hair very happy."

His good humor and smile were contagious. "Sounds like a plan."

She followed him to the back room, where he began to shampoo her hair, his fingers gently massaging her scalp in little circles, slowly draining all her tension. Just as she was about to start purring, TJ zeroed in on them.

"Rollie, I know you ain't gonna like this, but I have to tell you I brought Lisa here for more than a 'do."

Roland said nothing as TJ whispered their real purpose in visiting the salon. He rinsed Lisa's hair, wrapped her head in a towel and had her sit up. She felt his fingers tighten on her scalp as he spoke softly. "TJ. I told you no one other than the people involved could ever know about it. I understand why you told Lisa, but you should have discussed it with me first."

An hour later, Roland, wearing faded jeans and a leather jacket, came into the coffee shop and sat down next to Lisa.

"TJ, I'm sorry I got upset with you, but you should have talked to me about this first, instead of putting Lisa in the middle. When you get this list of missing women I'll tell you which women we did not help. That might not make sense to you two, but then I'd feel like I didn't actually give you names."

Lisa frowned. "We can work with that. But you said 'we.' I thought you worked alone."

Roland snorted, looking at TJ. "Well, at least you didn't tell her the whole story."

"Roland, we can do it any way makes you comfortable," Lisa said. "I understand if you don't want to give me any details. The important thing is that we find something we can go back to the police with. And eliminating women who left willingly is a necessary first step."

Lisa realized she'd committed herself. Someone had to find out what was happening to these women.

"I'm glad you feel that way, Lisa," Roland told her. "I'll tell you this much—I do this by myself, but sometimes there are things I can't do alone. I have a few close friends who help out, but on an as-needed basis, and they're never given names. The process can get expensive, and the women most in need are always the ones with the least funds."

Roland paused when the waitress appeared with their coffee. "About five years ago, when I first started doing this, I paid all of the expenses myself. The first time a close friend was beaten so badly by her boyfriend that she nearly died. I helped her leave town, and now she's happily married and living in another state. She's repaid me for what I covered when she left, but not everyone has been able to do that.

"My partner and I are going to buy a condo together in the third ward and that's cut down on how much I've been able to contribute. I've only been able to help out two women the last year or so."

"It sounds like there are quite a few people who know about this."

"They're all friends who care about women. Our world is different. In our network of friends, there are never betrayals."

"Never is a long time," Lisa said.

TJ interrupted, before Lisa and Roland could argue about it. "Lisa, hope you're goin' out tonight. You'll really turn heads with that great hair."

TJ was right. Lisa loved what Roland had done with her hair. Before she left the salon she'd made an appointment to have her hair colored.

"No plans. I don't go out much."

"Why not?"

"It's a long story."

Roland dropped a bill on the table. "I'll leave you two ladies to finish your coffee. Let me know when you want to go over your list."

Lisa watched him walk out of the shop. "He's an impressive man."

"Yeah. Rollie and I go way back. So what's your story? You gay, too?"

Where did that come from? "No. Although life might be simpler if I were."

"Simpler how?"

"I was married a long time ago. It ended badly and left me with a young daughter to raise. I wasn't a great mother—well, not really a bad mother—I just wasn't there for her emotionally during the important years. After my marriage ended, I went on a quest to find Mr. Perfect. I was gone a lot." Lisa felt a tug of guilt, remembering.

"So what happened with your girl?" TJ listened eagerly, leaning forward with her elbows on the table.

"I raised her on my own." Talking or even thinking about her inadequacies as a mother was difficult.

TJ studied her. "Funny, you and me have more in common than I woulda' thought. Me, I have commitment issues. That's why the good detective and I have lasted so long. We're alike that way."

"Have you ever discussed it with him?"

"Sounds like a shrink question, so I'm gonna ignore it. Save it for our 'therapy' session." She snickered. "So what do you do for male companionship?" TJ raised her eyebrows for emphasis on the word 'companionship'.

Lisa didn't want to get into the details of her poor choices in men or confide she was a forty-two-year-old romance junkie. "I'm just coming out of a relationship. It didn't end well. I guess you could say I'm taking a break right now."

"Yeah, best to take a breather." TJ stood up and stretched. "I have plans tonight, so better be moving on out of here. Thanks for comin', Lisa. Wasn't sure you would. Now that we know Rollie's gonna check off his ladies, our next step has to be the list. If you have any problems gettin' it let me know and I'll see what I can do."

"What if it leads us nowhere?"

"There's always plan B."

"And that is . . ."

"Didn't want to mention it, but I have a friend who works at the Journal if we get desperate."

"Using the media occurred to me, too. Hopefully we won't have to go that route."

When Lisa got home, she took Phanny for a walk along the street bordering the lake. The days were getting shorter, and the damp evening air carried the scent of decaying leaves and the approaching winter. As she walked she noticed the glow of warmly lit houses embracing what she perceived as happy families. Lisa felt a twinge of regret she'd never been able to provide Paige with a similar scene. Lisa's talk with TJ at the coffee shop had brought back all the guilt-laden memories she preferred to keep under cover.

As she walked she considered why she'd felt such a strong kin-ship with Jamie Denison. Jamie had gotten out of that lifestyle in time and found a loving husband. And, in spite of its problems, her marriage still had a good chance for salvation at the time she'd been seeing Lisa.

Lisa had given up the club life only after she'd begun to fear it had become an obsession. She'd given it up, focusing on her work and her daughter. But unfortunately, after years of therapy and the emptiness of her life without a man, she'd stumbled back into a cycle of futile relationships once Paige left for college.

A shiver ran through her when Phanny woofed softly and began to growl. Lisa didn't see anything. *Why did fall evenings have such a sinister feel to them?* Thanks to the moonless night, Lisa imagined it must be the gnarled branches of bare trees reaching out to her. And this quest she'd just committed to wouldn't be without its risks. She hurried Phanny back to the safety and warmth of home.

Lisa fed the dog and fixed herself a grilled cheese sandwich on some wonderful bread she'd found at a bakery on North Avenue. The sandwich, made with the nutty, grain-filled bread and her favorite cheddar cheese, went perfectly with the bowl of tomato soup she'd heated up.

When she finished eating, she went into the garage, pulled out a ladder, and used it to climb into the storage rafters. Moving aside some Christmas decorations, she found what she sought—a small, metal security box. She carried it back down with her and took it into the house. She opened the box and dug under a stack of papers until her fingers brushed against the .22 caliber pistol still in its place next to a box of bullets.

9

Eric Schindler, the former Dr. Schindler, obstetric surgeon, sat in his office, one of the few places he indulged in his favorite cigars. Owner of Kristy's Classics now, Eric enjoyed working with the old cars, but today thoughts of his former career plagued him. Maybe it was time—time to explore a re-emergence. He could make a few calls and see if anything had changed. Or call TJ, ask her if she'd heard anything new on his case.

His cell phone rang, jarring him out of his reverie. He opened the phone.

"Hey you, what's happenin'?"

"Not much. To what do I owe the honor?"

TJ said, "Well, you haven't bugged me in a while, so I thought I'd call and catch up."

"You're right, I haven't. But you never call to 'catch up.' What's on your mind?"

"Need to talk to you about somethin'. You gonna be around tomorrow?"

"You can't tell me what this is about?"

"Long story. Can't be told as well on the phone."

"If you have time tomorrow I'll pick you up and we'll go somewhere for lunch. A great '53 Corvette just came in today, and I need to take it for a drive. I know you love Vettes. We could take it out to Port Washington."

"Sounds good, Doc. How is the old car business going?"

Kristy's Classics, a Milwaukee area classic car dealer and show-room, had been a favorite hangout for him since his father had brought him there as a young boy. He heard the business had been struggling to survive, and when the dealership came up for sale, he'd jumped at the opportunity. He'd been at loose ends with his medical career on hold.

"The old car business is doing fine. Sure you won't give me a hint of what's on your mind?"

"Sorry, Doc. Have to run now, so it'll have to wait till tomorrow."

Eric suspected TJ's need to talk to him could only have some-thing to do with his wife's disappearance. Kayla. Obsession was the only word to describe what he'd felt for his wife. A model when they met, she'd never accepted that her career didn't hit the big-time. Brandy stingers, discovered on a skiing trip in Vail, became her method of coping with her disappointment.

After nearly two years in prison, where dwelling on it was all he had to do with his time, Eric finally understood their relationship hadn't been healthy for either of them. When TJ accused him of not being able to let go of Kayla's memory, she'd told him he would always compare other women to Kayla. He'd let her think what she wanted, although Eric believed his inability to stay with a relation-ship had more to do with how he'd lost his wife.

The next day Eric came home from his outing with TJ unsure which excited him more, TJ's 'plan' or the actual involvement of another person, Lisa Rayburn, even if it meant setting aside his ongoing dislike of therapists.

After all these years, maybe he would find out what had really happened to Kayla. Someone had abducted her; nothing else made sense.

It sickened him to know there was another missing woman, possibly many. TJ wouldn't give up the husband's name when Eric suggested he talk to the man. The guy's name wouldn't be too hard to find though; he'd simply have to go to the online newspaper archives.

It took only minutes on the paper's website to find the reference to the missing woman, and he quickly found Jeff Denison's phone number listed in the phone book. Risking TJ's wrath, Eric dialed the number.

Jeff Denison answered on the first ring. "Hello?"

"My name is Eric Schindler. You don't know me, but I was arrested five years ago for killing my wife. You might remember—the story ran in the papers off and on for years. Anyway, I got out on an appeal after two years. I didn't kill my wife, Mr. Denison."

He knew Denison didn't really know TJ, but wanted to give his call some validity. "A mutual friend told me about your situation—a friend who believes neither of us had anything to do with our wives' disappearances. I'm calling because your circumstances now are so much like mine were that I thought I could give you the benefit of my experience."

Still not giving Denison a chance to speak, Eric asked, "Would you like to meet for a drink sometime?"

Denison quickly said, "Sure, how about tonight?"

Eric hadn't expected that. But if Jeff Denison were anywhere near as troubled as Eric had been, he *would* want to meet right away. Eric remembered all those miserable nights he spent alone: drinking, staring at the TV, and agonizing about Kayla.

He invited Denison to Kristie's and lit up his last cigar of the day.

When Jeff Denison arrived at the dealership, Eric gave him a tour of the cars on the showroom floor, their glossy appeal brightening Jeff's face. After they'd made the rounds, Eric took him into the conference room and offered him a beer.

He accepted one and asked, "What made you call me?"

"I thought you might need some moral support."

When the other man said nothing, Eric asked, "Have the cops had you under the bright lights yet?"

"Not really. They still think Jamie left me. I know that's not what happened. She wouldn't just run off—not for this long, anyway, and not tell anyone."

Eric thought Jeff looked choked up. Nervous that the other man might actually cry in front of him, Eric gave him time to collect himself.

After a minute, with a grimace, Jeff went on. "My wife and I have a 911 call on record. I didn't get charged with anything, and Jamie told them I hadn't hurt her. I'll never forgive myself for frightening her enough to make the call. She did get hurt, but it was because I grabbed her arm. When she pulled away from me, she lost her balance and fell on a corner of the granite counter. She broke a rib. When they questioned me after she disappeared, they were looking at me like something that crawled out from under a rock."

"Have you called an attorney or put one on retainer?"

"No. Like I said, the police think she left me."

Denison was being pathetically naïve. "Do what you like, but it might be a good idea to have an attorney lined up." He didn't want to push; he'd let Denison think it over. "You know, in a way our cases are similar."

"They are?"

"My wife and I had a 911 call on record too. But I never laid a hand on her. And they thought she left me, too–at first." Eric wondered just how much to tell the guy. So far, he liked him. Denison

45

appeared sincere, or was Eric the one being naïve, thinking he could assume the man's innocence based on one brief meeting?

He considered the similarities in Kayla and Jamie Denison's disappearances too similar to be a coincidence. Eric decided to tell Jeff everything. TJ would be angry he jumped the gun, but he'd deal with the consequences later.

"Jeff, if you're feeling anything like I was, you'd do anything you could to find out what happened to your wife . . ." Eric began telling Jeff about Lisa and TJ's plan.

When he'd finished, Jeff looked like he'd been hit in the stomach with a battering ram. "If there is a killer, it means Jamie won't ever come back; she's out there somewhere, hurt, maybe dead." Jeff paled.

Eric suggested ordering some food, relieved the other man agreed.

After Eric ordered takeout, Jeff asked, "So, these women are going to try to find this killer?"

Eric said, "No, they want to find evidence that there *is* a killer. Force the police to do their job and find the guy."

"Why is now any different?"

"Now they have statistics proving something is going on with these women."

"You said you intend to persuade them to let you in on it?"

"That's another reason I wanted to talk to you. I figured you'd want to help and I thought if the two of us approached them, it would be more convincing. And think about it, two women interviewing abusers, possibly murderers? I'd sleep better at night knowing they weren't out there alone."

Jeff sighed. "This therapist. There's something you don't know about her."

"What's that?"

"Lisa Rayburn was the one seeing Jamie before she disappeared. I called her and pleaded with her to take me on as a client. She finally agreed."

Eric nearly choked on the unlit cigar he held in his mouth. "That's perfect. How could she say no?"

10

Seven years earlier.

The night with Nicole replayed in his mind like an old phonograph record. He'd stayed at her apartment until nearly four in the morning before he dared to take her body from the building. While he waited, he'd removed every trace of himself, anything that could possibly link him to her.

For months he'd watched the papers, never finding anything about a missing woman named Nicole. She must have been the kind of person everyone expected would just take off one day. He was home free.

Unsure whether he would feel compelled to such an extreme measure of retaliation again, he nonetheless found great pleasure in remembering every detail of their evening without dwelling on the conflicting emotions the memory aroused in him. That he'd go unpunished made it even sweeter.

He remembered her fondly. In a recurring daydream, she kissed him good-bye as he left her apartment, making him promise to call her the next day. The real ending to their encounter always popped up at the end, exciting him far more than the imagined good-bye scene.

11

When Lisa entered the waiting area to invite Jeff Denison in for his next appointment, she couldn't hide her surprise at seeing another man sitting next to him.

Jeff stood. "Lisa, I'd like you to meet Eric Schindler,"

Lisa ushered the men into her office. She remembered the name Eric Schindler and realized he must be TJ's 'Doc.' Why would he be here with Jeff?

Schindler, about an inch shorter than Jeff, was broader, built as solidly as a wrestler. His face revealed nothing as he took a chair next to Jeff in front of Lisa's desk. She thought she detected an odor of cigar smoke on him, a smell she hated only slightly less than the skunk spray Phanny brought in the house with her after meeting up with one of the little critters.

Jeff said, "I apologize for springing this on you. Eric's told me about TJ and what you two are planning. I'd like to use my session today for the three of us to talk."

She did feel like she'd had something sprung on her. "We can do that, Jeff, but first I'd like to talk to you alone."

Eric left the room.

She asked, "Why didn't you call me about this before just showing up with Eric Schindler?"

"You're right. I should have. But Eric told me about you and TJ—what you're doing. If there's anything I can possibly do to find Jamie, I need to do it. I was afraid you'd say no."

Irritated, but more at Schindler, who she was certain had orchestrated the ambush, she said, "Jeff, I understand why you feel that way, but it's not my decision to make. You should have asked TJ, not me. And I'm sorry, but finding your wife is not what this is about."

"But it could lead to that," he argued.

Under other circumstances, Lisa might have seen his assertiveness as positive.

Jeff said, "Eric did talk to TJ. She'll be here in about half an hour, but Eric wanted to talk to you first."

At least TJ would be on hand to deal with the situation. "All right," she said, "bring him in."

Eric came back in with his hands in his pockets, wearing a subtle smile. Schindler, in his fifties, had a compelling rather than handsome face and his black, coarse hair had only a few streaks of gray. He looked uncomfortable. He took a seat next to Jeff. "I wanted to meet you as soon as TJ told me about you, but I was afraid you might refuse to talk to me. The rise in missing women is horrifying, but it's given Jeff and myself hope. We want to find answers."

Aware of the sincerity in his plea, she said, "I'm not surprised that either of you would want to take part. But I have reservations about getting anyone else involved."

Eric sat back. "If I can't be actively involved, maybe there are other ways I can help. TJ won't go back on my payroll; she said this is something *she* wants to do. If nothing else I'd like to pay any necessary expenses."

The man could be persuasive; she'd give him that. He appeared confident and in control. *A little too slick?* He'd been a doctor after all; maybe it was just his built-in professional smoothness coming through. Or arrogance.

When she didn't speak, he continued, "Jeff and I want to help in any way we can."

Jeff nodded, looking relieved to have someone else plead his case.

Eric met her gaze. "I'm perceived by many people as just another wife-murderer who got off on a legal loophole. I'd like to get out from under that stigma. I want whoever is responsible for abducting my wife to pay for it."

Lisa raised an eyebrow. "I'm curious why you had to see me without TJ."

He leaned toward her. "Two reasons. First, I wanted to plead my case with you. Beg, if necessary." His smile eased his rugged features. "The second is my concern about the two of you meeting with men who are known abusers and maybe even murderers. I'd be more comfortable if we could go with you, but I know TJ is going to object. She perceives herself as perfectly capable of taking care of both of you. I'm afraid if I were to voice my concern, she'd be insulted."

"How do you know I'm not insulted?"

His eyes narrowed, as if contemplating her comment.

She said quickly, "We both know how TJ would react to that. As for me, I guess I hadn't thought about the safety issue yet. Considering TJ's background, I'm not sure your fears are necessary."

"You're right. And I apologize if I've offended you. Or TJ. Maybe I'm being old-fashioned. Or chauvinistic?" He looked at Lisa from under heavy, dark brows.

Her mind raced, trying to decide what it would mean for these two men to be part of their search. It would certainly be a positive for Jeff, desperate to play a role in finding his wife. He'd have to be willing to continue his therapy with someone else, of course. But there was something about Eric. Something that put her off.

The door opened and TJ entered the room. "Hey guys, what's happenin'?"

TJ sat at her desk, gazing out the windows. Her ninth floor apartment east of downtown Milwaukee didn't have a lake view, but she loved the glitter of the city's lights after dark. She'd take this over the endless steel blue of Lake Michigan anytime.

She'd been ticked-off earlier by Eric's rush to talk to Jeff and Lisa without her, but the end result satisfied her. He'd made a more convincing argument to Lisa than she could have, forcing her to admit that she and Lisa would need all the help they could get. Eric's safety concerns were a different matter. Well-intended but unnecessary. Demeaning even. Eric knew she could take care of herself, but she'd let it go. Only results mattered.

Lisa's point made sense. She and TJ had professional interviewing skills, so going out separately, each accompanied by one of the men, would get a lot more accomplished.

They agreed to keep the investigation to themselves as much as possible. From TJ's point of view, they had to keep it from the MPD for now. The last thing she wanted was for Richard Conlin to find out—at least until the search bore fruit. She had no doubt it would.

The next morning Lisa met Amanda Hawkins at the Women's Center in Oconomowoc. They shared small talk over a cup of coffee before Amanda handed Lisa a folder containing the list of names Lisa had asked for.

"I reviewed the statistics before I met with the directors of all the centers. Your grad student did an excellent job; I couldn't fault her work. I don't know if she told you she used to be an intern here. I had to have a talk with her before she left. Her extreme shyness makes her a poor candidate for counseling. That's probably what kept her from coming to us with what she found.

"The meeting went surprisingly well. The powers-that-be are behind you one hundred percent."

Relieved, Lisa said, "I can't thank you and the others enough. This file will be an immense help in finding out what's causing the disappearances." She accepted the folder. "I was afraid you might have gotten some resistance."

Amanda said, "You have to remember we're a group of women who've had a lot of experience with abuse. Some of us even have first-hand experience, unfortunately.

"The centers are going to revise the pamphlet they hand out to women, adding a section cautioning them about new relationships and acquaintances. It's been long overdue for a rewrite, and now they're going to rush it to print. That's as far as they're willing to go right now."

Lisa couldn't have asked for more from the centers. "That's wonderful."

Amanda's smile faded. "Right now there's no certainty what we need to warn women *about*. But from the reaction in the room, they'll have no reservations about putting out a more explicit warning if and when you learn more."

Lisa met TJ for lunch in a McDonald's near the bank where TJ worked. They were discouraged to see the list contained 48 names.

TJ griped, "Man, I hope some of these ladies are back home by now. I know Rollie won't have many we can cross off."

"Are we still meeting him tomorrow night?"

Obviously, TJ had something else on her mind. Her usual snappy talk was absent and her infectious smile missing. "I got some bad news today. Charles Morgan, Rollie's partner, is in the hospital. He got mugged the other night outside their place and he's real messed up. Rollie's out of his head, not sure he'll be up to meeting us. Don't think he's left the hospital since it happened."

"My God, that's terrible! I'm so sorry."

"Yeah. Talked to him this mornin'. Don't know when we'll be able to meet with him.'

Lisa hated to start without Roland's input. "TJ, why don't we go to him? We could meet him at the hospital cafeteria, give him some moral support and maybe bring him some decent food."

TJ took a bite of the cheeseburger she'd set aside. "You're right. Might be good for him to see us." She grinned. "Let's bring chicken soup."

12

Saint Mary's Hospital sat on a small bluff above Lake Michigan, just east of downtown Milwaukee. Late Thursday afternoon Lisa met TJ outside the hospital cafeteria. They bought sodas and walked over to a table where Roland sat reading a newspaper.

When he looked up, Lisa's heart went out to him. Dressed in a loose sweatshirt over old jeans, he looked nothing like the animated man with the flashing smile she'd met on Saturday. His eyes not only had dark circles under them, they held the aching look of someone fearing they could lose a loved one.

"I promised to do this, so let's get it done. I want to get back upstairs. Charles is still critical."

When TJ put her arms around him, he clung to her, tears streaming down his face. "How could this have happened? He's always so careful!"

TJ asked, "Did they catch the guy?"

Roland's expression hardened. "No. And they probably never will. You know how the cops feel about us."

TJ sighed, sympathetic. "I'll make some calls, see what I can find out."

"Thanks, TJ. But in all honesty, it was late when it happened. The street is dark along that part of the block. Charles didn't see who attacked him because they came at him from behind."

Lisa served the hot chicken noodle soup and put out a bag of biscuits. The three of them ate in silence.

When Roland finished eating, he said, "Thanks, I actually feel better now." He took a deep breath. "Okay, show me what you brought."

He pored over the names on the two sheets. "It's funny. I wouldn't have had to worry about this at all."

"What do you mean?"

"I had qualms about telling you which women I helped. Some of them are on this list, but there are some I happen to know aren't missing. The dates they went missing are next to their names and I know I've seen a few of these women since then. So I'll draw lines through them too, and you won't have any way of knowing which ones I helped out and which ones I've seen around." He took a few minutes to peruse the list and handed it back to Lisa.

Lisa looked it over. "This leaves us with 39 names to check out. It's good of you to take time out to do this, Roland. Please let us know if there is anything we can do for you and Charles."

TJ turned to him. "Rollie, let me stay with Charles for a couple hours so you can go home and change. Maybe grab a nap."

"Thanks, but I'm not going anywhere 'til he's out of danger. His brother and some of our friends are going to be here soon. Thanks for the offer, but don't worry about me, I'll have lots of support."

"We'll be prayin' for him." TJ hugged him once more. After Lisa followed suit, they walked out of the cafeteria.

When they reached the parking lot, TJ asked, "Wanna go to Vinnie's?"

"Sure. I'll meet you there."

Vinnie's bar, located on the east side of downtown Milwaukee, catered to the working crowd during the week and the clubbers on the weekends; it had been a popular spot since the '60s.

A buffet bearing a huge spread of hot and cold hors d'oeuvres was displayed across from the bar. Lisa spotted TJ walking toward her carrying a plate heaped with its offerings. "You just ate."

"Forgot to tell you—I got great metabolism—one of those folks who pisses off everyone else 'cause they can eat anything they want."

"That does piss me off," Lisa muttered.

They carried drinks to a booth in the back. TJ raised her glass. "Here's to catching the son-of-a-bitch."

"I'll drink to that. But keep in mind, you and I won't be doing the catching."

"Yeah, but I been thinkin', and there's something botherin' me. Richard says any serial killer thing goin' on is a fantasy of my overactive female imagination. But I can feel it in my gut—this ain't some online thing like the cops are pushin'. If we was goin' out on a limb, we'd have to ask, what would we find perched there?"

Lisa sipped her drink. "Just speculating, I'd wonder how he's singling them out, finding abused women to prey on. Do you think it could be a cop?"

"Sure. Or someone who works for one of the centers, the police department or emergency services, or even a 911 operator. Or anyone with a police scanner." She picked up a chicken wing, pointing it at Lisa. "Narrows it down to thousands."

Lisa took out the two copies of the list. They divided the list with a minimum of squabbling, assigning half of the names to Lisa and Eric, and the other half to Jeff and TJ.

"Rollie didn't narrow it down a whole lot," TJ grumbled.

"Stay positive. There are nine fewer than we had before."

TJ dabbed at her lips with a napkin. "Been thinkin'. What if Rollie's not the only one helpin' women out?"

Lisa took a deep breath. "I doubt it's likely, but only because I haven't gotten wind of even one in the area. Do you think it's worth calling James Wilson? Feel him out on whether he knows more about it than he told me?"

TJ snickered. "Lotta women would like to feel *him* out. Least they would if he wasn't such a prick."

"Can't hurt to try. I'll give him a call."

When TJ left Lisa in Vinnie's parking lot, she walked across the street to her apartment. The building, nearly forty years old, had passed its prime; though no longer considered an elite address, it was still respectable and well maintained. Years back, after so many newer places sprang up on the east side, the managers started making tenants super offers on long-term rentals. TJ had negotiated a sweet ten-year deal.

As she walked into the apartment, she noticed a message on her landline from Jeff Denison. Crap. She'd promised to call and set up a time to meet him on Saturday, the first day of their interviews. Even though it made sense, the buddy system still irritated her, and she'd put off calling him. She picked up the phone and dialed his number.

The phone rang so many times, TJ was about to hang up when he finally picked up. "Jeff?"

"Yes," he said, his voice thick and a little breathless. Had he been sleeping?

"This is TJ. Sorry I didn't call sooner, but been busy."

"Can you hang on for a minute?"

She thought she heard him blow his nose. Damn. Was he crying?

"I'm back. Sorry for the interruption." He sounded better, but nasal.

"No problem."

TJ wasn't quite sure what to say. Should she ask if he was okay? Lisa was the one who should be working with this guy.

"Just met with Lisa and we divided up the list. Gonna call a few tonight and see if I can get us some appointments lined up for Saturday. Most of 'em will be in this part of town, so why don't we meet somewhere 'round here for coffee at about eight and go over the schedule?" She mentioned the name of a pancake place across the street.

He said, "I'll be there. I could make some calls for you tonight, if you want to give me some numbers." His voice sounded quivery and he asked her to hang on for a minute again. In no mood to play therapist to a grieving husband, TJ hoped he really was just getting a pen.

When he picked up the phone, his voice froglike, TJ sighed and said, "What's your address, Jeff?"

After he gave her his Brookfield address, she was somewhat relieved. At least he lived close to the interstate. If she had to drive in this crappy weather, at least it would be on a salted highway. "Tell you what. I'll be at your place in thirty minutes. We can get things set up for Saturday."

The relief in his voice when he said he'd put on coffee and have the outside light on should have made TJ feel good about her offer. Instead, she felt a twinge of guilt. She understood the importance of his participation, but she still felt like she'd set herself up for a caretaking gig. Grudgingly, she put her coat back on and left her apartment before she could change her mind.

Jeff's townhouse took up half of a large brick duplex on the edge of a cul-de-sac lined with stately homes. When she arrived at his door, he'd pulled himself together, but he'd obviously been crying.

She followed him into a pleasantly decorated living room furnished with soft, warm-brown leather furniture, beige shag carpeting, and bright red accent pieces strategically placed throughout the room. A floor-to-ceiling fireplace flanked with bookcases and a large entertainment center covered one wall. The bright fire crackling in the fireplace made the room warm and inviting.

They made calls, drank coffee, got some appointments set up for Saturday, and made a separate list with names of anyone who refused to make an appointment. Those were the people they would just drop in on if time permitted. Their calls ended on a high note when one of the "missing" women answered her sister's phone. TJ crossed her off their list.

Jeff offered, "Would you like a glass of wine?"

Probably a stalling technique. He wasn't ready to be alone. Well she'd known the risk. "Sure."

Jeff was the first to break the silence as they drank their wine sitting in front of the fire. "You know, I was pretty upset when you called."

TJ gulped a mouthful of wine. "Yeah, thought so. "

"Today at work someone started playing songs from the '60s and '70s. I like all kinds of music, and I was into it for a while." He paused, looking down into his glass.

"One of them got to you."

"I'd heard the song before, but it didn't have any meaning for me until now. It's from the '70s I think. It's called 'She's Not There.' Have you heard it?"

Recalling the lyrics, a tingle spread over her skin as she realized how well—or how creepy really—the song described Jeff's situation. She said, "Yeah, by the Zombies."

"The music was so haunting; the words sounded like they'd been written for me. By the time the song ended, I had to leave my desk and walk around for a few minutes. You know how a song keeps running through your mind when you don't want it to."

He put down his wine and took off his glasses. Staring into the fire, he rubbed his eyes. "Tonight the song came back to me and sent me into what Jamie used to call a pity party. I had a good start on it when you called." He looked at her. "Thank you for coming over; it really helped."

TJ, who didn't do well with things like gratitude and compliments, said nothing. They finished their wine in comfortable silence. She stood to leave, and wondered why she hadn't noticed his boyish good looks. His deep-set, gray eyes behind the wire-rimmed glasses were fringed with thick lashes. His curly, light-brown hair was neatly styled. He brought out what little maternal instinct she had—even though they were probably about the same age.

Jeff walked her to her car and helped scrape off the layer of ice on the windows.

Impulsively, she hugged him when he opened the door for her and said, "I'm sorry about your wife."

He clung to her for a moment as she'd known he would, then pulled away and walked back toward the house.

13

The weather turned cold and drizzly. By evening, the snow threatening to fall on the city of Pewaukee only managed to mesh with rain, forming a thick sleet.

Shannon had been in the office all day with papers spread across the conference room table, organizing Earl's real estate transactions before he left in mid-November to spend the winter months in Florida.

Not long after taking a quick dinner break, she heard the wind beating at the walls of the old building, howling softly, eerily insistent. She shivered, wishing Lisa was working tonight. Just as she moved a stack of folders to the file-cabinet, she heard a noise coming from Lisa's office. She put down the files and went for the Taser she carried in her purse.

Weapon in hand, she opened the door to Lisa's office. Nothing appeared amiss. Through the large bay window, she saw the oak trees straining against the wind, a stygian scene highlighted by the dim light in the parking lot. The wind must have tossed something against the building. Spooked, but not enough to curtail her progress, she went back to her work.

It was still sleeting a half hour later when Shannon left the building. Though not easily frightened, she was glad she'd parked on the street so she could avoid the parking lot. Grateful the nearly deserted streets had been salted, she scraped at the ice buildup on her windshield until she'd removed just enough to see out.

Secure in her locked vehicle, she drove into the parking area behind the building. Her blood froze when she saw a shadowy form moving through the oak trees. It vanished so quickly she wondered if she'd really seen it.

She turned the car around, making sure everything was in order as her headlights lit up the building's rear entrance. Nothing looked out of place. She decided it couldn't hurt to drop in at the police station on her way out of town. She knew most of the Pewaukee police from seeing them in the deli across the street. She'd tell them what happened and ask if they would check the place during the night.

14

Six years earlier

She's the one—the woman of my dreams—the one woman I can trust. Allyson.

Intrigued by the anonymity and simplicity of meeting women online, he found her in a chat room for singles. They'd exchanged emails for weeks before their first meeting late at night in a small coffee shop. Thrilled when Allyson turned out to be as lovely as the picture she'd sent, he suspected his own good looks put her off—she'd been nervous and shy the entire time they'd been together.

Two more such meetings ensued, both under the cover of night, both in out-of-the-way places. He decided not to pressure her for more; the right time for them to be together would come soon enough.

He'd wait.

The next time she wanted him to meet late at night, he asked if she was married.

"I'm not. But there is something I have to tell you. I'm going to my class reunion Saturday. If you can pick me up after the dance Saturday night, we can spend some time together and I'll explain everything."

Anticipating an intimate evening with her, he sloughed off her mysterious words and booked a hotel suite near the college. He imagined her in bed with him and could almost feel her silken skin against his; hear her crying out his name when he made love to her.

But another, darker, image kept imposing itself over the bedroom scene—an exciting image, enticingly wicked. He couldn't wait to be with her.

15

Friday morning when Lisa arrived at the office, Shannon stood waiting for her at the door with a cup of coffee. "I thought about calling you when I got home last night, but you said you were going out, so I had to wait until this morning to tell you the news."

"Tell me what?"

"We had an intruder last night!" Shannon's dark eyes sparkled with excitement.

"An intruder?"

"Sure seemed like it." Shannon repeated what she'd seen and heard the night before.

"You must have been terrified. What did they say at the police station?"

"Stan was there. He promised he'd have whoever was on patrol last night check out our building every time they passed through town." She paused, breathless. "He said we needed a security system."

Lisa snorted. "For what? No one keeps money here and neither of our computers are anything a thief would want."

"Yeah, I told him that."

Frowning, Lisa looked around the room. "You've succeeded in spooking me. Now I'm seeing things that look out of place." She glanced over at her file cabinets. Top-of-the line, they were equipped with an ultra-secure lock system, and appeared untouched. But some of her things looked out of order.

"Are you sure? Do you want me to call Stan?"

"No, I'm not sure, and don't call Stan yet. Wouldn't the lock be broken or something if someone had gotten in?"

Shannon's pale complexion turned white. "Oh my god! What if when I thought I heard something, it wasn't someone trying to get in but someone already in, leaving?"

"The door looks all right, and it's still locked, so that couldn't have happened."

"But it could have," Shannon argued, her voice rising an octave. "That door has the kind of lock you can lock on your way out."

"Maybe you were just spooked by the wind."

"Lisa, you haven't got a real complicated lock on that door. I bet I could open it with a screwdriver and a credit card."

Shannon had a point. Lisa hadn't worried about security because she didn't keep any valuables on the premises, but her files were another matter. "All right, but forget calling Stan. Nothing's missing. Call a locksmith and have the locks changed to something more secure. It was probably just a kid from the neighborhood out for a thrill, but it feels intrusive."

Shannon persisted. "There's a good locksmith close by and I'll call him right away, but we still have to tell the police. And you have to be sure nothing is missing. You know, the prowler could already have been in there when I came in. I had some errands to do so I left for a while about five. I stopped to eat and got back here about six-thirty. He could have gotten in while I was gone. I'm glad I had my Taser. I'm calling Stan."

Shannon had purchased a Taser through an Internet dealer. Lisa had warned her about the illegality of carrying it and was waiting for an "I told you so."

"Okay, call Stan, but try to get the locksmith here sometime after two."

By the time Stan, a fiftyish, rather rotund police officer with thinning gray hair, arrived at the office, Lisa was sure they hadn't taken anything, but someone had been in her office.

After hearing their story and carefully inspecting the premises, Stan said, "Whoever broke in was probably looking for cash. When he didn't find any, he ran out when he heard someone else in the building."

"We called a locksmith to have stronger locks put on, "Shannon offered.

"Good. We'll keep a close eye on your building for the time being. Call us if anything else happens."

Stan, visibly taken with Shannon and obviously trying to placate their fears, advised them to park on the street when they worked after dark. To Lisa's relief, his cell phone buzzed, and he left before her first client arrived.

At noon Lisa and Shannon rewarded themselves with lunch at a lovely inn on the other side of the lake. Over the special of the day, a red pepper and sausage soup served with fresh, warm popovers and spinach salad, Lisa told Shannon about the group and what they hoped to accomplish. As Lisa expected, Shannon was eager to help with the online research.

She said, "You'll get to go out on interviews with one of those guys that were in the office. Which one, the nerdy one or the older, dark, mysterious-looking guy?"

"This won't be a social event, Shannon. I'm going with Eric Schindler, and on a personal level, I don't really care for the man."

"Who knows, he might turn out to be a real nice guy."

"He isn't. He's arrogant and annoying. Not to mention the fact that he spent time in jail for murdering his wife. And even worse, he smokes cigars."

"Are you afraid to be alone with him?"

"No. He's irritating, not threatening. TJ has spent a lot of time with him and is convinced he's innocent. I trust her judgment. For now."

"Have you heard from Tyler?"

Lisa was trying to forget about Tyler, but it was difficult, especially on sleepless nights. "Tyler isn't up for discussion. Back on the subject at hand, we're meeting Sunday morning to go over what we accomplish in Saturday's interviews. If you have anything for us that soon, let me know."

Shannon nodded. "I have to go into the office tomorrow for a closing, and when I'm done I can get started. Just let me know what you need."

The locksmith arrived promptly at two. Lisa was working on a client's file when the scream of the locksmith's power drill masked the entry of a visitor. She looked up to see James Wilson standing in front of her desk. Startled at his presence, Lisa jerked back in her chair, reflexes on alert. "You frightened me."

"Sorry about that. I got your call this morning and I decided to drop in since I was going to be in the area."

Lisa had forgotten she called him before coming into the office that morning and wished she'd prepared for her talk with him. He wasn't someone she wanted to reveal her hand to, merely wanted to maneuver information from.

"Have a seat, Mr. Wilson. I'd offer you coffee, but I'm afraid we don't usually keep it going after lunch."

He sat in one of the chairs in front of her desk, casually draping one long leg over the other knee. "No need for coffee. And call me James."

James Wilson's good looks and his surprising drop-in put her on edge. Lisa wasn't sure whether her unease came from her libido's response to him or if she just didn't like him. The division between attraction and repulsion could be as narrow as the one between love and hate. He was engaged, she reminded herself—to the police chief's daughter.

She'd limit her explanation to what had taken place at the center's meeting. He'd find out about it soon enough. "I wanted to let you know I talked to Amanda Hawkins from the Center in Oconomowoc about the increase in missing women. She hadn't been aware of it yet but moved forward with it and met with the heads of the other women's centers in Milwaukee and Waukesha County. They're all concerned. Unfortunately, the most they can do is caution women on developing new relationships."

"And you thought I needed to know this, why?"

Her attraction to him downshifted to ire. "I believe when I talked to you at the station, I mentioned I would be taking this up with the centers, and I wanted you to know I'd followed through."

He shrugged. "Ms. Rayburn, I shouldn't have to tell you that as far as the Milwaukee Police Department is concerned, that changes nothing. There still is no hard evidence of a crime—not enough for us to employ our scant resources to it considering the budgetary problems we're facing."

Lisa fought back her frustration. "Mr. Wilson, you alluded to knowing about a group that assists abused women in relocating. It would be helpful for the centers to know if one does exist and is affecting the statistics. Anything you can tell us could make a difference."

"I'm afraid I don't know any more today than I did when we talked. We heard about it from a reliable source, which of course I cannot reveal."

Lisa studied him carefully as he talked, undecided whether he was lying or just not telling her the whole story. The fact she couldn't tell made her uncomfortable; her inner radar for deception rarely let her down.

She got nothing helpful from the rest of the stilted conversation and when he walked out the door, she expelled a rush of air she hadn't realized she'd been holding in during his visit.

After dinner, Lisa left the house with Phanny, keeping their walk restricted to well-lit areas. She hadn't admitted it to Shannon, but the break-in rattled her.

Eric Schindler and James Wilson were on her mind—both exasperating men. No wonder she preferred younger men; they hadn't lived long enough to develop any kind of high-and-mighty attitude.

Lisa considered Eric Schindler. She remembered TJ saying he was still hung up on his wife even though it had been years since the woman disappeared. She had only TJ's instincts to substantiate he wasn't a murderer. But what did a murderer look like? Or act like? Would a guilty man be working this hard to find out what happened to his wife?

Lisa had agreed to work with him, so she'd have to set aside any reservations. Put up with his irksome manner and disgusting cigar smell.

16

Saturday morning, Lisa arrived at the diner to meet Eric. She'd spent more time than usual on her appearance. Her hair, newly shaded by Roland to a soft ash-blonde with pale platinum and golden blonde highlights, fell to her shoulders in loosely curved layers. The gray slacks and white Irish knit sweater she wore complemented her figure. She donned a pair of mid-heeled boots, high enough to be fashionable but not too difficult to walk in.

She looked damn good. She'd seen a photo of Eric's wife, the woman's beauty startling. Lisa suspected it's what had intimidated her into fussing over her appearance.

Waiting for her at a table near the back, Eric had a newspaper opened in front of him. He wore jeans and a white shirt with thin blue stripes covered by a pale blue sweater that contrasted with his dark hair. When she joined him, she noticed the scent of his pleasant, woodsy cologne—must not have had his first cigar of the day. A waitress hurried over to pour her coffee, asking if they wanted breakfast. They ordered omelets with side orders of pancakes.

Lisa brought out their list and told him she'd made three appointments for the day and explained she planned on using her book on abused women as a cover story for interviewing the friends and relatives of the missing women. The book, a textbook for clinicians on treating abused women, had been in the planning stages for nearly a year.

"I've enlisted Shannon's help. She's the assistant to the attorney in the office next to mine. She's good at computer research and is

71

going to look up the women's spouses and boyfriends to see if any of them are currently in jail."

"I suppose if any of them are, they'll need to be interviewed, too." He sipped his coffee. "I should probably be the one to do it. I think they'd open up to me because of my background."

He'd started making decisions already. "That may be true, but we'll need to discuss it with the others when we meet tomorrow."

"You're right. I already irritated TJ when I insisted the two of you not do interviews without Jeff or me. She thinks of this as her project, you know. I do like to humor her. Although I can't deny it'll be hard for me to sit back and act like a worker-bee."

Lisa had to respect his openness. "You're right about TJ, but I'm sympathetic to her resistance regarding our agreement of never going out alone. I made these appointments Thursday night. One of the women I called lives close to me in Oconomowoc. She's eager to talk. It's hard not to just run over there and meet with her right away. We have an appointment with her at one."

"Good. That'll give us time to devour all this food we ordered."

As if on cue, the food arrived, and they tucked into it with no more talk of missing women, jailed spouses, or interviews.

Lisa rode with Eric in the old fifty-two Cadillac that had been his father's.

"I try to take it out at least once a week," he explained.

The car looked like new. Riding in it, Lisa felt like she'd drifted back in time and should have been wearing a full skirt fluffed with crinolines, topped by a perky, ducktail hairdo a la Doris Day.

They drove to the first address, located in an old section of Waukesha. It turned out to be an aging apartment building on a street lined with mature elm trees which had somehow escaped the Dutch Elm scourge.

After a jerky ride to the fourth floor in a tinny old elevator, they entered a dim corridor reeking of bacon, coffee and used diapers. The muffled sounds of voices, cartoons, and laughing children emanated from the thin walls.

Elaine Blume appeared hastily dressed in tan slacks and a white blouse. Her brown hair, streaked with gray, hung in a ponytail, and her sockless feet were shod in a pair of red moccasins. Her daughter, Colleen Hamill, had been missing for nearly three years.

"You must be Lisa," she said, and asked them to have a seat. Like the rest of the apartment, the brown velveteen sofa they sat on appeared clean, but worn. The well-used furnishings looked like they had come with the apartment and barely survived all the years of tenant turnover.

Lisa introduced Eric and explained why they needed the information about her daughter. "What I have to ask you first is whether you've heard from your daughter since she went missing or if you know whether anyone else has."

Eyes shiny with unshed tears, Elaine said, "It's still hard to talk about. She and I were so close, and my life fell apart after she disappeared. Her father left me about a year later. Not that I blame him; I was depressed for a long time. But then he hired an expert divorce lawyer who made sure I ended up with nothing. I never saw it coming. Now I work second shift at the plastics plant down the street for ten dollars an hour and can barely pay the rent on this crummy apartment." She pulled out a rumpled tissue and dabbed at her eyes.

"I'm so sorry, you didn't come here to listen to me go on about my problems. No, I haven't heard from Colleen, and . . ." she stopped for a few seconds to wipe her nose, "I know I would have if she was still alive."

Feeling terrible about adding to the woman's pain, Lisa asked, "Do you have any idea what could have happened to her?"

Elaine sniffed, drying her eyes. "Well, her husband was a horrid man, but I never thought he did anything to her like the police suggested. I knew he hit her sometimes, and she always forgave him. I don't think he would have caused her any serious injuries, at least none bad enough to keep her from working. Colleen was his meal ticket. She worked as a dental hygienist and made good money. Joe worked construction and he always seemed happiest when he got laid off. I suspected he chose jobs that would be as temporary as possible. I never understood what she saw in him, but he could be charming when he wanted to be."

"Elaine, do you know where Joe is now?" Eric asked.

"I haven't heard from him in years. But I heard a rumor he's living in Milwaukee with a divorcee and her two kids. She gets big alimony payments; that's right up his alley."

Lisa noted the source of the rumor and asked Elaine for a photo of her daughter.

"We won't take up any more of your time." Lisa handed Elaine her card. "Call me if you think of anything else."

They made an unscheduled stop in Elm Grove, an upscale area north of Brookfield. They turned onto a street lined with stately homes, not quite mansions, but brick and elegant, with mature trees and professional landscaping. The house they stopped at had a curved brick pathway leading to a heavy stone step in front of an oak door with windows of leaded glass.

A tall brunette wearing gray sweats opened the door to them. She panted, out of breath. "What can I do for you?"

Lisa said, "I'm sorry to bother you, but we're looking for anyone who knows the whereabouts of Deanna Knowles."

She exclaimed, "Whereabouts? I'm Deanna Knowles. Who's looking for me?"

In an effort to finesse their way back to the car as quickly as possible, Lisa said, "I'm writing a book on women who've gone missing. Your name came up on our list. I'm sorry. There must have been a mistake."

Deanna Knowles frowned, her mouth pressed into a straight line. A tense moment passed. "My husband and I had some problems in our marriage a couple years ago. I stayed with my sister in California for a few months while I decided what I wanted to do with the rest of my life. I was gone for about two weeks before I called my husband."

Eric and Lisa thanked her, apologized again for interrupting her workout, and returned to the car.

"One down," Eric said, moving ahead of Lisa to open the car.

She turned to face him. "Not really. Did you notice her neck?"

"I didn't. Women wearing sweats don't have much appeal to the male eye. Sorry."

Lisa gave him a sharp look. "She had a nearly healed bruise below her jaw line and another above her collarbone. There's still a crack in that marriage."

A few minutes of silence passed.

Eric asked, "We have an hour till the next appointment. Do you mind if we stop at the showroom? I'll give you a free, three-dollar tour."

17

Eric's business remained Kristy's Classics, its name since the seventies when George Kristofferson opened it with six cars badly in need of repair and a dream of making classic car sales profitable. For a small admission, the public could visit the showroom.

The old cars, showroom new, dazzled Lisa as their bright colors gleamed in the sunlight streaming through the floor-to-ceiling windows. Eric explained the muscle cars from the sixties and seventies were the most popular and most lucrative models. Lisa decided they weren't her favorites; she loved the old coupes from the thirties. They reminded her of the black-and-white gangster movies she liked. She could visualize Al Capone leaning out a window, machine-gun in hand.

Quite a few people milled about the showroom, among them a striking young woman being shown the cars by a man who appeared to be giving her a sales pitch for an old sports car Lisa couldn't identify.

The woman, resplendent in tight, chocolate-brown jeans, low-cut orange sweater, and impossibly high heels, called out, "Eric! I'm so glad you're here." She did a little teeter-shuffle toward Eric, probably all she could do in her ice pick heels.

"Hello, Danielle. Glad to see you came back for a second look." Eric turned to Lisa. "Excuse me for minute. I need to take care of this."

Terrence Young, Eric's general manager, a tall, slim man with silver hair and a faint European accent, came over to Lisa and continued her tour while Eric and the young woman laughed in the background.

Peeved at being set aside, Lisa thought the woman didn't look more than thirty years old, and she was obviously putting the moves on Eric. He wasn't exactly batting her off with a dipstick. But then, it wasn't any of her business what the man did. She couldn't point fingers after all—Tyler was much nearer her daughter's age than her own.

By the time Eric tore himself away Lisa had grown seriously angry. They'd only come here at her agreement, and he'd rolled her aside like an old tire. She'd noticed he'd even taken time to light up a cigar in his office before joining her again. From the look of things, they'd be late for their one o'clock appointment.

"Sorry about that, Lisa. But I had to get a sale lined up."

Before Lisa could stop herself, she muttered, "Yeah, it looked like she had something to sell."

After leaving the showroom, Eric and Lisa arrived at their meeting in Oconomowoc fifteen minutes late. Helen Mueller, the woman Lisa had talked to on Thursday, was the mother of an Emma Fischer, who'd disappeared about a year ago. Helen lived in a small, ranch-style house located a few blocks off the lake close to the downtown area. The house looked well maintained and had an arrangement of pumpkins on the porch. A late model SUV sat in the driveway in front of an attached garage.

Helen Mueller greeted them with a strained smile as she invited them in. They turned down her offer of refreshments, but the coffee table in the center of the tiny living room held a plate of cookies. Lisa noticed Eric grab one as he sat down in a chair at the far end of the room. Helen chatted about Halloween and the weather, while Lisa wondered at the change in her manner since she'd spoken to her the other night.

She was about to remind Helen of the point of the meeting, when a man entered the room. Short-statured, he had thick reddish-brown hair and narrow, lizard-like, green eyes that took in everything without noticeably scanning the room.

"This is my son-in-law, Steven Fischer. He came over to help me with the windows. When I told him about your visit, he offered to be here, too."

"Mom says you're writing a book about missing women."

"Yes," Lisa said, "*abused* women." Like all the women on their list, Emma Fischer had a 911 call on record. Fischer ignored the comment.

Something about Steven Fischer set off Lisa's warning bells. "Right now we're trying to establish how many abused women reported missing are truly missing. Have either of you heard from Emma since she disappeared?"

Steven answered. "No, and we don't expect to. Emma cleaned out her checking and savings accounts before she left and took her coin collection. There'd been signs she'd been seeing another man. I couldn't get her to talk to me about it, and then one day she disappeared."

Lisa had been watching Helen's face during his speech, and it was oddly expressionless, her eyes examining the carpet.

The son-in-law, in khaki pants and a green polo shirt with sleeves stretched tight to accommodate muscular arms, looked like he spent a lot of time working out. *Small Man Syndrome*, Lisa thought. Odd, he was dressed to play golf, yet supposedly here to help with storm windows. Also strange that Helen, who'd been so eager to talk to Lisa when she'd called her, now had nothing to say.

Lisa stood. "Well, thank you for seeing us. Sorry to have intruded on your afternoon." Lisa handed Helen her card and asked her to let her know if anything changed, making eye contact with Helen on the word "anything." Helen walked them to the door. When they were out of range of Steven's reptilian eyes, Helen pulled a photo of Emma out of her pocket and slipped it to Lisa.

As they drove away, Eric said, "It wouldn't be too hard to make it look like Emma Fischer took her money with her."

"That man sent up red flags for me. It was strange he didn't comment on the abuse, or at least make light of the 911 call."

"Maybe he couldn't—guilty as charged."

"No doubt. But I'm wondering why Helen would have said anything to him about our visit."

"He must have found out about it somehow, but that would mean he keeps real close track of her."

"I don't know why he'd care, unless he thinks she suspects he had something to do with her daughter's disappearance. Which might indicate he did."

Eric frowned. "Something isn't right in that house. We have to drop by again sometime when we know Helen's alone."

They struck out at their next two unscheduled stops. At the first, no one related to or knowing the missing woman lived there. At the other, a For-Sale sign stood in the yard and the house looked vacant.

A little after four, Eric dropped Lisa off. She got out of the old Cadillac with an abrupt goodbye and hurried to her car. If today was any indication of how much their interviews would accomplish, things weren't going to move quickly. Lisa drove home, discouraged.

18

TJ and Jeff started out with five appointments. Two of the women listed as missing turned out to be accounted for. One they found at home, had even answered the door. The woman was still living with the same loser. TJ would have made book on the woman still being knocked around. How could women be so stupid? She thought of what she and her sister had been through with Janeen's husband, Mario. But she wouldn't dredge up ancient history; she had to stay focused.

Two husbands of the women on their list had still been at the same addresses as when the wives went missing. The first one, Rodney Whitman, had gotten a divorce after his wife disappeared, and the replacement wife answered the door followed by three little kids. Their house on west Capitol Drive had been neat and well kept, and the wife had no signs of scars or bruising. Rodney had been interested and respectful, had given them no attitude, and quickly dug out a photo of Kayeesha when they'd asked if he had one he could spare.

"Listen, I'd never hurt Kayeesha. I loved her. That 911 call was a mistake."

"Mistake? How so?"

"My brother, Trent? He's a nice guy, but he was using then. After he got out of rehab, he begged to stay with us for a few days. Him and his lady. She's the one made the call—about him. He was still on parole, so they took off together as soon as they heard the siren approaching. That's the God's truth."

TJ would have to find out who'd caught the case back then and get their impression of Rodney's story. He wouldn't be the only one she'd have to check out with MPD. She'd have to do a lot of ass kissing, or buy a lot of drinks. Buying drinks sounded like the better option.

The next husband, Ames Jackson, had been another story. TJ chuckled to herself at Jeff's reaction to the huge, thick-muscled, ebony-black man who'd answered the door. Jeff practically hid behind her. Who was safeguarding who?

Lot of attitude from that one. He admitted to slapping his wife around, but said she needed it. "The bitch had an eye for the dudes, ya know?"

TJ wanted to throttle the bastard. The big man remained adamant, however, on the disappearance of his wife Tonya, and told them if he found out who killed her, or who she ran away with, he'd "kill the motherfucker." TJ didn't doubt the claim.

Jeff, who hadn't said a word since they walked in, said quietly, "That must have been difficult for you when she disappeared. I'm sorry for your loss."

TJ cringed. She'd told Jeff to stay dummied up. For a moment, the big man looked at Jeff like he was from another planet, then his dark features slowly relaxed. When she'd introduced Jeff, TJ had mentioned he also had a missing wife.

Jackson stuffed his hands in the pockets of his jeans and sat down in a worn leather recliner. He looked up at Jeff. "Yeah, it's been rough. My mom keeps the kids for me during the week, but they really miss their mom."

Before they left he gave them a photo of Tonya and wished Jeff well, saying he hoped his wife showed up. TJ was amazed Jeff had actually been an advantage.

At the fifth appointment, the woman's sister answered the door. Becca Wright had been missing for three years. Her husband had taken off a year ago and left the sister, Marissa, to raise the child, a girl who looked about ten.

"Yeah, Jess punched her out a few times when he'd been drinkin'. He'd be a good guy the rest o' the time. But his buddies always got him started. Told him he was 'whipped.'"

"Do you think he had something to do with her disappearance?"

"Nah, he didn't have the balls to kill anybody, not even Becca." Marissa handed them a photo as they left and told them she missed Becca and still hoped she'd come home one day soon.

All in all, it had been a successful day. Jeff had been in good spirits, even bought TJ lunch at her favorite rib place on Silver Spring Drive. Nothing like Richard, who was always catching her off-guard with his moods, Jeff seemed to be a pretty easygoing guy, except when a wave of sadness hit him.

Normally, when TJ found herself alone on a Sunday night, she'd call Richard; they'd go to a movie or maybe out for a few drinks. She had too much on her mind tonight to sit through a movie, or worse, hang in a bar. Keeping things from Richard had become more difficult as the days passed. She didn't always share everything with him, but this was the kind of thing she'd have liked his input on.

The meeting that morning had gone well. They had four possibles on their short list and photos of all four. Three without Emma Fischer, but TJ wasn't ready to acquiesce to Steven Fischer as Emma's murderer.

There were no commonalities among the four women, except their all being strikingly pretty. She hated how they were going to be sidetracked by the Steven Fischer situation. TJ wanted to find the jerk and deal with him herself, convince him he'd be happier living in Podunk, Arizona.

But they were bound to come across scum-suckers when re-searching abused women. She just didn't want them to lose sight of their goal.

19

Six years earlier

After he checked into his hotel, he put a bottle of wine in the refrigerator to chill and made sure he had everything ready for his evening with Allyson. When he left to pick her up after the reunion dance, it started to snow, big wet flakes that stuck to the ground, layering it with slush. At the campus, it didn't take him long to find the building hosting the reunion; across its front a large sign, soggy with the wet snow, welcomed the attendees.

At eleven, when people started coming out of the building, the snow was coming down harder than ever. They gathered in groups, saying their goodbyes and laughing at finding themselves in the middle of a snowstorm in April. He grew impatient. He'd been waiting since ten, cruising the parking lot regularly before finding a spot near the exit she planned to use. He watched as she came out of the building, walking with three other people.

She glanced his way. Just when he was sure she'd seen him, a dark-haired man approached her and grabbed her arm. Allyson pulled away from him. He reached for her again until some people from the group next to them interfered, forcing the guy to leave Allyson alone.

When the black-haired man walked away, she ran for the car and jumped in next to him. "Hurry! Drive away from here."

Mystified, he drove away from the college, while Allyson crouched down in the seat, trying not to be seen. "I'm sorry—I should have told you. I just broke up with my boyfriend last month and he won't leave me alone. I filed a restraining order, but he ignores it."

He drove to the hotel, checking the rearview mirror to be sure they weren't being followed. The situation with the ex was troubling. If she'd gotten a restraining order and the guy wasn't complying, why wasn't his ass in jail?

Allyson, over her fright, kept talking about what a hero he was for being there in time to save her from the creepy ex-boyfriend. She kept touching him, her face bright with excitement.

When he was finally alone with her, he opened the bottle of wine and filled two glasses. He couldn't wait to undress her and carry her to the king-sized bed in the next room. After a few sips of wine and first tentative kisses, he relaxed, deciding to take things slow. He sat on one of a pair of chairs across from the sofa. Allyson sat down across from him, happily chattering about the reunion, how many people were there, who was successful, who wasn't, and how much some of them had changed.

He tuned her out, instead picturing what their lovemaking would be like, when something she said grabbed his attention. A guy from her class who had a big crush on her in school had followed her around all night at the dance.

"He was such a loser, I used to avoid him as much as possible. Who would have guessed—he's even ickier now."

She went on to describe him—short, with unkempt hair, big nose, dressed like a nerd, bad complexion. She told him all the funny little names they'd called the poor slob behind his back. As he listened to her, his anger built like the slowly forming eruption of a volcano until he thought his skin would burst. She'd nearly described how he'd *looked in college.*

He knew what he had to do.

Unable to look at her, he stood and walked behind her to the desk where he picked up the bottle as if to pour them another glass of wine. Clearly she wasn't the pure, lovable woman he'd imagined. When he turned, she had her back to him, her mouth still describing the poor fuck who had the audacity to have a crush on her.

Lovemaking forgotten, he lifted the bottle and slammed it into her skull.

20

The sun had barely risen when Lisa arrived at the office on Monday morning. Too wired to get much sleep the night before, by the time she'd been sure sleep would be impossible, it had been too late to take a sleep-aid. At five she gave up and took Phanny for an early walk.

On the way to the office, sleep-deprived and feeling sorry for herself, she stopped at a little German bakery and picked up a box of pastries. On the day after a sleepless night, her food cravings became too urgent to ignore. She needed sugar. Heck with her waistline.

Lisa's only client was at ten. She was playing her messages when she heard Shannon come into the building. A minute later she walked into Lisa's office holding a cup of coffee in one hand and a napkin-wrapped cruller in the other.

"Nothing like treats from Volkman's to perk up a Monday morning. What's the bad news?" Treats were usually brought in as a solace when one of them was having a bad day.

"One of my limited-sleep nights, I'm afraid. Too much going on."

Shannon sat down in a chair across from Lisa's desk. "That's too bad. What's on your mind?"

"Well, everything really, but we have to do something for Helen Mueller even if it isn't a part of what we had set out to accomplish. I thought about calling someone I know at Social Services, but I'm afraid a home visit could make her situation worse."

"You're right. If the creepy son-in-law goes on the alert, she may be at risk."

Lisa cringed. "That's what I was thinking, but I figured I was just being paranoid for her."

Shannon took another bite of her cruller. "Nope, and I wasn't even there."

"I drove by her house on my way in this morning. Fischer's car wasn't there. I called the Oconomowoc Police Department and asked to talk to the detective who had been in charge of her daughter's disappearance. They didn't say who it was, but said he would get back to me. I'm hoping it's someone I've worked with. It'd be nice if we didn't have to hide behind the writing-a-book excuse, but then we'd be tipping off the police about what we're doing."

"Do you think it matters? I mean since they aren't investigating it?"

"TJ seems to think it's best for now. She's going to use her contacts in the department to get information for us, so I don't see how we can keep it quiet for long."

The door opened, admitting a tall woman wearing a short, gray tweed blazer over a black turtleneck sweater and perfectly tailored black slacks.

"Hi." Lisa smiled and shook the woman's hand. "Shannon, this is Detective Maggie Petersen from the Oconomowoc Police Department. We worked together when I was a full-time counselor at the center.

"This is fast service, Maggie," Lisa said. "I called about thirty minutes ago."

"I stopped over on my way to the station."

Shannon offered her a sweet roll, poured coffee, and the three of them went into the conference room. Lisa noticed silver stud earrings and a silver watch were Maggie's only jewelry. She'd pulled her shiny, black hair into a simple braid that trailed down her back. Lisa always envied women who could look put together so simply; for her it always felt like a chore.

Lisa told Maggie their story, omitting the part about their gathering evidence to force a police investigation. She told the detective they were checking out disappearances of abused women for a book she was working on and believed some of the disappearances to be suspicious. Then she related what they'd observed at Helen Mueller's home.

Maggie Petersen listened without interrupting. The detective took a deep breath. "What I'm going to tell you is off the record, but under the circumstances I believe it's necessary to tell you about Emma Fischer, Helen's daughter. My partner and I interviewed Helen and the daughter's husband many times after Emma disappeared. There was no solid evidence the husband had anything to do with her disappearance, but David and I are certain he did.

"We thought the financial aspect suspect and tried to trace it to him. If he made it look like she took all her assets with her, he did a good job. She had an insurance policy, but it wasn't big enough to be a concern. I think you're right about the mother. We suspected like us, she believed he was somehow responsible for her daughter's disappearance, but she didn't think her suspicions could help us convict him."

Lisa asked, "What should we do? We're worried about Helen and feel responsible for stirring things up."

"I understand. I'll talk to David, but I'm afraid we're going to be in the same spot we were then. We need more. Helen has to be open with us, and I'm thinking you may be the one who can get her to do that."

"I'll do whatever I can."

Shannon blurted, "We need to get Helen out of that house."

Maggie smiled. "In a perfect world, it would be a good idea.

But it would require cooperation by Helen for one thing, and police resources to put her up somewhere, which Oconomowoc doesn't have.

"Lisa, I'd like you to call her. See if you can get her to come to your office so you can talk to her away from any possible influence by Fischer. Then, if you feel the timing is right, you can call me in. If the situation seems to warrant it, we'll encourage her to stay somewhere else for a time."

Lisa said, "I'll call her right now."

Standing, Maggie said, "If you're able to set up a talk with her today, let me know. Here's my card. My cell number is on the back. I need to get to the office and tell my partner about this. He despised Steven Fischer."

21

Later that morning, Shannon and Helen Mueller walked into Lisa's office and sat on the sofa. Shannon had offered to pick Helen up when she'd told Lisa her car was in the garage. Dressed neatly in a pair of jeans and a white-collared sweatshirt with a cardinal on a pine branch embroidered across the front, Helen's gaze darted about the room, betraying her nervousness.

After offering her coffee and what remained of the morning's treats, Lisa asked, "Did Shannon tell you why I wanted you to come in?"

Helen looked at Shannon, who smiled encouragingly. "She just told me you wanted to talk to me. I was so looking forward to talking to you about Emma when you came to the house. Steven stopped in right before you came. He saw that I had cookies set out for company and quizzed me about it until I told him. I didn't want him to stay, but I couldn't ask him to leave."

"Why is that, Helen?"

"I wanted to be able to tell you everything. If I asked him to leave, he'd suspect that I'd tell you what I really thought. I know in my heart he had something to do with Emma's disappearance."

"Helen, did you tell this to the police?"

"Well, not really. You see, I had no proof." She twined her fingers together on her lap, her eyes bright with tears.

Not wanting to cause her any more anguish, Lisa said, "You're right, they couldn't arrest him on suspicion. But if there's no proof, why do you think he'd be concerned about anything you would say?"

Helen blinked back tears. "I know it was foolish, but after she'd been gone a few days, I accused him of doing something to her. I was just so upset. He denied it, but since then he watches me like a hawk."

Lisa nodded, but wondered why Helen tolerated the man. "Helen, did you ever ask Steven to stay away?"

"Oh, no. I know he used to hit my daughter; I saw the bruises. I'm afraid to make him angry, he frightens me. I miss Emma so much! He keeps saying she'll be back any day. I know he doesn't really believe it, just like he's lying about Emma taking her savings and collection with her. She was afraid of him too. She wouldn't have left without telling me. I talked to her every day."

A tear spilled over and rolled down her cheek. "Now I'm even suspicious he did something to my car. I wasn't having any problems with it until after he left Saturday."

Lisa and Shannon exchanged a look. "Helen, I'm afraid we might have provoked Fischer into doing something rash. I've spoken with the detective who handled the investigation into Emma's disappearance. She'd like to talk to you again, try to stimulate your memory."

Helen's mouth set into a firm line. "Oh, I don't know . . ."

Lisa tried another approach. "Helen, we're concerned for your safety. We think it might be wise for you to go away for a while, at least until the police can prove Steven had something to do with your daughter's disappearance. Hopefully, with your help, they can put him in jail."

"You're right. I don't trust him. But leaving my home! Do you really think that's necessary?"

Lisa said, "I do. Maybe if you go over everything with Detective Petersen again, they'll find something new to go on. There could be something you didn't consider important at the time. There must be, or your son-in-law wouldn't be concerned about you talking to us."

Helen shrank back into the couch. "All right. I'll talk to her."

Lisa thought the others should know what had developed. Eric picked up on the second ring.

He said, "If you can convince Helen to leave, I don't think she should even go back to get her things. One of us can go over there and get them for her."

"She called her sister in New York and made plans to go for a visit. We can get her on a plane tonight. Maggie's going to be here any minute now to talk to her."

"I'm on my way."

Eric drove back to his office after he and Lisa had picked up suitcases and clothes for Helen, feeling relieved the police were going to work the Emma Fischer case again, and Helen would be safely in New York, out of harm's way.

At the office he found an urgent message from Jeff. When Jeff answered his phone, he told Eric the police had found his wife's car.

Eric's first reaction was concern that Jeff would end up in a jail cell as he had. "Do they want to question you again?"

"No, they only told me they found the car. They didn't even tell me where they found it."

"It's time to get an attorney, my friend. They *will* question you again. Finding the car makes it look like she didn't leave on her own. And they won't tell you anything until the car is processed."

"I drove around for days looking for her car," Jeff admitted.

"Yeah, I know. I did the same thing myself. Listen, Jeff, get an attorney on retainer—now."

22

Although he preferred to think of her death as an accident, five years ago Eddie Wysecki murdered his wife. A diabetic, Rita had been prone to drinking in excess and forgetting to take her insulin. Eddie, who worked as a bartender, often came home in the early morning hours after the bar closed to find her in a drunken, diabetic stupor. The first time it happened he'd rushed her to the emergency room.

During one of their subsequent trips to the ER, the nurses instructed him on how to bring her back by himself. He listened raptly, even took notes. Eddie would have done anything to avoid another endless night in the ER.

As a young man, Eddie had been in and out of trouble, culminating in a two-year jail stint after a botched robbery. In prison, he'd had a lot of time to dwell on his life, coming to the realization that being a criminal wasn't paying off. He didn't have the necessary attributes for a successful life of crime—balls and intelligence. After prison, he worked dozens of crappy jobs, proving himself a good employee, then moving on to one a little less subservient. When he finally landed a job as a bartender in the corner bar near his apartment, he knew he'd found his niche. Both the hours and the atmosphere suited him.

Rita Claussen, a regular at the bar, was five years older than him. A petite woman, she'd put on a few pounds over the years and wore her bleached blonde hair in a high concoction on top of her head, reminiscent of something from the '60s. He liked her bubbly personality, which became even more so as she drank. She often hung around till everyone else left, leaving with him after the bar closed for the night. An alcoholic, she nevertheless managed to get to work every day, where she held down a good job at one of the local breweries.

When they got married and moved into the lower flat of a nice duplex in West Allis, Eddie knew he had turned his life around. He wasn't exactly sure when things started to go south, but thought it began on that first night he came home and found Rita passed out. She knew she had to take her insulin regularly and shouldn't be drinking so much, but despite the many promises she made, her good intentions were short-lived. The frequent "revivals" Eddie performed wore on him.

After a couple years with no change in the pattern of their lives, Eddie wanted out, but felt like a real ass for thinking about divorcing Rita. He felt sorry for her and being married still had its advantages. Two paychecks ensured he could save part of his wages every week, and Rita, a union employee, had good benefits and carried him on her healthcare plan.

He got over the idea of divorcing her, but then the owner of the bar he worked in decided to retire and move to Florida, telling Eddie he'd give him first crack at buying the place. Eddie had worked there long enough to know the bar provided a decent income. He'd been hoping for the opportunity for a long time. But with only a little over ten grand saved, he'd need at least another twenty-five to swing it.

Rita, as part of her benefit package at work, had the exact amount as her life insurance payoff. The money it offered started niggling at him. Their marriage had become joyless, but she'd joined AA and was making an effort to take better care of herself.

A few weeks later the bar went up for sale. Then Eddie came home on a Friday night and found Rita passed out on the couch. Again. His first thought was pity—she'd really been trying this time. Then he remembered the life insurance. It occurred to him this could be his out. He didn't have to divorce her—just not revive her.

23

Jeff had just returned to his desk after a long, trying meeting with the other engineers when his cell phone vibrated.

"Jeff, it's Lisa. Is this a good time?"

"Sure, what's up?"

"Helen left for New York this morning. She'll be staying there indefinitely, while Maggie and her partner are working Emma's case again. Maggie and Helen went through Emma's things, and they think they found something incriminating Fischer. Maggie couldn't tell us what it was. They're trying to get a search warrant for his place."

Jeff looked up to see two detectives from Brookfield PD standing at the door to his office. He cut Lisa off. "Sorry, someone's here to see me. I'll get back to you."

He motioned them in and they seated themselves in front of his desk. Jeff knew this would be bad.

"Mr. Denison, we're here to talk to you about your wife's car."

Jeff dreaded what was coming next, wishing he had taken Eric's advice and called an attorney. Maybe he shouldn't say anything. Attorneys always advised their clients not to. Or at least they did on TV. But it was too late; he'd talked to them already, multiple times. He had nothing more to add.

"Your wife's car was discovered behind some deserted warehouses in the inner city, totally stripped."

He handed Jeff photos of the car, which looked like a mere shell of the flashy car it had been. The car, sans wheels, had been wedged between an old loading dock and a decrepit storage shed. Jeff felt like he'd been kicked in the gut. Jamie never would have left her beloved car behind.

"Please don't bother trying to find her—she's not there . . ."

Christ, that song again. Lines from it ran through his mind at the worst times. Fighting back tears he didn't want the detectives to see, Jeff put the photos down. "Do you believe me now? Jamie didn't just leave. She never would have given up her car."

"It *is* looking like she was abducted. Have you thought of anything else that could shine some light on this? Something she said? Did?"

It wasn't paranoia—they were looking at him like he was a suspect.

"No, nothing."

When they left Jeff had no doubt he'd been put on a very short list of suspects—probably their only one. He had a quick flash of gratitude for his role in the group and their work to identify what was happening to abused women. Swallowing the lump in his throat, he opened his phone to call the attorney Eric had recommended.

Early Friday morning, TJ got a call from Jeff Denison. He told her he'd finally called a friend he'd been avoiding since Jamie disappeared, and they were going to play a round of golf the next morning if the mild weather held. Worried the police were trying to find enough evidence to arrest him, golf would be a pleasant diversion. He hoped she wouldn't mind if they scheduled their interviews later on Saturday. "We could do some of them tonight if you have time."

TJ knew how devastated he'd been since they'd found his wife's car. "I'll see what I can get lined up and call you later."

She spent the rest of the day checking with her sources at MPD, begging information on the domestic calls described by their interviewees. She managed to get two interviews scheduled for that night. It had taken a few calls to find someone to talk to about a missing woman named Shirley Moran. When she finally reached the woman's brother, it turned out he lived in a building right across the street from her. Since he was nearly a neighbor, she decided to break the "rules" and trot over there by herself.

TJ felt like cruising on her own. Maybe drop in over at Vinnie's and see what was happening after she met the brother, since he lived right around the corner. The next appointment would take her to the south side in a popular Mexican restaurant off of Mitchell Street. She wouldn't need a sidekick; there'd be a lot of people around.

That night when she crossed the street for her appointment—it was actually on the side street around the corner from Vinnie's—TJ got a prickly neck feeling; it usually came on when she was being watched. She probably was—the come-get-me outfit she wore invited attention: tight black velveteen jeans with a black cami, black ankle boots, and a new geranium-red sweater-jacket, knit of fluffy angora, made her look like she was wearing a tiny red cloud. The jacket had the added advantage of hiding her sleek, custom-made leather shoulder holster.

The area, always busy, tended to be even more so on weekends. She scanned the street, but didn't see anything out of the ordinary. Broad oak trees lined the dark side street. An occasional car drove by slowly, looking for a parking place. Just when she found the apartment building, a big three-story, old brick affair, her cell phone buzzed. She checked the number. Jeff. Grumbling, she opened the phone. "Hey."

"TJ, it's Jeff. I thought we might be getting together tonight."

Now she was on the spot. Damn, she hated the fucking rules. And how this guy always made her feel sorry for him. Finding out about his wife's car had to be painful.

"Turned out one of the folks I found lives right across the street from me, so I'm there. Meeting him in a minute."

"Tell me this isn't one of the husbands."

At least he hadn't lectured her about going alone. "Nope, her brother. Listen, I thought I'd stop in at Vinnie's when I'm done here. Do you want to meet me there? Got another appointment at 9:00." *Maybe he'll say no.*

"I'll be there in half an hour."

TJ sighed and put the phone back in her pocket. She walked up the small flight of steps to the vestibule of the building. The feeling of being watched tweaked her again, and she turned quickly to see if someone had come up behind her. A few buildings from where she stood, a young couple walked toward the busy street. Nothing.

Shirley Moran's brother was a tall, thin, gawky guy in his late twenties, visibly put off by TJ. She obviously wasn't what he'd been expecting.

The apartment looked like a typical single-guy place, short on furniture, but packed with the latest in video and sound equipment. She turned down his offer of a beer, and sat at the dining room table, piled with mail, old newspapers, and magazines.

When she asked about his sister, he said, "No one thought she had any reason to take off. And her husband's a great guy. We still do stuff together, you know? We play on the same softball team and hang at the same bar. We even go hunting sometimes."

"If he's such a great guy, how come the cops had to come out to their place?"

He shifted in his chair. "Hey, she wasn't perfect. Shirley had a real bad temper, you know?"

"Yeah, so?"

"She liked to pick fights with him. Throw things. Sometimes, sharp things."

TJ knew about such women. As a cop, she'd been on more than one call where the abuser turned out to be a female. It had nothing to do with size; most men shied away from hitting back.

"She was hurting him?"

"That night she came at him with his baseball bat. She was pissed because he went out drinking with the guys after a game."

She asked for the husband's phone number, names of his sister's friends, and a photo he could part with. She gave him one of her cards and went out into the night.

Hurrying around the block to Vinnie's, she was glad to be back on a busy street. She didn't think she'd been followed, but the sensation of being watched remained. Uneasy, she looked forward to meeting Jeff.

In Vinnie's, the after-work crowd was starting to stagger home and the buffet table had been picked clean. TJ took a seat at the bar. Minutes later, Jeff walked in looking engineer-like in jeans and a dark-brown leather jacket over a white shirt open at the neck.

He sat down beside her. "How did the interview go?"

"The guy said no way the husband did it. Turns out the wife went at him with his own baseball bat, which explains the 911 call. The brother said he still hangs with the husband. Says the guy hasn't even had a date since the wife disappeared, 'cause he's still waiting for her to come back. Chatted him up for a while. Didn't get any lyin' vibe from the guy. Have to talk to the husband, too, but he's out of town now."

Jeff turned to her. "For what it's worth, I agree with Eric. You shouldn't go on these interviews by yourself."

"I hate it when someone starts out sayin' for what it's worth. Can always figure it's gonna be something that'll piss me off."

"And did it?"

"Sorta. But right now I'm glad to see you."

"Then I'll try not to do it again."

"Got the creeps walkin' over to his apartment. Had a feeling someone was watching me."

Jeff pondered for a minute. "Let's forget the drink and go for a walk. See if anyone follows us."

"You crazy? I don't go looking for trouble. We'll see what happens when we leave."

24

When Eddie got the money from Rita's life insurance, the bar was still on the market. He hadn't told anyone about the money and acted surprised when he found out about it. He even got another few thousand from her 401K he hadn't planned on. Her death had been ruled accidental, Eddie's negligence undetected. Things were going his way.

The purchase of the business went through and provided him with a comfortable income. Life was good again. He had enough money to drive a decent car, do a little gambling, and even thought about buying the duplex he lived in.

Then his gambling got out of control. He racked up some serious debt and had to take out a second mortgage on the bar. Life wasn't as much fun with money worries thrown into the mix and his business jeopardized. Desperately trying to get out of the hole, Eddie let one of his bartenders go and began working longer hours.

One night at closing everyone had left except a man sitting at the end of the bar, staring into his beer. Eddie thought he'd seen the guy now and then, but didn't remember ever talking to him. Eddie reminded him it was past closing and asked him to leave.

The man looked around nervously, making sure they were alone. "Do you know someone who could take care of my wife?"

Take care of his wife? Was she sick? It took a few seconds before it dawned on Eddie the guy wasn't interested in healthcare. As a bartender, he heard and got asked just about everything—but this?

"You're puttin' me on, right?"

The guy stared at Eddie and shook his head. Before Eddie could tell the creep to leave, he leaned across the bar and whispered, "It's worth seven grand to me."

Christ, seven-fucking-grand! Here was an opportunity dropping into his lap but did he have the stones to take advantage of it? He had to stall the guy, give himself time to think, make sure the asshole was on the level.

"I may know someone," Eddie replied cautiously, "but it'll cost you ten." *Fuck, did I really say that?* Eddie broke out in a cold sweat, hoping the guy didn't notice his shaking hands. He quickly picked up a damp rag, wiping the already spotless bar. Ten grand would take care of his problem.

At first the guy just nodded at the price, then leaned across the bar again. In a loud voice, droplets of spittle landing on the gleaming bar, he raised his voice for the first time. "For ten, she'd better fucking disappear—and on the weekend I'm in Green Bay at the fucking bowling tournament!"

Eddie discovered not only could he do the deed, over the next few years he performed it repeatedly. Solicitation hadn't been necessary. Each time, the opportunity just sort of happened. He found it amazing how many morons wanted their women out of their lives, overlooking the fact he'd been one of them.

Forty grand later, the bar was solid again. Eddie contained his gambling to an occasional poker game and weekly lottery ticket. Comfortable again, he started seeing the woman who delivered snacks to the bar every week. Doreen Wade was a good woman. A tall divorcee, with red hair and a wide grin, she had two kids, both over eighteen and living on their own.

On a Tuesday night, busy with the after-bowling crowd, Eddie went into the back room for a case of beer when he became aware someone had walked in behind him; a short, thin, weasely looking guy with patchy hair and beady eyes. Eddie recognized him as one of the losers he'd referred to the imaginary hit man. Shit, now what?

"What the fuck is going on?" the guy demanded. "Some bitch detective is nosing around asking questions about my wife's disappearance!"

"I told you I have nothing to do with it," Eddie snarled.

"But you know this guy, right?"

"Listen, asshole, I'm just the middle-man. The best thing you can do right now is shut the fuck up. Nothing goes back to you as far as I'm concerned. You need to keep your yap shut and forget about it."

The guy looked doubtful, his lips curling. "I guess you're right. But can you tell the guy someone's asking questions?"

"I told you before I don't even know the guy. I haven't heard anything from him in a long time, and there's no fuckin' way to contact him. He's probably long gone."

The little man didn't question Eddie about how he'd contacted the guy in the first place. His face set in a dark scowl, he shoved a white business card at Eddie. "It's on you now, pal." He turned and stepped back out into the bar.

Edgy, but feeling like he'd dodged a bullet, Eddie went back to the task of restocking beer. Later, when the drinkers had all left for home, he pulled out the card the guy had thrust at him. On it was the name of the detective who had been asking questions.

Teal J. Peacock. *What the hell kind of name is that?*

25

TJ and Jeff finished their drinks, talked a bit, and left for the Mexican restaurant. They located the restaurant on a corner across from three other popular spots on the adjacent corners, in a neighborhood seedy except for the trendy shops and restaurants dotting the main streets.

Jeff drove past the restaurant, the street in front of it lined with cars. "I don't like the looks of this neighborhood. I'll drop you off and look for a parking place on a side street."

"You're such a pussy," TJ scoffed. "I should drop you off!"

Jeff found a spot about halfway down a side street, dark, except for the low light coming from some of the houses. Glad TJ carried a gun, he thought maybe she was right—he was a pussy. At least if being cautious earned you that label. He'd never understood the popularity of restaurants located on their fringes.

The place was jammed. They put their name on a waiting list for dinner and went to the bar, filled with people drinking margaritas while waiting for their meal. Jeff squeezed up to the bar and ordered their drinks, while TJ excused herself, heading for the ladies room.

A tiny table by a window had just been vacated. He quickly took a seat, sipping the tart, icy drink. When Jamie's car had turned up, he'd hit a new low. And the damn song repeated in his brain.

"Let me tell you 'bout the way she looked..."

TJ wound her way through the crowded restaurant and entered a long, dark hallway leading to the back of the building. She could see two short hallways branching off about halfway to the exit, each with a sign directing patrons to one of the restrooms, Banditos on the left, Senoritas on the right.

It happened so fast TJ barely had time to react. A large figure came at her after bursting through the door to the alley. She thought she saw the glint of a knife before leaping to the side. She felt the blade meet its mark before she managed to give her assailant a sharp elbow jab to the diaphragm. In a heartbeat, she had her gun out, but he had dodged quickly, already at the exit to the alley.

Ignoring the searing pain in her side, TJ ran to the door, gun raised. She took a shot at his retreating shape as she stepped out into the alley. When she reached the side street she saw the rear lights of a car speeding away from the curb. He'd gotten away. Swearing to herself, she stumbled into a recessed doorway, where she put her hand to her side and felt the warm trickle of blood seeping from her body.

Above the sound of the salsa music and loud conversation, Jeff was certain he'd heard a scream. Panicked, he pushed his way through the crowd, looking for TJ. Across the dining room a cluster of women gathered around the entrance to a hallway. Looking into it, they talked excitedly in Spanish.

When he reached the opening into the dim hallway leading to the restrooms, he forced his way through the group of women.

One of them cried, "She shot a guy!"

Jeff's heart lurched as he ran out the exit door leading into an alley. He didn't see TJ, but drops of blood on the pavement led toward the street. He found her in the doorway of a defunct appliance store. She was leaning over, gun in one hand, the other clutched to her side. *Was she shot?*

When she saw him, she gasped, "Some fucker tried to grab me in the hallway. Got a knife in my side before I could get my gun out. Wanted to nail his ass, but he's long gone."

Jeff took out his phone. "I'll call 911."

"No fuckin' way! Let's get out of here before the cops come." One arm clutching her side, she started walking toward the car.

Jeff stopped her. "You need a doctor. I'm taking you to an emergency room."

"Not going to any ER. Ain't as bad as it looks, I know about these things—isn't my first time getting stuck." She glared at him. "And we know a doctor, don't we?"

Supporting her as she moved, Jeff argued with her as they moved to the car. Sure she'd never agree to go to a hospital, he opened the trunk and pulled a towel out of his gym bag. He handed it to her. "If you won't listen to reason, at least don't bleed all over my car."

When Eric got the call from Jeff, he was at a gourmet restaurant in Delafield with Danielle Ventura. She'd turned him down when he asked her out the first time, the day he'd brought Lisa to the showroom. The next time he'd asked she'd been coy about setting a date. With her finally, he found himself distracted.

As hard as he tried to change the subject from her divorce and all the things she did or did not receive in the settlement, she kept finding a way to pick up where she'd left off. They'd just finished their entrees when he felt his phone vibrate. He opened it and saw it was Jeff calling. He apologized to Danielle and took the call.

"Eric, TJ's been stabbed. She won't go to a hospital. We're headed to Waukesha."

"Give me a minute; I'll call you right back."

Eric looked over at Danielle. "Sorry, but I'm going to have to run. I have an emergency to deal with."

Her mouth opened to protest.

"I'll call you tomorrow and explain." Eric tossed a few large bills on the table, another in front of her for cab fare and hurried to his car, where he called Jeff. "Jeff, TJ knows where my house is and where I keep my spare key in case you get there before I do. I should be home in about the same time it'll take you to get there."

Eric heard TJ complaining in the background. *She can't be hurt too badly if she still has the energy to gripe.*

Eric arrived first, turned on the lights, and got out his medical supplies, glad he still had the things he'd need. He put on a pot of coffee, took out a bottle of brandy and an old bathrobe.

They came in minutes later, TJ leaning on Jeff, a towel clutched to her side.

Jeff said, "I tried to get her to go to the emergency room, but she insisted on calling you instead."

Eric helped Jeff bring her into the room. "That was stupid. You should have been treated immediately. If the wound is too deep, I'm taking you to a hospital."

They put her down on a long leather couch in front of the fireplace. Eric brought over a bright lamp to work by.

TJ whined, "Can't be too bad, he only got me a little. I moved pretty fast when I saw him. Hope I got one in him."

Eric started. "You shot him?"

"Tried, but he was running too fast. Couldn't go to the hospital. Didn't want the cops nosin' around yet. Wasn't anything worth telling them, anyway. He had on dark clothes, a cap pulled low, and sunglasses. Go figure."

Eric moved the towel and examined the wound, realizing she was right, it wasn't very deep, the bleeding already diminishing.

"Jeff, I put some coffee on. Would you go see if it's ready? Give me a few minutes. Then bring us the coffee and that bottle of brandy."

Jeff left the room.

Eric said, "You're lucky as hell, you know. If this was deeper it could have punctured your liver. I'll give you a local anesthetic, then I'm going to clean it out."

He froze the area, then cut open TJ's black silk camisole. She was naked underneath it.

"I knew you always wanted to see my tits."

"Honey, I've seen more breasts in my lifetime than most men can even dream of. They're just another pair. Nice, but just another pair."

TJ laughed, then groaned in pain. Eric put a clean towel over her breasts and set up the things he'd need on the table next to the couch. He washed the wound, using antiseptic on and around it before stitching it up.

"I think you're all right for now. But there's always a chance of infection setting in, so I'm going to give you an antibiotic shot."

He helped her into the old robe he'd brought out. "Take off your jeans.

"Thought they didn't do those butt-shots anymore."

"They don't. I just want a peek at your ass, too."

She clutched her midsection. "Don't make me laugh. It hurts."

By the time she quit complaining, he'd given her the injection.

When Jeff came back, the three of them had coffee with brandy. After he saw her nodding off, Eric picked TJ up and carried her to the guest room.

He came back and poured himself another brandy.

Jeff asked, "Do you think we should call Detective Conlin?"

"No. She's not seriously hurt. She can tell him herself if she wants to."

"Don't you think it's time to get the police involved?"

Eric had mixed feelings. "This incident could have nothing to do with our interviews." Jeff tried to object. "Let me finish. Do I think it's related? Of course, but proving it would be impossible. All we'll have to show for it is TJ's wound. Neither of you saw anything. I'm worried about everyone's safety. And we still aren't free of that psycho, Fischer. I'd suspect him except he never met TJ."

Jeff said, "That policewoman who's trying to get something on him—you said she sounded sympathetic. Maybe Lisa could have a talk with her."

"That might be the best way to test the waters. We'll have to talk about it."

Later, Eric emptied the coffee pot and checked the fire before stepping out on the patio for his last cigar of the day. Afterward, he looked in on TJ, sleeping peacefully, the butt of her gun sticking out from under her pillow. He'd never seen her looking so serene.

The call from Eric, reporting what had happened to TJ, had stoked Lisa's fears. She checked the windows and doors for the second time, glad she had Phanny close by. If anyone actually broke in, the dog would probably lick him to death, but Phanny had a huge warning bark that would deter most prowlers.

Lying in bed with her mind spinning, she worried about TJ, about all of them, and tried to focus on something pleasant. She thought about Thanksgiving, usually one of her favorite holidays. It was only two weeks away, and she hadn't heard from her daughter.

And Tyler kept calling, trying to persuade Lisa to keep seeing him. His engagement hadn't worked out. But Lisa knew things wouldn't be any different. Exciting, yes. Great sex, sure. But beyond that, she'd be waiting for the next nubile young thing to lure him away from her. But tonight his warm body lying next to her would have done wonders for her troubled soul, despite her determination to move on.

26

Eddie Wysecki had no luck finding an address for Teal J. Peacock. After giving it a lot of thought, he called the number on the business card the guy had given him. He pretended to be a storeowner in need of security. Good thing he always kept a throwaway cell phone for emergencies. Like calling his bookie.

With no intention of showing up, he arranged a fake meeting so he could check out her car and license plate. He'd follow her when she gave up on the new "client." With a little luck he'd get her address. He hadn't thought any further ahead. Eddie wasn't sure she posed a threat to him, but he wanted to find out as much as he could about her. Just in case. He couldn't afford to have anyone snooping around the bar.

The ruse worked, and she agreed to meet him at a restaurant on the outskirts of West Allis. He only had the guy's description of her as a mixed-breed babe who dressed like a slut. When he saw a woman getting out of a small red car, one of those weird, fast little things, a mini-something, he wasn't sure it was her. As she walked to the door, he noticed her security guard's uniform, and knew he'd spotted the right woman. Parked in the back of the lot between cars, Eddie waited.

A mere twenty minutes later, she gave up on the fictitious client, left the restaurant, and drove out of the parking lot. Eddie followed at a discreet distance to a bank across from the shopping center in Brookfield. She parked in the back, entering the bank by a rear door after waiting a few seconds. Someone inside must have let her in.

Now that he knew where she worked, it'd be easy to follow her home.

When Peacock left at five, heavy traffic made it easy for him to follow unnoticed. In downtown Milwaukee, he watched as she pulled into underground parking beneath a high-rise apartment building. She might just be visiting someone, so he hung around for a while.

He got lucky at six when she left the building on foot. She'd changed clothes, so he knew he had her address. Eddie left his car and followed her. There was a lot of activity in the area so he wasn't concerned about standing out. But suddenly she stopped and looked around, as if she sensed him following her. Crap. All he could do was keep walking and act normal; being five-ten, brown hair, gray eyes, medium build — maybe a bit overweight — conservatively dressed, wearing glasses, and, as they said on the cop shows, no distinguishing scars or characteristics, all allowed him to blend in on the busy street.

Peacock's movements made no sense. After she went into Vinnie's, he got in his car and parked nearby. He tailed her when she left the area in an SUV driven by a skinny young guy wearing a brown leather jacket. He followed them across town to a Mexican joint on the south side, then followed them into the restaurant. After a minute or two, he saw her walk through the restaurant, heading toward the restrooms.

When he heard the screams, he rushed over to the hallway, and saw her running out the back door into an alley. Eddie nearly dumped in his drawers when he heard a gunshot. Ears ringing and heart pounding, he slithered out, trying to look casual. The last thing he needed was attention drawn to him anywhere near violence.

He couldn't believe his luck when he entered the side street where he'd parked and saw her moving down the sidewalk, leaning on the guy he'd seen her with. When they got to their car, the guy opened the trunk and handed her something, then they got into the car and drove off.

Was she hurt? They'd be heading to the nearest hospital, but why hadn't they waited for the cops to show? Odd, he thought, odd enough to keep following them.

Mystified, he followed them all the way out to Waukesha, then outside of town, where they pulled into a huge estate. The house sat far back on a wooded lot, barely visible from the street. *Shit. Who are these people?*

The best course of action would be to forget about them. Unless something else happened close to home, he was probably off the hook. *This chick has bigger problems than me.*

27

After they finished their interviews on Saturday, Eric and Lisa drove out to Eric's to check on TJ. Lisa approached TJ, relieved to see her sitting by the fire wearing a headset and weaving to music only she could hear.

She pulled off the headphones. "How'd it go?"

Lisa, knowing TJ wouldn't want a fuss made over her, didn't inquire about her health. "Good. I think we're almost at the halfway mark."

Wearing a pair of black jeans and a sweatshirt hanging nearly to her knees—no doubt belonging to Eric—TJ got up off the floor with a grimace. "Got skewered like a frickin' pig at a luau."

"I think we should report it."

"Nothin' to report. Didn't see nothin'. No way to tell if it's connected to all this."

The ensuing argument ended when Jeff came in and asked how she was doing. TJ replied, "I'm good. Eric's taking me back to my place tomorrow as long as I'm not infected." She wrinkled her face, looking over at Eric.

Jeff asked, "Do you think you'll be safe by yourself?"

TJ gave him a glowering look.

Lisa said, "TJ, on Monday, Maggie's coming in to give me an update on Steven Fischer, so I'm thinking I'll broach the topic of what we're really working on here. If she seems sympathetic, we can try to enlist her help."

They continued to discuss whether to get the police involved until pizzas arrived. When only a few corner pieces sat untouched, Lisa said, "What about Thanksgiving week? I think we should skip the Saturday after the holiday. I'll have time to set up some appointments for the following week."

Jeff groaned. "My folks are in Florida, and Jamie' parents invited me to have dinner with them. I'm not sure I can handle that."

"If you need an excuse to get out of it, you're welcome to come to my house," Lisa offered. "All of you are welcome. I don't think Paige is going to make it. I'm cooking even if it ends up being just Phanny and me."

TJ looked up from the last corner of pizza she was nibbling on. "Usually spend the day with my sister and her kids."

"Bring them too," Lisa suggested. "It'll be great to have kids around."

Later, TJ, Lisa and Eric lingered in front of the fire, sipping coffee. TJ sat tilted back in a big leather recliner, feet up and eyes at half-mast, a mug of coffee balanced on her chest.

"TJ," Lisa began, her voice soft, "I know you didn't see your attacker's face, but did you see anything noticeable about him?"

"When I went out that night, I had a feelin' like I was being watched. Didn't see anybody suspicious, but I have sort of a radar for that kinda thing."

"And you think whoever was watching you could be your attacker. Could it have been the person you were supposed to meet at the restaurant? Or maybe the guy you'd just talked to?"

"Nah, I had the feeling before I talked to the first guy, the one in my neighborhood. And I called the other one this morning. He was pissed 'cause we didn't show up at the restaurant. He claims his wife's friends have heard from her. It checked out, so no, not him. And he's too short."

Eric leaned forward. "So this guy was tall?"

"Yeah, and something about him is buggin' me. Can't tell you what, though. Somethin' . . ."

Lisa perked up. "If you didn't see his face, it had to be his posture—or his gait."

"Oh yeah, right, I can call the cops now. Tell them his 'gait' was familiar." She sat up in the chair, setting her empty mug on an end table.

"Sorry, just frustrated. Pissed me off I didn't put a bullet in his ass."

Lisa realized TJ had no way of knowing for sure she hadn't hit her assailant, but let it drop.

TJ stood. "Gonna go back to my cell and hit the sheets. Night all."

When she'd left the room, Lisa turned to Eric. "Her cell? Is she that angry with you for keeping her here?"

"No. That's just TJ being TJ. Someone had to convince her to take time to heal, even if she won't admit she needs it. She'll be fine; the wound isn't serious."

Lisa stood. "I'm kind of tired, too. Do you mind taking me back to my car now?"

"Sure, but I'm either going to take you to your car and follow you home, or drive you home and get you to your car tomorrow."

"I suppose I'll sound like TJ if I object. Will she be all right here alone?"

Eric chuckled. "She sleeps with her gun under the pillow. And I have a state-of-the-art security system, approved by Ms. Peacock herself. She'll be fine."

After dropping Lisa at her car, Eric followed Lisa home. When she pulled into the garage and got out of her car, she saw him walking toward her.

"I'd like to meet Phanny."

Phanny wiggled with delight. She greeted him with a wet, lightning-fast kiss.

"I forgot to warn you about the tongue," Lisa laughed.

"That's okay, I love dogs. I'm thinking about getting one."

"I'd recommend adoption. Someday I'll have to tell you the story about getting Phanny. There are so many dogs that have been abandoned and need homes." He followed Lisa into the house, where he insisted on going through all the rooms.

Grateful for his protectiveness, she realized he hadn't annoyed today. She had a feeling his negative attitude toward her had more to do with her profession than herself, but he'd yet to tell her why. She'd noticed the only calls he took during the day were business calls and suspected the others had been from a woman. Either he was avoiding the woman's calls or didn't want to have a personal conversation in front of Lisa.

Eric looked in on TJ when he got home. She was asleep, lying on her side. He bent over, slid the gun out from under the pillow and set it on the nightstand.

28

Two years earlier

There wasn't a book on serial killers that described him. They were all a crock. He fit none of their DMS-III groups, or popular stereotypes. Supposedly, they tortured their victims, wrote puzzling letters to the police and/or press, left their victims intriguingly postured, and ultimately, escalated and went wildly out of control—this last factor making them easy to track down.

He'd done none of those things. His ladies rested comfortably on his property up north. Respectfully buried—no shallow graves for the wildlife to dig up.

For him, killing had become a hobby, not an obsession. After they arrested Allyson's abusive boyfriend for her murder, he'd been successfully ferreting out abused women. It offered the perfect way to commit murder—the police always had a prime suspect.

Abused women were vulnerable, easily manipulated into keeping their meetings with him hidden. Some he dated once or twice then never saw again. They were the ones he determined didn't need to be eliminated, kind souls with low self-esteem who gravitated toward men who abused them. He pitied them, leaving them to their miseries. He sought women who deserved to be treated badly—beautiful on the outside, but ugly on the inside–where it mattered.

29

Detective Maggie Petersen walked into Lisa's office early Monday morning.

"No doughnuts?"

"No time to work them off today."

"I thought you'd like to know Steven Fischer will be in custody by the end of the day. We discovered some interesting things in his financials thanks to information from Helen. There's no doubt he tampered with his wife's accounts to make it look like she left on her own."

"That's wonderful news."

"We haven't found her daughter's body yet. We've traced Fischer's charge card purchases and found he's staying at a motel near Madison. We suspect he's getting ready to bolt. The motel is close to the airport."

"You're sure he's still there?"

"Yes, the Dane County sheriffs are watching the place. And my impression of the man is his ego's a lot bigger than his brain. He'll be certain he's crafty enough to be one step ahead of us."

"Helen will be so relieved."

"I'll let you know when he's in custody. As soon as we get the warrant, we'll pick him up."

"Maggie, thank you for taking care of this so quickly."

"No thanks necessary. We're glad to have this creep off the streets. Thanks to you, Helen's life will be her own again."

"What if he gets out on bail?"

"There's always that. We'll have to take it one step at a time."

Lisa sat back, contemplating how to begin. "Maggie, there is something else I'd like to talk to you about. Do you have time for a cup of coffee?"

"Sure. We won't be leaving for Madison for a while."

They sat across from each other in Lisa's office looking out at the nearly opaque lake, unwelcoming under a sky the color of poured concrete.

"Maggie, we haven't been entirely open with you about why we met with Helen Mueller in the first place."

"I didn't think so," the detective replied, "but I knew your concern for Helen was genuine, so I didn't push it."

"Is it possible to have an off-the-record conversation?"

Maggie nodded. "I don't see why not as long as you aren't going to confess to a crime."

"We haven't done anything illegal." She told Maggie the story of their group, beginning with the statistics on missing women and her visit to the MPD. Maggie listened without question or comment.

"After what happened to TJ, we decided maybe it was time for some type of police involvement. TJ doesn't want to tell Detective Conlin any of this until we have more than our suspicions to offer the Milwaukee Police. I would agree with her, except things are getting dicey. It's possible the attack on TJ could have had nothing to do with all this, but I think it's highly unlikely."

"I'd have to agree, Lisa. What are you hoping to find that will convince the police to investigate?"

"We're trying to identify women whose disappearances are unexplainable; those we're sure didn't leave on their own or were killed by their abusers. So far we have about eight. We hoped once we had the list completed, we'd be able to find common factors among these women that would tell us what happened to them."

Maggie frowned. "Are you thinking one person is responsible?"

"Yes, but we haven't ruled out more than one. And there *are* other possibilities, as James Wilson was so quick to point out."

Maggie gazed out at the lake. "I know you're all determined to see this through, so I'll forgo the warning speech and any expression of my concern that two of your group could be murderers. Do you have any idea how much longer it'll take to finish all the interviews?"

"We're thinking another month."

"If you aren't ready for this to be official, what can I do for you?"

"I don't know. Suggestions, maybe . . . Advice." Lisa stumbled. She should have been prepared for that question.

"I'd like to share this with David. Is that all right?"

"Sure, if he can also be an off-the-record consultant."

Maggie grinned. "It's what he does best. He's not a by-the-book kind of cop, which is why we get along so well—and *not* so well at times. I'll talk to him and get back to you. Are you going to be around tonight?"

"Yes. Let me give you my home phone number." She wrote it on the back of one of her business cards and handed it to Maggie.

Maggie walked out, her long braid trailing down her back. Lisa breathed a sigh of relief. She refreshed her coffee, wishing she'd made a bakery trip on her way to work. Food was so damn comforting.

A Sunday brunch with Danielle turned into an overnight at the Radisson, and Eric didn't arrive at his dealership until eleven Monday morning.

At eight that night he was still at his desk, updating the website when she called and invited him to dinner. The invitation seemed like too much too soon. But he'd enjoyed the night with her, and he had to eat, didn't he?

The food at Merino's was delicious and Danielle was lovely, but he declined her offer to spend the night at her place. She'd looked disappointed when he told her he was going to be busy getting ready to take some cars to an auction in Texas the following week- end. He explained all the planning that went into getting ready for an auction before realizing she was waiting for him to invite her along. Uneasy, he ended the evening as gracefully as possible and walked her to her car, promising to call her before he left on Friday morning.

30

Lisa made great progress on her calls Monday evening. By eight o'clock, she had more than six interviews set up for Saturday and one for Friday evening. The sister of one of the missing women told Lisa her sister was alive and well and living in Montana. Another one eliminated from the list.

Lisa got up from her desk and saw Phanny looking at her with hope all over her face that there may be a walk in her near future. Lisa felt bad for the dog because lately she'd been nervous about after-dark outings and had just been letting Phanny out for a few minutes before she went to bed.

Maggie called to give her the good news—Steven Fischer was in jail. The bad news was he wasn't talking and had an excellent criminal attorney representing him. Lisa didn't really care. Although she hoped to see him pay for what he'd done, their main goal had been keeping Helen safe.

Lisa's doorbell rang at five after eight, and she opened the door to Maggie and her partner. She brought them into the kitchen where she had hot cocoa waiting.

David Lassiter looked about ten years older than Maggie, making him near forty. Lisa didn't think she'd ever seen him before, and she knew most of the Oconomowoc police by sight. Maggie introduced them, and they sat down at the table as Lisa poured steaming mugs of cocoa.

Maggie stirred marshmallows into her mug. "I told David about your group and what's been happening since you started the interviews. I'll let him give you his impressions."

David stared raptly into the cup he held in front of him. "I don't think anyone's made me cocoa since I was five.'

Maggie laughed. "I guess that's one impression."

Lisa crossed her legs under the table. David's sensual looks made her uneasy. He smiled at her, and ridiculously, she felt her face heat up. She didn't doubt he knew the effect he had on women.

"I'm sympathetic to your mission," he began, looking directly into her eyes. "But I'm not comfortable with civilians playing detective games. That said, like many other people, domestic abuse played a large part in my life growing up. My father's favorite pastime was hitting my mother. She died of cancer at forty-two. I've always believed it was because he took away her spirit to live. So, when Maggie told me your story, I had mixed feelings about it." He paused, adding a few more marshmallows to his cocoa.

Maggie flashed him an impatient look. "David and I have decided to do whatever we can to help you. Let us know what you need, and if it's something we are able to help you with, we will. But there will be a couple conditions."

"I expected there would be," Lisa said, "and I think I can speak for everyone and say, given what happened to TJ, we won't be objecting to whatever conditions you feel are necessary."

David said, "Good, because they're non-negotiable. The first is that all of you remain safe. You've started by pairing up, but it's not enough. You must never leave the other alone—not even for a minute. Your friend TJ's untimely trip to the ladies room? I don't think we need to tell you nothing like that can happen again. You'll all have to be extremely vigilant in protecting each other."

Lisa hadn't felt completely safe since the incident. "You won't get any argument on that, Detective."

"The other condition may sound extreme, but Maggie and I are in agreement on it. Since all of you live alone—we want you to pair up together until you reach the point of handing this over to the police."

Lisa felt her face burning again. "You're not serious!"

Maggie explained, "Lisa, TJ's been attacked and you've unearthed a murderer. It's likely TJ's attack had something to do with your interviews. If nothing else, it was an attempt to get you to back off. It could be one man you've interviewed or someone else who's involved in these disappearances. It doesn't matter which it is; you all live alone—you're sitting ducks."

"I'll have to talk to the others about it."

"Lisa, you can't do this fast enough as far as we're concerned," Maggie said. "We don't recommend you stay with friends or relatives for the obvious reason none of you would want anyone else jeopardized."

Lisa busied herself by bringing out a plate of cookies.

David grabbed one. "I don't want any of you alone during the night, and no one goes out at night alone. For any reason. I know this will be a big sacrifice, but with Maggie and myself on board, you should get this done faster than you'd planned."

"What about your concern that we're working with two men who might possibly be murderers? This would force us to live with them."

Maggie frowned. "You've already told us you trust these men— you can't argue it both ways, Lisa."

Weeks of forced togetherness. Lisa got up from the table muttering, "Living with TJ will be interesting as hell." She turned to the stovetop to refill their mugs.

David expressed a sly smile. "Why stay with TJ? You could do the boy-girl thing again; you're all adults."

She bit back a sharp retort. "I'll talk to them tonight. Anything else?"

His gaze met hers. "Our involvement is officially not happening. If anything goes wrong, we know nothing. Nothing we do for you will be traced back to us. I'm sure you understand; our jobs could be on the line."

Phanny had been sitting with her head on Maggie's knee. Maggie, enjoying the doggie affection, had been stroking her head. "Lisa, I wouldn't leave your dog alone—just a precaution."

"Right. I'd been thinking that, too."

Lisa walked the detectives to the door, her head whirling at the implications of this new wrinkle. She wasn't looking forward to breaking the news to the others.

At nearly eleven, Lisa's phone rang. It had to be Eric; she'd already talked to the others.

"I got your message, Lisa. Is it about Maggie? Did you talk with her?"

"I arranged with Jeff and TJ that the four of us meet tomorrow to discuss it."

"Can you give me the highlights?"

"We knew if they agreed to work with us on this, they would have conditions."

"How bad is it?"

"It's the safety issue."

"The safety issue has been a big concern of mine from the get-go. We're already pairing up; what else do they want?"

Lisa decided she might as well tell him. "They don't like the fact that all of us live alone and think we need to do a roommate thing until we turn this over to the MPD."

She wasn't sure what she expected when she told him the news, but certainly not the raucous laughter she heard on the other end of the line. It was contagious. Lisa started to giggle. And burst into laughter. God, it felt good!

When they managed to contain themselves, Eric said, "It's really not a problem. Everyone can stay here; there's plenty of room. I'll park my cars at work so all of you can all have a spot in the garage. How much safer could we be? I have to be out of town this weekend, so I'll feel a lot better knowing the rest of you are together."

It could work. Lisa didn't relish living under the same roof as Eric, but he'd been more tolerable lately and it would be a temporary arrangement. Maybe when they told TJ and Jeff, it wouldn't be as much of a shock, knowing they already had a solution. "That's very generous."

Eric went on, "It may be a good idea to have someone watching the house for a few days. What do you think?"

"Seems a little extreme, but let's talk about it when we get together."

"It might be better if I just do it, rather than give anyone the opportunity to nix it. At least while I'm gone. Then no one ever comes into an empty house by themselves."

"You're probably right. Go ahead and arrange it for the weekend. We can see where we are on the subject when you come back."

"I'll put it in place."

31

The next morning, relieved to find out Maggie Petersen and her partner were willing to help, everyone reluctantly agreed to the terms set out by the two detectives.

Living together quickly became a new item on TJ's complaint list—another, Eric's decision to hire a security guard to watch his estate the weekend he'd be gone. She claimed it undermined her skills, but Lisa wasn't buying it.

She knew TJ's confidence had been shaken and suspected she was secretly glad for the additional protection.

Everyone settled in at Eric's with a minimum of fuss. TJ claimed the guest room she'd stayed in over the weekend, and Lisa took the maid's suite over the attached garage, an apartment with two small bedrooms. Accessible from the loft above the kitchen, it also had its own entry from inside the garage. She found it to be a cozy chamber, decorated in a woodsy flavor with pine furniture and dark green fabric. Lisa tossed Phanny's bed in front of the gas fireplace in the living room. Excited by the newness, the dog ran from room to room, sniffing and exploring.

The master suite on the first floor had his and hers bedrooms, one on either side of two gigantic closets and a shared bathroom the size of a small house. Eric put Jeff in what used to be his wife's room. Jeff commented the house looked like something belonging in the mountains of Colorado. With log siding, stonework, green-tin roof and leaded windows, the house fit perfectly into the wooded surroundings.

Over takeout food served hastily on the huge, granite-topped island that separated the kitchen area from the living room, Lisa handed out schedules for the next weekend's interviews.

"There are only about nine left after these. Those are women we couldn't find current addresses or contacts for. I'm going to call Maggie tomorrow and give her the names. If she comes through with something on them, we can try to get everything done by next Wednesday so we can focus on the short list over the holiday weekend."

Jeff's gray eyes narrowed. "Once we have this 'short list' won't we be handing it over to the police?"

TJ scoffed. "We'll need more than our list to get Milwaukee's finest off their dead butts."

Lisa said, "I thought we planned to find some threads connecting the women before we turned over the list."

Jeff frowned. "If we do that, we'll be here for weeks."

Eric stood. "Come on, people, where's your sense of adventure? We need to keep Maggie and David happy for the time being, but once we no longer need their help, anyone who's comfortable on their own can leave."

"Can't be soon enough for me," TJ muttered.

Explaining the living situation to Richard could be touchy for TJ, but other than that, Lisa had a feeling TJ would be content right where she was.

The lights were still on in Eric's house when Danielle drove by a little after eleven. She knew Eric carried his cell phone with him. Panicky, she suspected he'd been dodging her calls. Their time together had been so special. Was there another woman?

Gripping the steering wheel with wet palms, she slowed enough to see; the house sat too far back from the street to make out anything other than the lights. *Ridiculous, driving by his house.* She was acting like a teenager.

Obviously, he wanted to take things slower than she did. She'd foolishly thought that by keeping him at arm's length for a while before she'd finally agreed to go out with him, he'd be positively enchanted with her after she said yes. *So much for my stupid plan.*

She turned around, once more driving slowly past the grounds. From that angle she could see any cars in the driveway. When a dark shadow moved toward the house, she stopped the car, looked again and saw nothing. It must have been her out-of-control emotions playing tricks. She took a deep breath and headed for home.

Fearing sleep would be elusive, Lisa put on a robe and slippers, then went back downstairs to sit by the fire for a few minutes until the sleep aid she'd swallowed took effect. As she descended, she realized Eric's house held no aroma of his disgusting cigars—apparently he kept his habit outdoors—or had a smoking room somewhere.

Surprised to see TJ sitting on the sofa and staring into the fire, Lisa sat down next to her. "Are you okay?"

"Yeah. Never would have guessed things would end up this way. And we still have a long way to go."

"It seems to me we've accomplished a lot."

TJ sighed, eyes staring at the glowing embers of the fire. "You're right. Suppose I'm not done beating up on myself."

"That's not like you, TJ. Will it help if I give you permission to be officially done beating up on yourself and let it go?"

TJ laughed. "Not sure why I'm letting this drag on. But go ahead—work some shrink magic on me."

The request for help took Lisa by surprise. "Well, absent any magic or time for therapy, I could take you through a relaxation exercise."

"I'm ready to try anything. Gotta snap outta this."

Lisa had TJ put her head back, her feet up on the ottoman, then close her eyes and take deep measured breaths until she felt at peace and relaxed. Then she talked her softly and slowly through a visualization of TJ confident, proud, and focused on all the wonderful things she'd accomplished.

When she finished and eased TJ back to their conversation, TJ started giggling.

"I don't believe it. I wanted to crawl in a hole until all of this got over. I feel great. You did work magic."

Amused, Lisa said, "Slow down. What we did is just a way to deal with stress. You'll need to do it more than once, and you can do it without me anytime you like. The trick is to relax as much as possible and stay focused."

"I'm glad we had a chance to talk. I haven't had much time with you."

TJ rose from the sofa. "Neither has Richard. He thinks I'm staying with my sister for a few days to help with the kids."

"Do you do that often?"

"Yeah, sometimes when she's having a hard time. It ain't easy raising two kids alone. Well, you know how it is."

"She's lucky to have you around to help." Lisa felt the pill kicking in. "Richard's okay with you being gone?"

TJ stretched as far as her stitches would allow. "He's been pulling nights to cover for a friend of his. Makes it less likely he's wonderin' about me."

Wednesday morning when Eric finally returned her calls, Danielle apologized profusely for calling him so often the day before. "I've been looking at a BMW at the dealership in Delafield, and I wanted to check the price with you before making an offer."

It was a plausible excuse. He knew she'd been looking at cars since she'd gotten her divorce settlement. "I'll fax you some figures from our books."

She said, "Tell you what—I'll treat for lunch at the Machine Shed. You can give them to me in person."

After their lunch, Eric thought he'd been diplomatic. He'd explained to Danielle he didn't want a relationship. It had been the right thing to do, but he didn't feel good about it. Had he gotten through to her?

Funny how he'd been comparing her to Lisa. The two women were about the same height with similar coloring, but other than that there weren't many similarities. Lisa wore her intelligence like a cloak of honor, and Danielle kept hers carefully hidden under expensive designer clothing and chic hairstyles.

He turned into his dealership, glad to be distracted from thoughts of women. He had cars to prepare for shipping.

32

The present

It had been weeks since he discovered Lisa Rayburn and her evidence posse trying to root out the reason abused women were disappearing. Meddling cunt. He watched her—and her little band of followers. He didn't know her well enough to be sure if the world would be better off without her, but his world would and that's all that mattered.

After he'd found out they'd all taken up residence at Eric Schindler's estate, he knew he'd have a difficult time singling out Lisa. But she represented the head of the snake—without her, the rest would shrivel and desist.

He'd been watching Schindler's place for a few days when he noticed someone else staking it out. Sitting in an old Buick, the guy couldn't have been part of security. Probably nothing to concern himself with, but he remained aware of the watcher's comings and goings.

33

Danielle had been separated from her husband for nearly two years before the divorce. Eric was the first man she wanted in a long time. She knew there had to be another woman in his life. He hadn't actually said he didn't want to see her again, just said he didn't want a relationship. In her experience, it all translated to another woman in the background.

Thursday afternoon she sat in her car, discreetly parked in a lot across from Kristy's Classics. She could tell by the flurry of activity that they were getting ready to go to the auction. Two car carriers were being loaded with classic autos, most of them muscle cars. After all the cars were loaded, Eric drove off in his Delorean.

Danielle felt ridiculously adolescent following him to his house, but she had to know if was in for the night, not on a date. Shortly after Eric pulled into his driveway, another car drove in behind him. In the beam from her headlights she saw the silhouettes of two women. *Two women! Is he having a party? But he'd hardly be throwing a party the night before he leaves for the auction.*

Danielle parked her car on a side street. Clutching a tiny flashlight she kept in her purse, she got out and crept along the edge of the heavy woods that extended behind Eric's property. Darkness fell before five now, the visibility nil in the damp woods. Her imagination flickered back to the shadow she thought she'd seen when she drove by the other night. She shivered, progressing clumsily through the thicket of the woods.

Eric's property was covered with mature pine and spruce trees, and the house backed up to a wooded area that spanned about a square mile. Prime real estate—he was a wealthy man. Her determination to snag him mounted.

Glad she'd worn dark clothing, but hoping not to ruin her new leather boots or snag her cashmere jacket on the thick, thorny undergrowth, she continued toward the house. Edging quietly onto a patio running along the north wall, she peeked into the side of a bay window and counted three people. Two women. Damn, which one could he be seeing? Both attractive women, one of them even reminded Danielle of herself, except for the dowdy figure. *God, the woman must wear a size fourteen. Couldn't be her, must be the tiny one with the short, curly hair.*

Danielle, moving slowly in her narrow heels, stumbled her way back to the car, embarrassed at her behavior. Her mind reeled with possibilities, none of them attractive.

Hard as he tried to forget about the Peacock woman, Eddie had a difficult time letting it go. Even though common sense told him he was safe from detection, his curiosity about her drove him to distraction. But he'd be seeing Doreen tonight. Maybe an evening out would get his mind off things he'd rather forget.

At six, she called with an excuse about spending the evening with her daughter who needed a shoulder to cry on because her boyfriend dumped her. What was with kids today? They weren't independent like his generation.

Now what to do with his evening? He had the bar staffed for the night in anticipation of his date. It had been a while since he'd seen a porno-flick; that usually cheered him up. He headed to the adult bookstore to get a video, then on a whim he got on the interstate and drove to the last place he'd seen Peacock.

He staked out the house he'd seen her and her friend drive into the week before after all the excitement at the Mexican restaurant. It wasn't long before he saw her turn into the driveway in her little car.

After an hour Eddie thought he'd give it another thirty minutes then take off. An old woman walking a dog strolled past his car, giving him the stink eye. Nervous because of her obvious curiosity, he hunched down lower in the seat.

Twenty minutes later, no one had left the house. The hag with the ugly dog still hovered, the dog lifting its leg to anything standing still. Bored, Eddie drove away, looking forward to a quiet night in his recliner with a six-pack and porn. He'd have to think of another way to get info on the broad.

34

When Eric called Danielle before he left, she read into it what she wanted, still believing in the possibility of a relationship with him, yet disturbed he hadn't told her what he'd done the night before. What she'd seen in his house still bugged her.

Shopping, a favorite pastime on Friday nights, led her to the high-end boutiques, where she found a great dress for her next date with Eric, a date she was sure would occur as soon as he got back from Texas. But as she drove home on I-94 and passed the exit for Waukesha, she couldn't resist driving past his house again. She noticed lights on; maybe he'd left them on for security. But no one left that many on. She told herself she wouldn't go sneaking through the woods again; last night had creeped her out.

Disgusted with herself, but out of control, she parked on the side street again. She covered the same route to the window she'd peeked through the night before. When she looked in, her stomach lurched. The same people were gathered in the kitchen. They looked comfortable with one another, obviously making dinner. What the hell?

Across the street from Eric Schindler's estate, Eddie Wysecki sat in his car, watching for any sign of TJ. Doreen had bailed on him again, still using her daughter as an excuse. Maybe she was getting ready to move on. Might be for the best if she did. In case he had to leave town in a hurry, running would be easier without any ties. He felt pathetic, sitting here for two nights, stalking some chick he'd never met. And on a Friday night to boot.

Since he'd arrived, he hadn't seen anyone come or go. Stupid to keep sitting there. He wasn't going to find out anything this way and his butt was starting to cramp. Maybe another fifteen minutes.

In the kitchen, TJ and Jeff laughed as they made chili, arguing about how much, or if any, cumin should be added to the recipe. Lisa sat in front of the widescreen TV, having agreed more than two cooks in the kitchen were too many.

When Phanny came around wanting to go out, Lisa took her to the door off the kitchen.

"If you're taking her out, I'll go with you," Jeff offered.

"Thanks, but I'm just letting her out for a minute. She's good about staying close by."

Any plausible explanation for why those people were staying in Eric's house eluded Danielle. Eric had said nothing about having houseguests. She started to back away when she heard a door open. Had someone spotted her? It would be impossible to get back to the woods without being seen. Squeezing into a corner between the side of the house and a large, stone chimney, she hoped for the best, her heart pounding.

Relief poured through her when she saw a black dog being let out to do his business. Damn, was he going to bark at her? Instead, it saw her and ran over, seemingly looking for affection. Danielle gave the dog's head a quick pat, then turned toward the woods with the dog at her heels. She whispered at it to go home, but the canine followed her into the blackness.

As she moved into the dark woods, her small light began dimming. Without adequate light, the dog's presence was reassuring. She hadn't gotten more than fifty feet in, when the dog started to growl. She stopped in her tracks, wondering if she should turn back when a figure rushed out from behind a wide oak tree. Danielle felt herself pulled against her attacker's body, her arms pinned to her sides as the dog backed away, whimpering.

Strong, gloved hands circled her throat. She clawed at them, uselessly trying to halt the viselike tightening. Thrashing wildly, she kicked at him in an effort to free herself, praying the dog would come to her rescue. But the dog was hurrying back to the house, tail pointing toward the ground.

When Lisa opened the door to Phanny, the dog rushed in, whining. Lisa tried to calm her as the dog frantically circled the kitchen but Phanny's strange behavior persisted.

Worried, she said, "I hate to interrupt the fun, but Phanny just came in whining and won't settle down. I'm afraid something isn't right outside. Maybe we should go out and have a look around."

Jeff said, "Call the security guard."

TJ sprang from the couch. "He's not going to be here until eleven. I'll go out. You two stay put." She put on a jacket and checked her gun. Jeff, not waiting for permission, put on his coat to follow.

"I think I saw a lantern in the garage. Let's grab it," Jeff suggested.

"Fine." She turned to Lisa. "Stay here. I'll call you if anything is off."

Lisa's cell phone rang only minutes later. "Lisa, there's a woman's body out here. I called 911. Do you know if Eric has a gun in the house?"

Lisa had avoided telling them about her handgun rather than explain why she owned it. The moment of truth had arrived. "I have one."

Not asking for an explanation, TJ told her to find some plastic rope and meet them in the woods about a hundred yards behind the house.

"I'll be right out."

After locating the rope and picking up two lanterns she found in the garage, Lisa hurried out to the woods with Phanny leashed at her side. Aided by the light of the lantern Jeff held, she quickly found TJ and Jeff standing over the body of a woman.

The woman lay on her side, wearing dark slacks and a black leather jacket, her face turned away from where Lisa stood. Feeling like it would be disrespectful, Lisa didn't try to get a better look at the woman's face; she couldn't possible know her. Instead, she asked, "Did either of you recognize her?"

"No, but she's a damn good-looking woman," TJ said, wryly. "Give me the rope. I'm going to tie off the area before the scene gets messed up. Don't get any closer." Jeff and Lisa stepped back, watching as TJ circled the trees with the plastic rope.

After she finished, TJ said, "Lisa, we'll stay here. Why don't you go back? Someone will have to call Eric."

Lisa asked, "Someone must have dumped her body here, don't you think? She wouldn't have been out for a walk in the woods this late dressed like that."

"She's still warm. Had to have been killed right here, that's why I'm trying to preserve the site for the police."

Lisa wanted to get as far as possible from the death scene. She'd broken out into a cold sweat under her clothes; she'd never seen a body that had been murdered. Clutching her gun in one hand and a flashlight in the other, she made her way back to the house with Phanny, nervously looking from side to side.

She hadn't been back long when Jeff appeared at the door. The sound of sirens filled the night as Lisa let him in.

Breathless, he said, "TJ wants to know how you want to spin this for the cops."

"Spin it? Are you serious?"

"TJ's right. We have to have an explanation ready for what we're all doing here."

"That's easy," she said, calmer. "We're house guests, keeping an eye on the place while Eric's gone."

"That sounds kind of lame, doesn't it?" asked Jeff.

Lisa rubbed her stress-knotted neck. "Isn't that actually what we are? *Why* we're houseguests is what we leave out. If anyone can think of something better, let me know. We should call Maggie and David. This is out of their jurisdiction, but maybe they can give us some advice on how to handle things."

"Good idea. I'll tell TJ." Jeff turned to go back out until the police arrived.

Lisa watched him leave, dreading the call to Eric. The auction in Texas started tonight. He'd probably have his cell phone turned off until he got back to his hotel room. She'd leave him a message to call her when he got in.

Still parked in front of the house, and nearly dozing off, Eddie jolted up when he heard sirens, quickly aware of their wailing drawing near. *Fuck!* Had the old lady from last night reported him as a prowler? He had to get the hell out of there and never come back. He'd make sure to get all his ducks in a row and blow town if he had to.

35

Detectives Maggie Petersen and David Lassiter showed up soon after Lisa called, while what looked like the entire law enforcement population of southeastern Wisconsin gathered outside the house. Maggie and David exchanged glances after they'd been given the details of the night's events.

Lisa said, "We feel terrible about this woman, but we have no idea if is related to what we're doing."

When they looked skeptical, she added, "We called you because we aren't sure what to say to the police. We're just going to tell them we're houseguests." She looked from one to the other for some sign of understanding.

David took a deep breath, a frown forcing his dark brows together. "Assuming that would pacify them for now, how are you going to explain the security guard?"

"We called the service and told them not to send him yet. When he comes later, it'll look like a response to the murder."

Maggie, her face unreadable, said, "That may be overkill. Waukesha is sure to station a car here." She looked at David, who stood stiffly at her side, his hands in his pockets. "What do you think?"

Looking over the room and its furnishings, he said, "Judging by the looks of this place, Eric's a wealthy man, so it wouldn't be a stretch to say he'd act to protect his friends by hiring a guard, even with a police presence. But I'm not comfortable holding anything back that could help with the investigation of this woman's murder."

Maggie said, "You can tell the Waukesha police whatever you want, but if it turns out this murder is related to your investigation or ambiguous in any way, we won't have a choice—we'll have to contribute what we know. As officers of the law we can't withhold anything that might be evidential."

The detectives accepted their silence as agreement and went outside to make their presence known.

The relationships among the departments bordering Milwaukee were amicable. As a result, when Oconomowoc detectives Maggie Petersen and David Lassiter explained to the other officers that they'd come over when Lisa, a friend of Maggie's, had called, no one objected to their presence.

As the body was carried away, the officer in charge, a short, burly detective from Waukesha PD, handed them a photo of the dead woman's face. Neither of them recognized the woman.

TJ, who'd been allowed to remain behind the rope when one of the county sheriffs remembered her as a former Milwaukee cop, walked over to them, her rigid posture the only sign of her stress. The three of them stepped aside.

"Have they questioned you yet?" Maggie asked.

"No formal statement, but yeah, they asked me a few things. Told them I never saw the woman before and that we're friends of Eric's, staying here for a while."

"We'll give you twenty-four hours. If this isn't wrapped up by then, we'll have to share what we know about your interviews."

TJ looked away. "Gotta do what you gotta do."

When the Waukesha police came into the house to take the group's statements, they talked to TJ first in Eric's office.

When they called Lisa in and they passed her a photo of the dead woman, her face burned with recognition. *It's Danielle, the woman I met in Jeff's showroom.*

Seeing Lisa's reaction, the detective asked, "Is she someone you knew?"

"I met her briefly. About a couple of weeks ago."

"Where?"

"In the showroom at Kristy's. Eric took me there. I saw her looking at an expensive car; I don't remember what kind." Lisa took a deep breath, wondering if her suspicions had been right; was this the woman Eric had been seeing? Unwilling to voice her female suspicion, she didn't feel the need to share her thoughts. "Her name was Danielle. I can't remember her last name, although Eric did introduce us. Sorry, I'm really upset, but I think it'll come to me."

The statements were brief since no one really knew the woman. They'd been in the house at the time of the murder and heard nothing. It was clear the detectives thought the housing arrangement odd, but the group's explanation placated them for the moment.

36

Except for a lone squad car parked in the drive, by 1:00 a.m. the police, sheriffs, and crime scene techs had all gone, the only reminder of the night's violence the bright yellow crime scene tape encircling the trees. The media presence had rushed back to their caves to report the sensational murder.

Jeff stood at the stove stirring the nearly forgotten chili when TJ walked into the kitchen. She bent over the pot, sniffing the spicy mixture, amazed to discover she was hungry.

Jeff turned to her. "We need to talk about the possibility this woman's murder is related to us."

"Possibility?" she scoffed. "You kiddin' me?"

Frowning, he put down the spoon. "It's possible there's another explanation," he insisted.

"Yeah, you go on thinkin' that, and I'll go on thinkin' about what I'm gonna do with my millions when I win the lottery."

Jeff served himself chili, then sat at the island staring into his dish, poking through the food with a spoon. TJ filled a bowl and sat next to him, berating herself for her thoughtlessness. The woman's murder had to be plaguing him with images of what might have happened to his wife. "Sorry. Just seems obvious to me, that's all."

An hour later, a teapot Lisa put on had just started whistling when her cell phone rang.

Eric sounded out of breath. "Is something wrong? I just got back to my room and noticed your message."

"I don't know how to tell you this . . . " she started.

"Is everyone all right?"

"Yes, we're fine." She blurted, "We had to get in touch with you before the police did—a woman was murdered in the woods behind the house."

"Did anyone get a look at her?"

"TJ and Jeff did when they found her. The police showed the rest of us her photo."

"Can you describe her?"

There wasn't an easy way to break the news. "I'm sorry, Eric. The woman was Danielle Ventura."

Lisa heard him catch his breath. She carried the phone to the laundry room, shutting the door behind her.

Minutes later, she came back out to find everyone looking at her.

"So, what did he say about her?" TJ probed, following her into the kitchen.

"He can't come back until Sunday morning. That's the soonest he can get away and leave his manager in charge. He'll hop a red-eye after the auction tomorrow night—tonight, actually—and get here early Sunday."

TJ persisted. "Who is she?"

Lisa hadn't shared her suspicions about Eric's love life with any of the others. "She's a divorcee he's been dating. He told me she'd become very possessive. Whenever he told her he'd call her, she couldn't wait and would call and pressure him. Before he left he explained to her he wasn't looking for a relationship, but didn't think he got through to her. He'd planned on talking to her about it again when he got back."

"Crap. Good thing he's in Texas. It would look bad for him—another woman in his life murdered."

Lisa added, "He only dated her the last couple weeks. Not a lot of time to have a motive to murder someone." Eric would be devastated. He'd feel to blame somehow no matter who was responsible for the woman's death.

TJ's cell phone buzzed. She walked out of the room, speaking in low tones. Lisa wondered if Eric had called TJ to ask for more details.

When TJ came back in the room, she busied herself picking up the used bowls, rinsing them out and putting them in the dishwasher. She kept her eyes down, arranging dishes on the top shelf. Finally, she turned to face Lisa and Jeff. "Eric called back. He asked me if anyone noticed the dead woman resembled one of us. Told him no. No one noticed."

Lisa felt a tightening in her stomach. Her voice at least a pitch too high, she asked, "Who does he think she looks like?"

"You."

Lisa stepped back, her heart pounding, a lizard of fear crawling through her. It hadn't occurred to her—she and Danielle were about the same height. And Danielle's hair. She'd had it pinned up when Lisa met her, but she imagined worn loose, it would look like hers. She moved to the couch and sat down hard with a loud swoosh of its overstuffed cushions.

She looked up at TJ. "That would explain it, wouldn't it? Whoever is killing these abused women knows about us. He thinks getting rid of one of us will stop us from pursuing our inquiries. It's time to tell the police what we're doing."

Lisa heard a soft knock on her door. She opened it to TJ, who walked in wearing a red plaid nightshirt with worn brown slippers.

"Got a question for you. Did you know Eric was seeing this chick?"

Lisa hadn't really known. "He didn't say anything about her when we were doing interviews."

"I kinda thought maybe you and Eric . . . "

Lisa stopped her. "Not in this lifetime."

"How come you never told me you have a gun?"

Lisa didn't want to talk about it. She'd been hoping she could tell them all at the same time, carefully doling out a sanitized version of the truth.

"I'll tell you some of it now, but it's a long story. The rest can wait."

She followed Lisa into the living room and sat next to her on the sofa.

"I bought the gun after my divorce and learned how to use it."

"You were afraid of him?"

Maybe there was no simple version. "Not really."

TJ persisted. "But you wanted to shoot him."

"He threatened to sue for custody of Paige." The hatred she'd been burdened with for so long ago still boiled within her. "I never knew I could despise anyone so much, even wish him dead." Her eyes hardened in remembrance.

TJ shrugged. "Anyone can kill under the right circumstances, especially to protect their kid. I'd keep bugging you to tell me more about it now except we only have a few hours before we hafta go out again."

"We do have to keep going, don't we? This has to end—soon."

Back in the guestroom, TJ discovered she was out of toothpaste. She went to Eric's room, intending to look for an extra tube in his bathroom cabinet. When she walked into the spacious bathroom situated between the two master bedrooms, she heard a sound in the adjoining room where Jeff slept. She moved closer to the door. Was he crying? Seeing Danielle in the woods must have hit him hard— reminded him Jamie could be dead, too. TJ wanted to turn around, pretend she hadn't heard anything. Instead, she eased into the room. *Damn, I'm getting soft.*

"Hey, everything okay in here?" Knowing it wasn't, what could she say?

"Yeah," he replied, his voice thick.

She sighed. He'd settled on the end of the bed fully clothed. He sat bent forward, his face in his hands, his glasses on the nightstand next to the bed.

Tough love, first. "You wanna talk, or should I leave you to wallow?"

Sitting up straight, he rubbed his face. "I've tried not to think about what must have happened to Jamie, but when I saw that woman I couldn't help but think she's probably in a woods somewhere—just like her. I keep seeing pictures of it in my mind when I close my eyes."

TJ suspected he was right about his wife. "I'm sorry you're hurting."

She turned to leave the room. Maybe he needed to be alone to grieve. She got as far as the bathroom, then turned around and walked back to the bed. Sitting next to him, she put her arm across his back. Jeff moved into her arms. She held him until it became natural for them to lie back on the bed. Later, when he fell asleep in her arms, she eased off the bed, covered him, and slipped out of the room.

37

At 7:00 a.m. Saturday, Eddie Wysecki woke with a start when his doorbell buzzed. The half-eaten bowl of greasy popcorn on his lap overturned, landing bottom-up on the floor. He'd fallen asleep in the recliner the night before and as he struggled to get out of the overstuffed chair without stepping on the mess, nausea swept through him. Not sure if his stomach objected to the buttered popcorn or all the mugs of beer he'd ingested the night before, he swore as he struggled to get to the door.

Through the peephole he saw two men wearing clothing ominously formal for a Saturday morning. *Fuck, cops*. The contents of his intestines rolled. The dog lady must have given the cops his license number. But, shit! What could she have said to make them show up at his door at this ungodly hour? Parking on the side of the road wasn't a crime, but he'd have to give a reason for being there. What could he say?

The doorbell rang again, followed by two sharp knocks. Eddie opened the door.

"Edward Wysecki?"

"Yeah." They flashed their badges and IDs. Detectives. Everything in his intestines liquefied.

"We need to ask you a few questions. Do you mind if we come in?"

When he nodded, the men barged inside, introducing themselves as Waukesha detectives Greg Zabel and Max Feinstein. *Christ, Jewish cops now?* Bad enough they'd started letting women into their

149

ranks. His digestive system in turmoil, Eddie clenched and asked, "What can I do for you gentlemen this morning?"

The younger guy, Zabel, said, "Someone reported seeing your car last night on Larkspur Drive outside of Waukesha."

His insides churned; his ass was about to spew. He had to get to the john.

The dick went on, "Sorry. I have that wrong. They saw your car parked there on Thursday night, and last night, at about the same time both nights."

Eddie interrupted before the guy could say another word. Without waiting for their approval, he excused himself and bolted down the hall to the bathroom. In his urgency, he didn't notice Max Feinstein quietly following him to make sure the bathroom had no windows.

As Eddie relieved his wringing intestines, he had a few minutes to think about what to say to the cops. The old bat couldn't prove he was there. He'd just have to deny it, wouldn't he? But no, she'd given them his license number, so he was seriously fucked. He had to find a way to buy himself time to get out of town. It wouldn't take long; he had money stashed and a fake ID that had cost him three weeks' profits.

He couldn't deny he'd been there, but what could he tell them to get them to leave and give him enough time to bolt?

It came to him. The Peacock woman. She'd be his cover.

After they left Eddie's apartment, the detectives didn't speak until they got to the car. Greg Zabel had sensed Wysecki's nervousness. When he'd gotten a whiff of the man's disgusting breath and seen the popcorn on the floor, it hadn't taken any great detection skill to see the guy had slept in the stained recliner. The scene didn't seem to fit a guy who'd committed murder the night before, but he'd seen stranger things in his ten years as a homicide detective. The guy had definitely been edgy.

Greg started the car. "That guy looked green."

"Shit, did you get a whiff of his breath?" Max settled his wide girth into the stiff seat of the unmarked. "We have to talk to this Peacock chick. Name like that, must be a spade."

After three years partnering with the man, Greg had grown immune to his partner's racial slurs. "If she backs up his story, it doesn't necessarily get him off hook."

38

When Maggie's phone rang Saturday morning, she rolled over. But she'd awakened enough to remember the events of the night before. She and David had words on the way home last night—they weren't in agreement about withholding the group's activities from the Waukesha detectives. David, willing to stick his neck out because of the abuse in his family history, insisted on giving the group their twenty-four hours, unlike Maggie, who regretted giving them *any* time. Their relationship, still in its early stages, had yet to be tested by a difference of opinion on the job, at least one causing a rift. They hadn't parted on the friendliest of terms.

When the phone stopped ringing, then immediately repeated its wailing, Maggie picked up. It was her boss, and she could tell by his raised voice, he wasn't happy.

"I hear you barged in on that murder in Waukesha last night."

Already a reprimand? "I can explain."

"Forget it! You know a Teal Peacock? One of those 'guests' staying at the Schindler place?"

"Not well, but yes, I know her."

"Thought you might," he said sarcastically. "Schindler's neighbor gave Waukesha the license number of a car with a guy in it that happened to be parked across from the place about the same time this woman bought it. Turns out he's some barkeep from West Allis, Eddie Wysecki. He told them the reason he'd been there is he suspects his girlfriend—this Peacock woman—of cheating on him and was keeping tabs on her. Waukesha hasn't been able to get in touch with her to confirm his story. Anyway, I know this is your day off, but they're shorthanded, so I'm sending you over there for the day. After you get in touch with Peacock."

"You want me to work Waukesha?" It was unheard of—they never crossed boundaries. She decided not to question it further since at least he wasn't reaming her out about being at Schindler's the night before.

"They're in a bind because two detectives were in an accident yesterday and are still in the hospital. Find this Peacock broad and get over there."

Maggie told him she would report to Waukesha right away and would call David too if he wanted. He wanted.

She knew exactly why TJ's cell phone was off but had no clue about a boyfriend from West Allis. Lisa had told her TJ was seeing an MPD detective, but it didn't mean there weren't a few wannabes hanging around.

She called David and told him she'd pick him up on her way to Waukesha, then tried Jeff's phone as she pulled on her clothes. "Jeff, is TJ with you? Her phone's not on."

"Yeah, she's right here. You caught us between meetings; we're at Dunkin Donuts having coffee." She heard him say, "Maggie," followed by the sound of the phone changing hands.

TJ asked, "Hey, what's up?"

"Waukesha got a report of a suspicious car with a man sitting it, parked across the street from Eric's last night and Thursday night. The guy's name is Eddie Wysecki; he owns a bar in West Allis. They talked to him this morning and he claims he's been seeing you. Says he's worried you're cheating on him, so he was trying to find out what you're up to. Do you know him?"

"Shit, no, I never heard of the asshole. Never been in a bar in West Allis—that town is a shithole."

"That's what I thought—about Wysecki, not West Allis. Damn. He had to know his story wouldn't check out, so he must have wanted to stall us. He's probably in the wind by now."

"Well, for Christ's sake, why did they leave the guy alone?"

"I guess because they really didn't have anything on him. And remember what day this is."

"Well, it ain't my fuckin' birthday!" TJ's language grew increasingly colorful as her anger escalated.

Maggie was in too big a hurry to pacify TJ. "David and I are assigned to the investigation. For today, anyway, because it's the first weekend of deer hunting season. You must remember what it was like when you were a cop."

"Yeah right. Ten long days of cluster-fuck."

TJ closed the phone and handed it back to Jeff. He'd been admiring the way her sweater hugged her body—and how her amazing blue eyes flashed when she was angry. She'd been so good to him last night. It was hard to meld the woman who'd held him until he fell asleep with this person next to him slinging smut. "You eat with that mouth?"

She gave him a dark look and ordered two more donuts.

39

Just beginning to break a sweat, he fought to keep from dropping the 125 pound weight he was pressing when he heard the announcement on the morning news. The woman in the woods—she wasn't Lisa Rayburn. He'd fucked up. Who the hell was Danielle Ventura and what was she doing in the woods?

He hated it when he failed to accomplish something he'd set out to do, but he dared not act again so soon. Schindler's house would be as secure as Fort Knox now. It would be impossible to get to Rayburn. If he was lucky, she and her band of followers would figure out she was the real target and back the hell off.

The scene in the woods had stoked an urge to resume his hobby. He needed an outlet, but it couldn't be Rayburn.

He'd have to choose carefully.

40

Maggie and David met Zabel and Feinstein at the Waukesha station, where the four of them went over the details of the case while they drank charred, police-station coffee out of Styrofoam cups and waited for the search warrants on Wysecki's bar and apartment. Wysecki was still nowhere to be found.

When the warrants came in, the other officers asked which one they wanted. Surprised at being given a choice, Maggie and David ended up at Wysecki's bar.

The bar was in a blue-collar neighborhood of aging, two-family duplexes and taverns on nearly every corner. Two West Allis uniforms stood sentry, and informed them that Wysecki hadn't shown. His bartender pulled up a moment later. A tall, stoop-shouldered man in his seventies, he hurried to the door and held it open for them.

The place smelled overwhelmingly of stale beer, but the floors and the surface of the bar were spotless. An ancient manual cash register stood open and empty. The bartender explained that he'd taken the receipts the night before and dropped them in the night deposit after closing.

In the back of the building was a tiny, unisex bathroom across a short hallway from a combination office and storeroom. A stained, wooden desk piled high with papers, receipts, advertisements, and an overflowing ashtray took up most of the room. The rest was piled to the ceiling with cases of beer, soda, and kegs. On the wall behind the desk hung the ubiquitous girlie-calendar.

A door at the back of the room, nearly hidden by a stack of old signs, opened to a cellar reeking of mildew. David called the bartender in and asked what they used the cellar for.

"Not much. The vendors don't like hauling deliveries downstairs for a small account. Just a buncha' old junk down there."

After moving the signs aside, Maggie and David made their way down sagging wooden steps lit by a single light bulb suspended from the cobwebbed ceiling.

Maggie wrinkled her nose at the musty odor. "Probably hasn't been used in years. Should I go to the car for flashlights?"

"No, I think there's another light. Let's see if it works." David turned on a hanging bulb in the middle of the room. The bartender had been right—the cellar was filled with junk. Mostly old bar stools, their stuffing oozing out like hernias. And enough beer signs to be a collector's dream except for the rust and mold marring their surfaces.

Maggie hated old basements; they tended to be ripe with disgusting things like spiders and rats. "Let's get out of here."

"No, we'd better go through everything. I'll finish here if you'd rather wait upstairs." He poked through a stack of old cardboard boxes filled with ancient, yellowing papers from the business.

"Man, it's stuffy down here," complained Maggie. She couldn't wait to get out of the cave-like cellar. "David, stop a minute. Do you smell that?"

"Smell what?"

"Your nose must be plugged. I'm getting a whiff of a really nasty odor. Something died and it smells like it's still here."

David walked to the back of the room. "Yeah, I'm getting it now." He walked closer to an area behind the furnace and pushed aside a stack of boxes. "This metal door in the wall is for an old coal chute. Let me see if I can get it open." He tugged on the metal handle, stumbling when it opened easily in his hand.

An undeniable odor of death wafted from the dark interior. Human or animal? It remained to be determined since there wasn't enough light to see inside the opening. Maggie's face scrunched up in revulsion as the smell diffused toward them through the doorway. The blackness beyond the opening was absolute, the odor palpable.

"I'll go up for the flashlights and make sure the bartender stays put," Maggie offered.

"All right. Bring the Vicks, too. Have those patrolmen find out if there's anyone from the Medical Examiner's office who hasn't gone deer hunting."

When Lisa and Jeff returned to the house Saturday, there was still a patrol car parked at the curb, and the security guard's car sat next to the garage. Quickly deemed "robo-cop" by TJ, the guard circled the grounds and house at regular intervals, effectively protecting the residents from the media.

TJ arrived next, her arms full of Chinese takeout. The rich, spicy odor of ginger and soy filled the room as they busied themselves getting out napkins and plates. A call from Maggie interrupted the preparations. Lisa put the phone on speaker.

Maggie told them about the suspect, Eddie Wysecki. "We haven't found him yet, but he may be your killer. We searched his bar and found an old coal chute in the cellar. We found the bodies of three women inside. This will be a field day for the media and take you folks out of the spotlight."

"Do you think they'll find more bodies?" Lisa asked.

"They're still looking. If he's your killer, he'll have more bodies stashed somewhere else. Three wouldn't account for the stats on missing women."

Lisa, disappointed, rubbed the back of her neck. "No, they wouldn't." She'd been hoping with this discovery, it would all be over. *But a second killer?*

"Do you know who any of them are?" Jeff asked.

"No. And identification could take some time."

TJ asked, "Do they know if he's the one who killed Danielle?"

"His car was seen in the area two nights running. Everything points to him, but we don't have a motive."

After they ended the call, TJ said, "We're off the hook. Won't matter if this Wysecki isn't our guy. The cops will put it all on him whether they find more bodies or not."

41

The security guard sat quietly in the back seat as Jeff drove to a late-night appointment, an extra safeguard insisted on by Lisa since there was still a squad stationed in front of the house. The address, on a street southwest of downtown Milwaukee, was in a neighborhood past its prime—if it ever had one. Now mostly Hispanic and transient, the houses were shabby and ill-kept, a far cry from its beginnings as an oasis for Polish immigrants. Known as a high crime area, the guard asked why the need to go there so late.

"We gotta go when we gotta go," said TJ, offering no explanation. "Hope this dude shows."

Jeff asked, "What's his name?"

TJ turned on the reading light to get a look at the note Lisa had given her. "The guy is Raoul Lopez. This says he's a friend of the missing woman's brother and the only person Lisa could reach. Note says don't expect much of this one." She turned off the light. "Great. A wild goose chase in a crappy neighborhood. Way to ruin a Saturday night."

Because of the late interview, TJ had been forced to tell Richard she already had plans with her sister. She hadn't told him just what those plans were, but promised to meet him the next day. He hadn't sounded upset with her, but she could tell he was getting suspicious.

At their destination, a dark street lined with aged, two-family homes, TJ and Jeff walked up to a worn-out duplex, its siding painted a hideously brilliant shade of blue. No lights appeared in the lower flat as they walked around the side of the house to the entrance of the upper where they'd seen a faint light coming from the front window.

With no operable lighting on the stairs leading to the upper flat, they had to rely on the small flashlight TJ carried. At the top of the stairs, TJ knocked on the door. No one answered. They hadn't seen Raoul enter, so he might already be inside. She spoke the man's name loudly, knocked again, and tried the door. It wasn't locked.

"Maybe we'd better get the guard," said Jeff before TJ could open the door any further.

"Nah, it's okay, nobody's here." But she handed him the flashlight and pulled out her gun as she walked through the door. "Or maybe not," she whispered.

A dim light from a TV broke the darkness as the sound of a laugh track came from a small living room to the right of the kitchen where TJ and Jeff stood next to a yellow, Formica-topped table.

TJ called, "Hello, anyone home? We're here to meet Raoul."

No answer. They edged carefully into the living room. Still holding the gun, TJ reached over and turned on a lamp perched on a packing carton next to a ratty sofa. In its dim light they saw a small child, maybe four or five years old, curled up on the sofa, knees bent up to the chin, staring at them with fearful, dark eyes. TJ couldn't tell if it was a boy or a girl. The kid wore blue jeans and an oversized sweatshirt; its dark hair covered most of his or her face.

Jeff squatted down to make himself eye level with the child. "What's your name?"

The child didn't answer, just stared up at them through dark, stringy hair, something gripped tightly under its arm, as if trying to keep it hidden from them.

"Can I see what you have?" Jeff asked softly. Clutching it with both hands, the child reluctantly pulled out a baby doll wearing a tattered pink dress.

He sat down next to her. "She's real pretty. What's her name?" The girl hugged the doll to her chest, silent.

TJ left the room to make sure the child was the only occupant of the apartment. The kitchen's cupboards were empty and the refrigerator held nothing but a few cans of beer. The only edible thing TJ found was a package of elbow macaroni. An open garbage can overflowed and the table in the middle of the room sat under a layer of grime and fast food wrappers. A look in the two small bedrooms revealed more squalor: the beds unmade, sheets gray and unwashed. Some moron had left the kid alone in this cesspool.

TJ walked back to the sofa where Jeff offered the girl a granola bar. The child reached for the bar slowly, her gaze never leaving Jeff. She looked as if she feared he might snatch it away from her.

Jeff looked up at TJ while the girl ripped open the pitiful offering. "We have to get her out of here. Someone left this poor kid alone with no food and the door unlocked, for God's sake!" His face was stiff with anger.

"Seen worse in my time."

"Call Lisa. She'll know what to do about her."

TJ's sympathy for the girl conflicted with her annoyance at having yet another distraction. "Go out and tell the guard what's going on. Don't want to have a problem if Raoul shows up. The bastard." She sat next to the girl, wondering what to do next. She knew they couldn't call Lisa. Lisa's answer would have to follow procedure. And at midnight on a weekend before a holiday, TJ knew what would happen to the kid if they had to do things by the book.

Jeff came back in with Robo, aka Chad, in tow and asked, "What did Lisa say?"

TJ diverted the question. "Tell you about it later. We gotta get her out before Raoul shines around."

The girl still wasn't talking but had eaten the granola bar in record time. She stared at Jeff, silently asking for more food. He explained to her they had to leave and they would like it if she would come with them. He promised to get her something to eat, offering her his hand. The girl stayed put, burrowing further into the sofa.

TJ bent down to the girl's level and whispered in her ear. Her eyes widened. She followed TJ, hand-in-hand, out to the car. Chad got behind the wheel. "I saw some activity down the block. We need to put some distance between us and this dump."

TJ and Jeff got in the back with the girl. The car moved quickly from the curb.

TJ leaned over to Chad, "Take us to 27th and National."

On the corner of 27th sat a brightly lit McDonald's. TJ saw Jeff grin as he figured out what TJ had whispered in the kid's ear.

"Pull in the drive-thru," said TJ. "I'm cravin' a Big Mac."

They ordered food—Big Macs and sodas for the adults, and a cheeseburger, French fries and chocolate shake for the girl. TJ hoped the kid wouldn't puke after eating all the greasy food. They drove away, the girl eager for the food TJ handed her. The fries went first. She'd eaten nearly half of it all before she fell asleep, the milkshake still clutched in her hands.

TJ looked down at her. "Wonder how Eric feels about kids?"

Eric, who'd just come in from Texas a few minutes earlier, sat at the island when TJ and Jeff walked in carrying the sleeping child. He looked up from his coffee, eyebrows raised in question.

TJ looked at Eric. "It's a girl."

His expression giving away nothing, he got up and studied the girl in Jeff's arms. "About five years old. Neglected, right?"

"Someone left her alone in an unlocked apartment with no food. We found her there when we went to what we thought was going to be our appointment. Someone must have given us a phony address."

"Put her in your room, TJ. The sofa opens into a bed and the linens are in the chest. I'll look her over and you can get her settled. Then we'll talk."

Eric had a bottle of brandy on the counter when they came back into the kitchen. His expression looked grim. "All right. I'm a doctor if the kid needs medical attention and we have plenty of room here. If we're able to help out a neglected kid, that feels like good news compared to everything else going on."

TJ smiled, relieved. "Right, taking care of a kid will be good for us."

He looked doubtful, his eyes dark. "Have you talked to Lisa about this?"

"Nah. Jeff wanted to, but I knew what she'd say. The kid would have been put in a group home, maybe even in detention temporarily until the system could find a foster."

He raised the bottle and poured himself a generous drink, offering it to TJ and Jeff when he'd finished. "Technically, you're kidnappers." He wiped his face with his hands. "And the rest of us are aiding and abetting."

An hour later when Lisa came downstairs to make tea, Eric was sitting on the couch, staring into a crackling fire. "You're back."

He acknowledged her presence with a weak smile.

She put water on to boil, then sat next to him. "Eric, we're all so sorry about Danielle. We feel like we're the ones who put her in harm's way."

"If I'd been honest with her from the start, she'd still be alive."

"Eric, no one could have foreseen this. No one is to blame but the person who did this to her. We can't forget that."

He turned to her. "You know he meant it to be you. I can't keep you safe anymore."

"Keeping us safe isn't your responsibility. You brought us to your home to protect us. It's possible Danielle's murder had nothing to do with us. Someone could have been after her—a stalker, maybe."

He rubbed his eyes. "You're right. Maybe the cops will get some answers for us."

"You should try to get some sleep."

"I don't think that's possible."

42

Sunday morning, unhappy with how TJ and Jeff had handled the situation with the child, Lisa grudgingly acquiesced to let TJ take the problem to Conlin. She wasn't sure he could smooth it over for them, but it made sense to ask for his help since they'd found the girl in Milwaukee.

Lisa worried Jeff felt too responsible for the child. She knew he hoped that the Milwaukee Department of Health and Human Services would keep him informed of their progress in finding a good home for the girl even though she'd warned him it would be unlikely.

Eric announced, "I'm going to the Waukesha Police Department to be interviewed, then I'll go to an office supply place to pick up a couple whiteboards. We'll be ready to categorize the women's habits."

Lisa poured pancake batter onto a large griddle. "Don't you think that should wait until they find out more about Eddie Wysecki?"

"He ain't our guy," yelled TJ from across the room, where she sat reading the Sunday paper. "If he was, there'd have been a lot more bodies in that cellar. He's just a dumbass West Allis barkeep. Where's he gonna stash all those bodies?"

Jeff pointed quietly to the girl, motioning for TJ to watch her language.

"Sure she's heard worse," TJ grumbled.

"I agree with TJ," said Lisa. "I don't think he's our killer either. From what we've heard about him, I'm not sure he would have the wherewithal to ferret out abused women, especially such attractive ones."

"You're right. The women on our short list are all hot. Wouldn't have had nothin' to do with a loser like him," TJ added.

The child turned out to be a needed distraction. And Danielle's murder was having the opposite effect Lisa thought it would; it had made everyone even more determined to finish what they'd started. She'd have to try again to find someone who knew the woman who had led them to Raoul's apartment. That someone may know where the child belonged.

After they'd eaten, Eric said, "I know all of you hoped to be back home for Thanksgiving, but I think we need to stay here.

The room went silent. "I'll pick up a big turkey today. Lisa, you can give me a grocery list and I'll bring home anything you need. And TJ, please invite your sister and her kids. They can stay the night if they want. I'm going to put on a second guard for the weekend. But you'd still have to warn your sister about the risks— even with the beefed up security, they'd have to stay inside."

Lisa wasn't sure about the wisdom of bringing anyone into their midst. With Tyler out of her life, and Paige not coming home, celebrating the holiday at Eric's would be better than being alone. *To hell with fear.*

TJ drove to Richard's apartment early in the morning, hoping a visit would pacify him. As long as their names stayed out of the Ventura woman's murder story, there'd be no need to tell him anything—yet. She wanted her moment, the big moment when she could drop the evidence in his lap–evidence of a crime that both Richard and that prick Wilson refused to acknowledge.

When she arrived, she found him sitting at the kitchen table reading the paper. When he saw her he stood up, taking her in his arms, his kiss warm and tentative, almost questioning.

It had been too long since they'd been together. Feeling horny, TJ wanted to go to the bedroom—have hot sex immediately with the ulterior motive of delaying any unwanted discussion. Breaking from the kiss, he picked her up and carried her from the room.

Their lovemaking had an intensity brought on by weeks of abstinence. TJ gasped as he entered her, all the fervor they'd enjoyed in the past adding to the pleasure of the moment. His thrusts were slow, then urgent with built-up passion. TJ felt her tension dissipate, wondering why it had been so long since they'd enjoyed each other like this—but the return of reality interrupted her bliss when she remembered her purpose in maintaining her distance.

Hours later, wearing bathrobes and reading the paper, they decided to stay in for the night.

TJ felt Richard watching her. "What?"

"Nothing, just looking. How's your sister doing?"

Here it comes. "She's fine."

"Are you going back there tomorrow night?"

TJ remembered her cover story had been staying at Janeen's. "Not sure yet." *Where is he going with this?*

"I thought since you usually spend Thanksgiving with her, you might stay there this week."

He's fishing. She'd play it cool. "Yeah, probably. But we got invited to one of her friends for Thanksgiving. We won't hafta cook. How about you, goin' to your folks' place?"

"No, I don't think so. Thought I might go with you this year but since you're going somewhere else, Justin and his wife invited me over—you, too, by the way—so I may do that."

His parents lived in Chicago, and Thanksgiving was one of the few times Richard went home to visit. TJ hadn't met them. By an unspoken mutual agreement, meeting relatives was something they didn't do, although Richard had met Janeen a few times.

Is he fishing again? She wasn't sure, but his hint to go along with her was something new. "Too bad. Janeen always asks me to bring you, and I always tell her you're going to Chicago." She didn't extend the invite for him to accompany them to the "friend's" house, hoping he'd drop the subject.

She said, "Let's do something special next weekend. Let's drive up to the Dells and go gambling in Black River Falls like we did last year."

Aware Richard knew a diversion when he heard one, TJ reminisced about how much she'd enjoyed their weekend in the Dells. Before long, he agreed to make the plans. It had been a long time since they'd gone anywhere together, and she could already picture the two of them in one of those great suites with a hot tub and a king-sized bed. Maybe things would get back to normal for them—she just needed to decide if it was what she wanted.

43

TJ left Richard's apartment the next morning knowing she had to move fast. If she didn't report in to Lisa and Jeff about Richard's advice concerning the child, her phone would be ringing.

She hadn't said a word about it to Richard. She'd bought the kid some time by convincing the others she'd have him handle it. The more she'd thought about group homes and foster parents, she knew she had to act. Richard would have had no choice; he'd have to turn the kid over to DHHS and they would find her somewhere to stay. Not that there weren't places which actually improved a child's circumstances, but the kind able to fit a kid in the week of Thanksgiving wasn't likely to be one of them.

Playing within the lines wasn't TJ's style, and she'd been living by the group's rules for too long.

Red lights were the only traffic signs she honored—and some of them just barely—as she pushed the Mini to the south side of Milwaukee. Luckily, she had a good memory for directions and easily found the old duplex they'd rescued the child from Saturday night. The place looked even crappier in daylight, the siding splitting off in places and the windows badly in need of repair.

She drove past and parked in a lot behind a run-down apartment building at the end of the street. At the duplex, she crept up the steps to the upper flat, finding the door still unlocked. Didn't these idiots ever learn?

She entered the apartment, where she heard faint snoring from the direction of the bedroom. Peering into the room, she saw a form in the bed, a dark-haired man, sleeping with his back to her. Had to be Raoul. She cased the room for a weapon. The snoring remained steady.

TJ walked to the foot of the bed and gave the bed frame a sharp kick. A second passed before he rolled over, face scrunched from sleep, eyes narrow slits. He did a violent double take when he saw TJ standing at the foot of the bed. He reached over, his hand fumbling on the nightstand.

"It ain't there, asshole." Baring her teeth in a wicked grin, TJ held up his gun—in her other hand she held her own, pointed toward the bed.

He growled, "You gotta' death wish, bitch?"

"I just might." She held her gun higher, directed at his face. "What were you doing with that kid Friday night?"

"The kid?" His face darkened with anger. "You took her? You almost got me killed, you cunt!"

"Listen, asswipe, you really don't want to piss me off. Answer my questions and I'm outta here." She felt him plotting his options, certain that grinding her into dust was one of them.

He started to get up from the bed. She did not want to see his naked butt. "Whoa! Keep your bony ass right where it is."

He flopped back onto the bed. "She ain't my kid. She belongs to a friend of mine, okay?"

"Not okay. Who's this friend and why were you keeping the kid here?"

The guy looked pale and hung over. Probably coming off a big weekend high. "He asked me to."

TJ sneered. "You know what, you piece of shit? I haven't shot anyone in a while, and I'm gettin' the urge. And you know what

else? I think the cops might be interested in this piece you're using."
She waved his gun in the air.

His pallor turned an ugly mottled puce. "No cops! I'll tell you—
she's Julio Mandela's kid. His bitchin' wife left him, and he took the
kid to get her to take him back."

"What's the wife's name and where can I find her? If you lie
about it, I'll be back and I won't be smilin'. Get my drift?"

"Yeah, yeah. Her name is Teresa. I don't know where she's living,
but she works at the Red Roof on twenty-seventh."

With a last threat of returning if his information wasn't accurate,
TJ backed out of the room, checking to be sure no one else had
arrived.

Raoul sat up, reaching for his pants. "Hey, bitch! Leave my gun!"
She moved toward the door. "I'll mail it to you, asshole!"

At the Red Roof Inn, TJ parked in the back just in case the lowlife
called Mandela decided to show up. Rather than waste time with a
nosy manager, she walked the halls looking for the woman named
Teresa. After questioning three maids in various stages of cleaning
the stale-smelling rooms, she found her.

Teresa was shorter than TJ, Hispanic, with dainty, feminine features. Her long hair, held back by a red plastic headband, fell nearly
to her plump waist. She practically hid behind her cart when TJ
asked if she was Teresa. She whispered, "Yes, I'm Teresa."

"Listen," TJ said, keeping her voice low. "You have to come with
me. My friends have your little girl and I want to bring you to her."

"Tina! You have Tina! Mother-of-God, is she all right?" She
dropped the feather duster she'd been holding, her cleaning forgotten.

"Keep your voice down. She's fine now, but the creep who had
her knows I'm here. Let's go." TJ towed her out to the car, shoved
Teresa in, and jumped behind the wheel. She'd just turned onto the

street when she ordered Teresa, "Quick, duck down." A rusty old Camaro moved slowly across the parking lot. Had the asshole called the girl's father? TJ wasn't taking any chances. The Mini took off like a rabbit.

When TJ's little car turned into Eric's driveway, she heard Teresa muttering in Spanish, her eyes wide with wonder at the magnificence of the grounds and the huge log home.

"Who lives here, a movie star?" she asked, in heavily accented English.

"Nah, a real nice guy."

When they walked through the door, opened by a very curious Lisa, Teresa gaped at the house's spacious, well-appointed interior.

In the living room, Jeff and the girl sat on the floor playing cards. She looked up from the game when TJ and Teresa walked in and jumped off the floor, crying, "Mama!" She ran to Teresa, practically climbing the stunned woman.

Jeff looked on in amazement while mother and child embraced. He shook his head in wonder at the sight and got up off the floor. TJ, wanting to give Teresa some privacy, grabbed his arm and led him into the laundry room.

As soon as the door shut behind them, he asked, "How did you find her?"

TJ hadn't planned to reveal what had actually gone down. "While all of you stewed about DHHS, I was thinkin' you were going about it wrong. Had to go back to the source—the dump where we found her and go from there."

When she'd finished telling him what happened, he put his hands on her shoulders and said, "You took a big risk for her. But I'm so glad we have her mother here. You're amazing."

TJ found praise and criticism equally difficult to accept. "No thanks necessary."

Lisa called Eric and told him the news about the girl.

"We'll just have to add them to our little commune until we know it's safe to send them home." He didn't ask her how TJ managed to pull it off. Or maybe he didn't want to know.

"How about if I put them in the guest room where TJ's been staying and have TJ move downstairs?"

"I'll let you handle it. Is the mother willing to stay?"

"We haven't asked her yet, but I'm sure she will be. She's terrified of her husband and that he might try to take Tina again. Are you coming home right after you close?"

"I'm planning on it, why?"

"I'm making a pot roast. I thought we could all use some comfort food."

After dinner, Eric drove Lisa home to pick up some things she wanted for the preparation of their Thanksgiving dinner.

Lisa had lost much of her enthusiasm for the event. Maggie had called earlier to let them know the police had no bead on Wysecki and it would be at least a few days before they identified the bodies. Maggie admitted she couldn't see Wysecki as being able to carry out the complex plot hatched by the person the group sought. With TJ still insisting Eddie Wysecki probably didn't know how to do anything more complex than mix a dry martini or read a racing form, Lisa finally had to admit he wasn't their killer.

Eddie was, however, being sought as Danielle's murderer, and Maggie warned them it wouldn't be long before the police would be around again to interview the group, especially TJ. She reminded them they would have to be open with the police about their investigation into the missing women.

Eric interrupted Lisa's thoughts. "You're awfully quiet. Problems other than the obvious?"

"Other than the fact someone wants to kill me?" Lisa was terrified Danielle's murderer would find her and finish the job. "Sorry, I didn't mean to snap at you. You're right; there are other things I'm wrestling with."

When they arrived at her house, Eric opened the car door for her. At his insistence, she'd added timers to her outdoor lights, and the place was lit up like a going-out-of-business sale. At the entrance to her house, a plastic bag containing a gift-wrapped package hung suspended from the doorknob. Its unexpected appearance stopped them where they stood.

"Maybe we should call Maggie," said Eric, stepping protectively in front of Lisa.

"No. Let's take it in first and see if I can tell where it's from. Paige could have arranged to have something sent."

Carefully, they carried the package into the house and set it on the kitchen table. As they edged the box from the plastic, the logo of a local florist became visible next to a large, red bow. Eric handed Lisa a card that had been attached to the bow.

Lisa, I'm feeling terrible about the way we left things. Please, let's meet for a drink and talk. Love, Tyler

Lisa hadn't heard from Tyler since the night he called to tell her he'd broken off his engagement. She'd told him it was over between them and knew she'd done the right thing. But at this moment, she'd have given anything to be with him, wrapped in the sanctuary of his embrace if only for one night.

"I assume we don't have to call the bomb squad?"

Lisa shook her head, mortified to find she couldn't speak around the lump rising in her throat.

Eric placed a hand on her shoulder. "Are you all right?"

"I'm fine." She reached into the box and lifted out a small crystal bowl filled with a bouquet of pink tea roses and babies' breath.

Eric gave her a handkerchief to catch the tear rolling down her cheek at the sight of the flowers. He led her to the sofa, and after locating a bottle of wine, poured her a drink. Lisa cradled the glass in her hands, wishing she were alone to have a good cry.

He sat down across from her. "All right, I'll play the shrink, you can be the patient."

Confiding in Eric was the last thing she wanted to do, but absent the opportunity to be alone for a good cry, his presence would have to do.

"It's everything. All of this couldn't have come at a worse time for me. My daughter's not coming home for the holiday, and a relationship I enjoyed just ended, and even though the parting was inevitable, it's left a void in my life. And this fear—it's almost more than I can handle."

"This is the first time I've seen you show any sign of weakness. But I know you're a strong woman."

"I'm a strong person in a lot of ways, but there's been too much all at once. Maybe it's time for me to have some therapy of my own. I've been putting it off since my therapist cut me loose."

Eric leaned forward, his elbows on his knees. "A therapist would do that?"

"Therapy only works if the patient is willing to make the changes necessary to improve their life—I wasn't." She took a deep breath. "But I'm also feeling a little guilty talking about me when you're feeling bad about Danielle."

"Forget about me. I'm intrigued—tell me the rest."

She'd opened Pandora's box; she might as well tell him every-thing. "I don't do well with relationships—mature ones, anyway. I like the excitement of meeting someone new, the challenge of the hunt, the highs. If it starts resembling stability, I leave. I gravitate toward men who are unattainable. The latest, the one who sent the roses, is fifteen years younger than I am. We ended when he became engaged. Then, after his engagement didn't work out he called and said he'd like to pick up where we left off. I turned him down. The flowers are an attempt to change my mind."

He chuckled softly. "I think we actually have something in common."

44

It was after eleven when Maggie and David left the Waukesha station. Their differences of the evening before had been forgotten in the day's events, and David asked to spend the night with her. Too wired for sleep, they had a beer in front of the TV, neither of them paying much attention to the old movie playing on the set.

David, still angry that Waukesha had let Wysecki out of their sight long enough to run, still complained about it. "We don't have enough manpower to be sure every possible route out of town is covered. Crap, it's impossible, anyway. If Wysecki has an alternate ID, we're screwed."

Maggie sighed. "They didn't have anything to hold him on, and he didn't seem important enough to put on a tail."

She leaned back, her head on David's shoulder, and closed her eyes. She should get some sleep, close down her mind for a few hours. She heard David flipping through the channels, finding the usual late night drivel, stopping at a poker tournament.

He said, "Wysecki doesn't have much of a life outside of his bar. He's a gambler. If he gets his ass to Vegas, he might as well be on the moon; any idiot could disappear there."

Maggie opened her eyes and sat up. "Didn't someone say he liked to play the horses? Wouldn't a guy like him head somewhere with a track?"

"Might be a place to look. Most of the tracks in the Midwest close for winter, but isn't there a track in Florida that's open all year?"

"Florida and California, I think. It's worth a shot. We could call the tracks and get his picture circulated, have them keep an eye out for the guy." Excited, Maggie had a burst of renewed energy and went for her computer.

David groaned. "Not now."

"It'll only take a minute. I'll find out which tracks are open this time of year, and we can alert them in the morning." Maggie already had her computer open, quickly tapping keys.

"You do that. I'm going to take a shower. I'll keep the bed warm for you."

After fifteen minutes online, Maggie discovered a lot of racetracks open during the winter months. She thought it best to go with the big ones and decided on Hialeah in Florida and Aqueduct in New York. She didn't think the smaller tracks would be as attractive to a gambler, but she liked Arizona and New Mexico for their proximity to the border, and selected three from those states. She settled on a list of five to contact first thing in the morning.

At 7:00 a.m., they got a call from their boss to report back to Oconomowoc. When Maggie told him she had something on the Wysecki case that might be a promising lead, he told them to go ahead and check in with Waukesha, but be back by afternoon.

Zabel and Feinstein acted grateful to have help, even if only for the morning. Maggie showed them the printouts of the racetracks she'd pinpointed as places Eddie might gravitate to and suggested they get in touch with track security at each of them, fax them a photo, and ask them to watch out for Wysecki.

"I like it," said Zabel. "But we were just going over to the Medical Examiner's office to find out how close they are to identifying the bodies. Then we have meetings set up with some of the bar regulars and Wysecki's girlfriend."

179

Feinstein's brow wrinkled all the way up his bald head. He looked at Maggie. "Why don't you two stay here and do the track thing and we'll cover these appointments. I think you both know your way around pretty well."

Maggie felt David's irritation. He hated phone work, preferred to be out on the streets. But she wanted to make sure her idea was in place, and ignored his negative body language. "Sure, we can do that."

Feinstein looked them both over, and folded his arms atop his round stomach. "On second thought, I've never been real fond of autopsies. If one of you would rather go out with Greg, I'll stay and help with the racetrack angle."

David jumped on it. "Bodies don't bother me, I'd be glad to go out with Greg. That is, if Greg doesn't mind."

Zabel nodded toward David and stood up to leave. They left the station, headed for the medical examiner's office.

As soon as they were out of earshot, Max Feinstein turned to Maggie. "I hate seeing stiffs getting cut up, and my bad knee is bothering me. So anything that'll keep me out of the morgue and on my butt is what I'd rather be doing."

45

The temperature hovered in the low seventies in Hialeah, overcast but warm. Hardly a breeze ruffled the palm trees decorating the racetrack.

Unless the track had a big race scheduled, Mondays brought a small crowd. Despite the low attendance, no one was looking for Eddie Wysecki. At least half of the photos handed out to the security guards rested in the bottom of freshly lined trash bins. Except for Fitz Herrera's. He'd memorized the photo, pulling it out from time to time to compare it with a face in the crowd.

Herrera's job mattered to him. His goal was to become a police officer, but openings were hard to come by. The gig at the track had taken him years to get and could lead to a coveted position with HPD. He'd figured with security experience, he'd have a shot.

As he moved through the stands, he thought about Wysecki and wondered if he'd really killed all those women. Fitz loved women. He couldn't imagine anyone hurting one of them, but in Miami it happened all the time. Sometimes even here in Hialeah.

He tried to think where someone like Eddie Wysecki would hang out if he were here. Probably in the grandstand where it was most crowded. The mutt would most likely stay outside and only go in to place a wager. For sure he'd use one of the new automated machines so he wouldn't have to face a teller. Fitz's eyes scanned the crowd. On his third pass through the grandstand, he noticed a man sitting on a bench about three up from the space in front of the fence outlining the racetrack. He wore large mirrored sunglasses, a goofy-looking hat like a guy might wear to go fishing, and a jacket with the collar turned up even though the temperature had hit eighty degrees. He held a racing program in his lap, and a copy of every tip sheet sold by the vendors—a serious player. Fitz decided to keep an eye on him from a distance.

Eddie hated the automatic wager machines. Working the damn machines while wearing the fucking reflector glasses was a pain in the ass, although hiding his face would be worth it until he could make the right connections for his escape to Mexico. He sure liked the easy life: gambling, hanging at the track, frequenting the dozens of titty-bars in the area, the endless, balmy weather. But his money wouldn't last long here; he had to get to Mexico where he'd be considered a wealthy guy.

He was on a winning streak and finding it tough to stay low-key. Without sitting with a track buddy, the wins weren't quite as savory. Throwing a fist in the air and pantomiming "Yes!" had to suffice.

He'd overheard what he considered a hot tip in the eighth race. He planned to scoot out after its finish. When the bell for the eighth race went off, Eddie hung on the rail. He'd bet some serious change. It turned out to be an exciting race, the horses bunched up coming around the final turn, with the favorite beginning to lose ground. Eddie was ecstatic as his horse, at 15-1, approached the frontrunner. Forgetting his cool, he shouted, "Come on six, come on six!"

When the three lead horses thundered over the finish line, they were synchronized like a Swiss watch and Eddie's number six was one of them. Even with a photo, the decision would be a tough call. Eddie went to a bench, sat for a minute, then came back and paced in front of the rail. When the photo finish of the race went up on the giant monitor the crowd went wild. Number six, Perry's Pride, had won the race with only one, well-bred nostril nipping ahead of the other two horses.

Eddie went wild. He pulled off his hat and performed a frantic dance, looking like some kind of mystic tribal chief without the feathers. Halfway through his wild performance, the silver shades flew off his face.

His mania ended abruptly when two iron fists grabbed his arms, snapping on a pair of cuffs.

The press quoted Fitz as saying he acted on automatic pilot when he recognized Eddie Wysecki. In real time, however, as Fitz grabbed the guy, all that went through his mind was, "This is my shot!"

46

TJ opened her phone.

Maggie said, "TJ, I wanted to talk to you about this first because I know you understand how the system works. We just got word they've picked up Wysecki in Florida, but it'll take a while to get him transferred here, maybe a few days. And he's not talking. He asked for an attorney right away."

"Fast work."

"We haven't turned up anything in his financials or from interviews to give us any indication he had another place where he could be stashing bodies."

"Never thought it was him doing the missing women."

"Well, he may have disposed of the bodies someplace we haven't discovered yet. You can tell the others he's in custody, but it's not for publication.

"I know you don't think he did the Ventura woman, but you know the blame is going to swing his way. You folks will be under the microscope if they start trying to find a connection between Eddie and Danielle."

"Yeah, I figured that."

TJ closed the phone. After she shared the news with the group, she would need to forget about all this shit and have some fun. Jeff's suggestion that they go out for a while after dinner would be a welcome relief from murder and mayhem. She pulled on a pair of jeans, a bright orange sweater, and boots with spiked heels. A good time was in order.

Jeff drove them to the Sombrero Club, a bar and restaurant on Pewaukee Lake, not far from Lisa's office.

"They have great margaritas," he promised.

"You ever been to this place?"

"No, but I've heard about it."

TJ laughed. "Figured."

They sipped margaritas, sitting at the bar listening to the band play music from the sixties and seventies. Jeff surprised her when he asked her to dance. While he wasn't what she would call a good dancer, he managed himself well on the dance floor, a feat few men could pull off. As she moved her body with the beat of the music, TJ realized she'd really needed to unwind.

When the final notes died out, the music continued with one of her favorites, "You Are So Beautiful to Me." Jeff put his arms around her waist, and they began to dance to the slow, molten sounds of the love song. They weren't exactly pressed together, but she put her arms around his neck, resting her head on his shoulder, while reminding herself they weren't on a date. But he felt good.

When the song ended, the band took a break.

Back at the bar, TJ picked up her drink. "You were right—they make a great margarita."

Jeff frowned. "TJ, I think you put yourself at risk too often."

TJ had forgotten they were out to celebrate her discovery of Tina's mother, but hadn't expected a lecture on her methods. "That's how I live my life. Used to be a cop, you know. That's when I really lived on the edge."

Wisely, Jeff let the subject drop. When the band resumed, a tall, well-dressed black man approached them and asked TJ to dance. She looked at Jeff.

"Go ahead."

Jeff watched her leave, thinking he'd never known anyone remotely like TJ. But he and TJ were just friends, weren't they? A twinge of disloyalty struck him as he realized it had only been two months since his wife disappeared.

He watched them dance; they looked awesome together. It didn't take long before the rest of the dancers circled TJ and her partner, watching their performance. Maybe this guy was someone TJ should get to know. Jeff hadn't liked what he'd heard about Richard, her detective boyfriend.

When the song ended, TJ's partner grabbed her to dance with him to the next song. Jeff downed his drink, trying not to watch her every move. Overcome with guilt, he ordered another drink.

After TJ finished the second wild dance with the other guy, the lights went down, signaling a slow dance. The song began.

"No one told me about her, the way she lied."

Jeff nearly dropped his drink. He should have been prepared— they *were* playing old songs. Before he could react, TJ appeared at his side, asking him to dance. He knew she was probably just worried about him because of the damn song, but he wanted to feel her in his arms again. To hell with the damn song. On the dance floor, when she rested her head on his shoulder and he felt her warm breath on his neck, he knew—she felt the attraction too. The song ended all too quickly—it had lost its hold on him.

When they returned to their seats at the bar, Jeff felt like he needed to say something, but what?

"So," he asked, "are you having a good time?" Lame. He should have kept his mouth shut.

She smiled at him. As she started to speak, a woman approached them. "Jeff? Jeff Denison?"

"Yes," he said, not recognizing the woman. About his age, she was short with long, reddish hair.

"I thought it was you. I'm Susan Jaster. You probably don't remember me, but I met you last year at our Christmas party." Jeff looked at her blankly.

"You know, Lifetime Insurance, the place where Jamie worked." Jeff still didn't remember her, although his memory of the party was not a fond one. He'd never felt like he fit in with Jamie's friends. "Sure, I remember that party."

"You know, when I saw you I remembered something from that night." She moved closer to him. Her breasts, loose under a thin, satiny top, grazed his arm.

"Something about the Christmas party?"

"About the night Jamie went missing."

She had his attention. Jeff could feel TJ leaning forward, waiting to hear what Susan had to say. He asked, "What do you mean?"

"Well, it was kinda weird. We were all drinking a lot and dancing, and I wasn't even sure it was her."

They listened raptly for more. Jeff asked, "Are you saying you saw Jamie that night?"

"Yeah. I think I did. We were sitting at that booth over there." She pointed to a booth across the room. "It was real crowded that night. I thought I saw her standing at the bar. "

"Here?"

"Yeah."

"That's it? You *think* you saw her?" Jeff wished she'd get to the point if she had one. He didn't think it likely Jamie had been at the Sombrero Club the night she disappeared.

"I'm pretty sure I saw her. But it was more than that. I met this guy, you know? We decided to go somewhere else for a while. When we left I thought I saw her car in the parking lot. It like—stood out, you know?"

Jeff did know. When Jamie bought the expensive little sports car, he'd said nothing even though he'd disapproved of the purchase.

"Are you sure about any of this?"

"Well . . . pretty much."

"Did anyone else see her?"

"No, just me."

Jeff wanted to shake her. "Did you tell this to the police?"

"I wasn't there the day the cops came around at work. No one believed I saw her that night—we always asked her to come with us and she never did. I had a lot to drink so I figured the cops wouldn't believe me either."

It made sense; she didn't come across as very credible. She'd been looking questioningly at TJ. Jeff finally introduced her as a friend.

TJ helped wrap things up. "We need to get going. Gotta be at work early tomorrow."

Jeff rose from his seat, tossing bills on the bar.

"Well, I just thought I'd tell you," Susan hissed, obviously irritated Jeff hadn't been more interested in what she had to tell him. She stalked back to her table, her short suede skirt barely covering her narrow hips.

When the door closed behind them, TJ stopped, her eyes gleaming. "We got a lead!"

47

The guest list for Thanksgiving dinner had grown exponentially. Who'd have thought so many people had nowhere to go? Lisa kept busy planning the meal, and Eric hired a second security guard for the weekend. Her schedule minimal due to the holiday, she immersed herself in culinary concerns.

Lisa was alone in the kitchen when TJ came in on Tuesday night.

TJ hadn't looked her in the eye. She had her back to Lisa as she hung up her coat.

Lisa asked, "Hi, what's up?"

"Wish I knew."

"Anything you'd like to talk about?"

TJ sat down at one of the kitchen stools. "Got any coffee?"

"No, how about tea?" TJ made a face but accepted a cup of the green tea Lisa was fond of and stared into it without sipping.

Lisa poured herself a cup and sat next to her. "Did you have a good time last night?"

"Something real interesting happened last night." TJ told Lisa about the conversation with Susan Jaster. "We're gonna need to go back there with a picture of Jamie and see if anyone else saw her. Could be a great lead."

"It could, I suppose. But why the mood? Isn't that good news?"

TJ sighed heavily. "Might be time for me to come see you for therapy."

Lisa laughed. "Okay, what's going on? It has to be serious if you're thinking about therapy."

"It's Jeff."

"Jeff? What about him?"

"You know."

"Are we going to play twenty-questions?"

TJ stood, carrying the tea she still wasn't drinking, and walked over to the window. With her back to Lisa, she said, "I'm startin' to get feelings for the guy. Well, lust anyway."

Lisa held back what would have been her first response. "How do you feel about that?"

"I could give you a buncha reasons why it's bad. Let's see, he still misses his wife, we're even more opposite than they were, I ain't good at relationships, and he's too goddamn white!"

"White? Conlin's white. Since when does that matter to you?"

"Not that kind of white. I mean vanilla-white. The guy goes to church every week. He's an engineer. He likes old movies. And what would he want with someone like me?"

Lisa walked over to TJ and turned her around. "TJ, we can't help who we're drawn to. You and Jeff have spent a lot of time with each other and gone through a lot together. Being drawn to one another is understandable. But Jeff is very vulnerable right now. Your friendship has been good for him, but I'd hate to see you get hurt. He still has a lot to work through before he can get involved with someone again. And what's this 'someone like me' comment? I've never known you to have an ego problem."

"I know. An' don't even know what I want anyway. Guess I'm just confused."

Lisa said softly, "Maybe Jeff has some qualities you wish Richard had."

TJ didn't comment.

"Do you want advice?"

"Sure. You'll lay it on me anyway."

Lisa smiled. "Don't let it go any further for now. He isn't ready. But he needs your friendship. Talk to him about it. There's no reason you can't go on being friends. If there is a chance of something more developing between you, remember it has to happen slowly. For both of you, not just Jeff."

TJ wrinkled her nose. "Don't usually put things off; if I want it, I go for it, you know? Don't like waiting. But, you're right. We need to talk. Course if he doesn't feel the same way, I'm gonna feel like an idiot."

"Do you think he feels the same way about you?"

TJ stood up and emptied her cup in the sink. She grinned. "Yeah."

Teresa used leftover beef roast to make beef sandwiches and a pot of soup for dinner. After Eric invited them to stay she'd insisted on cooking for them until she decided what to do. She had a brother in Florida and was contemplating moving there.

Lisa, Jeff, TJ, and Eric gathered in Eric's office later to go over the information they'd gathered so far and placed on the whiteboards.

Each of the fifteen women on their short list had her own column with her photo posted at the top. So far the only things the women had in common were their attractiveness and the 911 calls.

TJ had added, "Possibly seen at the Sombrero Club the night she disappeared" in Jamie's column. Everyone shared her excitement about the lead, and they discussed how they would proceed with the interviews at the club.

Jeff wanted them to act on it immediately. "Why are we waiting to go over there?"

TJ cut him off. "Called there today, and found out this week lots of the regular help is off because of hunting season and the holiday.

Makes no sense to go now. The manager is checking their records so he can let us know just who was working that night."

Jeff wasn't giving up easy. "Well, what about Tina's father? What are we doing about him?"

Lisa pacified him with, "Got Shannon working on that. What we know from Teresa is he stays with friends, so it's hard to locate him. I did call Maggie today and let her know what's going on. She told me Teresa has to go to the MPD and get him picked up for taking Tina."

TJ looked at Jeff. "Think we should talk to any other women from Jamie's office?"

"It didn't sound like anyone else saw Jamie. And the Jaster woman seemed kind of flaky. There is one woman I know who Jamie worked with and went to the gym with. I'll call her and see if she was at the club that night."

Most of the women on their list were computer literate, and one of the avenues they were working on was to find out if any of them made a habit of meeting men online. Some of them frequented the clubs, some worked out, and some cheated on their husbands. They weren't finding any commonalities, but had a lot of people to talk to in each woman's circle of friends.

Jeff left the room and called Amy Hayes, Jamie's friend from the office. When she answered, he explained how he'd run into Susan Jaster and what Susan had told him about seeing Lisa the night she'd disappeared.

"Sorry, Jeff, I wasn't there. I usually go with them on Fridays, but I had a date. The day the police were at the office they talked to everyone. When we compared notes later, the girls who were there said they hadn't seen Jamie and weren't at all sure about Susan's powers of observation. They said she'd been drinking a lot. That's why no one brought it up to the police."

Maybe the great lead was going to be a total bust after all. Jeff exchanged a little small talk with Amy and answered a few of her questions about Jamie.

Just as they were about to hang up, she said, "Wait. I just remembered something. You know Jamie and I used to do an aerobics class together, but I quit going for a while. She mentioned meeting a new guy at the Y—not that she was interested in him—she just said he was new and really nice, but I don't think she'd talked to him much, you know? She said he was real good looking, too. At the time I thought she might have made him up to get me to come back."

When Jeff came back and gave them the news, TJ volunteered to go to the gym to see if she could find someone in Jamie's aerobic class who might remember the guy and point him out.

Lisa said, "You know, folks, I think we have to make a list of just what kind of things we're going to research from these women's lives." She pulled out an easel with large sheets of post-it paper and began recording.

When they ran out of ideas, they spent some time fine-tuning the list, weeding out any that were unnecessary or repetitive.

TJ complained. "Shit! Gonna have to start from square one with this list!"

Lisa said, "It might seem like a lot, but with this list we'll have a better handle on what to ask their friends. You just never know what may be a link between them."

Finding a link, if one even existed, looked like an insurmountable task. The group was discouraged.

Lisa was certain she'd never again have a good night's sleep. She got out of bed and went downstairs for some of her Forty-winks Tea.

She found Eric sitting at the island eating a sandwich, the day's paper spread out around him.

"Did you go back to work?"

"Yes. Three new cars came in today, and we're having some problems with the website. Bad night for sleeping?"

Lisa laughed, looking down at her robe and slippers. "How could you tell? And I think I've lost a dog—Phanny hasn't left Tina's side since she arrived."

Lisa put on a kettle for her tea and sat down next to Eric.

"I'm sorry you couldn't sleep."

Lisa thought he looked tired. "It's been difficult with everything that's been happening."

"How are things going with Teresa and Tina? Are they comfortable staying here for the time being?"

"Of course. Teresa was thrilled with your offer to stay."

"Tina's going to be okay, isn't she?"

"Yes, she's doing better by the hour now that she has her mother."

"Thanks to TJ. Did she ever tell you how she managed that?"

"Yes. She said don't ask and she won't tell."

"That's what I thought."

They sat for a few minutes without talking. Then Eric turned to her and said, "I've always wanted to ask you something. Haven't you ever been at all uncertain about Jeff and me?"

"You mean about the possibility one of you killed your wife? After I had a couple sessions with Jeff there was no doubt in my mind he had nothing to do with his wife's disappearance. And I respected TJ's opinion of you." She'd already admitted to herself his being a pain in the butt didn't make him a murderer. Lisa hadn't told anyone she had moments of distrust for the man, despite their getting along better.

"I wish the rest of the world agreed with TJ's opinion."

"Is that why you're no longer practicing medicine?"

"More or less. When I got out of jail I found out my name was anathema in the medical community. They revoked my privileges at the hospital, but I still have my license to practice."

"There must have been somewhere you could have worked."

"Sure, if I wanted to live in a desert or a jungle and travel by camel. But seriously, I enjoy what I do. When I was still practicing I made some very wise investments which allowed me to live this way. I've been fortunate."

Lisa pushed herself away from the counter. "I'm finally feeling sleepy."

Before she could get up, he covered her hand with his, gave it an affectionate squeeze, and said, "It was nice talking with you."

As she went up the stairs, the hand he'd touched felt warm, and Lisa had to shift her thoughts to something else before she started to reflect on her sudden attraction to Eric Schindler.

48

The following morning Teresa came into the kitchen to start the first pot of coffee. She scooped out the coffee, stewing about her daughter. Tina's nightmares were probably normal under the circumstances, but Teresa worried about the girl. It had taken nearly an hour to get her back to sleep after the last one. Teresa couldn't find the bear Jeff had given Tina, which had made matters worse. The girl loved it.

While the coffee did its thing, she looked around for the bear, stopping at the closed door to Eric's office. Eric had warned her not to let Tina go inside, but you never knew with kids. Teresa entered the room, flicking on the overhead light.

She froze at the sight of the whiteboards spread out in a semi-circle in the middle of the room, photos of women's faces heading them. Fifteen pairs of eyes stared at her. Teresa wanted to run but stopped in her tracks. "*Madre de dios!*" Locked in place, she crossed herself. The fourth woman from the left was Diane Jadzewski, a woman she used to work with. She scurried from the room, praying for Diane's soul. She'd heard enough of their conversations to know — these women had all been murdered.

Jeff wandered into the kitchen, lured by the smell of the strong brew. Teresa stood at the stove, her arms tight about her abdomen. When she saw Jeff, she burst into a string of Spanish. He had no clue what she was saying, but knew by her hysterical speech, it wasn't good.

"Slow down." He took her shoulders and sat her down. "Tell me what's wrong."

She wrung her hands. "The pictures!"

"What pictures?"

She pointed to Eric's office. "In there. I was looking for Tina's bear."

"Couldn't you find the bear? Is that what's wrong?"

"No, no! Not that. It's Diane—she's one of them!"

Jeff breathed a sigh of relief as Lisa walk into the kitchen. She'd do a much better job of handling Teresa. He told Lisa what had happened.

Teresa grew silent as Lisa explained to her that right now, they really had no idea what had happened to her friend. "We talked to her parents and they think Diane ran away because of her husband. She may be perfectly fine; we don't know for certain what happened to any of those women."

Teresa pressed a tissue to her face.

"Teresa," Lisa said softly, "what can you tell us about her?"

"She was my boss. But nice person, we talked sometimes. About our men."

"Did she tell you anything about her husband?"

Teresa sniffled into a balled-up Kleenex. "Yes. He hurts her. We talked about it sometimes. But last time I see her, she was happy. She met someone and was getting divorce."

"Did she tell you anything about him?"

"No. Just that he very nice."

Lisa's hopes sank like a wet tea bag. "Anything you remember would help, Teresa. Did she say what he looked like?"

"Oh yes! I forget—she say he very handsome. Tall, big shoulders. Nice body."

"Anything else she might have said about him? How he dressed? His car? Any tattoos? Glasses?"

Teresa hugged herself, tears rolling down her cheeks. "Nothing else."

"Thank you, Teresa. You've been very helpful. We're trying to find your friend. And all those other women. If you remember anything else, just let us know."

Teresa sniffed, obviously relieved that the questioning was over, and went to give Tina her breakfast.

Lisa looked up. Jeff had left the room.

That night, filled with an anxiety that wouldn't let her drift into sleep, Lisa got out of bed and walked into the living room of the small apartment. Was fear keeping her awake? Loneliness swept through her, and with it, Tyler's face.

An excuse to call him popped into her mind—the flowers. She'd never acknowledged his gift. Forgetting there was good reason for her oversight, she opened her phone.

Tyler's voice, thick with sleep, answered. "Hey."

"It's me."

She heard the rustling of bedclothes. "Lisa."

"Yeah."

His response came lightning fast. "I miss you."

"Me, too." Her pride, what little remained, wouldn't let her be the one to suggest they meet. And she couldn't invite him to Eric's, didn't want him to know she wasn't staying at her own house.

He stood waiting for her in the doorway when she pulled up at his house. They grabbed for each other the minute the door closed. His mouth met hers, hungry on lips opening to welcome him.

They made their way to his bedroom without breaking the embrace, leaving a trail of clothing in their wake. Every ounce of her being became one with him, every compartment of her brain closing off to everything but the thrilling sensation of his body melding with hers, her eagerness to feel him inside her.

Moving together with the sweet familiarity of longtime lovers, they made love with a passionate urgency. Her climax, when it came, left her with a peacefulness she'd been missing for weeks.

As she drifted off in his arms, she told herself it would only be for a minute. When she awoke and saw it was nearly 4:00 a.m., she leapt out of bed. Tyler didn't wake up. Filled with a rush of guilt, she dressed hurriedly and ran out into the night, the dangers of being alone forgotten.

Lisa flinched at sound of the garage door opening, praying no one heard it. She opened the doorway leading to the apartment quietly, carefully disarming the alarm and resetting it behind her. She moved stealthily up to her quarters and opened the door.

Eric sat on the couch, a bottle of scotch on the coffee table in front of him. The room reeked of cigar smoke.

He stood, picking up the bottle, his dark eyes angry. "I was about to call the police before I saw your car was gone."

She wanted to ask why he'd come up here looking for her, but thought better of it. "I'm sorry if I worried you." Inadequate, but what could she say? She'd been lonely, horny? "I couldn't sleep. I felt like I needed to get out, so I went for a drive."

Eric moved toward her. When he spoke, he was close enough for her to smell the scotch on his breath. "A drive? Honey, I know what a booty trip looks like." He snorted. "Or should I say—smells like."

Unable to deny his words, Lisa's face heated with embarrassment. "I said I'm sorry." She sniffed the air and muttered, "Surprised you can smell anything."

"You're sorry. I worked late tonight because I spent the morning at Danielle's funeral. You know, the woman who was murdered in place of you? But you must have forgotten that in your rush to see your young stud."

"Eric, I know you must be hurting—"

He cut her off. "You don't know shit! And don't start throwing your psychology bullshit at me. All that therapy crap ever did for me was cost thousands of dollars and Kayla was still fucked up. It didn't stop them from sucking up the money, though, even when it did nothing for her."

When her tears came, Lisa had no idea why. For Eric, Danielle, Kayla, herself?

Eric's face reddened in a burst of fury. "Oh, sure, cry now." He turned from her, walking to the door.

Lisa grabbed his arm. "Please, let's talk about this."

He pulled away from her. "You disgust me," he said, slamming the door behind him.

49

The number of people who straggled in for Thanksgiving dinner amazed Lisa. TJ's sister, Janeen, turned out to be so unlike TJ, Lisa could hardly believe they were related. The cocoa-complexioned woman was soft spoken, her slightly plump body crowned by a head of short braids tipped with tiny red beads dangling about her smiling face when she talked.

The wonderful aroma of roasting turkey filled the kitchen as Janeen handed Lisa a casserole dish brimming with sweet potatoes topped with marshmallows, and another with her homemade cranberry relish. Her children, Lonnie, five, and Jazz, seven, carried in a large, cardboard box filled with games.

Tina hid behind her mother when she saw so many strangers but it wasn't long until, lured by the stack of games, she joined the other two children on the floor in front of the fireplace.

Lisa was putting finishing touches on the centerpiece when Eric walked into the room. They'd been carefully avoiding each other all day. He broke the awkward silence by asking her about Paige.

"She finally called me back this morning. Her boyfriend made it home yesterday, and they were invited to another couple's house for Thanksgiving dinner. She's promised to come for Christmas."

"I'm glad to hear it. Have you told her what you're doing here?"

"No. I'm going to wait until I see her at Christmas." Glad he'd broken the silence between them, Lisa was hoping to have a chance to talk to him alone, but knew it might not be possible with so many guests in the house.

The food was set out on the island buffet style, two large, golden turkeys proudly displayed, surrounded by all the traditional accompaniments.

When everyone was seated, their food steaming in front of them, Roland said grace. Charles sat next to him, fully recovered from the wounds of his attack.

The talk during the meal was spirited, none of it on the topic of missing women, abuse, or murder. Lisa had a passing, ironic thought how like a normal holiday gathering this scene would seem to an outside observer.

After the meal everyone able to stay headed for the living room to sit by the fire.

Once everyone had settled, Jeff said, "We forgot something important. We didn't say what we were thankful for this year. I'm sure everyone can think of something they're thankful for."

TJ tilted back in a recliner, eyelids drooping. "Go ahead."

Jeff grinned. "Sure, I'll go first. I'm thankful to be sharing this day with all you wonderful friends. And I'm thankful Tina and Teresa are back together."

Roland spoke next. "I'm thankful to be here, and thankful for TJ, who introduced me to all you people. And mostly, I'm thankful Charles is better and we were able to buy the loft apartment we've always wanted. We'll be moving after the holidays, and you're all invited to our housewarming party."

The thankfulness traveled around the room until the children followed suit, expressing thanks for all the games, the good food, and for the desserts still to come. Teresa, with misty eyes and a voice choked with happiness, said how thankful she was to have her daughter back and for the people who found her: TJ and Jeff. And Eric, for sharing his home with them.

Lisa was silently thankful for the children, Lonnie and Jazz, who'd done what none of them had been able to accomplish—turn Tina back into a child.

Tina wiggled nervously when the other children looked at her expectantly. She looked around the room, and then ran to Jeff, hugged him, then TJ. To each of them she whispered a shy, "Thank you."

The guests had all left by early evening. Lisa, dressed for the out-doors, went to the back door with Phanny.

Eric asked if he could join them. "I need to move. Burn off those two pieces of pie I ate."

They went out into the crisp, evening air and strolled the grounds, avoiding the area still cordoned off with yellow crime-scene tape. It loomed in the background, oppressive as a funeral wreath.

Lisa broke the silence. "I think we should ask Maggie if the tape can come down, don't you?"

"I don't know. It only happened last Friday."

It was hard to believe it hadn't even been a week since a woman had lain dead in that spot. Lisa didn't want to dwell on it, but knew because of their resemblance to each other, the other woman's death would weigh on her forever. Pulling her mind from the morbid, she focused on how much she'd enjoyed the day in spite of the tension she'd felt with Eric.

"Eric, this was such a special day. Thank you for everything you put into it."

"No thanks necessary. You're right. It was special in spite of everything that's happened."

"We can't overlook the good things we've done."

Eric stopped to adjust Phanny's collar. "No, but I've been thinking about Danielle's murder. Someone—and I don't think that someone is Mr. Wysecki—sees you as our ringleader and went after you hoping the rest of us would let it go once you were out of the picture. Danielle's murder makes me more certain that we're doing the right thing—this person has to be stopped."

Lisa's throat tightened. The fear she'd managed to set aside for the day crept through her like an oncoming case of the flu. She raised her gloved hands to her face to stave off a grimace. "You're right—about all of it. But you know what I can't make sense of— what was Wysecki doing here that night?" She exhaled, her breath creating a misty, white vapor in the cool evening air. "That's a mystery we may never have the answer to unless he explains it to the police."

Eric turned to her. "There is one more thing I'm thankful for today—you." When she remained silent, he added softly, "You are what holds all of us together."

She and Eric avoided the topic of the night before. They'd gotten back on normal ground, but what had happened needed to be discussed.

Lisa stopped walking. "I'm sorry about last night. I shouldn't have gone out without saying anything. I shouldn't have gone out at all."

He turned to her. "Lisa, I was way out of line—I felt like a real horse's ass today." He took a deep breath. "I was feeling sorry for myself last night, that's why I went up to talk to you. I hoped you'd still be up. I needed a shoulder to cry on, I suppose." He paused. "I needed your shoulder."

Lisa, bewildered by the rush of feeling that overcame her with his words, whispered, "I needed someone, too." She bent down to pet Phanny, who looked puzzled because they'd stopped walking.

"Everything felt so overwhelming last night. For me, being with Tyler was like getting drunk. I forgot about everything while I was with him. Not the best choice, but no hangover."

"I understand. Are we okay?"

Lisa felt like her next words would be critical to any friendship or relationship she'd ever have with Eric Schindler. She said, "Very okay," and reached out to him.

He took her in his arms. She felt safe nestled against his wide chest, and wondered why she'd never seen past her petty annoyances to how good a man he really was. They broke the embrace as the security guard walked past and wished them a good evening.

She had to admit Eric could be kind and generous. That's probably all there was to it. She didn't need the complication of having romantic feelings for a man. Any man. Or worse, a man described by TJ as being in love with a ghost. Maybe her feelings were only lust — *that* she could deal with.

TJ was sharing the lower suite with her sister and planned on driving them home the next day. She'd go back to her apartment where she'd meet Richard for their trip to Wisconsin Dells. After Janeen and the kids had settled in for the night, TJ went upstairs to get a nightcap.

She wanted to talk to Lisa. Grabbing a nearly full bottle of wine, she picked up two glasses and padded up the steps. There was a light under the door to the apartment. After tapping softly on the door, TJ walked in and saw Lisa sitting on the couch, reading a book.

Lisa looked up. "Unusual for you to be awake this late. What's going on?"

"Nothin', just needed to tell you something before I leave." TJ set down the wine glasses, and at a nod from Lisa, poured them each a glass of wine.

"Speaking of your weekend with Richard, are you sure it's a good idea?"

TJ frowned. "Why wouldn't it be?"

"I can think of a few reasons, but setting them aside for now, what's on your mind?"

"Rollie and Charles."

"What about them? They looked happy today."

"They're happy—it's somethin' else. Rollie told me he's pretty sure Charles' mugging wasn't a mugging."

"Do they think it was a hate crime because he's gay?"

TJ looked at her impatiently. "You aren't getting it, are you? Remember it happened a couple days after we met him at the salon?"

Lisa winced at the enormity TJ's words. "Rollie thinks it was about what we're doing?"

"Just sayin' Rollie thinks it might be."

"Why now, after all this time?"

"Seems like now that Charles is over the trauma, he remembered somethin'. After the guy worked him over, he said to Charles, 'Stay the fuck out of it!' Rollie hasn't told Charles what he thinks it means. Not yet, anyway."

"Why isn't he telling Charles the truth?"

"Well, there ain't no real truth here. It's just supposition, right?"

"But if it's about our investigation, the assailant mistook him for Roland, just like me and Danielle. They are about the same height and build. And it was dark."

"Yeah, yeah. But two mistakes? Well, there's nothin' we can do about it anyway. It's over and Charles is okay. I think Rollie's afraid if Charles thinks his attack had anything to do with Rollie's helpin' women disappear he won't want him to do it anymore. Or donate to the cause again. Don't want that to happen."

Lisa drained her glass. "Yes, but—a gay bashing? It's unconscionable to let Charles go on thinking that."

"Would you talk to Rollie about it?"

"Why me?"

"I dunno. Because you could do it better?"

Eric's words came back to her; "You are what holds us all together." It felt like a heavy burden. She'd have to be strong for all of them, and somewhere in that strength, find a little left for herself.

50

TJ and Lisa were eating breakfast when Maggie entered the room, her cheeks pink from the cold. "Sorry to disturb your breakfast. Security let me in." She nodded toward the food-laden buffet. "Is this really the day after Thanksgiving?"

Lisa asked, "Do you have news for us?"

"I do. Is everyone here?"

"No, just us. Would you like some breakfast?"

"Thanks, but I can't stay long. The women's bodies in Wysecki's basement have been identified. None of them are on your short list, but you had one of them on your original list. We had the woman's husband as the prime suspect, though he was never arrested."

"Do you think Wysecki might have killed the wife for the husband?"

"They're looking into it. Wysecki had financial problems from time to time, so I suppose it's possible he may have resorted to it. They're also looking into his wife's death, but it appears to have been an accident."

TJ scraped her plate. "What about Danielle Ventura? If Wysecki didn't kill her, who did? If it was someone who thought she was Lisa, then we must be on the right track; there is a killer and it ain't Wysecki. And get this—Teresa knew one of the ladies on our short list. Said she had a guy in her life other than her husband."

Maggie said, "Okay, we don't know who killed Danielle. Everything points to Wysecki, but we won't know anything for sure until we have him in custody, and that probably won't be until next week

208

sometime. If it wasn't him and her murder is related to your interviews, then I'd have to ask—who knew what your group was doing?"

Lisa choked on a bite of food. "Who knew? That would be a lot of people. Everyone we interviewed. "

"That's right. So, bottom line—you need to wrap this up as soon as possible. How long are all of you planning on staying here?"

Lisa shrugged. "I think TJ is planning to leave next week."

TJ nodded. "Have a life to get back to."

Lisa agreed. "I'd like to be in my own home again before Christmas. Shannon's offered to stay with me, but our plans aren't certain yet."

Maggie frowned. "I think you should consider going to the police after Wysecki is interviewed. Unless he admits to killing Danielle, the Waukesha Police will be back to talk to all of you, and this time their questions will be intense. It would pay to be proactive."

Before TJ could protest, Maggie said, "That may be a good thing for all of you. With it out in the open, there'd be no reason for the killer to go after any of you."

"We're making progress, Maggie. I think in a week we'll have enough."

"Good. They should be done talking with Wysecki by then. Until then, remind everyone to be cautious. It's unlikely your killer will go after any of you again. If he's the one who killed Danielle, he's probably feeling real good about having Wysecki as a scapegoat."

Lisa said, "One last question. Do you think there'd be any value in having a profiler look at our information?"

"A profiler? No, I don't think so, Lisa. Because, if I've understood your purpose here, you're not looking for a killer, you're simply trying to convince the police there is a killer, force them to begin a formal investigation.

"If, and I say this very emphatically, you folks believe you have an idea who is behind these disappearances, do not attempt to play detectives. I would hope an assault on one of you and the murder of a person who was supposed to be one of you, would be enough to prevent you from doing something stupid."

TJ and Lisa stayed silent, letting Maggie think she'd had the last word on the subject. Lisa didn't mention the stack of books on Eric's desk about profiling, the Internet search he'd done, or the long list of profilers for hire he printed out.

On a whim, Maggie stopped in Kristy's Classics. She found Eric out in the garage, bent under the open hood of a '57 Chevy.

"Didn't think you did the dirty work," Maggie jabbed.

Eric looked up, a clipboard in hand. "No, just recording the number from the firewall dataplate."

"I just talked to Lisa and TJ and decided I'd stop and see you."

"Why the personal visit, Detective?"

Maggie repeated what she'd told the others.

Eric said, "I'm not surprised. What happens if they find out Wysecki didn't kill Danielle?

"You'll have to tell them everything."

Eric grimaced.

She said, "How many of the women on your list are from Waukesha County?"

"Four, I believe, including my wife and Jamie Denison."

"I've been thinking; if you get nowhere with the MPD, I'm pretty sure Waukesha County would take the case. Once it's officially on Waukesha's books, Milwaukee would be backed into it whether they wanted to be or not."

"I like your way of thinking, Detective," Eric said. "But we'd still want to finish what we've started. Couldn't a profiler be helpful in finding a commonality between the women? Might move things along a little faster."

Maggie sighed. "I'm not a big proponent of profiling. But if it would get you folks away from police work, go for it. You might want to talk to David. He had a case in Chicago when he worked there, and they used a local guy to run a profile for them. David liked him, said he was good."

"Can you find out how to contact him?"

"Let me talk to David. I'll let you know what he thinks. He knows this profiler pretty well, so if you decide to go that route, I'm sure he'd call him for you."

"I'd appreciate it. I'll be glad to pay his fee."

"The others are talking about returning to their homes. I'm hoping you'll convince them to stay with you. And, include Shannon."

"I've been working on it. But I'm up against the holiday season, and they're a stubborn bunch."

51

TJ drove Janeen and the kids home from Eric's. As she drove, she kept a close eye on any vehicles following them for more than a mile or two. TJ hadn't told her sister all the details of what had been happening the last few weeks, only that they were trying to get evidence someone was abducting abused women.

Janeen had her own experience with spousal abuse, one which included her sister, and ultimately resulted in TJ leaving the police force. She hadn't been forced out. Her brother-in-law's shooting had been ruled a clean shoot, necessary to protect the lives of Janeen and the police officer who shot him—TJ.

Try as she might to squelch them, scenes from that night still played in TJ's mind: her sister screaming, Mario's knife pressing into Janeen's neck, the way his body hit the wall when TJ had shot him. TJ'd been eternally grateful her sister had had the foresight to send the kids down the hall to a neighbor before things escalated.

TJ eased up on her rearview-mirror observations when Janeen asked, "So, what time are you meeting Richard for the big weekend?"

"Soon as he gets off; probably leave about five."

"You don't sound too excited about it."

"Since when do you care about my plans with Richard?"

Janeen had never liked Richard and kept telling TJ to find a man her own age, someone to settle down with. Have kids even, despite the fact TJ denied wanting such mundane things.

"That Jeff guy seemed real nice. He's the one you've been work-ing with right?"

TJ should have known her sister would have picked up on her attraction to Jeff. Damn, she didn't want to talk about it. "Yeah, he's the one. Poor guy's real upset about his wife going missing. Gotta feel sorry for him." Maybe the sympathetic words would change the subject.

Her phone rang just as they stopped at a light. Richard said, "Sorry, babe, but I'm still in Chicago. Some family things are going on and I have to stay for a couple more days. We'll have to do our weekend another time. Tell you what. Why don't you take your sister and the kids and go to the Dells anyway? I'll pick up the hotel tab."

"Not necessary." TJ said, annoyed at the last-minute cancellation. But Janeen had been right; TJ hadn't been excited about their trip. But she suspected there was more to his call than a family thing; Richard wasn't a family kind of guy.

He said, "Should I reschedule?"

"Sure. No problem." Did he really think she'd bought his weak excuse? The jerk probably met someone in Chi-Town who he couldn't resist. But she needed a weekend alone. Alone, in her own place.

It had been two years since Lisa had stopped seeing her therapist, Robert Bernstein, but after what had happened with Tyler, she knew it was time—time to sort through her ongoing love affair with exciting, albeit unfulfilling, relationships.

"Lisa. It's been a while."

"I know. Sorry, Robert, you probably have a lot going on, but I'd like to see you."

"Something urgent?"

"Not really. Can you fit me in?"

"I'm not in the office today. I'm actually off for the weekend at my wife's insistence."

"I don't want to take you away from your family."

"No, no. Mother and daughters are at the mall indulging in their favorite pastime. I'm about to go for a run. Want to join me?"

They met on a hiking path in the Kettle Moraine area, a state park north of Oconomowoc. Lisa found him at the side of his car, doing deep stretches. "I maintain a very slow pace. The better to hear you speak, my dear." He laughed. "Baby steps, you know. I'm trying to get rid of some of this gut." He patted his middle. A tall man, Bernstein carried the extra pounds well.

"I know what you mean. I stuffed enough food in my mouth yesterday to hibernate for a month."

They started off walking, then picked up the pace to a slow jog. There weren't many people on the paths, a few dog walkers the only people around.

"Robert, you're doing a great job with Jeff. He speaks highly of you." Lisa had sent Jeff to Robert when she stopped seeing him.

"I'm not sure I can take all the credit."

"Being busy has helped, too, I'm sure."

"Lisa, I know you aren't here because of Jeff."

"No. I'm not sure how much Jeff has told you about what we're doing . . . It's been intense."

"Intense? It sounds more like life-endangering lunacy to me."

"Something had to be done. Too many women have been victimized by this person."

"How do you know it isn't persons?"

"We don't, I suppose."

"Other than the obvious, what's bothering you?"

"Nothing in my life has changed a whole lot since we last talked—since you gave up on me." *That's what it had felt like.*

"Gave up on you? I wouldn't put it that way, Lisa. You'd given up on yourself; there was nothing more I could do for you. Taking any more of your hard-earned dollars for therapy would have made me a charlatan."

"I guess you're right." Professionally she'd known it, but it had, nevertheless, made her feel deserted.

"You know I'm right. Only a quack keeps seeing a patient who won't make the necessary effort to get better. You're here, so what's changed?"

"It's a long story, but I'm not happy with my life, my relation-ships."

"Lisa, if you're serious about working on it now, I'll be happy to start seeing you again."

Lisa stopped to retie a shoelace, glad for a break in the conversa-tion.

Robert ran in place. "I'm surprised you aren't putting therapy on hold until this investigation of yours is over."

Lisa sighed. He knew there was more. She'd never been able to hold out on him.

They resumed their pace. "It can't be easy for all of you, holed up together like you are."

"You've guessed it, haven't you?"

"Hey, your life is in danger, you've been forced to live away from the home you love, Paige is gone, and you're trying to break away from the addiction that's always kept you going. It's only natural you'd want to reach out to someone when you're in such a vulnerable place."

"All true. But Eric Schindler can be such an exasperating man."

"Eric Schindler?"

"You didn't think I'd be attracted to Jeff, did you?"

Robert laughed. "Jeff is in your usual age range."

Lisa grinned. "Guess I deserved that one."

"So what's happening with Eric?"

"Nothing yet, but there's beginning to be an attraction there. For me, anyway."

"What's holding you back? That's not like you."

"Eric and I are both broken, Robert. Two jagged pieces don't make a whole."

"Lisa, I've always maintained you are not a relationship addict. Not in the true sense." When she started to protest, he said, "You aren't. I know it's how you label yourself, but you know as well as I do not every little foible can be labeled a personality disorder. Everything in our profession is not black or white."

He was right. But labeling it made it feel inescapable, unfixable. It allowed her to enjoy the excitement of the new and the pain when it ended; even a painful breakup made her feel alive. "Then what is the solution for my not-a-relationship addiction?"

"You know the answer as well as I do, Lisa. You have to break the pattern, learn to find joy in a relationship not destined to be terminal. One both exciting and comfortable with someone who loves you, who'll be there for you."

"Right. Meanwhile I'm trapped in limbo with a man I'm both attracted to and despise."

"Are you sure about that?"

"Despise may be a little harsh. He has some good qualities."

Robert chuckled. "So, what would be wrong with just going with the flow for now?"

"Are you suggesting I hop in bed with him?" She laughed at the thought, but it intrigued her.

"As your therapist I would never do such a thing. As your friend, I'm concerned about you and think connecting with another person might be good for you right now. I'm not saying it needs to be a sexual connection."

She stopped running and broke out in laughter. "Oh, Robert, I almost said, 'You're screwing with me, right?' but the absurdity of the pun stopped me." Lisa wiped away the tears brought on by her own joke as Robert looked on, smiling.

"Lisa, call my office and make an appointment. I think you're ready to work on your issue."

"My man-diction?" Her play on words sent her into another fit of giggling.

52

In her apartment after she'd dropped off Janeen and the kids, TJ reviewed what they had so far on the missing women; there just weren't any real commonalities among them. A few had had a hint of a new man in their lives, but nothing certain. They needed something concrete.

Eric didn't think Kayla had been seeing anyone, but she'd been a party girl, so maybe anything could be possible. When TJ had interviewed Kayla's two running partners neither claimed to have known about her seeing anyone. Maybe she needed a rematch with those bitches. It was, after all, Friday night—their night to prowl the clubs. TJ wasn't ready to let the group know she and Richard cancelled their weekend plans. She didn't want to tell them and listen to a safety lecture about being alone, but she wasn't feeling up for going out by herself either.

She dialed Shannon's cell. The woman was always eager to be included. When she picked up, TJ said, "You aren't talking to me. Get it?"

"Sure. Lisa said you're gone for the weekend."

"My plans changed."

"Okay. I heard you went to the Y this morning. Did you find anything?"

"Nothin' much. Found the woman who talked to Jamie from time to time. She remembered Jamie mentioned a new guy she'd seen around the Y, described him as a real hottie, but that was about it. Checked with management to see if they had a new membership right around that time, but there weren't any new sign-ups that fit the description. So either he was already a member at some other location or passed himself off as a member."

"Too bad we couldn't find someone who remembers him."

"Yeah. Don't think there's anything more there."

"How about the Sombrero Club?"

"They said next week would be better. You know, folks gone for the holiday now."

"Well, employees might be, but this might be a good weekend to find the regulars hanging out."

Great. Now Shannon thought going out was her idea. "Wanna meet me there?"

"Uh . . . sure."

"Park in the overflow lot across the street. I'll meet you at ten."

A country-rock band was playing at the Sombrero Club when TJ and Shannon walked in. The place was busy, but not as crowded as she'd expected, even better for her purposes. The clubs got the biggest crowd after eleven, so now would be a good time to talk to the bartenders.

Every barkeep they talked to either hadn't been working that night or didn't recognize the photo of Jamie Denison. TJ noticed another guy working the waitress station at the end of the bar. When she showed him the photo, he studied it for a long time.

"I think I saw her that night. Yeah, I noticed her 'cause she was just standing by herself near the end of the bar." He grinned. "I'm partial to blondes. She wasn't dancing or talking to anybody. She just stood there holding a glass of wine and watching the crowd."

"Did you notice when she left?"

"No." He reached over to fill an order for a waitress who'd slapped a drink slip on the bar.

When he finished, he said, "I saw her talk to somebody."

"A guy?"

"Nah, a woman. She's a regular—name's Kimberly. She's out on the dance floor now. The one with the tight pants and shiny top."

She was easy to spot. Doing a wild hip-hop, the other dancers gave her and her partner a wide berth.

TJ stopped the woman as she came off the dance floor. Moving fast, it looked like she was trying to shake off the guy she'd been dancing with.

"Excuse me, Kimberly?" TJ introduced herself. "Mind talking to me a minute?"

Leading her into the restaurant with noise level more conducive to conversation, they took a seat in the waiting area. TJ handed her the photo of Jamie, explaining the bartender had seen them talking the night Jamie had disappeared.

Kimberly's dark brown hair, cut short on the back of her neck, tapered dramatically longer to fall into giant commas around her face as she looked down at the photo. "Yeah, I talked to her. Probably a Friday night, but I can't say which one. Couple months ago, maybe. Might have been that night."

"Can you remember what you talked about?"

"She was just standing by the bar watching, not dancing or talking to anyone. Then Willie came and asked her to dance." When TJ looked at her questioningly she said, "Oh, yeah. Willie's here all the time. He's a real loser—kind of a nut-job, you know? Anyway, this chick in the photo turned down everybody who asked her to dance. When Willie kept asking her she got real pissed."

"Did you hear what she said to him?"

"I don't think she said anything really bad. When he finally moved on, I said something to her like 'He does that to everyone.' That's when we talked."

"Do you remember what you talked about?'

"She said something like 'How could a creep like that think I'd dance with him?' I told her not to feel bad, he hits on everybody; no one dances with him unless they're desperate. 'Cause he dances like he's having some kind of seizure."

"That's all she said to you?"

"I don't remember anything else. We didn't talk much, but mostly we talked about getting rid of guys who won't take no for an answer. And losers like Willie always hit on the hottest girls. Go figure."

TJ asked, "He here tonight?"

"I haven't seen him yet, and he's always the first one here if he's around."

TJ figured Kimberly was done talking; her gaze kept drifting toward the bar. "Did you see her talk to anyone else?"

"Uh-uh. I didn't see her again. After I talked to her, she left the bar, went into the restaurant."

TJ found Shannon and repeated the interview with Kimberly. They went into the restaurant and asked for the manager. When a baby-faced guy wrapped in a white apron walked out to talk to them, TJ didn't think a guy who looked like he hadn't had his first shave yet could possibly be the manager. His nametag, however, read, "Jason Turnbill, Night Manager."

A deep, husky voice contrasted with his youthful appearance. "What can I do for you?"

"I'm looking for anyone who saw this woman on a Friday night about two months ago." TJ handed him the photo of Jamie and gave him the date. As he looked at it, she added, "She was seen entering the restaurant at about eleven."

"She doesn't look familiar to me, but I'm not out front too much at that time of night. I can check my records and get back to you in a couple days."

"Listen, this is really important. Could you run this by the people who are here now and see if anyone remembers her? And we'll need a list of employees who worked that night."

Baby-face frowned. "Is this that woman who's missing?"

"Yeah, and we need to know about her movements that night."

"Okay, I'll be right back."

Shannon said, "She probably just got something to eat and left."

"Dunno. She didn't go back home."

"Right. She probably wouldn't have gone to another club if she ate."

The back of TJ's neck tingled. "Somethin' happened *here*."

Jason Turnbill came out accompanied by a petite young woman wearing jeans, a T-shirt and an apron about five sizes too big for her, so long it dusted the floor. "This is Carly. She remembers something."

Carly didn't look a day over fourteen. She held the photo of Jamie, and then looked up at them with baby blue eyes too large for her tiny features. "Um, I got off early. About nine, as soon as the big dinner-rush ended." She hesitated, pulling at her apron.

Jason placed a reassuring hand on her shoulder. "Just tell them what you saw."

Carly flickered a small nervous smile. "I have a friend who's older than me and she comes here to dance. I snuck over into the bar to meet her after I got off." She stopped talking, and stared at the floor.

TJ tried to put her at ease. "Go ahead, girl. We're only interested in finding out about Jamie. Her husband is worried sick."

She looked up at TJ, her forehead wrinkled with worry lines.

"Carly, how about you and me talk alone over there." TJ walked the girl over to an empty booth in the front of the restaurant.

Carly said, "I just wanted to have some fun, you know?"

"Honey, just tell me about Jamie. If you get any crap from the boss, call me and I'll talk to him for you." She handed the girl a business card.

"Thanks. It's just . . . I really need this job, you know? So, anyway, my friend never showed up. I knew I shouldn't have stayed. Then this really cute guy asked me to dance. We danced for like a really long time, and then we went out on the deck to talk. It was so cool, you know, the moon shining on the lake."

"Then what?"

"We talked and, you know, stuff. I saw this woman walk out on the deck. We weren't real close to her and it was kinda dark, but she stopped in the light when she walked out. I'm pretty sure it was her." Carly took another look at the photo of Jamie. "Yeah, it was her." She sighed. "The guy I met turned out to be a real loser. He walked me to my car, then when I wouldn't go with him to his place, he went back in the bar." She huffed. "I meet all the losers."

"Did you notice how long she stayed?" TJ asked, trying to keep the girl on track.

"Right. When she came out she had a glass of wine and she sat down on one of the chairs facing the lake. She looked sad. Well, I couldn't really see her face—I guess it was just the way she moved. She kept staring at the lake. Then the next time I looked over her way, there was a guy sitting in the chair next to her. He had a drink too, and they were talking."

"Did you notice whether they left together?"

"When we left they were still sitting there."

"Did you see what he looked like?"

"Old. Maybe forty? He looked tall, big shoulders. I never got a look at his face. I think he had gray hair."

"Were they still talking?"

"Yeah. And he was holding her hand." She closed her eyes and wrinkled up her face as if trying to recollect something, and said, "Oh, yeah, something weird—they had two boxes of takeout sitting on the table next to them. Not opened or anything."

TJ thought she'd gotten everything she could from the girl, but asked, "How about other people? Anyone else out there closer to them who may have overheard what they were talkin' about?"

"No. It was late and there wasn't anyone out there except some little kids running around. They must have been waiting for their parents to get done eating."

"Any idea who the parents were?"

"No, lots of people come in with kids, and I wasn't waiting tables that night."

TJ slid out of the booth. "Thanks for talking to me, Carly. No one's heard from this woman since that night and we're afraid someone may have taken her." TJ leaned over, her mouth inches from the girl's ear. "So if I were you, little girl, I'd keep in mind there are some scary people out there and be real careful who you walk with into a dark parking lot."

Nodding assent, Carly gave her a sheepish little half-smile.

After a few more passes through the bar, making certain Willie hadn't come in, TJ and Shannon went out to their cars. TJ briefed Shannon on her talk with Carly.

Shannon frowned. "It's going to be hard for Jeff—finding out Jamie was out in a bar alone. And met a guy."

"Yeah, but not as bad as finding her body."

Shannon looked thoughtful for a few seconds. "What about Eric's wife? Are you sure she didn't hook up with someone?"

"I was. Now I'm wonderin' again. Maybe we should give her lady friends another go-round tonight."

"Tonight? Isn't it a little late?"

"Nah, they're night creatures. I know where they hang, and it's not too far from here."

53

Secrets, the Brookfield nightclub frequented by Kayla's friends, was located off the lobby of a Radisson hotel across from the Brookfield shopping center. Snobby was the word that came to mind whenever TJ entered the place. She'd only been there a few times—once on a date with a dentist from the area, a man she met at the bank. There'd been no second date.

The other times were when she'd been trying to get a bead on Kayla—find out who her friends were and what made her tick. When she and Shannon walked into the softly lit bar, a live jazz trio played a mellow version of "The Lady is a Tramp." *Appropriate.* Dozens of the area's richest and most attractive mingled at the bar and in the booths positioned against the wall. The ambiance sported lots of mirrors, plants and a soft aqua décor, blending every shade of turquoise from the palest water to the deepest teal.

TJ hated the place. It was all about who had what and who was the prettiest—women *and* men. She and Shannon had dressed for the place, but looking like she fit in didn't make her want to be part of it.

Shannon took a seat at the bar next to a couple splendid in gold, diamonds, and designer clothes. As soon as TJ's eyes became accustomed to the dim lighting, she spotted Suzette and Diana, Kayla's running partners. The pair had been out of town the night Kayla Schindler went missing. TJ had questioned them more than once. They hadn't been helpful but she hadn't thought they held anything back, either. The friendship between the three had been a shallow one. TJ didn't think they knew much about each other's lives other than what they shared when making the rounds of their favorite clubs.

When TJ spotted them, the women appeared to be vying for the attention of a rather elderly man wearing a silver-gray custom-made suit and a matching rug. Two kinds of men frequented these places, the old and rich, and the not-so-old trying to be rich. The wannabes tended to be good-looking, the others looked like this guy.

The women gushed when they recognized her. "TJ!" She suspected their delight at seeing her hid a sense of rivalry. The guy with the rug eyed her and she shot him a look that sent him on a quest for more willing game.

"Hey, you two. Sorry to interrupt, but I need to talk to you again."

Suzette, the gray-eyed redhead, pursed her glossy, carmine lips. "What more could there be? You asked us everything imaginable and we weren't even in town that night."

Bitch. TJ couldn't stand these women. Not because of who they were but for what they represented—women with only superficial ideals. Money, looks, and rich men made up their entire purpose in life. *Disgusting.* "Some new information has come up and I've got some questions for you."

Diana, her hair in a shiny black bob set off by dangling, diamond, hoop earrings, actually looked concerned and told TJ to ask them whatever she needed to ask.

"Is there somewhere other than here Kayla would have gone by herself?" The women looked at each other. Diana's gaze settled on a woman sitting at the bar. Younger than most of the patrons, long, softly curled blonde hair trailed down her shapely back, exposed by a sleek brown dress cut nearly to her tailbone.

"See the blonde over there?" Diana nodded, her opinion of the woman obvious. "She's always trying to push her way in." She scoffed. "None of us like her; she was wasting her time. But if Kayla was out by herself, Amber might have glommed onto her. Maybe she knows something. But other than here, I don't know where Kayla would have gone by herself."

"And you're sure you don't remember her having a guy hanging around?"

"No. Men liked her, but she was only interested in her husband. She was confused about life, I guess. He was gone a lot. She got depressed about it—and other things."

Well aware of what the "other things" referred to, TJ said, "Thanks, ladies." She made her way over to Amber, wedging her way between the blonde and the trio of men surrounding her.

She explained to Amber who she was and asked if she could have a minute alone with her. Amber's heavy-lidded gaze cased TJ from head to toe, nearly leering. *Yuck.* She'd ask the snake her questions and get the hell out of here.

When they were alone in the lobby, Amber took a sexy pose on a light-blue divan that perfectly complemented her brown dress. As she crossed her long legs, the slit on the side of her dress opened high enough to expose her underwear—or would have if she'd been wearing any. Her eyes traveled over TJ again. "What do you want to know about Kayla?"

"Did you see her the night she disappeared?"

"Sure."

"Why didn't you come forward with that information?"

"It didn't seem important."

TJ resisted the urge to slap her. "Where did you see her?"

Amber sat back and crossed her arms. "I came in here at about nine that night. After about an hour, I got bored and decided to go downtown to Vinnie's. When I walked out to my car, I met Kayla coming in and told her nothing was happening here. So we went down to Vinnie's."

"You ride together?" So far this would explain no one at Secrets seeing Kayla the night she disappeared and why her car had shown up in an east side parking lot.

"No, we drove our own cars." Amber shifted position as two handsome men approached the club, making sure they'd seen her.

"Then what? Just tell me everything you remember."

"Vinnie's was packed. Couple guys at the bar gave us their seats, then hung around. They must have thought giving us the seats would get them in our pants. Fools. After we got rid of them we each did our own thing. I saw some friends and went over and had a drink with them. After that I don't know where she went. I didn't see her again, so I figured she either left or met someone."

"Are you sure you didn't see her with anyone?"

"Kayla always had guys around her."

"But no one in particular that night?"

"Not that I remember. It was a long time ago."

Crap, this got her nothing new. But she knew lots of the staff at Vinnie's. They'd tell her whatever they could remember, but the skank was right—it had been a long time ago.

"What about the two guys you blew off? How pissed were they?"

Amber's neatly penciled eyebrows shot up, her green eyes widening. "You don't think they could have done something to her?"

"I don't think anything. What do you remember about them?"

Scrunching her eyes, she seemed to be concentrating for a minute. "Not much, really. They were dressed like factory workers on a night out. Jeans, flannel shirts over T-shirts, work boots, like that. They thought we'd be impressed they were stagehands for some Broadway show playing at the Center." She snorted. "Like that would impress us."

"How did you blow them off?"

"We tried being nice first—told them we were waiting for dates—but they kept hanging around. They didn't get it so Kayla told them to disappear. We'd had a couple drinks by then and she was getting loose lips."

"Do you remember what she said?"

"Not exactly. Maybe something like, 'Thanks for giving us your seats, but you can move on now.' And when that didn't work she told them we weren't interested in losers like them. Might have been worse than that. I don't remember for sure, but they left."

Weird. It sounded like Jamie Denison's attitude at the Sombrero Club. Probably didn't mean anything. But they'd have to try to find the stage guys, see what they had to say. She thanked her and got up to leave when Amber offered to buy her a drink. There was no mistaking the question in the probing peridot eyes.

"Sorry, got other people to talk to tonight." *Shit.* TJ figured if she would ever be tempted to have a fling with a woman, this flytrap would be the last one she'd try it with. She shuddered and hurried back into the bar to get Shannon.

On the way to the car, Shannon asked, "Now what?"

"Think I'm gonna go back to Eric's."

Shannon stopped walking. "You're going back? Did you find something?"

"Maybe. But I'm not sure what it means." She made a face. "Might not mean squat. It's freezing out here. I'll call you on your cell and fill you in."

It was quiet in the house when TJ returned to Eric's. She put on a pair of sweats, and restless, went back upstairs and made herself a drink. She carried it to Eric's office, where she sat down and studied the whiteboards for a while, then got up and added the newly gathered information under Jamie and Kayla's names. She circled the new bullets under each name that said, "Blew off creepy guy." What could that have to do with anything when it was two different guys?

TJ sat down in Eric's plush, leather desk chair. They were missing something. Not missing something exactly; there was something there, something important they hadn't connected. What was it? TJ couldn't stand feeling like the answer hung there on the fringes of her consciousness, just beyond her ken. *Damn!* She knew nothing would bring it out now. She had to walk away from it. Do something else.

On her way back downstairs, she noticed the door to Jeff's room ajar and peeked in to see if he might be awake. He wasn't there. Strange. Maybe the others were out for the night. Back in the kitchen, she peeked into the refrigerator. She got out some turkey and bread, set it on the counter, and saw Phanny watching her. That dog was always hungry. She fixed herself a sandwich piled high with white meat, "accidently" dropping a piece on the floor the dog snapped up.

"I thought you were gone for the weekend."

TJ looked up from mid-bite to see Eric moving toward the refrigerator.

"Change of plans. Came back for a turkey sandwich."

He laughed. "You've got a friend I see."

"Yeah, this dog's always where the food is."

The turkey and bread came back out, and Eric sat next to her at the island with a double-decker turkey sandwich in front of him.

TJ knew his style. He was good at getting her to open up by saying nothing. "Forget it if you're waiting for me to tell you what happened."

He took a bite of his sandwich and studied her.

"Okay," she admitted, "Richard stayed in Chicago. Some family thing."

Eric kept eating.

TJ could tell he was resisting a smile by the way his laugh lines puckered at the side of his eyes. "You never did like him," she accused.

Eric put down the sandwich and turned to her. "The guy's a good cop."

She glared at him.

"I don't like him for you, all right?"

"Why?"

Eric looked surprised he'd asked him. "I suppose 'he's not good enough for you' isn't what you want to hear."

TJ kept glaring.

"I guess I always thought you deserved someone who made you his top priority. Not married to his job—someone younger, a little less street-worn."

"You sound like Janeen. May have run its course, anyway." She sighed. "I got somethin' to tell you—nothin' to do with Richard." She told Eric about their trip to the Sombrero Club, and what she'd added to the boards. "Somethin's naggin' at me, though."

"I hate that feeling. How do you pull it out?"

"Dunno. It's always different. But what do you think? Was Kayla capable of being nasty like that?"

"When she'd been drinking, sure. Do you think you can find the guy?"

"I checked the archives from the paper. Found out the name of the play. There should be records of who worked the stage that night."

"Seems like it gives us more new questions than answers, doesn't it? Maybe the profiler can give us some insight."

"Profiler—what the fuck?"

54

The afternoon the profiler arrived, Tina spotted the large, dark blue van as it moved into the circle drive and stopped in front of the door. She looked on in wonder when the side door opened as if by magic and a long ramp slowly emerged from the van, lowering to touch the ground. A thin, sharp-eyed man operating a motorized chair rolled down the ramp. Tina ran to get Eric, who hurried to put a portable ramp on the front step for their guest.

Like many of her peers, Lisa hated to admit anyone other than a practicing clinician could be so insightful of the forensic psyche as to actually be able to pinpoint a killer's profile, but she was determined to keep an open mind.

When he entered the room, Mason Orth appeared small, but Lisa quickly realized his position in the chair concealed his height. He wore a soft, taupe fedora, reminiscent of another era. When he took it off, hanging it on the back of the chair, she saw his hair was mostly silver, although he didn't look more than sixty.

Eric introduced them. Orth's eyes drew her to him, eclipsing the effect of his handicap. They were piercing, intense. When he looked into her eyes, she felt like he could see her deepest secrets.

He held his hand out to her. When their palms met, her feeling about him intensified. He would help them; she could feel it.

"Please, call me Mason. David told me you're a psychologist. We'll have to put our heads together and see what we can come up with."

Did he think he could win her over with that line? "It'll be a pleasure. David's told us wonderful things about your work."

"I hope I can live up to his praise." He laughed, the sharp planes of his face softening. He turned to Eric. "I want to thank you for your generosity in inviting me to dinner, but if you don't mind I'd like to see these information boards I've heard about."

Eric motioned toward his office. "Of course. We won't be having dinner for a while yet."

They showed him into the office. He guided his chair to the middle of the room, looking over each woman's photo and information without speaking. Eric excused himself while Lisa took a chair, silently waiting for a comment from the enigmatic man. Minutes passed.

Mason Orth's intensity filled the room, the silence almost eerie. The spell broke when he asked, "Lisa, are you convinced these disappearances are the work of one person?"

Lisa wondered how he'd known she was still in the room; he'd addressed her without moving from his position in front of the boards. Bewildered, she replied, "I wasn't at first. I was only sure something wasn't right. I never believed the rise in the statistics could be put off to chance—it was too high. The police think it's the work of one or more of a number of deviant online groups, or an organization helping women to leave abusive relationships. Their head of computer crimes, James Wilson, believes 'multiple factors' are responsible."

Turning to her, he asked, "What do you think?"

"I don't believe these women have run off or been killed by their husbands. The more we dig, the more it looks like there was a man on the fringes of these women's lives, a man careful to stay in the background, invisible. I'm convinced there's one person out there targeting this specific group of women."

"Quite fascinating, isn't it?" He turned back to the photos. "The obvious conclusion would be the key to this mystery lies with the victims. Find why he's targeting abused women, and you'll find your killer."

"You don't think we should focus on the obvious—why he's killing abused women?"

Observing the photos, he answered, "One would be inclined to think he had a grudge against them for some reason. However, it could easily be something as overt as he enjoys killing women—and these women are a group whose disappearances can be blamed on many factors. Rather convenient for him when there is a ready-made suspect for the law to concentrate on—missing women who can be explained away."

Lisa smiled, impressed. "We haven't thought of it that way. It's so simple it makes perfect sense."

He turned back to face her. "Yes, but there is nothing simple about your killer. He's an extremely complex man."

TJ was running late. By the time she joined the group, they were seated at the dinner table, sharing another of Teresa's sumptuous suppers. On tonight's menu, beef stew served with Parmesan cheese bread. It smelled wonderful. Teresa rushed to put a serving in front of her, shooing Tina back to their room.

They introduced TJ to Orth. The man's penetrating eyes made her uneasy. She'd been against bringing him on board, but if he could help them wrap things up, she'd hear him out.

After dinner, they gathered in front of the whiteboards. The profiler turned to TJ. "I understand researching these women was your idea. I always like to start at the beginning, so tell me why these disappearances piqued your interest."

TJ was taken off guard; she'd planned on being an observer. The nagging feeling she'd had when studying the whiteboards, remained. She'd been hoping a new insight might break it loose. "Goin' way back, my sister was abused by her husband until the police stopped him—permanently." She neglected to add she had been "the police" who'd stopped him.

"'Bout a year later Eric hired me to find something that might help to get him out of jail on appeal. After doin' all the legwork and getting to know Eric, I knew he didn't kill his wife." She explained the rest of her story, including what they'd been told about the statistics by Richard Conlin and James Wilson.

"A mutual friend told me Lisa was goin' in to MPD about the stats. Thought the police had blown the whole thing off, and when I heard someone else was interested, decided to see if I could get her to help me."

"The Milwaukee police are still ignoring it?"

"Yeah, so far. Dependin' on what we can give them, Waukesha and Oconomowoc are gonna rework Jamie Denison and Kayla Schindler's disappearances once we turn over our information. We'll hand over everything we got, including whatever you have to add. And we'd like you to be here when we do it."

TJ hadn't planned on asking him to be there. Something about Orth made him credible, assured her his expertise could improve their chances with the law.

Orth waited a bit before he spoke, his eyes appraising her. "Let me think about it. I'll get input from all of you tonight. I'll give you a written report eventually, but I'll be able to tell you my impressions before I leave. Then you can decide if you think it will be helpful to have me here when you address the police. And I would encourage you to include a representative from Milwaukee."

TJ grimaced. "Well, I know Richard Conlin would come. Not sure he'd bring an open mind."

"I'd think the fact the area police are going forward would convince them, if nothing else," Orth commented.

After dinner, they reviewed all the evidence and information from the interviews. TJ added that she'd located Tim Aiello, the stagehand who talked to Kayla at Vinnie's the night she'd disappeared. He admitted Kayla had pissed him off when she'd so rudely given him the brush-off. He had an alibi for the evening, however. The stagehands shared rooms and his roommate remembered him coming in before eleven because he'd interrupted an important phone call from his wife, who was almost ready to give birth. Aiello admitted he watched Kayla after she blew him off and had seen her leave with a man. The interesting part, he remembered, "The dude had gray hair."

Orth grew quiet after they'd shared everything they thought important. They left the room to have coffee and dessert in the kitchen. After he'd finished his coffee, the profiler started talking.

"I don't think what I have to say will be a surprise to any of you. I believe the Milwaukee police are wrong, and you folks have it right. This is the work of one man. There is always the possibility of an accomplice, but I think it's unlikely. Your killer could be a woman, although the odds are against it, and the missing bodies would leave us to deduce the killer had the strength to take them with him and somehow make them disappear. My feeling is the perpetrator is a male.

"Serial killers tend to be Caucasian men in the twenty to forty age range. If your witnesses were accurate about the gray hair, I'd guess he's not a lot more than forty and prematurely gray. He's not an attention seeker, or there would have been bodies found. Part of him isn't proud of what he is doing, but the other part wins out.

"He's successfully disposing of the bodies of these women, so I would expect him to own or have access to a vehicle which would make it possible—a van, an SUV with darkened windows, even a truck with a closed bed.

"He's organized. These murders—if indeed they are murders and he doesn't have the women stashed away somewhere as prisoners—are well planned. He's highly intelligent, most likely employed in a respected profession."

Lisa frowned. "What about what we've heard from witnesses— that some of the women were rude to men who approached them?"

Orth brightened. "That's the interesting part! All your victims are very attractive women. Vulnerable to their abusers, yes, but bright women, employed at above average jobs. Your killer convinced them to keep their liaisons with him a secret—probably by playing the safety card—and they went along with it. They would have feared repercussions by their abusers if it became known they were seeing him. It follows he's a charming, good looking man, and also manipulative."

Jeff said, "I thought all these guys were loners."

"He very well could be. He feels in control with these women, so he's free to be outgoing with them. His social skills may be limited in any other setting.

"To get back to your question, Lisa, here is what I find intriguing. If his trigger were these women's derogatory comments to men who are unattractive to them, it would seem to follow, he himself is unattractive. Since we know that to be highly unlikely, it reveals he either was unsightly at one time and carries a grudge, or has some kind of hidden handicap. Maybe he's bald and wears a wig. Possibly he has a sexual dysfunction or an abnormally small penis. It could be any number of things really, and when the police find him, it'll become apparent."

Lisa sighed. "*If* the police find him."

Orth looked at her sympathetically, a half-smile on his narrow face. "I understand you're discouraged. But the police will have to do their work, and without any bodies it will be difficult to find him. There's a good chance he owns property where he disposes of his victims. I'm afraid it's possible he could relocate as soon as he becomes aware the police are finally on to him." His last words were not what any of them had wanted to hear.

After Mason Orth left, TJ had to admit he'd been impressive. What she'd been most taken by was that he hadn't tried to wow them with any impossible little details. His profile fit with the amount of evidence they were able to provide. Most importantly, he backed up what they'd been trying to tell the police.

Orth's report would be their final coup.

55

Richard had tried to call TJ since the botched weekend, but she'd chosen to be unavailable. He had someone new; she knew the signs. But she needed to see him. It was after nine when she called him. When he answered she asked him to meet her at Vinnie's.

She got there before Richard and sat in a booth on the back wall. When he sat down across from her, she realized the usual sexual tension between them was absent. He wore a new sweater with jeans and a leather jacket, the red of the sweater emphasizing his gray-sprinkled hair. Funny, but he looked different to her now—older, tired. If he was seeing another woman, she wasn't perking him up any.

"Been a while," TJ opened.

"Sorry about our weekend."

She smirked. "No, you're not, but I didn't ask you here to bitch about it. There's somethin' I need to talk to you about."

"About time."

"Remember that Lisa Rayburn who came to see you about the missing women stats?"

Richard fumbled his drink. "Huh?"

Interesting. This isn't what he'd expected. Must have thought she was going to talk about their relationship and he was the one seeing someone else. He'd be back eventually, expecting things to go on as always. But this wasn't the time to tell him it wouldn't ever be the same.

"Lisa and me have been collecting evidence for you."

Now she had his attention. She knew him well enough to spot his anger even though his expression hadn't changed. The little vein traveling from the middle of his left eyebrow to his temple grew as his blood pressure rose, and it looked about to burst.

She began, "Patty Barkley told me about Lisa goin' to see you . . ."

As she talked, Richard listened without interrupting, but the vein in his forehead throbbed throughout her speech, his eyes ablaze with anger when she concluded by telling him they'd hired a profiler.

"You did all this behind my back? I expected more of you, TJ. Of us."

"What *us*? The us that was goin' away for a weekend? You think I haven't figured out you met some chick you're spending time with?"

Richard shifted in his seat. "Okay. We'll leave *us* out of this conversation. You know how I feel about you sticking your nose into police business."

She noticed he hadn't risen to the bait when she mentioned another woman. "What police business? You and that dickwad Wilson just blew it off."

Through gritted teeth, he said, "I told you before—there was nothing concrete to investigate."

Gotcha! "My point exactly. We're gonna give you something concrete. Tomorrow at Eric Schindler's place—10:00 a.m."

Smiling smugly, she sat back and sipped her drink.

Richard threw back his scotch and stormed out.

56

The next morning the group, along with Orth, Maggie, and David, gathered in Eric's living room. They were joined by the two cops from Waukesha and others from Brookfield, Pewaukee and New Berlin; all areas with victims on the whiteboards.

Eric had sent Teresa out with Tina for the morning, but she'd refused to leave until she'd prepared two huge urns of coffee and put out juice, bagels, and Kringle from a nearby bakery. Shannon had come out to take over for Teresa during the meeting. A fire roared in the hearth, welcoming everyone coming in from the frigid weather.

TJ wondered if Richard would arrive as promised. When she'd seen him the night before, she hadn't meant it to be personal—though, of course, it had been. Maybe he'd send someone else. She doubted it, though; he'd be too curious to stay away.

When the doorbell rang Eric went to answer the door. TJ heard Richard's voice as it opened and felt a sense of satisfaction because he'd shown up. For her, it gave more credence to their work than anything else that had taken place since they started. Her gratification died quickly when he walked in accompanied by that arrogant prick James Wilson. It was her turn to be pissed.

Swallowing her anger, TJ introduced them to the group. She'd deal with Richard later.

"Just so it's clear to all of you," Richard announced, "we are here as a courtesy only. Our presence doesn't mean we condone police work being done by civilians, or that we're committed to move forward with an investigation based on evidence presented to us

242

here. It's our understanding two departments from Waukesha County *are* going to begin an investigation based on today's information. If it turns out there is any solid evidence which would impel us to move forward, we'll work with the other departments."

The room went quiet after his speech. TJ seethed. Not that she'd expected anything more from MPD, but combined with Wilson's unwelcome presence, it really burned.

Maggie stepped forward and introduced herself and her partner. "Detective Conlin, the reason we've committed to this is because four of the missing women, two of whom are Jamie Denison and Kayla Schindler, lived in Waukesha County. Quite a few are from Milwaukee. It makes sense to join forces if there is a pattern here that crosses county lines."

Richard said nothing. He and Wilson moved toward the coffee displayed at the side of the room.

The whiteboards sat in a semi-circle in the living room, incongruous next to the plush, leather furniture and bright fire. Greg Zabel and Max Feinstein from Waukesha pored over them, careful to stay far from a developing pissing match between MPD and OPD.

After everyone had their coffee, TJ and Lisa made the presentation on what the group had collected, explaining their conviction the disappearances pointed to the work of one abductor.

Zabel raised his hand and asked, "What about Danielle Ventura? Is she one of your purported victims? Or is she connected to your research in some other way since she was killed right here in your backyard?"

They'd anticipated his question. Lisa answered, "We believe her death was intended to be one of us."

Their audience, silent at Lisa's revelation, watched as Eric brought out a poster he'd assembled presenting a photo of Danielle next to one of Lisa. The room hushed as the resemblance between the two women became apparent—Eric had been sure to find photos emphasizing their similarities.

Eric addressed the assembled officers. "As you can see, there is a striking resemblance between Lisa Rayburn and Danielle Ventura. As most of you know, I'd dated Danielle a few times before the night she died. Our best guess is she came here to find out who was staying at the house. In doing so, she took a short cut through the woods in order to be unobserved. Our killer, waiting for one of us to leave the house, mistook her for Lisa."

When no further questions came up, David introduced Mason Orth. Orth described the unsub as he had for the group. If his support of the group's theory made a difference to Richard Conlin and James Wilson, it wasn't evident in their stoic expressions.

After Orth concluded and answered questions, everyone broke into cliques, discussing just what the information meant to the various departments, and whether they would act on it. Richard headed for the coffee urn with TJ following.

She had to ask. "So what do you think?"

"I have to admit you people did a great job. But it doesn't change anything. There's no hard evidence. No bodies have been found; no one has identified your mystery man. You aren't even sure there isn't more than one perp."

TJ turned away from him and leaned on the island, staring sullenly out into the living room. "Why'd you bring Wilson?"

Richard poured his coffee and pointed at her with a slice of Kringle. "You know he's the one who did all the research on this when the stats showed up so high. And you of all people should know we don't have the staff to open an investigation when there's no hard evidence."

TJ tuned him out as she watched the interactions in the room. Wilson stood admiring the antique tools mounted over the fireplace.

She saw Shannon making a move toward him, engaging him in conversation. They sat down on the stone apron of the fireplace.

Shannon beamed. He was definitely a hot-looking guy. Backlit by the fire, his taupe hair gleamed silver and his handsome features glowed.

TJ had been ready to give Richard a sharp retort when it happened. Pieces of the puzzle came together, hitting her like a physical blow—the silver hair, Wilson's computer skills, the attack on Charles when no one else knew what they were planning. Turning away from Richard, she fled from the room, leaving him waiting for a comeback.

With the bathroom door locked behind her, TJ stood in front of the mirror, leaning on the vanity, collecting her thoughts. She wanted to run out and tell the others, but knew she had to hold back until she had time to think it through. After a few deep breaths, she opened the door and saw Jeff standing in the hall waiting for her.

"Are you all right?"

"Yeah, sure, I'm fine."

He didn't look convinced. "You want to go somewhere after this—maybe for a drink?"

It was unlike Jeff to suggest a drink this early in the day; he had to be worried about her. She couldn't be with him now; she needed to be alone.

"No, thanks. My stomach's a little queasy."

He said, "Maybe you should rest for a while before you go to work."

Rest didn't seem possible in her present state. She pacified him. "Sure. I'll grab a nap."

57

James Wilson sat in his office at MPD, seething. That bitch Rayburn and her cronies were getting too damn close. He had to get a grip—what did they have, really, but speculation? It had taken all the reserve he could muster to sit through their little presentation.

He needed to go home, get out on his sled and fly over Lake Winnebago at top speed. But he dare not do anything Conlin might see as the least bit unusual—not that Conlin had a clue—or make him pay any attention to James' comings and goings. He'd play it safe, though, stay in the office the rest of the afternoon and get some work done.

The disappointment he'd felt when he'd taken out Danielle Ventura instead of Rayburn had been offset by his good fortune when the police unearthed the bodies in Eddie Wysecki's basement. With a choice suspect like Wysecki, James remained invisible.

He'd been safe—until this.

He had to stay focused. For now, the most prudent course would be staying under the radar as he had been and do nothing. He had some reports to keep himself busy for the moment, but unfortunately they'd need a signature from Marian Bergman. James wasn't sure he could tolerate her in his present frame of mind. But today she was interviewing for a new position in their unit, and playing God would have her in a good mood.

When James entered Marian Bergman's office to have her sign the finished reports, he noticed Timothy Agazzo sitting across from her.

A small, nervous man with no personality, unwashed, thinning hair, and poor personal hygiene—James wondered how he'd ever been hired. His protruding eyes and full, pouty lips gave him the look of an undernourished frog.

James turned to leave, but Bergman said, "Stay for a second, James, we're done here."

By the look on the guy's face, he hadn't expected the brush-off. If Agazzo was here to throw his hat in the ring for the position, the interview hadn't gone well. He slunk out of the office, his normally bent posture even more so. His shoulders, narrow and rounded, looked like they couldn't support anything heavier than the dandruff dotting the shoulders of his uniform.

"I take it he won't be our replacement."

Bergman snorted. "Like I'd want to look at that face every day." She shuddered, shuffling some files on her desk. Probably put the poor slob's application on the bottom of the heap where it would lie untouched until she hired someone else. Without looking up from her papers, she said, "Why doesn't the man transfer to the evidence morgue in the basement where we wouldn't have to see him every day?"

Relieved it was a rhetorical question, James put the reports in front of Bergman for her signature. Even her looks bothered him. Her tightly wound chignon pulled up the ends of her eyebrows, giving them a winged, evil appearance. She might imagine the look fashionable, but with her perpetual expression of anger and disdain, James thought she looked like a witch.

The signed papers in hand, James left the room before his anger surfaced. He had no love for Agazzo, but the bitch had neutered the guy.

It came to him—*she had to be next.*

58

TJ woke up an hour later in Eric's office, tilted back in the soft leather recliner. She'd gone in the room to sit for a bit in an effort to pacify Jeff. A knit throw covered her although she hadn't fallen asleep with it. Across the room, engrossed in a leather-bound book from Eric's collection, sat Mason Orth.

He looked up. "You're awake. I hope you're feeling better."

TJ blinked back to full consciousness. She must have really been out; the whiteboards were back in place and she hadn't heard a thing. "I thought everyone left."

"They did. I said I'd stay until you woke up."

The enormity of what had sent her into a tailspin came back to her.

Orth watched her with narrowed eyes. "I have to admit I had another reason to stay. I wanted a chance to talk to you alone."

What does that mean? Orth was too damn intuitive. "I just didn't get enough sleep last night, told Jeff there was nothin' to worry about."

"He cares about you." It wasn't a question.

"I should get going." Part of her wanted to hear what he had to say to her, even though the other part wanted to rabbit. "Thought the morning went pretty good."

"TJ, I can see you're bothered by something. I believe it's about the case. In fact, if I were to make a wild guess, I'd say you had a sudden insight of some sort."

Is the guy psychic? TJ was torn. She really needed to bounce this off someone else, and knew it couldn't be one of the others. Not yet, anyway.

She ran her fingers through her hair. Orth had spun his chair over to her side. He was too close now. She had to either open up or shut him out.

She sighed. "How about a hypothetical?"

"That's fine. However you want to discuss what's bothering you."

"What if I told you I think I know who our perp is, but nailing him will be impossible?"

Orth set down his cup. "I could say what you'd expect me to say—anyone can be found out and charged, but we both know that's not always true." He studied her face, then said softly, "I can see you're in great pain, TJ."

She had the bizarre thought he sounded like a priest. His unexpected sympathy touched her and all the emotions she'd been holding back for so long broke the surface. Quiet tears poured down her face. Orth moved closer, and put his arm across her back.

Geo Turner lived in an apartment above a Laundromat on east North Avenue, not far from the University of Wisconsin-Milwaukee in distance, but light years away in social strata. The neighborhood, with its high crime rate, was populated with older, two-story duplexes and small businesses.

A computer crime felon, Turner had been brought in by TJ and her partner on his third arrest, more than three years ago. They'd staked out his apartment until he emerged, unaware of their presence, coming with them willingly once he realized they outnumbered him.

Since then, he'd been effectively staying out of sight of the law. When he opened his door and saw TJ standing there, he growled, "Fuck! Can't you cops leave me the fuck alone?"

She pushed past him into the ratty apartment. His office, located in what must be the dining room, was stocked with computers and related equipment probably worth more than the run-down building housing it. "Chill, asshole. I'm a private citizen now."

Turner slammed the door behind her. "Then what the fuck you doing here?"

She jabbed him in the shoulder. "A little respect, fucker, I still have contacts in the department. Could get your scrawny ass hauled in like that!" She snapped her fingers. "I have a job for you."

"Yeah, right. And I suppose its pro-fucking-bono," he snarled.

"I can pay. But the price better be right."

He snickered nervously, clearly worried it was some kind of set up.

"I need background on a guy. Everything from the day he was born. Detailed. Very detailed."

"Sounds too fucking easy. What's the catch?"

TJ took an envelope from her pocket, pulled out a photo of James Wilson, and slapped it on the table.

"Holy crap! You gotta be kidding me!"

Sneering, TJ got in his face. "If you're so fucking good at what you do, I guess who this is shouldn't be a problem. All you have to do is make sure your 'inquiries' are rock-solid undetectable. Got it?"

"Oh, I get it all right. You want me to fucking jeopardize my new life."

"Like you're one-hundred percent straight these days."

Turner stiffened. "It's going to cost you."

She reached into the envelope and took out ten, one-hundred-dollar bills, laying the money next to the photo. "This is what it's going to cost me."

He picked up the money, turning up his nose like it was a six-day old dog turd. "I suppose you want it yesterday."

"Nope, tomorrow works for me."

"Two days."

"Deal."

A deal with the devil, but worth the risk.

59

Mason Orth hated winter. And Christmas. He often wondered what kept him in the Midwest, but Chicago was where he'd worked. His job had been his one great accomplishment in life. Staying in the place where he'd been successful made him feel grounded.

A round trip ticket to the Bahamas sat on his desk. Three days before Christmas he would leave and come back after the beginning of the New Year. He had no work scheduled over the holidays. The balmy weather of Freeport, the beaches, and the casinos beckoned.

When the doorbell rang, he set down a glass of wine along with the novel he'd been reading. He rarely had visitors and hoped it wasn't another neighbor child selling their latest, useless fundraising item. When he opened the door and saw TJ standing there, he was peculiarly unsurprised. Without a word, she walked in as if she'd been invited.

She took a seat on one of the matching sofas positioned in front of a fireplace aglow with a cedar-scented blaze. He poured her a glass of wine, then left the room, returning with a plate of cheeses, crackers, and crusty bread, and placed them on the coffee table between the couches.

TJ passed him the envelope containing the report from Geo Turner. He pulled out the contents and selected the photo—James Wilson, aka Ronald Rommelfanger. The picture was grainy, but still revealed the misshapen features of his face, the rough complexion, and the gross obesity. "Imagine a child growing up with such a face. And name. It's no wonder food was his only friend."

TJ sneered. "My heart bleeds."

After reading through it, Orth looked up from the file. "The accident that nearly killed him destroyed his face; a plastic surgeon transformed him into James Wilson. It's understandable the man would have adopted a new name.

"It's strange. I didn't get any bad vibes from the man, but then I didn't really talk to him one-to-one. This information certainly supports your suspicions. What are you going to do with it?"

TJ looked at him quizzically, her brow wrinkled. "If I knew that, I wouldn't be here. Couldn't keep this to myself and not sure I want to tell the others."

Mason noticed how lovely she looked, her short hair tousled, her skin glowing a dusky, amber gold in the firelight; the only hint of her turmoil the dark shadows under her deep blue eyes. "I'm glad you came to me. I'm afraid it's not unusual in my profession—knowing who's responsible for an ugly crime, yet knowing you may never be able to bring that person to justice."

"So you agree, there's no real evidence here."

"You'll need more for a conviction even though he fits the profile of your killer."

TJ sipped her drink. "Everything fits. There's no doubt really. Least not for me." Her face hardened. "He has to be stopped. Stopped before he can keep on killing women."

"You don't think the police would act on this?"

"They've said over and over there's no evidence—no bodies. Fuck, he's one of them; no way they'll listen!" She poured herself another glass of wine, appearing to fight for composure. "No, tellin' them will just tip him off. He'd take off just like Wysecki did. Someone has to stop him."

With no doubt where she was headed, Orth took a deep breath, searching for the right words—if there were right words for a situation like this. "TJ, you're putting an impossible burden on yourself. Why?"

TJ squirmed under his gaze. She stood up, stoked the fire, and added another log. "There's something you don't know about me."

"I make it a habit to gather background on everyone I work with. I know you shot your brother-in-law."

She sat, hugging herself, then looked up at him. "There's somethin' that's not in anything you could have found."

"You don't have to put it into words, TJ. I understand. There are times when we're forced to make life-changing decisions in a split second."

She sat back, obviously relieved he understood.

"Do you believe your experience puts the burden on you now?"

She sighed. "Somethin' like that."

He spoke softly. "How do you think your friends would react if they knew about Mr. Wilson?"

She smiled for the first time since she'd come into his house. "They'd all want to waste his ass. But they'd have more confidence than me that the police would catch the bastard."

TJ's smile faded, her hands kneading a small pillow she held in her lap. "Maybe not Eric. The system screwed him, so he'd want to make sure the animal was stopped. I think he'd do it with his bare hands if he could. I can't let that happen; the cops still think he's guilty of killing his wife. It has to be me. I have to make sure he don't kill any more women. Or one of us."

"I can understand why you wouldn't want to unload this on the others, but what about Detective Conlin? Wouldn't he listen to you?"

"He'd listen. But his nose is out of joint over all this. He couldn't be objective. He sided with Wilson in the beginning and would have a hard time backing off, even though I know he isn't the creep's biggest fan."

Orth considered everything she'd said. There were no simple answers, no easy advice.

"TJ, while I admire your concern for the others, I believe you need to take at least one of them into your confidence. Vigilante justice is never morally right. You need their feedback. Your intentions are noble, but too dangerous alone, for many reasons. If you decide together you really want to do this, you'll have help carrying it out. And, more importantly, with the emotional impact of your actions."

TJ took the last sip of wine and the last bite of cheese. She looked over at him, meeting his gaze. "I'll talk to Lisa."

60

Happy to be back in her own home, Lisa kept busy getting things ready for the holiday: decorating, cleaning, cooking, writing cards, and making the requisite calls to relatives around the country. She missed the others, but knew they'd all needed a break. She'd invited TJ over for dinner and gotten a lukewarm acceptance. Something felt wrong. Lisa realized once more she had a strange sense of foreboding. What was it? Or did she even want to know?

A ham and noodle casserole baked in the oven when TJ arrived. She handed Lisa a bottle in a brown paper bag.

Lisa pulled out a bottle of tequila. "Thanks!"

"For margaritas."

"They do go with anything."

TJ took in the open room and the antique furniture. "Nice place." The colors were peaceful: soft blue, off-white, and cocoa brown. It comfortable room with an open floor plan, the farmer's table in front of a low counter divided the kitchen area from the dining area.

"Only two place settings. No Shannon tonight?"

"She had other plans. It'll just be the two of us. We need to talk."

You don't know the half of it. TJ decided to wait until after dinner to drop the bomb. Following Orth's advice made sense, but she still felt guilty involving Lisa.

Lisa took the steaming casserole out of the oven. The meal smelled and tasted wonderful—cheesy and hot, salty with the taste of ham. TJ mixed the margaritas—extra potent—while Lisa arranged the salad.

After dinner they finished their drinks sitting on the long plaid sofa in front of a big stone fireplace and covered themselves with furry throws. TJ broached the topic. "You ever wonder about the timing of your office break-in and Charles' mugging?"

"Sure. But even though Roland believed it was related to us, I always thought there could be another explanation, didn't you?"

"Yeah, for a while. And the office thing didn't seem to be a big deal at the time either, did it?"

"Now you think they're *both* related to our search?" When TJ didn't answer, she said, "But we didn't start the interviews until almost two weeks later."

TJ liked tequila. It gave her the push she needed to tell Lisa what she'd come here to say. *"Someone* knew."

"Good God! You don't think Richard has something to do with this!"

"No. I don't."

She watched as Lisa's face shifted with realization. "James Wilson is the only other person who knew early on." Lisa gasped. "Him—a murderer? How did you come up with that?"

TJ explained about the day of their meeting with the police, how something had been nagging at her. When she saw Wilson sitting with Shannon on the hearth, the firelight changing his unusual taupe-brown hair to glistening silver, she realized what it was. If the earlier events were connected—and thinking they weren't was too far beyond coincidence for TJ—then the killer had to be either Conlin or Wilson. And she knew Richard, knew it couldn't be him. And he didn't fit the profile.

"That's why you got upset the other day!"

TJ reached into the leather bag she'd brought, took out the file, and handed it to Lisa.

She glanced inside. "Where did you get this?"

TJ looked her in the eye. "You don't wanna know."

TJ watched Lisa read, her expression becoming one of absorbed interest. *Good. Your professional expertise is piqued.*

When Lisa finished reading, she looked up at TJ, who was watching expectantly, her body swaddled in the fur throw as if protecting herself from an unknown presence. "Amazin', isn't it?

"He fits our profile."

When TJ remained mute, Lisa said, "Are you going to tell Richard about this?"

TJ expressed a dry, mirthless laugh. "Yeah right. What do you think?"

Lisa swallowed the last of her drink, oblivious to the fact it was warm and diluted. "I think we need a lot more alcohol." Then it came to her—the reason for TJ's silence. "Dammit! There's nothing concrete here, is there?" Lisa threw down the file.

TJ shook her head, pulling the throw tighter around her small body.

Lisa sputtered. "But what about circumstantial evidence—the preponderance of evidence? Wouldn't the totality of everything be enough?"

"Nah. Might be if it was anyone else. I thought about telling Richard, but don't think it's a good idea. He wouldn't have an open mind being as how the beast is one of them."

Unable to turn off her psychologist's fascination with the man, Lisa picked up the photo of Ronnie. God, he'd been so ugly before his accident. And that name. Ronald Rommelfanger. His classmates must have been on him incessantly. What are the chances after his "rebirth" as the handsome James Wilson, he'd act out his pent-up rage against women? Orth had been right; Wilson, as their killer, was fascinating.

TJ lifted her glass, tilting the last few drops of the drink into her mouth. "I can hear the wheels turning over there. What are you thinkin'?"

Lisa took a deep breath. The new information felt like a bad dream. "We have to tell—"

"No," TJ interrupted furiously, abandoning the throw as she jumped up. "We can't tell anyone!"

"Why?"

"We can't tell anyone," TJ repeated.

"What do we do? Wait it out while he kills more women and hope the police come up with him as a suspect?"

TJ stood, walked into the kitchen and came back with the bottle of tequila and two shot glasses. She poured two, and handed one to Lisa. "Didn't see any limes in your fridge, so bottoms up." She raised the glass to her lips and gulped down the tequila.

Lisa picked up the shot glass and followed suit.

TJ sat down with her elbows on her knees. "Got a story to tell you. About me. And Janeen."

This must be serious. "All right."

"Everyone loved Janeen's husband, Mario. I did, too; he was a great guy. And talented. He sang with a group of jazz musicians who made it pretty big in town. When they broke up, he couldn't get another gig. He started drinking—turned ugly when he had too much. Started roughing Janeen up if she complained when he came home late, drunk. She didn't tell anybody about it for a long time. She even tried to hide it from me, but I noticed a nasty bruise on her neck one night. She tried to blame it on playing with the kids. I knew better, seen too many women like her, too many bruises just like hers. After a while, you can spot them a block away."

259

Lisa sighed. "I know. I've worked with many of those women." As Lisa listened to the unfolding drama of TJ, Janeen, and Mario, Janeen's abusive husband, she wanted to go to TJ and put her arm around her. But she knew the story had to flow without interruption, without any reaction, and most importantly, without judgment.

"He went to rehab after I took him aside and explained what I'd do to him if it happened again. But he was only there a week when they sent him home. Said he could work with them as an outpatient. What a joke. He started drinkin' again when he was still going for his supposed counseling. I told Janeen to leave him, get a divorce. But she loved him, still believed he would change. You know how *that* goes.

"Next thing, I get a hysterical call from her one night when I'm on shift. She told me she called 911. He had her trapped in the bathroom, bangin' on the door, yellin' at her to let him in. We just happened to be in the neighborhood at the time. I got there before the emergency responders, ran in before my partner could get out of the car. When I found them, he'd just busted down the door and was goin' for her with a knife. He lunged for me when I told him to drop it." Her knuckles whitened as she clutched the shot glass she held. "I shot him."

Lisa poured TJ another inch of tequila. "TJ, you did what you had to do. You saved your sister's life."

"I didn't have to shoot to kill. Had time to disable him. My gut took over—I wanted the bastard dead."

"That's understandable. She's your sister."

TJ snorted. "Yeah. Understandable. Only good thing happened that night is she got the kids the hell out before he went wild."

Lisa said softly, "That's a terrible secret to carry around all these years." The time had come—she had to tell TJ about her own past. She'd never told anyone the whole story, had carried it like a hidden birthmark all these years. "You aren't the only one with a secret in her past."

Looking a little less glum, TJ raised her eyebrows.

Lisa rose from the couch. "I have something to show you."

She led TJ to a room in the basement. In a dark corner behind the furnace, stood a tall, locked cabinet. She pulled out a key ring and opened it. Lined up inside were a dozen rifles.

TJ gaped. "These are yours?"

"They were my grandfather's. I inherited them with the house. I grew up with guns. All the men in my family hunted, and as soon as I was old enough to hold a rifle, my grandfather taught me to shoot."

"You hunted?"

"No. I never could do it. But I was fascinated with guns and loved to go to target practice with him." She picked up a rifle, holding it almost lovingly.

"That one's quite the cannon."

"It's a 30.06. He used it for deer hunting, but it's a bit of overkill for deer, although it's a popular weapon for the sport."

Lisa handed it to her. TJ held the rifle, admiring its heft. She passed it back, looking like she was wondering where Lisa was going with all this.

Lisa put the gun back, locked the cabinet, and gestured for TJ to follow her. They went upstairs, and Lisa handed her a coat. They walked across the driveway to a large shed where a motion-sensored light went on at their approach. Lisa unlocked the doors. In the middle of the shed sat a matched pair of shiny, dark blue snowmobiles.

TJ's face brightened. "We're going for a ride? Never been on one, might be fun."

"Not with all the tequila we drank. Some other time."

Lisa walked over to a large wooden box once used for firewood. She fumbled with a key, opened the padlocked box and lifted out a rifle identical to the one she'd shown TJ in the house. TJ took it from her and looked it over.

"Same rifle. No?"

"Same rifle, yes." Lisa said. "But what's different?"

"This baby has a special sight on it—like on a sniper's rifle." She looked up at Lisa. "Bet you were good. Must be a story behind this cannon."

Lisa took the gun back and reversed the process she'd gone through getting it out.

"There is. But it's going to take a lot more tequila to tell it."

Another shot of tequila later, Lisa and TJ sat across the table from each other. TJ couldn't imagine what Lisa would reveal about her past. How bad could it be? Lisa—all white bread and wasp—how bad could it be?

Lisa's hands gripped the bottle of tequila, her nails peeling the label. "I told you the short version of this, but there's a lot more to it. After we separated and my ex threatened to sue me for custody of Paige, I nearly lost my mind."

TJ reached over, took the bottle from Lisa, and poured them another drink.

"I talked to an attorney. He said nothing could prevent Lawrence from trying to get custody, even though it was unlikely he'd win. I couldn't live with 'unlikely.' Lawrence was a tyrant, a total control freak. He started disciplining her harshly before she was even two-years-old, I didn't want him raising Paige, and I couldn't imagine living without her."

She looked at TJ. "You must have some idea of what I was going through. You probably had similar feelings when your brother-in-law was alive."

TJ nodded.

Lisa said, "One night I dreamt I shot the bastard. The dream stayed with me for days. He threatened me again and warned me he'd contacted the best attorney in family law and said I wouldn't have a chance of getting custody of my daughter.

"After that I started thinking about it, about actually killing him. Whenever Paige was with him, I spent my time refreshing my skills with the 30.06. I had an elaborate plan in place, but the gist of it was I'd follow him when he went hunting. I'd find just the right spot, take him down, and then pray it would look like a hunting accident. Now when I think about it, I realize how naïve it was." She downed the shot TJ poured. Her words, while not slurred, had lost their usual crispness. "But you know what? It was a pretty damn good plan."

"What happened? The jerk is still alive and you got custody, right?"

"Yes, he's still breathing and I got custody of Paige. But it wasn't because I won a big legal battle or because Lawrence had a change of heart. Ironically, I was saved from my madness when he met someone else. He fell head-over-heels with a nineteen-year-old, and all of a sudden he couldn't wait to finalize the divorce. She wanted a big wedding, and a life with no encumbrances from his previous marriage."

TJ sifted through it, amazed at Lisa's story.

"Aren't you going to ask me if I would have gone through with it?"

"Figured you'd get around to it if you wanted to tell me."

"I believe I would have. I would have shot him."

"You sound pretty sure."

"I have to tell you everything I planned in preparation." Lisa put on a pot of coffee. When it was ready, Lisa cradled a mug of steaming coffee, and began, ""My plan to get rid of Lawrence began with the rifle. I started refreshing my shooting skills at a remote spot near

Beaver Dam. I was good with it, even won a few matches when I was a kid. I bought its twin, the one I have locked in the shed, from a dealer at a gun show—a parking lot deal. Scary, really, how easy it was to get as long as I had enough money to grease his palm. I'd dressed like a man for the occasion, mustache and all."

TJ couldn't help but chuckle as she pictured Lisa in disguise.

"I knew you'd get a kick out of that. I drove to Chicago one weekend to pick up the props and paid cash. Too bad I didn't know you then—I could have used some help with it. It took a lot of practice to get it right."

TJ grinned. "It's an art."

Lisa continued with her narrative. "I had the advantage of knowing exactly where Lawrence hunted, because he dragged me along once so they'd have an extra license just in case they had a good bounty. Lawrence liked to slip out after he and his buddies came back in for the day and do his own thing. It was an ego thing; he thought he could do something on his own the trio couldn't."

TJ's eyes narrowed. "Hmm. Your alibi?"

"That's where a stroke of luck came in. The opening weekend of deer hunting, when he and his buddies always went, coincided with a conference in the cities I happened to be registered to attend. It's a huge affair; no one would have been the wiser if I slipped out for a day. Not the perfect alibi, but rational.

"I found a little rent-a-heap lot in St. Paul. For a big enough cash deposit, they said I could rent a pickup with no questions asked. I planned on wearing the disguise when I picked it up."

TJ poured more coffee, feeling her senses slowly returning to a pre-alcohol stage. Lisa hadn't exaggerated. It had been a good plan. "Sounds like you thought of everything."

"Well, I knew I'd be the first one the police would question if they suspected his death wasn't a hunting-related incident. They'd take the 30.06, test it, and when it turned out not to be a match, hopefully I'd be off the hook."

TJ ran over it in her mind. "One question. Why didn't you dump the knock-off rifle?

"If I'd used it, it would be in the bottom of the Mississippi river gathering sand." Lisa paused for a sip of coffee. "It felt good to tell somebody. But it's nothing compared to what you've been burdened with."

TJ snorted. "Now you sound like Orth."

"Orth?"

She'd wanted to tell Lisa about her trip to his house and started by telling her how he'd come to her after the meeting with the police at Eric's—how he'd practically read her mind. She watched Lisa's face for a reaction when she got to the part about stopping Wilson herself, but Lisa's demeanor remained impassive.

Lisa pondered. "So you trusted him with this. I suppose I would have, too." She got up from the couch. "I think we need more coffee. And some sugar. How about dessert?"

"On top of all that tequila?"

Lisa set a plate of brownies on the table in front of the sofa. TJ picked one up but didn't take a bite. "We have to do something—hafta' get rid of the guy."

Lisa said, "I was afraid that's where we were headed. I think we have to give the police some time to put it together. Maybe they'll work it out."

Does that mean you're on board with it? TJ took a deep breath. "Yeah, in a perfect world. 'Fraid Wilson'll take off if he knows the department is working it."

"I'm not so sure. He'll believe there's nothing the police can find. But you're right, with his skills it would be easy for him to change his name and head for places unknown. But I think he'll revel in watching them spin their wheels for a while and do some gloating, enjoy feeling omnipotent. He doesn't know we're on to him, so he won't have a sense of urgency."

TJ had to agree with her logic. They probably did have some time. "If the cops don't get him, you'll help me out?"

"Help you out? I'll pull the trigger."

61

The nasty tidbit of office gossip revealing Marian Bergman's husband of three years had left her for his twenty-something, red-haired secretary couldn't have pleased James more. The fact that Marian had been off all week on personal leave added credibility to the second part of the rumor—Bergman had fallen into a serious depression. He'd been plotting an accidental death for the woman, now this gave him a ready-made plan.

He watched her condo for a few days. If he didn't hate her so much he might have pitied her. Bergman rarely left the house and when she did, only performed errands while wearing dark sunglasses and a wrinkled, khaki overcoat. Her normally slicked back hair hung limply on her shoulders.

The following week when Marian returned to work, she appeared gaunt, and behaved nastier than ever to everyone around her.

Via the Internet, James purchased a large quantity of sleeping pills from an overseas site not requiring a prescription. It had been a simple matter for someone with his computer talents to find out which brand she used. Ordering them in her name and arranging to receive them anonymously had been more challenging.

Obtaining an unregistered handgun hadn't been difficult. Luckily, his uncle had trained him in the use of guns, although curiously, James had never liked hunting.

After work on Friday, Marian stopped on the way home to visit the local liquor store, and walked out carrying a brown paper bag large enough to hold a weekend's supply of forgetfulness.

James watched.

He'd prepared well. The date he'd planned with a young woman in case he ever needed an alibi went so smoothly it bored him. Her name was Eden and she talked about herself incessantly. They had dinner at a restaurant in a woodsy setting near Oshkosh. The food was wonderful and the wine enticing. He didn't order a second bottle; he wanted her thirsty for a nightcap when they got to his house on Lake Winnebago.

When they arrived there, she gave him a mischievous smile and hurried to the bathroom to "slip into something sexy." While she changed he brought out an irresistible bottle of Dom Perignon and poured two flutes, adding his special recipe to her glass. She whisked back into the room, dazzling in a skimpy, pale blue teddy. He handed her the spiked drink and raised his for a toast. "To an unforgettable night with a beautiful woman." After she'd downed the champagne, he led her to the bedroom. She'd be out until morning.

Marian Bergman lay in bed propped on a bank of pillows, a TV remote in one hand, an empty glass in the other. Eyes closed, she snored softly, a noir, black-and-white movie playing on a flat screen TV across from the bed. A bottle of vodka, containing only an inch of the colorless liquid, sat on the nightstand.

She snorted suddenly, blinking her eyes several times as if releasing them from something sticky. She squinted, her face screwed up as if seeing a ghost.

James Wilson sat on the red, brocade chaise next to the window. The white shantung draperies behind the chair had been drawn, shielding the room from the moonlit night and any possible observers.

In a voice slimy with menace, he said, "Hello, Marian. Lovely evening isn't it?"

Aghast, she stared at him, mouth gaping, slack from the effect of the vodka. She sat up, pulling the comforter over her, although the room was warm and she wore a heavy fleece robe.

"You son-of-a-bitch. How did you get in here?"

His mouth stretched into a flat smile. "It wasn't difficult, Marian. You should've installed a security system."

She hissed, "What do you want?"

He pulled out the prescription bottle he'd brought along and tossed it to her. She caught it reflexively, and then held it up to the light to read the label. "This isn't mine—why is my name on the label?"

"I bought them for you, Marian, so you can put yourself out of your misery." He sneered. "Your husband will never come back. He probably hates you just like everyone who works for you. They call you the 'Granite Queen' when you're not around, did you know that?" James sat, legs crossed, ominously cool, speaking just loud enough to be heard above the murmuring sounds of the movie.

Marian stared at him, her umber eyes scorched with anger. Seconds passed. A minute. She fell back onto the stack of pillows. Her eyes had gone blank, unfocused. "I guess I can't deny the irony of this situation, can I?"

"No, you can't. You've been on a self-destructive spiral for nearly two weeks. I'm here to make things easier for you. I'll even give you a choice. The contents of that bottle—or this." He revealed the gun he'd brought to emphasize her alternate option, never doubting she'd choose the one that fit his purpose.

A lone tear trickled from the corner of her eye. She took a deep breath, exhaling loudly. "You're right, you prick. I just don't give a damn."

Two hours later James crept out of Marian's house, making sure he'd left behind no trace of himself after deciding not to get creative and make her leave a suicide note.

When he crawled back in bed with the drugged blonde, he rolled up against her back and nibbled on her neck, his turgid cock almost painful with the urgency of his hunger.

"Mmm," she purred, as she turned over and climbed on top of him.

62

With Christmas over, Lisa, like her clients, sunk into a post-holiday depression—that, and fretting about the bizarre pact she'd made with TJ the *night of the tequila*, as she'd come to think of that memorable night. But Eric's party was coming up; maybe she could scrape up some enthusiasm for the event.

The affair, a '50s-'60s themed New Year's Eve celebration, was held in the showroom of Eric's classic car business. The third year of the event, it came complete with a DJ playing rock and roll, dance contests, and partiers decked out in vintage costumes.

TJ shadowed Wilson whenever she had time. It wasn't an intense surveillance, but she'd wanted to get a feel for his routine. She'd heard from a friend on the force that he'd broken up with the chief's daughter Claire, but TJ saw the couple meet for lunch the day before Christmas. Not what she'd wanted to see; she didn't want to have to worry about the woman's safety. She knew Claire to be a good person. Even without knowing he was a murdering fiend, TJ wondered how Claire had ever hooked up with a creep like Wilson.

She'd agreed to go to Eric's party. Dressing in '50s style seemed absurd but might be fun. Lord knew they all needed—and deserved—some fun.

The thermometer dipped to minus twelve by six o'clock on New Year's Eve. The party was in full swing when TJ arrived, parking illegally in the lot next to the bank across the street from Eric's showroom. She shivered as she ran to the door, the bitter wind icy on her bare legs. One good thing about the ugly saddle shoes, they worked well on the slippery ground. The short leather jacket she wore did little to keep out the frigid air, but it was the only thing in her closet that had worked over the wide, pink poodle skirt.

Stanchions with red velvet roping bordered the showroom, arranged to provide plenty of room for dancing and still protect the cars. The dance floor already sprouted dancers trying to look—and dance—like teenagers from the rock and roll era.

"TJ!" Lisa laughed, when she saw TJ come in. "You look so cute!" Lisa wore another version of the skirt, yellow with a long Dachshund appliquéd above the hem. TJ had only agreed on the costume after Lisa offered to have them made up for them.

"Yeah, yeah. Rollie got my hair into this ponytail thing. I gotta return the hairpiece though."

She thought it all a little outrageous, but maybe with a drink or two she could get into the spirit of things. She hadn't seen Jeff or Eric yet. "Where are the guys?"

"Eric's been running around keeping everything going, and I don't know where Jeff is. They're going to have dance contests and karaoke later. He may be hiding out, trying to avoid getting roped into one of those." Lisa grimaced. "I'm not crazy about them either. Maybe he'll share his hiding place.

Shannon appeared, squealing, "We have to do a song together! It would be so neat!"

Lisa and TJ were saved from bursting Shannon's party bubble by telling her that wasn't going to happen, when a tall, young man sporting an Elvis-style pompadour asked Shannon to dance. She winked back at them as she followed him to the dance floor.

TJ turned to Lisa. "Let's go get a drink and get in the party mood."

"Sure. As long as it's anything but tequila."

TJ, worrying Lisa would back out of their arrangement, hurried her over to the bar. Thirsty guests, dressed in getups from the '50s, surrounded the bar, where the drink specials were the old favorites: Singapore Slings, Tom Collins, Screwdrivers, and Harvey Wallbangers.

After they'd picked up their drinks, TJ maneuvered Lisa to a quiet corner. "Been watchin' Wilson."

"What if he sees you?"

"He won't see me! I'm not following his every move. Just want to get to know his routine."

"It's dangerous. If he starts to suspect we believe he's the killer, he may try to go after you. Or me—again. Just because the police are working on the case now, it doesn't guarantee our safety."

"You're right, but I want to be ready to make my move on him."

Lisa gulped her drink. "*Your* move? Did you think I'd changed my mind?"

"Thought it was a possibility."

"I haven't. We can't allow him to continue murdering innocent women."

"He knows too much now—he'll change how he's doin' things. Anybody could be his next victim."

Lisa's hands trembled, the ice cubes in her drink rattling. "That's a frightening thought, isn't it? I've been hoping he'd be forced to lie low for the time being."

Jeff approached them wearing black slacks, white shirt with collar turned up, and black leather jacket. His curly hair was combed up on the sides, and rolled onto his forehead, Fabian style. TJ thought he looked sexy, but didn't voice the compliment.

"You two ladies look cool and solid," he said, attempting to mimic the parlance of the decade. He looked at TJ. "How did your hair grow so fast?"

"Magic!" She laughed. "Rollie magic."

Appearing fascinated with TJ's new look, he asked her to dance. She handed Lisa her drink, and followed him to the dance floor. The song, slow and sensual, encouraged couples around them to press together, arms circled about each other. TJ reveled in his closeness. He smelled so good. Not of any fancy cologne or aftershave, but his shirt smelled like soap and softener and his hair of shampoo. Clean, masculine smells. The dance floor thickened with couples, forcing them closer. TJ's arms crept up around his shoulders and she felt his arms circling her back, his breath on her neck.

He whispered, "You feel so good."

Aroused, she lowered her face to his chest, enjoying the moment. *This can't last.* She had to be prepared. The aftereffect of what she and Lisa had planned would involve separation from the others. *All the more reason to enjoy the night.*

Eric took a break from watching over the party long enough to go to the bar for a drink. He found Lisa there watching the dancers and holding two drinks.

"What have we here, a two-fisted drinker?"

"TJ went to dance." Lisa desperately wanted to have a good time tonight. Forget all about that monster James Wilson and what she and TJ had planned for him. She hadn't seen Eric in the two weeks since she'd moved back to her house with Shannon.

"This is a wonderful party. Everyone's gotten into the spirit."

He looked over the room. "The same guests come back every year, so I must be doing something right. I'm happy all of you are here tonight. I've missed our little commune."

He took the glasses out of her hand and led her to the dance floor.

By eleven-fifty, nearly everyone was on the dance floor, wearing shiny hats and blowing noisemakers. Clutching small cups of confetti, they stood ready to toss it in the air at the peak of midnight.

Though Jeff had been close to TJ all evening, he hadn't been smothery, backing off now and then to let her do her own thing. She'd had a great time dancing to the old style rock with one of Eric's mechanics. They'd even won the dance contest, dancing wildly to "Rock Around the Clock." Her head still spun from getting tossed around, but she'd managed to keep up and not embarrass herself, thinking she'd danced damn well for an old broad. Not that thirty-three was old, but her partner looked barely out of his teens.

Wondering if Jeff would find her for the midnight dance, TJ stood near the bar, imagining what it would be like to kiss him at the stroke of twelve. She scoped the room, looking for him.

At that moment, Richard walked in with a date.

Irritated, she wondered why Eric hadn't warned her. The woman next to Richard looked nearly his age and wore her dark hair straight, falling to her shoulders just above the scooped neck of a long, black dress. Richard wore a tux; they'd obviously come from another event. Funny they hadn't stayed there until midnight.

So what if he's here? She didn't give a rat's ass, and she didn't want Jeff to think it bothered her to see Richard with a date.

Her heart stopped. Standing next to Richard was James Wilson with Claire at his side. TJ froze in place while time stood still. In the background, the crowd began to chant. "Fifty-five, fifty-four…"

She had to get out; she couldn't be in the same room with the murdering freak—not on New Year's Eve. And she wasn't sure she was a good enough actress to remain visibly unmoved by his presence.

"Twenty-one, twenty, nineteen…"

TJ went for her coat and hurried out into the frigid night air.

On the dance floor, the countdown reached midnight. Couples embraced, kissed, threw confetti, and sang along to "Auld Lang Syne." On the dance floor with Eric, Lisa enjoyed his kiss as the clock struck midnight, disappointed when the couple next to them pulled them apart. She hated the tradition of being passed from person to person at midnight, and quickly edged through the crowd headed for the ladies room.

Shannon rushed in behind her. "Lisa! Did you see who came in?"

"No. What are you talking about?"

"Just before midnight—Richard Conlin and James Wilson came in. With dates!" She stopped to let Lisa process the news.

Lisa gaped. "Conlin and Wilson. Do you know if TJ's seen them yet?"

"Probably. She took off—didn't even wait until midnight. I think Jeff went after her."

Eric hadn't mentioned inviting Conlin and Wilson. Lisa wondered why he hadn't been more sensitive to TJ's feelings. Lisa knew TJ hadn't left because of Richard; Wilson was a shrewd bastard, and the last thing they needed was for him to have even a hint of their suspicions. Lisa took a deep breath and went back to the party.

She found Richard Conlin standing near the dance floor with a dark-haired woman in a black gown. Ignoring the woman, she asked, "Can I have a minute?"

He stepped away from his date. "What can I do for you, Ms. Rayburn?"

"Rather tacky of you to be here, don't you think?"

"Not that it's any of your business what I do, but TJ and I aren't together anymore."

Lisa snickered. "That's a poor excuse for acting like a jerk with no concern for anyone but himself." She'd been about to add a few more choice words when James Wilson and Claire approached them.

Dismissing Richard with an icy look, she turned and walked away, wondering when Conlin and Wilson had become double-dating buddies.

Heart pounding with anger, she found Eric. "Eric, I'm curious why you invited Richard Conlin and James Wilson."

He looked at her quizzically. "I didn't. Claire Thornton's uncle is a customer here. Claire comes every year. Did you know her father's Milwaukee's police chief?"

"I do, but what does that have to do with anything?"

He studied her, frowning. "I had no idea Conlin and Wilson would be here. Claire's uncle is invited every year. I don't question who he might bring, or pass an invite to. I'm sorry if TJ's upset. I'll explain it to her."

The cold air hit TJ like a blast from a fire-hose as she fled the party and ran for her car. Used to spending nights in a heated garage, it balked as she tried to start it. After a few failed attempts, she saw Jeff standing next to the car and opened the door.

"What's wrong?"

Shivering, she stepped out and slammed the door shut.

Jeff put his arm around her. "If you're sure you want to leave, I'll drive you home."

His car warmed up quickly, the heated seat toasty on TJ's cold butt. He hadn't questioned her, which had given her time to have an explanation ready. They were nearly to the interstate when he pulled over and stopped the car. "Happy New Year."

TJ leaned toward him and kissed him on the cheek. "Happy New Year, yourself." *Not very romantic.*

Jeff pulled back into the traffic. "Do you want to talk about it? You must be upset about Richard—I saw him come in."

277

TJ felt torn. She couldn't tell him about Wilson and didn't want him to think she was pining for Richard. "It was just a shock, seeing him with another woman. I'm not upset."

"TJ, come home with me tonight. You can stay in the guest room. I don't think you should be alone."

She *didn't* want to be alone, but not because of Richard. "Sure you're not the one who doesn't wanna be alone?"

He sighed. "I have my own baggage tonight, you know that. But the party helped me forget about it."

Baggage. He had no clue to the heaviness of the trunk-load she carried. When he turned off the interstate at the Brookfield exit and drove toward his townhouse, she was grateful he'd made the decision for her.

At nearly two, TJ crawled into the bed in Jeff's guest room. After a half hour of switching positions under the thick down quilt, she got up and went to the kitchen in search of milk. Finding a half-empty bottle, she gave it a sniff test. Heating some in the microwave, she carried it with her to a big recliner. The chair was comfortable, the milk soothing, and by the time she'd finished it, her eyes started to close. She eased the chair back into full recline, and nodded off.

She woke when she felt a blanket being spread over her. Jeff stood next to the chair. "I'm sorry, I didn't want to wake you."

He looked so cute with his hair mussed and wearing only a pair of red-plaid pajama bottoms. TJ crawled out of the chair. Wordlessly, she took his hand and led him to her bed.

63

James despised New Year's Eve, although tonight he'd enjoyed being with Claire. When he'd turned to her at midnight, she kissed him, but he'd felt the gulf between them.

That party—all those people dressed up like teenagers, pretending the year to come would be better than the last. Pathetic. He'd seen that smug bitch, Lisa Rayburn, dancing with big-shot Schindler, and censured himself once more for mistaking the Ventura woman for her.

Richard hadn't wanted to come to Schindler's party, and James had seen him looking over his date's shoulder for Ms. Peacock. Something about TJ had always rankled James. That whole bunch thought they knew how to investigate the missing women, but they had no proof of foul play. They'd done their meaningless little bit of damage. He was confident the police wouldn't find anything new, so why let them get to him?

After he took Claire home–she didn't ask him in anymore—he couldn't unwind. His hatred of Lisa Rayburn and her band of pseudo-sleuths kept eating at him, and the urge to resume his hobby clung to him like a cloak of leeches. He needed a new subject.

Risky or not, it had to be one of them.

64

On New Year's Day the thermometer remained stuck at twenty below zero. TJ woke up lying on her stomach in a strange bed, the delectable smell of coffee and frying bacon summoning her from under the covers. Turning over, she remembered where she was and why.

She wondered if Jeff had left the bed because he'd been feeling a twinge or two of regret for the night before. The last thing she wanted was to complicate his life—or hers. Too late, though, she'd already done just that. Remembering, she smiled and decided she wouldn't dissect it now, just enjoy. She stood, slipping into a white, terrycloth bathrobe she found at the foot of the bed.

He was setting the table for breakfast, and smiled when he saw her come into the kitchen. "I hated to leave you, but I was hungry. We never ate anything last night." He took her in his arms and held her for a few seconds before giving her a lingering kiss. "Last night was wonderful."

TJ read the question his eyes. He wanted her to agree, tell him they hadn't made an impulsive mistake.

She smiled back at him. "Yeah, it was." She held him, never wanting to let him go, but knew reality would soon intrude on their afterglow.

He broke the embrace. "I don't want you to think I'm sorry about anything. I know this is happening too soon, but it's not like either of us were planning it."

Best to keep things light. "Honey, I been plannin' this since the day we met."

Jeff laughed, pulling out a chair for her. "Sure you have."

He served her half of a fluffy cheese omelet sided with bacon, toast, and orange juice. She picked up her fork.

Back at her apartment that night, TJ experienced that lovely, after-new-sex mood that made a woman feel all warm and tingly inside. But soon, thoughts of James Wilson dispelled her good spirits. Hate was an ugly thing, and it was burrowing into her life like a maggot. She had to convince Lisa to up their timeline.

After TJ left, Jeff turned his energies onto his neglected home, wanting it looking its best for TJ's next visit. They'd agreed to take things slow, but he couldn't wait to see her. She'd suggested a movie Tuesday night, but it felt like weeks away.

He was surprised when the doorbell rang and walked to the door hoping it would be TJ surprising him. When he opened the door to James Wilson, he didn't know what to think. "Mr. Wilson. What can I do for you?"

James Wilson stepped inside. "I'm sorry to interrupt you, but I've been thinking about some of the things you and your friends talked about at Eric Schindler's place. There are a few questions I forgot to ask. I hope you don't mind."

"Sure. I'll answer them if I can. Come on in."

Wilson slipped his coat off and entered the room, taking a seat on the couch. "Nice place you have here."

"Thanks. Can I get you something? A glass of wine, maybe? I have a bottle of merlot open."

"Sure. Whatever you're having."

After Jeff left the room, Wilson reached for Jeff's glass, deftly adding a fine white powder to the dark burgundy liquid.

65

Shortly after ten Monday morning, TJ's cell phone rang as she was about to leave her apartment. She didn't recognize the number on the small screen.

A deep male voice asked, "TJ?"

"Yeah."

"You don't know me. My name is Jon Engel; I'm a friend of Jeff Denison."

"Sure, Jeff talks about you."

"This is probably nothing to get worried about, but—"

That spooky feeling crept up the back of her neck. "Probably nothing to worry about," usually turned out to be something for which the word worry was an understatement.

"Jeff's supervisor called me because Jeff didn't come into work today and didn't call in. They tried his parents first, but I think they're out of town. I know you're a good friend of his, so I thought maybe you'd know why he isn't at work. It's not like Jeff to be a no-show without calling."

It isn't. "No idea. I haven't talked to him today."

"I hope you don't mind my calling; I looked up the number of your security business. I'm getting worried; he's not answering either his cell or his landline. Maybe I should go over to his house and see if he's there."

Rivulets of fear trickled through her. "Do you have a key?"

"No. I hadn't thought that far ahead."

"I'm about twenty minutes away from Brookfield. I'll drive over and check it out."

"I'll meet you there."

TJ closed the phone and rushed out the door.

It took her longer than she'd counted on to get to Brookfield. Getting out of downtown Milwaukee quickly was hopeless during winter. Stacked snow, heavy traffic, and road closures turned the area into a maze. Her fear for Jeff niggled at her, while visions of them together on New Year's filled her thoughts. She didn't know what the two of them were all about; she just knew that right now she needed him in her life. When she finally pulled up at Jeff's townhouse, an extended-cab pickup sat parked in the driveway. A tall red-haired man approached her as she got out of her car.

He held out his hand. "You must be TJ. I'm Jon Engel. Did you bring a key?"

"Nah. I have other resources."

He shuffled from foot to foot in the frigid air and watched as TJ pulled out a small leather case. She selected a tiny silver tool and began working the lock on the front door. It didn't take long until it opened; she'd warned Jeff his security was pitifully inadequate.

Jon Engel frowned. "Maybe we should wait."

"For what?"

"I think we should call the police. His car is in the garage. He could be injured—or sick."

"Has he told you what we've been workin' on?"

Engel froze in place. "You think something's happened to him because of that?"

TJ read concern in his face, but nothing would keep her from entering the house. "I'm goin' in."

She stopped in the opened doorway. "Wait here. If this place turns out to be a crime scene, the fewer people in here the better."

TJ edged into the foyer, letting the front door swing shut behind her. "Jeff? Jeff?"

The palpable silence drew her into the living room. An all too familiar smell permeated the warmth of the room, its presence in Jeff's home a terrifying message of doom. TJ's throat constricted as she entered the room, which appeared to be in order. She glanced at the recliner she'd slept in only two nights ago, the one she'd vacated to share her bed with Jeff. The memory of their lovemaking failed to dispel her fear.

She looked up to see the body of a man hanging suspended by the neck from the railing of the loft, the body dressed in Jeff's clothes. TJ felt like she'd been hit in the stomach by a cannonball. Her knees buckled as she screamed, "No!"

It was too late for paramedics; Jeff's face was the color of winter twilight. Silent tears poured down her face as she collapsed to her knees, struggling to remind herself to respect the room as a crime scene. When her legs would support her again, she walked, sobbing, back into the winter air.

Jon Engel took her in his arms, drawing her away from the door.

She managed to croak, "Jeff's dead," then sobbed against his chest, fighting nausea, berating herself for not preventing Jeff's murder. She wanted to scream out the name—James Wilson.

She hadn't thought Wilson realized her suspicions. But what if he'd seen her following him? If he had, then Jeff's death rested on her.

Jon trembled against her, struggling to stay in control of his emotions. She had to get a grip on hers.

She wiped her face on her sleeve. "I have to call Maggie. She's a detective we've been working with. And the Brookfield guys, too." Her fingers fumbled for her cell phone, while her every instinct wanted her back in the house, searching for evidence.

After the calls, she said, "Jon, don't judge me for this, but I have to go back in." She quickly explained it appeared Jeff had committed suicide. Before he could protest, she said, "I know he didn't. Don't know how much he's told you, but we've all been in danger. I know he's been murdered, but the police might not see it that way. I have to know if he—or someone else—left a note."

Jon handed her a handkerchief. "Whatever you think. I'll wait here for you."

TJ entered the house. *It's only a crime scene. It's only a crime scene.* The repeated mantra kept her focused while she bent her head down, scanning the room for a note. Nothing. She hurried into Jeff's office. The room was immaculate, but his laptop was open. She tapped the return with a fingernail and a Word screen opened. It was there—the note.

To my family and friends,
I'm sorry to leave you this way. I can no longer live with my guilt.
Believe me, this is the best thing. TJ, I'll miss you. Please try to
understand.
Jeff

The note's brevity would give it credulity with the police. They would assume the guilt he referred to would be an admission he'd done something to Jamie. But TJ knew Jeff would never have left a note on his computer. To him, computers were machines; he wasn't a gamer, an emailer, or social-site user. The electronic note had to have been Wilson's idea.

As she turned to leave the room she saw the open door to the guest room where only two nights ago they'd made love, slept together, and discussed the future. She could feel his arms around her as they'd been the night before, see his golden brown eyes searching hers for shared feelings. God, she had to get out of here. She couldn't be in the house when the law arrived. Somehow, she'd have to convince them to test his keyboard for residue from rubber gloves. The bastard would have been way too careful to leave a print.

66

Lisa excused herself when Shannon tapped on her door, certain it wouldn't be good news; Shannon had never interrupted her while she'd been with a client.

Shannon, her face tear-stained, pulled her into the conference room. "TJ just called. It's Jeff—he's dead. It looks like suicide."

After the initial shock, Lisa's first thought was, suicide—no way. But he could have slipped into a depression if his guilt about Jamie and his attraction to TJ pulled him over the edge. Or maybe that was just easier to imagine than the alternative—an alternative Lisa could have prevented if she hadn't convinced TJ to give the police time before the two of them intervened. She wanted to scream and throw things, at the very least sit in a corner and cry. But Lisa had to stay calm. Hysteria and grief would have to wait. "TJ found him?"

"Yes, but a friend of Jeff's was with her. She says she's staying until the police leave. Maggie and David are there too."

"I have to go to her. I'll end this session and cancel the rest of my appointments."

"I'll make the calls for you. Go ahead and leave."

On the drive to Brookfield, Lisa took out her phone. She normally didn't use her phone as she drove, but there were calls that couldn't wait. She called Eric first and told him the little she knew about what happened. "I'm headed there now."

"I'll meet you there."

Her next call was to Robert Bernstein. Since starting their interviews, Jeff had been in therapy with Bernstein. His answering service picked up and she left a message, explaining it was an emergency.

Five minutes later, her cell phone rang. Glancing at the number, she pulled into a parking lot to take Bernstein's call.

"Lisa? What's wrong?"

"Jeff Denison is dead."

"Good God! I'm so sorry."

"I have to talk to you about it—call it a consult if you need to, but trust me—it's important." She waited while Bernstein considered her request.

"I have about twenty minutes between clients at one o'clock, if that's enough time."

"That's perfect. What I need from you won't take long."

Filled with a sadness quickly evolving to rage, Lisa moved back into traffic, all her instincts screaming Jeff had not killed himself. That monster James Wilson had to be projecting his madness on them again. On TJ. He'd screwed up once when he attacked TJ at the Mexican restaurant—actually, screwed up twice including Danielle Ventura.

He probably wanted to punish them for putting his freedom at risk. They'd been mistaken in thinking the pressure would be off them once the police opened an investigation.

Police cars filled Jeff's street; an emergency vehicle sat in the driveway. TJ, Maggie, and a tall man wearing wire-rimmed glasses stood next to the van. The three stood close to each other, red-eyed and clutching to-go cups of coffee.

She rushed over to TJ. "Honey, I'm so sorry." She took her in her arms. Lisa felt hot tears travel down her cheeks and turn icy in the frigid air. She whispered, "You don't think he did this, do you?"

With her lips against Lisa's ear, TJ rasped, "I know he didn't," and broke the embrace.

They had to talk before Eric arrived—and without Maggie and Jon.

TJ introduced Jon to Lisa. He held out his hand, smiling sadly. "I've heard so much about you. I wish we weren't meeting because of this."

TJ said, "Jon agreed to stay with me till you got here. He's going to try to get in touch with Jeff's parents. They're on a cruise somewhere."

Jon left, promising to keep in touch and let them know what he found out about Jeff's parents. They'd need to make arrangements for a service. TJ didn't tell him there would need to be an autopsy, and if they found anything suspicious, it would be days before the coroner released his body to the family. That bad news could wait.

Maggie said, "I'm going to go in and find David. They haven't told us much yet, and I haven't been in since the tech crew arrived. TJ, why don't you and Lisa sit in the car where it's warm?"

Attempting to avoid the attention of the media, TJ and Lisa walked quickly to Lisa's car. Lisa cranked up the heat. "I don't think Jeff would do this either, but we have to consider the possibility."

Nostrils flaring, TJ nearly shouted. "No! We won't consider it." She paused a moment. "There's something I haven't told you. New Year's Eve—we slept together. And before you ask, no he wasn't feeling all guilty. We talked about it, about us, and you know how I hate that. He was happy about everything."

Lisa asked, "Your talk—what did you say to him?"

TJ shot her a dark look. "I didn't tell him he was just another fuck if that's what you're thinking. We agreed to take things slow. We were gonna see a movie tonight, and . . ." she choked on her words and pulled a crumpled tissue out of her pocket.

"I'm only saying we need to be sure."

TJ wiped her eyes. "Being sure don't change anything. We still have to get Wilson. He did this."

Lisa pulled a small box of tissues from the glove compartment. She took one out and handed it to TJ just as Eric pulled up in front of them and got into the back seat of Lisa's car.

He reached over and put his hands on TJ's shoulders. "I know Jeff wouldn't do this."

TJ turned to him. "Tell me somethin' I don't know," she said bitterly.

"Come home with me. I'll give you something to calm you down and you can stay as long as you like. Lisa, I think you should come back too. And bring Shannon. I don't like this. If we're right about Jeff, we're all still in danger."

TJ acquiesced. "Okay, but we can't leave here until we know if they've found anything. Gotta make sure they don't just put this off as a suicide. I called Richard. He and his partner are going to be here any time now—talk some sense into these Brookfield cops if Maggie and David can't."

Eric's suggestion that they move back in with him had given Lisa her out. "Eric, if you can stay with TJ, I'll pick up Shannon. We'll pack up and come out tonight."

Lisa hurried to Bernstein's office. As she drove, her cell phone rang. She glanced at the number. Shannon.

"Lisa, all your appointments are taken care of for tomorrow and Wednesday. Your two Wednesday morning clients said they would skip this week and see you the same time next week."

"I appreciate that Shannon, thanks. Eric wants us to stay at his place again. You, too. If Jeff didn't kill himself, then all of us are still at risk. I couldn't argue—we'll be safer there." Moving back into Eric's estate would complicate things for her, but Lisa would have to make the best of it, work it to her advantage.

"How is TJ? Is there anything I can do?"

"She's fine for now—Eric is with her."

"I can finish up here and leave pretty quick. Should we go to your place now to get some things, then go to Eric's together?"

"No, I have some errands to do first. I'm getting a terrible headache. It feels like a migraine and it's going to be a bad one, I'm afraid."

"I didn't know you got migraines."

Lisa hated to lie, but this one was necessary. "I haven't had one in years. All this is just too much; my body's telling me to slow down. After I'm done running around, I'm going to go home and lie down for a couple hours. That's the only thing that works. I'll meet you at Eric's later."

"Do you think it's a good idea to be alone?"

"It'll only be for a few hours. I'll be fine. You go ahead to Eric's. Don't take Phanny with you; she'll be my protector. As soon as I'm feeling better, I'll be there. I'll call you before I leave home." Lisa feared she was over-explaining, but Shannon had no reason to suspect the lie.

Lisa walked into the Bernstein's waiting room two minutes past their scheduled time. His eyes looked sympathetic, but she couldn't let him make this about her. She took a seat and said, "They think he committed suicide. You know what I'm going to ask you."

"Of course. You want my opinion on whether Jeff could have been suicidal." Noticing his reddened eyes, Lisa realized she'd been selfish in her haste to find answers—he was feeling the pain of Jeff's suicide, too.

He continued, "The answer is no, I don't think he was at all suicidal. But you know quite well what we see on the surface doesn't always tell the entire story about a person's mental state. Our clients don't always tell us everything."

"True enough. But there's something you don't know. He and TJ slept together New Year's Eve. I'm concerned he may have felt guilty."

Bernstein's forehead creased. "Lisa, Jeff was wrought with guilt after his wife disappeared, and as you're aware, on the verge of a serious depression. His work with your group, and the friendships that came with it, pulled him out of it. In my opinion, he was past the stage of obsessive guilt." He sat back in his chair, studying her.

"Most of our time together was spent examining his relationship with Jamie. I believe they were both trying to be the person the other wanted them to be and as a result, found themselves uncomfortable with their relationship. They tried to make it work, but it never had a chance."

Lisa thought his words made sense with what she knew about the couple. "But he and TJ didn't have any more in common than Jeff and Jamie."

"No, they didn't. But they had developed something very special—a strong friendship. Would it have resulted in something lasting? Who knows? I don't believe sleeping with her would have made Jeff feel so guilty he'd commit suicide."

Lisa released a pent up breath. "I didn't think so either."

"Lisa, are *you* all right?"

"I'm upset about Jeff and what this means for the rest of us." She felt him evaluating her response.

"I can see there's more to it, Lisa. But if you don't want to discuss it, I'll respect your wishes. You know you can talk to me about anything. I want you to come and see me when you have time."

She took his hand in hers when he walked over to her. "I'll do that, Robert. Thank you."

67

Eric had talked to Jeff on New Year's Eve as they'd set things up for the party. Nothing in the conversation or Jeff's demeanor had revealed a hint of depression. No, their killer wanted to punish them. Eric wanted to find the man and tear him apart. He felt helpless, but what could he do? He could only try to keep the rest of them safe.

Before they left Brookfield, Maggie joined Eric and TJ. "Richard Conlin's here and he's talking to the Brookfield guys about doing a more thorough search. They seem convinced Jeff killed his wife but never had enough evidence to arrest him for it. They see this as a guilt-ridden suicide, so they aren't going to be easy to convince his death might be suspicious. I'll let you know how it turns out."

When Eric and TJ got back to his place he put her in the guest room and gave her a sedative, refraining from telling her it was strong enough to put her out until morning. She needed the rest.

Teresa chattered in the background, mumbling TJ needed to eat first. Food, Teresa's cure all, bubbled on the stove; she'd made a pot of chicken noodle soup. When Eric walked into the kitchen, Tina had just come in from the yard. God, he'd forgotten about the child. The smile on her face dimmed when she noticed the serious looks on their faces—and her mother's tear-stained cheeks. Eric was grateful Teresa would be the one to explain Jeff's death to her.

Shannon, who'd been staying with Lisa since she'd moved back home, had left for Eric's by the time Lisa pulled into her driveway.

Phanny greeted Lisa with a wet kiss, but she shooed the dog away as she opened the thick, brown envelope TJ had handed her earlier. She spread its contents over the table, seeing TJ had plotted out every move Wilson made while she'd been watching him.

A germ of an idea had sprouted in Lisa's mind after the night she told TJ about James. What she saw on the pages in front of her proved it was doable.

A photo of James Wilson driving a snowmobile had been taken with a long-range lens. His sled appeared to be the latest and fastest, probably a custom model. TJ had documented his habit of whipping across the lake and the trails near his place on Lake Winnebago every day when he came home from work. Wilson commuted to his lake home from Milwaukee during the winter months, leaving his apartment in the city vacant.

Lisa studied the maps TJ printed out. Wilson's home, fifteen miles north of Fond du Lac, sat on the east side of Lake Winnebago in an area sparsely populated with pricey homes. A snowmobile trail drifted past, webbing out from the eastern shore of the lake and branching out into the countryside. According to TJ's notes, Wilson had a pattern of moving northeast from the lake, taking a trail that swung out into a wooded area near the marshlands.

He'll be full of himself tonight; the fiend will be proud of what he's done to us. Lisa hadn't felt so much rage since Lawrence threatened to sue for custody of Paige.

With a few adaptations, the plan she'd devised for Lawrence would work just as well for Wilson. The bastard was sure to be racing his sled tonight.

Although she'd never loaded the snowmobiles by herself, it wouldn't be impossible. She'd take them both. Two wouldn't be as suspicious if anyone saw her in the area after the shooting. Paige usually helped her load them, but Lisa would manage alone. She could make it to his place in a little more than an hour providing her grandfather's old truck started. A lot of maybes, unfortunately, but she couldn't wait for certainties. This had to be done now, while TJ was with the others and had an ironclad alibi.

68

James couldn't stay at work a minute longer after he heard Jeff Denison's death had hit the media. Elated, he headed north to his lake house, eager for the speed and release sledding gave him. The new, custom sled had been a great investment. He couldn't get there fast enough to celebrate his victory by racing across Lake Winnebago.

The motor of the high-powered engine growling in the breeze, James pulled out onto the lake. He'd barely picked up speed when he realized there were so damn many ice-fishermen on the lake, whose shanties and trucks would encumber his ride.

Turning the sled, he pointed it in the direction of the trail.

69

TJ had marked a deserted cul-de-sac where she'd made a habit of leaving her car when she watched Wilson. As Lisa drove into it, she saw it would be a perfect spot to leave the truck and trailer; they wouldn't be visible from any of the nearby roads. Now she had to hope she made it to the trail before Wilson and in position on her snowmobile when he drove by. Her attack had to be a surprise; her sled wouldn't be able to outrun his. The aerial map indicated a low rise adjacent to the trail not too far in from its inception near his home—an ideal spot to wait and get off a shot without being seen.

Last winter Paige had convinced Lisa to buy a new set of matching sleds to celebrate her graduation. Glad now she'd acquiesced, and grateful for the power of the new machine, Lisa drove one of the snowmobiles off the carrier and sped to the beginning of the trail. About a quarter of a mile in, she found the place where she planned on watching Wilson, a low hill next to the trail where she could wait hidden by a stand of pine trees.

Sitting on her snowmobile in the frigid air, the wait dragged on endlessly although not more than ten or fifteen minutes passed. Light snow showers began a steady fall over the area, icing the exposed areas of her face, sticking to the false beard and mustache she'd glued in place. The fat-man stuffing under the men's hunting clothes she wore did little to keep her warm. The damp air seeped in, the insulation serving to maintain the cold against her body.

I have to stay focused, forget the discomfort. Lisa did a mental exercise, reviewing and visualizing the steps of a perfect shot. She was ready.

When the black sled with its gold detailing rounded the bend below the rise where Lisa waited, she had a nanosecond's hesitation. There was no mistaking the custom sled, the rider wearing the coordinating suit he'd had on in TJ's photos.

Lisa raised the rifle. She had him–James Wilson–in her sights. Like people whose lives flash in front of them the instant before death, the faces of Jeff, Danielle Ventura, and the missing women flickered in Lisa's vision. She steadied the rifle and planted three shots into Wilson's chest.

Sixteen-year-old Tommy Rennicke had split only a few sections of oak when he heard the shots. He dropped the ax and looked up, wondering who'd be shooting this time of day. The shots sounded like they came from a powerful gun. He didn't think there was open season for anything warranting a weapon that size at this time of the year.

He looked toward the snowmobile trail. A sled driven by a big guy wearing a hunting jacket, with what looked like a rifle sticking out of it roared by on the trail, full tilt. Too far off to see much more, he couldn't even be sure about the rifle. The guy was high-tailing it toward the beginning of the trail.

Tommy turned back to the woodpile and began to stack what he'd chopped when a thought came to him. The only other rider he'd seen on the trail was that asshole on the black, high-powered sled. He usually rode the trail at this time on weekday afternoons.

It'd started to snow, big flakes adding a thicker blanket to the foot or more of snow already on the ground. His mom wouldn't be home for a while yet; he'd have time to snoop around. Slipping into his snowshoes, he set out for the trail.

70

Heart pounding, Lisa rode her sled off the hill. Back on the trail, headed for the truck, she accelerated the sled to top speed. She couldn't make herself look back. Above the roar of the engine, she didn't hear the sound of Wilson's sled crashing through pine trees, its motor buzzing in the quietly falling snow after it overturned.

Driving without lights was risky, but she couldn't take a chance on being noticed. She'd seen someone chopping wood at a house she'd driven past, but felt confident he'd been too far away to see anything more than a sled speeding past. Within minutes she turned back onto the dead-end street where she'd left the truck.

She'd taken too many chances. But everything had gone as planned. She'd left the ramp down on the carrier and easily drove back up onto it in the falling snow. Securing the snowmobile next to its mate and starting the balky truck went a lot easier than the loading process.

Whatever Lisa imagined she would feel after shooting Wilson, it didn't come close to the reality. She'd never have believed she'd be experiencing the elation of a job well done. *A monster no longer roams free in my world—I've made sure of it.*

Driving back to Oconomowoc, she felt sure the heady feeling wouldn't last.

She had to get home quickly and call Eric and Shannon before they became concerned about her. At the moment she had only one concern–the person she'd seen chopping wood.

But what could he have seen? Her face hadn't been visible under the helmet she'd been wearing. He would have seen nothing but an overweight man in hunting clothes driving a snowmobile. Speeding. Speeding, right after he'd heard shots. But he couldn't have seen anything that would identify her. She'd had the foresight to smear the plates with paste, making it appear like frozen snow. The numbers on the truck and the sleds were indecipherable even if anyone had been close enough to read them.

The snow thickened, coming down faster. She'd take the back roads in order to miss the evening traffic on I-94. It was sure to be a mess in the heavy snow. She'd be home, showered and ready to leave for Eric's before ten.

When Lisa pulled into Eric's garage it was nearly ten. He stood waiting for her when she got out of the car with Phanny at her side. Tail wagging, the dog ran for him. Eric bent down and patted Phanny, rubbing her ears as she wriggled in delight at seeing him.

"How's your headache?"

"The worst is over. Taking a nap really helped. Did you bring TJ here?"

"Yes, she's here and down for the count; I gave her something to keep her sleeping through the night. And I called her sister—let her know what's going on. There's a pot of chicken soup on the stove if you're hungry, or would you like something stronger?"

Chicken soup sounded surprisingly good. "Let's start with the soup. I'm famished." Lisa hadn't eaten since her morning granola.

After she unpacked, she joined Eric, who'd put out two bowls of steaming soup and a plate of biscuits. Eric was a perceptive man; she'd have to be careful not to give him any cause for concern other than the headache she'd lied about.

"You waited for me. Thanks."

He smiled, but she saw the pain in his dark eyes. "Sure."

Eric and Jeff had become close. He probably didn't want to be alone with his thoughts any more than she did.

Lisa sat next to him at the counter rather than across from him where he could observe her. "Did Maggie tell you and TJ anything?"

"Not really, but things got interesting after you left. Conlin showed up."

"TJ said she'd called him."

"Yeah. He was good with her. The Brookfield police wanted to write this off as a suicide. Richard reminded them about your investigation and got them to agree to have the whole place gone over. They even gave in when TJ insisted they check his computer keyboard for prints and possible residue from rubber gloves."

"His computer?"

"Sorry. Forgot to mention they found a suicide note on his computer screen. The usual 'I'm so sorry' thing."

Distracted, Lisa said, "I can understand why TJ would insist on them checking. Jeff never would have left a note on his computer. He didn't even use email."

It suddenly occurred to her none of it mattered anymore. They were safe; she'd ended the nightmare. But she couldn't share it with Eric. Not now—maybe never.

When Eric suggested they put on an old movie, Lisa was relieved to have an excuse not to go to bed. Even her prescription sleeping meds wouldn't put her out tonight. A movie might not turn off her thoughts, but at least she wouldn't have to talk. Or try to sleep. And best of all—she wouldn't be alone.

71

The next morning, TJ staggered out of bed, woozy from the powerful sedative Eric had given her. She pulled on a robe and walked out to the kitchen.

Lisa looked up and rose from her chair. "TJ, how are you? Let me get you something to eat."

"Nah, just coffee. Still a little foggy. Anything from Maggie yet?"

"She told us the forensic unit went over Jeff's house, but we won't know anything for a few days."

TJ looked around to make sure Teresa and Tina weren't anywhere nearby and took a chair at the island. "I'm gonna kill Wilson, the son-of-a-bitch!"

Lisa poured her a cup of coffee.

Listlessly, TJ clicked on the TV, wondering if Jeff's death would be on the news. It opened on a local station where the weather girl, wearing a fur-trimmed parka, stood in front of a giant drift of snow, describing what they were in for during the week—more snow, alternating with sub-zero temperatures.

TJ couldn't stop thinking about Jeff: his smile, his affectionate nature, and his warm embrace. Tears welled in her eyes, remembering their night together. In the middle of a moronic commercial portraying diapered toddlers discussing the stock market, the station broke in with a special announcement.

A second newswoman stood in a setting of new-fallen snow, stiff tendrils of her auburn hair fluttering in the frigid breeze, an upended black snowmobile in the background. She gripped a microphone in her mittened hands.

"Early this morning, on a snowmobile trail in Calumet County, the body of a man identified as James Wilson was discovered shot, his body lying near this overturned snowmobile believed to belong to the victim." She stepped further aside and let the camera pan in. "Mr. Wilson was employed as a computer crimes consultant for the Milwaukee Police Department."

Dazed, TJ turned up the volume and shuffled from the island into the living room where she stood, mouth agape, in front of the giant screen.

The reporter continued. "An early snowmobiler discovered the scene and dialed 911. Calumet County Sherriff's Department is examining the area and has not made a statement. The Milwaukee Police Department will issue a press release later this morning and it will be covered by this station." They broke to an interview with the man who'd found the body, a young man with a nervous facial tic and two days' growth of stubble.

TJ turned around to see if Lisa had seen the announcement. She stood at the stove facing TJ, a wooden spatula gripped in her hand.

Outraged, TJ asked, "Did you fucking hear that? The fucker couldn't even wait for me to destroy his ugly freakin' ass!" She puzzled over an odd look on Lisa's face, one she couldn't read. If TJ hadn't known the rest of them had been gathered here at Eric's the night before, she would have suspected they'd gotten rid of the bastard themselves. She mumbled, "At least the son-of-a-bitch is dead—can't hurt anybody no more." TJ stepped in front of Lisa, who hadn't spoken. "Leaves us off the hook—that what you're thinking?"

"It may not be as satisfying, but I'm relieved we didn't have to go through with it. Aren't you?"

"Maybe." But TJ felt like she'd been robbed. Brimming with hate, she wasn't ready to share Lisa's relief.

The doorbell rang as Shannon entered the room, her eyes squinty from sleep and dressed in a navy blue sweat suit over bunny slippers. She looked from TJ to Lisa. "What's going on? Feels kind of intense in here." When neither of them answered, she said, "I'll get the door."

When Shannon returned with Richard Conlin, Lisa was making more coffee, while TJ sat at the island, scowling.

Richard looked at TJ. "Are you okay?"

TJ snarled, "What do you think?"

Lisa broke the ensuing silence. "Do you want some breakfast? Teresa always makes enough for a crowd."

Richard asked for coffee and sat across from TJ. "I'm glad the three of you are here. I have a question for you."

TJ looked over at him with an eyebrow raised, her dark look replaced with curiosity. What was he doing here?

"Have you heard the news about James Wilson being shot?"

TJ snorted. "Was just on the TV. Who'da thought?"

Shannon dropped a dish. "What?"

Richard brought her up to speed on James Wilson's death. "I've been assigned to investigate his murder. I'm a skeptic when it comes to coincidence. His murder, added to your suspicions about Jeff's suicide and what happened out here to Danielle Ventura, seems like too many deaths not to be related. We're even reopening Marian Bergman's suicide."

"Well, maybe if you and the rest of the MPD would have gotten off your lazy asses, some of these folks would still be kickin'."

305

Richard sipped his coffee, ignoring TJ's insult. "I'm thinking maybe after we met here last month, James might have started some inquiries of his own into the disappearances. He could have stirred something up and someone decided to stop him.

"So what I'd like to know is if he contacted any of you to discuss the case after we met with the profiler."

TJ sniped, "You gotta be kidding me. Like that asshole would discuss anything with us."

Lisa broke in. "No, we never heard from him."

Richard stood to leave. "Thanks, ladies. I'm going up to Fond du Lac from here. I'll be back if I need to talk to you again." He stopped to kiss TJ on the cheek and moved toward the door.

After Shannon left the room, TJ said, "Shee-it. He thinks the 'killer' did Wilson? How off-base is that?" She snickered and looked at Lisa, watching as she tidied up the kitchen. Lisa seemed different this morning; maybe just relieved it was over. "So what do you think? Who beat us to him?"

Lisa kept stacking the dishwasher. "Didn't you say he also did private consulting? He might have had some shady business dealings that caught up with him."

TJ wasn't sure what to make of it. Lisa still wasn't looking her in the eye. But then things were so seriously fucked up it was hard to tell what anyone was thinking. "Never heard any of his business dealings being on the dark side. But with him, anything's possible."

Lisa sat down. "Think about it. Any one of his victims' relatives could have found out about him—decided to take the law into their own hands."

"I s'pose. Still wish we coulda' offed the bastard."

Lisa winced.

TJ didn't miss Lisa's expression. What was she avoiding—and why?

TJ put her head in her hands. She couldn't worry about Lisa. If the pain of losing Jeff weren't bad enough, now she'd have to worry about the cops coming after them. Richard had an agenda—and it wasn't just Wilson.

72

Lisa sat at her desk doodling, feeling at loose ends. Maybe she shouldn't have cancelled her appointments. Her group met tonight; that should take her mind off things for a couple hours. Catching up on paperwork did little to squelch the distractions in her head. She was about to go across the street for a sandwich when the door from the parking lot flew open.

TJ burst into the room wearing faded jeans under a stressed, gray hoodie, her dark curls matted. Despite the cold, a navy pea coat hung unbuttoned from her thin shoulders. Her blue eyes, streaked with tiny red threads of pain, were circled by dark shadows. She snarled, "You did it."

Lisa's pulse stopped. "Did what?"

TJ chuckled as she moved closer to Lisa's desk. "You're good. Anyone but me might believe you."

"What's this about? I thought you were spending the day with Janeen."

"Cut the crap. I'm not in the mood for screwing around. You didn't show up at Eric's until ten last night—it wasn't too hard to put together."

TJ had talked to someone. Shannon? Eric? No use avoiding it, it didn't matter how she'd heard it. "I was going to tell you."

"When? When it fucking snows in hell? I thought we had a deal."

Lisa walked out from behind the desk. "We did. But things changed with Jeff. You know that. I didn't want to tell you yet—you were so upset. I wanted you to have an alibi and I believed it would be simpler if you didn't have anything to hide."

"An alibi? No one knows we had a reason to take out the creep. We're the only ones who know he killed Jeff."

Lisa rested her hands on TJ's arms. "They will—it's only a matter of time."

TJ walked over to a chair and flopped into it. "Yeah. Seems like it has to come out, but I dunno, the bastard covered his tracks pretty good. They won't believe he was our killer unless the bodies turn up." She shifted in her seat. "Now what? Do we need to be worried about anything?"

"You mean did anyone see me? I don't think so. But there was someone chopping wood near the trail—it looked like a kid. He might have seen me driving away."

She relayed everything about her afternoon, including what Bernstein had told her, that in his opinion, Jeff hadn't been suicidal. Under the circumstances, a breach of confidentiality involving a person already deceased, didn't seem important.

TJ agreed the kid couldn't have seen anything linking them to the shooting. She looked at Lisa. "I'm impressed. Didn't think you had the *cajones*."

"I just got lucky nothing went wrong. It had been so long since I shot a rifle, I wasn't sure my aim was still on."

"You know this is gonna catch up with you, right? Now you're all full of yourself for gettin' it done. You'll feel like crap when the high wears off."

Lisa swallowed. "I know. I have an appointment next week with Bernstein."

"You can't see a shrink! He'd have to turn you in."

"No. Not unless he thought I'd be a danger to others—or to myself." Lisa rubbed her face. "I feel bad we can't tell Eric and Shannon. I hate pretending we still have to worry about our safety."

"We don't have to pretend. Think about it. We could tell them—no, I'd tell them—I suspected Wilson. Then after Geo Turner got me the report on him I didn't tell anyone because I didn't have hard proof it meant anything."

"They might buy it. There's so much to think about. And we haven't even had to face Jeff's funeral yet. Do you think they'll ever have conclusive proof he didn't commit suicide?"

"He didn't. We know that."

"Is Janeen waiting for you?"

"Nah. She took me to get my car. Had to get away from her. You know how it goes—she'd smother me with good intentions and all that warm, fuzzy shit."

Lisa smiled. TJ was sounding better.

73

The medical examiner's report pronounced Jeff Denison's cause of death asphyxia by hanging, manner undetermined.

Positive in her own mind Jeff had been murdered, TJ had mixed feelings about its revelation. Except for the fact the missing women's bodies might never be found, it would be in her and Lisa's best interest if Wilson's career as a murderer never came to light. It wouldn't be fair to the families of the women though, if their bodies were never found—or to Eric if he could never prove his innocence.

TJ knew if the asshole had left even the tiniest clue linking him to the missing women, Richard would find it. But now she had something else to deal with—Jeff's funeral.

The service was held in a tiny church just outside of West Bend, a small town northwest of Milwaukee where Jeff had grown up.

Jeff's face remained etched in TJ's thoughts, but at least he wasn't on display, a ritual she detested. She wouldn't have wanted to see a funeral director's attempt to make him appear asleep, postured in a coffin, his hands crossed on his chest. He would have been nothing like the real Jeff, who tossed about in his sleep, hogged the bed, and clung to her during the night.

Jon Engel stood by her side along with the members of the group. Eric, their protector, was experiencing Jeff's death as a personal failure. He stood on her left, devoid of emotion, but TJ knew he was grieving. She knew better than to try and convince him it wasn't his fault.

After the service, a gargantuan selection of food was on display at Jeff's parents' house, another custom TJ abhorred. There must be a lot of people comforted by food when they were sad, but TJ, who normally had a nonstop appetite, thought it barbaric. The sight of all that food made her queasy.

Jon appeared at her side. "Nothing appeal to you?"

She shrugged. "Just don't get the food after the funeral thing."

"I never have either, but I suppose bringing food is something people can do for the family other than just ask, 'Is there anything we can do?'"

"I guess."

"TJ, I have to tell you something. Let's go out in the sunroom for a minute."

Unlike its name, the sunroom's atmosphere was chilly from its expanse of windows facing the frigid, January wind.

Jon turned to her. "I know this is going to be unexpected, so I'll come right out and tell you. Jeff made you beneficiary of his life insurance."

"What?"

"I advised him to change his will after Jamie disappeared. Jeff was too upset to think about practical matters. Since I drafted his will and handled his legal concerns, I reminded him to do it. Most people aren't aware how complicated an estate can get if everything isn't in order. So we changed his will and his life insurance. He left everything else to his parents on the off chance Jamie ever reappeared."

Speechless, TJ stared at him, her eyes wide.

"Jeff had deep feelings for you, TJ. You saved him from himself when he was overcome with grief. He said if anything happened to him, he'd want you to be able to start that business you told him about."

312

TJ didn't know what to say. Jeff had thought enough of her to arrange this gift even before the night they'd made love.

"This is so . . ."

Jon smiled. "Of course it is."

"Can I turn it down?"

"He wanted you to have it, TJ. The insurance company will automatically send it to you. It'll take a few weeks, so you'll have time to decide what you want to do with it."

When she started to sob, Jon reached out and took her in his arms, his large body dwarfing her. Lisa appeared at her side followed by Eric and Shannon. The group—ever protective. What would happen to their camaraderie if everyone knew what had really happened to James Wilson?

Richard Conlin sat in a back booth of the cops' favorite watering hole, nursing a beer and wondering why Jerry Chang, the newly appointed head of computer crimes, had left him a message to meet here at the bar.

When Chang sat down across from him, he turned down Richard's offer of a drink. *Must be serious.*

"What's going on?" Richard asked.

Chang shrugged out of his heavy winter coat. "Maybe I will have a drink—something strong—a shot and a beer."

When Richard came back with the drinks, Chang had a brown file folder sitting in front of him.

He raised the shot glass. "Bottoms up." The shot disappeared, followed by large gulps of the beer.

Richard frowned. "All right. What gives?"

Chang opened the folder and pushed a photo across the table. Richard glanced at it. "That's an *ugly* guy."

The face in the photo was that of a young man with a lumpy, bulbous nose, complexion scattered with blemishes and scars from pimples past, sagging eyelids, and receding chin. Even the stubble of his beard looked patchy as a mole-infested lawn. The guy was hideous. "So who is this mope, and why should I give a crap?"

Chang produced a blue, legal document.

Richard scanned the pages. "You've gotta be fucking kidding me!"

"Don't I wish. No, I dug this up today, unfortunately."

The document recorded a name change awarded by the court over ten years ago in Ashland County.

"I assume the freak show in the pic is Rommelfanger."

"You assume right."

The chief would be livid when he found out the personnel department hadn't found this. Or that his former "future son-in-law" had been a sideshow candidate.

"Are you sure this is news, this wasn't in his file?"

"I'm sure on both counts."

Richard chugged down the rest of his beer. "It's not *illegal* to change your name. Or your face."

Chang snorted. "Yeah, like it'll make a difference to the chief."

He handed Richard a newspaper article from a small town in northern Wisconsin, detailing an accident on a remote highway and the injuries suffered by Rommelfanger ten years ago.

Chang waited while Richard read, then said, "He wasn't expected to make it and while he was still out, an intern took it upon himself to work on Rommelfanger's face. I hunted him down. He told me he had Tyrone Power in mind, whoever the hell that is."

When Chang left the bar, Richard sat in the booth staring at the photo, amazed a face could be changed so dramatically. It didn't seem possible, but there it was.

Sipping his third beer, he realized something was twitching at him. What was it? He sat staring at Wilson's before photo, when it came to him, something the profiler had said. The killer, assuming you believed he existed, had a grudge against women for rejecting him, most likely because of a handicap. With a face like that, he'd have a grudge all right; women would have run from him. But he couldn't see Wilson as a serial killer—an asshole, maybe, but a murderer?

It occurred to him what the revelation could mean—TJ and her friends—this put them on the top of the suspect list. If they'd uncovered this information, despite a lack of proof, they'd have thought he was their killer.

How could he find out if they'd had suspicions? He'd start by calling Chang in the morning. Ask him just how difficult it had been to unearth the dope on Wilson.

74

Two days later, TJ and Lisa met in Waukesha at a Chinese restaurant known for good food and a serene atmosphere. They chose a booth in the rear and ordered a pot of tea while they waited for their food.

Lisa asked, "Have you decided what you're going to do with the insurance money?"

"Gonna put it in something safe—for now."

"Makes sense."

TJ said, "We gotta figure a way to handle this so we don't hafta live like jailbirds in Eric's house forever now we know we're safe and they don't."

"I've been thinking about that, too. Like you said before, we could tell Eric and Shannon we were starting to suspect Wilson, but didn't say anything since it was just that—only a suspicion."

"Hunh." TJ sighed. "All right. If this is gonna work, we have to have our stories straight. We'll tell them I was starting to suspect Wilson. Then I got the background on him and felt sure in my own mind he was the one. And I just now told you—you didn't know anything about it before he was killed. We can go from there. But I'll do the talking, so by the time you have to say anything, you'll be ready."

The next time they all got together, TJ began spinning the tale of her suspicions of James Wilson. She avoided looking at Lisa while she followed the script they'd agreed on, concluding by bringing out Wilson's "before" photo.

After Eric and Shannon's shocked faces returned to normal, she explained why she'd been reluctant to tell them—there just wasn't enough proof. When she'd finally confided in Lisa, she'd insisted they tell Shannon and Eric.

Lisa, as agreed, had stayed quiet during TJ's discourse, letting the narrative play out. She'd been concerned about Eric's reaction, and as expected, he was first to question the story's content.

"How sure are you he's the one? And who killed him?" Eric was angry. Lisa knew why; if he'd known, he'd have gone after Wilson himself.

TJ said, "I'm sure. Anybody coulda killed him. Somebody related to one of the women, a client, maybe even a relative of Bergman."

"Bergman?"

"His boss at MPD. Right before Christmas she overdosed on sleeping pills after her husband left her. They ruled her death a suicide, but who knows? Everybody hated her guts."

Eric stood and glared at her. "Now we won't find any of those women's bodies, and I'll never be able to prove I didn't kill Kayla." He stood in front of TJ, his arms crossed. "You know, if I hadn't sedated you myself, I'd think *you* killed him."

TJ met his gaze without blinking, matching his dark look with one of her own. "I woulda' done it if somebody hadn't beaten me to it. But here's the rub—if the cops find out he's the killer, who do you think will be on the top of their suspect list?"

Shannon said, "Us? No, they couldn't think we did it. We didn't even know about him until now. And we were here that night."

TJ faced them. "Wait—wait a minute! I just thought a' somethin.' If the women's bodies turn up, and they find out Wilson did them, they won't give a rat's behind who knocked him off. We'd be home free." Her blue eyes flashed. "We've gotta find the bodies."

Richard called TJ, demanding they meet. With the temperature still below zero, she wasn't eager to leave the comfort of Eric's home. Since she'd told Eric about Wilson earlier, he was still agitated, shooting questions at her she couldn't or didn't want to answer.

She pulled on her coat and made a fast exit as soon as Eric left the room. Now she had another irate male to deal with. She could handle it, though; it was Lisa she'd been worried about. But Lisa had been great. No one would have suspected she had a secret.

One look at Richard's face when he opened the door of his apartment confirmed she had another fire to put out. He had all the signs of suppressing his fury.

She threw her coat over a chair and took a stool at the kitchen counter. "What's going on?"

He didn't offer her a drink—another bad sign. Definitely pissed about something, he tossed a photo at her. "Guess who?"

Rommelfanger. TJ knew it wasn't a question. He assumed she knew. Should she play dumb? She'd left behind an angry Eric. There was no need to exacerbate that—she couldn't let on to Richard they knew about this. Not before discussing it with the others.

She looked up from the photo. "Ugly fucker. Think I'd remember that mug." TJ, who prided herself on being an excellent liar, was sure she'd given nothing away.

"So that's the way you're going to play it?" Red-faced now, Richard steamed, the vein at his temple prominent.

TJ stood up. "I didn't come out tonight and freeze my ass off just to play guessing games. You want to tell me what's going on? Then fine, we can talk. If not, I'm outta here." She picked up her coat, aware of him scrutinizing her. Clearly he was torn between stopping her from leaving or letting her walk out.

Until the door clicked shut behind her, she'd been certain he'd ask her to stay.

75

The next night at seven, Richard and Justin, his partner, stood on Eric Schindler's doorstep. Eric, dressed casually in jeans and a hooded sweatshirt, greeted them at the door. "You have news for us?"

"We need to talk to you. All four of you."

"Sure. Come on in. You're just in time for dinner. We can set two more places."

"Thanks, but we can't stay long. Just a few questions and you folks can get on with your meal."

They accepted coffee while Lisa and Shannon put the finishing touches on the table setting.

Lisa knew Richard watched the reactions of all four of them. "We've come across something that could possibly throw suspicion on James Wilson as the person responsible for the missing women. If he were your killer, it would also implicate him in the Ventura murder and Denison's dubious suicide. We thought maybe Marian Bergman, too, but we haven't uncovered anything proving her death wasn't a suicide."

Richard scrutinized their faces. "There's nothing really conclusive; the only thread is this." Richard tossed a photo of Ronnie Rommelfanger's face onto the counter. "This is James before plastic surgery. He grew up as Ronald Rommelfanger. He looked like this before having his face destroyed in an accident and a plastic surgeon turned him into a good-looking guy. Makes him fit the profile Orth came up with—the killer having some kind of handicap, now or in the past, giving him a serious grudge against women. James wouldn't have had any problem attracting women, and tracking down abused women would have been a cakewalk."

They gathered round the island. Lisa said, "He would have been bullied mercilessly as a child."

Richard waited patiently until they'd finished discussing Wilson's former appearance. "Whether he's a murderer or not, we have to investigate his death. That said, I have to ask all of you where you were when he was shot. The autopsy report narrows the time of death to roughly from 4:00 p.m. to 9:00 p.m. the night Jeff Denison died."

TJ crossed her arms over her chest. "You know where we were that night—we were all here. None of us knew about this Rommelfanger thing."

Justin said, "Sorry, we're going to need details."

Eric volunteered, "Since we believed Jeff had been murdered, I brought TJ back with me after we left you. I increased security again and asked Lisa and Shannon to move in. They had been staying at Lisa's. We were all spent the night here again.

"TJ and I left Jeff's townhouse together sometime around two, after you arrived on the scene. I drove to her apartment so she could pick up some of her things and we came back here sometime before four. I gave her a strong sedative and she slept until morning.

"If you want further confirmation, Maggie Petersen stopped in later, and so did Jon Engel."

Richard frowned. "So TJ was down for the count, and the rest of you were here all night?"

Shannon stood up, irate. "We explained that already. Somebody killed Jeff and who knows which of us would be next? You're treating us like suspects and all we've ever tried to do is find a murderer for you."

Visibly surprised at Shannon's outburst, Richard had no comeback.

"I'm the only one without an alibi," Lisa offered. She took a sip of wine. "I was with TJ at Jeff's until about two when I left to do some errands before going to Eric's. I developed a migraine. When I got home the pain was so bad I had to lie down for a while. I fell asleep and didn't get out here until sometime around ten."

Richard and Justin exchanged a look.

Shannon shifted in her chair. "Uh, there's something I have to tell you. Well, tell Lisa actually."

The room went quiet as the morning after a ten-inch snowstorm.

"After it stopped snowing that night, I went out to pick up a prescription. Sorry Lisa, but I didn't want you to think I was checking up on you, so I never said anything about this. I stopped at your house to be sure you were all right. I was worried about you and wanted to ask you if you needed me to drive you over here. I let myself in. You were really out of it and didn't even wake up when Phanny barked. I figured you needed the rest, so I left. I didn't tell you because I was afraid you'd think I was being overprotective."

Lisa explained, "I took something to make me sleep. Maybe that's why I didn't hear you. I had an alarm set for nine."

Lisa sighed, relieved when Conlin and his partner left, but realistically she knew it wasn't over. But if the worst happened and she ended up behind bars, it would have been worth it.

When Lisa went up to bed carrying a pot of tea, Shannon, who was staying with Lisa in the second bedroom of the apartment above the garage, said hopefully, "Hope you brought me a cup."

She wondered if Shannon would bring up the lie Lisa told. Shannon had either been there, seen Lisa was gone, and decided to cover for her, or not gone at all and told the lie. Either way, she was sheltering Lisa.

Shannon put down the book she'd been reading. "I was upset they actually thought we might have killed somebody. I did go out for a bit that night—but I didn't go to check up on you."

Lisa exhaled—it worked out better if Shannon didn't know she'd been gone.

"I thought about it, but I was afraid Phanny would bark like she does when someone comes in and wake you up. I hope they'll leave us alone now."

"They'll probably be back sooner or later."

"It felt weird to lie to a cop, but I knew you were there. They might have made a big deal of it otherwise. Then where would we be?"

76

With Wilson dead, the group had decided it might look suspicious if they all returned to their respective homes, although TJ had started spending time at her apartment. Their determination to locate the bodies came to a stalemate when everyone balked at another visit to Geo Turner, TJ's computer guru. That's the only way TJ thought they'd find out if Wilson owned property where he might have buried the missing women. If they rested on the bottom of Lake Winnebago, they might never be found.

TJ didn't work at the bank on Fridays and took advantage of her time to breathe some life back into her business. When her cell phone buzzed, seeing Richard's number surprised her. She hadn't heard from him since he'd questioned them at Eric's. She opened the phone. "Hey, what's shakin?"

"I haven't talked to you in a while and thought I'd see how you're doing."

Yeah, right. Richard never called without a reason. "So, how's the case coming? Find out who killed the asshole yet?"

Richard laughed. "Is that any way to speak of the dead? Nah, the damn thing is going cold on me. The county guys don't have jack, and I think the chief is losing interest. He's assigning us other cases."

"Hunh! What a shame no more taxpayer money's gonna be spent finding out who killed the killer. Guy should get a medal. Hey! Maybe it was Charles Bronson."

"Funny. I didn't say I'd given up on it, did I? In fact I'm driving up to Fond du Lac again to question a witness once more. A kid."

The witness might be the person Lisa saw. "What kid?"

"A kid who lives near the snowmobile trail saw Wilson drive by the day he got shot. That's how we pinned down the time of death. We questioned him a couple times. The second time he admitted he'd seen Wilson go by, but I still have the feeling he's holding something back. I have the day off, so I'm going to drive up there, pull him out of class. Shake him up a little."

Should she be concerned that the kid might have seen Lisa's truck? If he did, it might point the investigation their way. "What were your partner's thoughts on the kid?"

"Justin thought he was just being a kid. He said all kids have something they'd like to keep from the cops."

"Probably right."

"Yeah, but I'll give it one more shot. Not anything else to go on. Cops up there haven't found a damn thing. Thought I'd see if you wanted to ride along."

TJ's mind raced. Was he expecting her to react? She couldn't pass up an opportunity like this; her other work would have to wait.

"Sure, what time?"

"I'm leaving from my desk so I'll be there in about twenty minutes."

Richard thought she looked good, definitely better than the last couple times he'd seen her. Gaunt and weary, she hadn't looked like the TJ he knew. Denison's death must have hit her hard. Jealousy needled at him before he reminded himself the guy was dead. It might not be too late for him and TJ, although he doubted things could ever be the same.

When they got to the school, an assistant principal put them in a small, cluttered conference room to wait while she found Tommy Rennicke. Richard hated the atmosphere in schools. The stale smell of food, sweat, and too many bodies in too small a space reminded him of his own days in school—which he'd hated.

When Tommy entered the room, Richard noticed the kid looked edgy. It had been a smart move to pull him out of his comfort zone.

"Have a seat, Tommy. Good to see you again."

Tommy placed his arms on the table, trying to look cool. Richard wasn't fooled. The kid was nervous.

"Thought I'd come to see you, try to pick your brain a little more—you know, see if you'd remembered anything."

"No. I told you everything."

"Sure about that? You look a little nervous."

Tommy didn't reply, just sighed and folded his arms across his chest. Might be a wasted trip, but coming here with TJ could be a start to mending things between them. Richard felt his cell phone vibrating and took it out. Justin.

"Sorry, I have to take this." Richard stepped out into the hall.

TJ thought the kid was acting like any teenager, given the circumstances, his gaze nervous, on everything in the room except on her. She decided to kill him with silence— that always worked.

He asked, "So, are you a cop too?"

TJ considered how to play him. "Nah, I'm a PI. I'm working the case for the family." The lie came easily and the kid looked relieved. "So you didn't see anything?"

"Just saw the guy drive by before he got shot. He was speeding. That's about it."

TJ read the kid as lying: no eye contact, fidgeting with his bracelet and the zipper of his jacket. She'd have to move fast; Richard would be back soon. She handed him one of her business cards. "You know, if something comes to you, you can call me. I'm not a cop, so anything you tell me can be just between us."

He didn't look her in the eye, but took the card and stuck it in his pocket.

Over lunch, Richard asked if Tommy had said anything to her.

She went with the necessary lie. "Nah, but I think you're right, he's got something on his mind. Have to agree with Justin, though—it's probably just a kid thing."

"I suppose. Which leaves me with nothing. I'm tempted to go to the chief with my suspicions about Wilson. At least we'd have a shot at finding the bodies if he is the killer." He observed her closely. Part of his intent in bringing her along was to see if he could detect anything hidden in her manner. Not surprisingly, he hadn't.

"Opens a big can of worms for the chief, doesn't it? He could kill the messenger."

Richard sighed. "Yeah, but you know that's never stopped me. And don't forget he's retiring pretty soon. He may be long gone before we find the bodies—if we do—then it'll be on someone else's watch."

TJ waited for Lisa to get back to Eric's and confronted her in the garage. "You'll never guess who I spent the day with. Richard."

"How'd that happen?"

"He called me. Brought me with him to talk to a witness–a kid. Pulled him out of his class at high school."

"That's surprising. Sure he didn't have an ulterior motive?"

TJ chuckled. "Course he had one. Knew it at the get-go. Didn't do him any good, though. I was stone, pure stone. Didn't give him squat."

"Then what happened to make you drive all the way out here to tell me about it?"

"First of all, the kid didn't have nothin'. Just saw Wilson drive by. But on the way home, Richard let somethin' slip."

"Tell me."

"Kinda wanted to drag out the suspense a little."

Lisa tossed a paper clip at her. "Spill it."

"Claire Thornton inherits everything–Wilson's whole estate."

"That is big. But what can we do with it?"

TJ said, "What do we do with it? Got it all figured out. You go talk to her all shrink-like, get her to trust you, and find out if the prick had any property we don't know about. Then we find the bodies."

77

Claire's home sat on a street bordered by tall oak trees, lined with lovely old homes built early in the twentieth century, many inhabited by academics from the nearby campus. A broad porch aproned the front of the dark brick house.

Lisa couldn't imagine anything she wanted to do less than interrogate Claire Thornton, the police chief's daughter, but TJ had been convincing.

She arrived at the scheduled time, wearing a tailored pantsuit with her tawny hair pulled back into a demure twist; TJ had "suggested" a professional look and conversational manner.

Claire answered the door sans makeup or styled hair, but still as lovely as she'd been in formal dress on New Year's Eve. "Come in."

Dressed informally in jeans and a white sweater, she led Lisa to a room on the left of the entry decorated in pleasing shades of green, with a shiny wood floor and shaggy, off-white throw rugs. An aria played softly in the background—Madame Butterfly. The poignant notes suited Claire and the room they graced.

Lisa took a seat on one end of a long sofa. "Claire, I'm not here because anyone from the police sent me."

"I suspected as much. My father's kept me sheltered from the investigation."

Lisa had planned her opening words. "I'm not sure if you know about this, but along with some friends, I've been working on a case of abused women gone missing. I consulted James about it a few months ago."

Claire nodded. "I knew about the statistics. James told me they didn't believe there was any cause for alarm."

Lisa watched Claire for signs of a closed mind, but she merely looked curious. She took a deep breath and told Claire everything that had happened in their search to find evidence of a crime.

She concluded, "We've come across something about James I wanted to discuss with you." Lisa reached into her briefcase and handed Claire the picture of Rommelfanger.

She looked at it sadly. "This is James as a young man."

Taken aback, Lisa said, "You knew?"

"My father felt I should. He told me about the facial reconstruction James had after the accident, but he didn't show me this. What could this have to do with his murder?"

"Claire, what if I told you there might be something about James no one knew, not even your father?"

Her eyes widened, her face animated for the first time since Lisa walked into the room. She leaned forward, eager. "I knew there had to be something from his past that he kept to himself—I never did discover what it was. And something . . . something tortured him. When my father told me about his face, it did answer some questions I had, but part of me knew there had to be more."

Lisa knew what she had to say wouldn't be easy for Claire. The woman perceived James' hidden background as something painful, not evil. If she loved him she'd be shattered. Based on TJ's reports, though, their relationship had evolved into something other than a love match. She had to tell her their suspicion about Wilson and let Claire decide its plausibility.

She asked, "Did James tell you we hired a profiler and he and Richard Conlin were there when he gave his report?"

Claire shifted her weight on the chair, looking wary of what Lisa would say next. "No."

"Based on everything we'd found, the profiler believed there *was* someone abducting abused women—a man with a grudge against women—a man women were attracted to, but who had a hidden defect, or possibly had something in his past which would make him turn on them. Something that would have made them reject him."

Claire's fresh-scrubbed complexion paled.

"We think it's possible James could be the one responsible for the missing women. And not just because of what he used to look like– there are other indications."

Claire leaned her head on the back of her chair. As if sensing her pain, a longhaired tabby-cat leapt into her lap.

"Claire, I'm sorry I had to tell you this. Our theory about him needs to be either validated or disproved. We'd like you to help us— you're the only one who really knew James."

"What does it even matter anymore if you're right about him? He's dead."

Claire's manner implied she wasn't shocked. Something about Wilson had her wondering about him. Sexual proclivities? Maybe. But Lisa could hardly ask her about their sex life. She waited, hoping Claire would open up to her.

Claire buried her face in the cat's soft fur. The cat, appearing un-nerved by the intimate gesture, quickly jumped down and left the room.

"When James and I first met, we just clicked. I believed I'd found my soul mate. We got engaged only a few months after we met; I couldn't wait to marry him."

"Did something happen to change things?"

"It was all my fault really." She reached over to a side table cov-ered with silver-framed photos and handed one to Lisa, a picture of Claire with James. They were laughing and had their arms around each other. Then Lisa noticed Claire's face. In the photo, a long, rather hooked nose dominated her face, but she'd still been an attractive woman. She looked at Claire, now every bit as beautiful as a model on the cover of Vogue.

Claire said, "I went through a phase in college when my looks plagued me, but the surgery I needed to change my face frightened me. So over time, I accepted my looks and became comfortable in my own skin."

"Did James encourage you to have the surgery?"

"No, not at all. I mentioned it once and he said he loved me just as I was."

"Then why did you decide to do it?"

Claire sighed. "For all the wrong reasons. James was such a handsome man and women were intrigued with him. I suppose I wanted to be his equal in that way. I had it done in New York when I went there to visit a friend, and I made the mistake of not telling him until I came back."

"What happened when you returned?"

"I was excited about surprising him. I surprised him all right, but not in a good way. He didn't say anything really, but nothing was ever the same again. Finally, we agreed to take a break from our relationship."

"But you started seeing him again."

"I did. I'm not sure why. Nothing had changed. There was still a void between us."

"That must have been painful for you. Did you try to get him to talk to you about it?"

Claire smiled mirthlessly. "Many times. He refused to discuss it." She turned to Lisa. "What are you hoping I can tell you?"

"The women's families deserve to have closure. If James is responsible for the disappearances, it's possible he owned land under another name, in a remote area where he could have hidden the women's bodies. As his sole inheritor and executor, you're the only one who can help us. We need to find out if it exists."

Claire wiped her face with her hands. "It exists. I don't know exactly where—somewhere in the northern part of the state, close to Lake Superior. I can't tell you any more; everything is still with the attorneys." A tear trickled from the corner of Claire's eye. "James told me about it. He said he went up there when he needed to be alone and clear his head."

Lisa's pulse quickened.

Claire asked, "Does my father need to know about this?"

"He'll have to, eventually, I suppose. This is really just speculation on our part at this point."

Claire took a deep breath and looked into Lisa's eyes. "I'm afraid it isn't just speculation. It explains everything."

78

The trip to northern Wisconsin happened sooner than expected when in the last week of March, temperatures in the sixties graced the state with an early spring thaw. The grass was greening in spots and the highways exploded with people rushing north to take advantage of the mild weather.

Richard rode next to Eric in the Silverado, and Claire, who'd insisted on coming with them, sat quietly in the back. They'd secured two of Eric's ATVs on a trailer behind them. It seemed like only yesterday he'd agreed to be part of this wild goose chase, but it had been nearly six weeks since they'd agreed to wait until the snow melted.

If someone had told him he'd be riding to the ends of the earth with Schindler, hoping to resolve a case he'd promised Chief Thornton he'd drop—a case he himself had scoffed at not too long ago—he'd have questioned his or her sanity. Maybe he should question his own. But the chief had been retired nearly thirty days—his fair-haired daughter now an accomplice in an unauthorized search for the bodies of the missing women. As far as Richard was concerned, this was a fishing expedition. The bodies could be anywhere, assuming they even existed.

Eric talked about resorting to cadaver dogs and even ground-penetrating radar, GPR, if today's search came up with nothing. *GPR. Christ, the guy must have an endless supply of money.*

They were headed for Ashland County. The county's upper border ended at Chequamegon Bay, an offshoot of Lake Superior.

Mellen, a tiny town in the northwestern end of the county, was home to the hospital where Rommelfanger had lain close to death so many years ago. Wilson's property, which had been owned by his uncle until he inherited it, lay about five miles north of Mellen.

Richard suspected the group's involvement in Wilson's timely demise, but had yet to figure out how it could have been accomplished. He had to admit, Schindler moving heaven and earth to recover the bodies of Wilson's victims didn't seem to fit with Schindler as a murderer.

The police forces had moved on to other things as the investigation into the missing women became cooler every day. It was too early for the statistics to have gone back to normal, but Richard had become a grudging convert to the theory of Wilson as the killer. Even his partner didn't know he'd joined the group in their search— Richard was on his own time with this one.

Claire stood in the rustic farmhouse, watching as Eric and Richard rode off on the ATVs. The small place remained neat and clean; she hadn't cancelled the contract with the property management service that maintained it. There was little here of James. It looked like he'd never been in these rooms, although she knew he'd spent many weekends here, away from the city. And her. Poring through the old-fashioned house, she wondered if she'd find anything more personal than the furniture. She came across a dusty photo album in an old pie safe and carried it over to the round, oak kitchen table. The album had to have belonged to James' uncle. His uncle's family name and the date were written on the inside of the front cover.

Leafing through the musty pages, she found a photo of a woman labeled as Lorraine, James' mother, holding a baby in her arms. God created all babies beautiful. Sadly, James' beauty as a baby had been fleeting. On a following page, as a toddler, his features had already begun shaping into those of Ronnie. Claire noticed photos missing from each photo event, leaving blank spaces on many pages. Her heart softened with pity as she realized which photos were missing and why. Ronnie had destroyed the photos of himself.

Eric knew the bodies, if found on the grounds, would quickly be linked to Wilson. The group had speculated that the longer it took for the connection to be made to Wilson, the less likely it would be any of them would be linked to his murder. Eric had his doubts. James might be outed as the killer, but the members of their group would still be prime suspects in his shooting, regardless of the time frame. James had been a member of the Milwaukee Police Department after all, and even though they would be resistant to acknowledging one of their own as such a heinous killer, they'd still be determined to find the person responsible for his death. Or not—Eric realized paranoia crippled his judgment.

They covered the acres of wooded land, watching for anything which could indicate a burial site. Eric's heart nearly stopped when they saw a matted, bloody disruption in a last drift of snow tucked under a grove of pine trees. On closer inspection, it turned out to be the remains of a deer that had become dinner for a wandering predator. Its rib cage lay in the shadows, a forgotten remnant of what had once been a beautiful animal. The sickening smell of death permeated the air as they left the scene behind.

Straddling the ATVs hours after beginning their search, Eric and Richard rested on a low hill overlooking a small meadow surrounded by tall pine trees. The trees blocked out the setting sun, even though it was barely four in the afternoon. Guided by an aerial map of the land that covered nearly three square miles, this opening in the trees would be their last stop before returning for Claire.

Richard alit from the vehicle, stretching his limbs. "Man, I feel like I've been on a horse. I don't think we've covered half of this land. It could take days to go over it all."

Eric squinted into a ray of sun spiking through the trees. "We didn't expect to find something right away." The meadow below, thick with growth, was pungent with the scent of the surrounding pines. Something about the seemingly innocent visage made him uneasy.

Richard turned to him, following his line of sight. "What do you see?"

"I don't know. Those shrubs in the meadow look like Blackthorn bushes. I had to get rid of some near the house last summer; they have nasty thorns. Not sure I'd expect to find so many of them bunched together in the middle of the woods."

"Why not?"

Eric squinted in the direction of the meadow. "They're pretty common, but those look like they're in a pattern of some kind." He shuddered at the thought of such a lovely scene being the site of a mass burial. "Come over here and take a look at them from this angle."

Richard walked over to Eric. "I see what you mean. The outer ones almost seem to form a circle. Too perfect to be random growth?"

Eric tried counting the shrubs. "Hard telling, but that would be my guess." Eric's gut told him they'd found the women's bodies, resting in the meadow, buried under the Blackthorns. *Wilson's private cemetery.* His chest tightened with a sickening dread of what they'd find underneath the thorny branches. "Let's try digging below one of the smaller ones."

He drove down into the meadow, the trailer behind his vehicle bouncing noisily behind him on the rough terrain. When they reached the meadow, Richard asked, "Sure you're okay with this?"

Eric sat on the ATV, wondering if they'd find Kayla.

Richard offered, "I can do this, Eric. Why don't you wait back at the house with Claire?" Richard jumped off the ATV and stood next to the smallest bush. There'd been rain the last few days, making the ground spongy and easily tilled by the spade he retrieved from the trailer. After he lifted out the first few shovelfuls of soil, he repeated, "Sure you want to do this?"

Eric, standing at Richard's side holding a spade of his own, *wasn't* sure. It was one thing to be looking for graves, but knowing one of them could be the resting place of his missing wife was something else. But he'd known what he risked—had gone looking for it—done everything in his power to make this day happen. He started digging beside Richard. The fresh smell of the disturbed soil filled his nostrils, sickening him as if the scent were that of rotting flesh.

The bush itself came out easily, its spidery roots trailing a scent of hewn earth, reminding him of hunting night crawlers as a kid. But they hit frozen ground about a foot down. They unzipped their jackets and continued to work their way into the hardened soil. Forty minutes later, about two feet into the ground, Richard's spade hit something solid. They carefully exposed a heavy, green plastic tub about five feet long, the kind kept on patios to store things like cushions and gardening implements.

Richard tossed the shovel aside.

Eric said, "Open it."

"We can't open it. If it's what we think it is we might compromise the evidence. It's time to call the local authorities." Richard took out his phone and dialed the number of the county sheriff he'd talked to the day before.

"This is Detective Richard Conlin from the Milwaukee Police Department. I talked to you yesterday about the former Morehouse land. We're on the property now."

Eric couldn't hear what the other person said, but Richard's next words were, "I think we found them. If we did, I'm guessing there's at least twenty, maybe more. They appear to be marked with Blackthorn bushes. It's getting dark fast. I'm not sure we can do much more tonight." He paused, listening. "No, we can't do any more here until a forensic team arrives. I'll call in to my people; they'll get the state crime scene techs to come out." Then in response to something said on the other end, "We don't want a media blitz, so keep it quiet. Bring tape and lights. We'll keep watch until the experts get here, however long it takes."

Richard closed the phone. "He's coming over to see what we have. I need to make a couple more calls. Why don't you go back to the motel we saw in town and check us in. Unless you want to stay here at the house."

"Sleep here?" Eric shook his head. "No way. I'll make the arrangements for us at the motel, but I'll be back. I'm not leaving this spot until they're all brought up. It's the least I can do."

79

Six days later the exhumations were completed and every inch of the grounds examined. The bodies, which had been carefully wrapped in heavy quilts before placing them in their coffin-like plastic tubs, were transported to the state crime lab for identification.

Milwaukee's new chief of police had stayed in constant touch during the process, and thanks to Richard and the group, submitted the names and photos of the women they assumed to be the victims. The formal ID process, once started, would take weeks to complete.

Because of a four-karat, emerald-cut diamond ring still on her finger, Kayla Schindler was the first to be tentatively identified. The ring, along with the designer dress she'd been wearing the night she disappeared, cinched the ID for Eric, but the authorities wanted conclusive DNA evidence before making a positive ID. With the discovery of her body among the others, they had no doubt that Kayla's death had been at the hand of the same perpetrator.

80

Lisa walked into Bernstein's office for a scheduled appointment. Sitting across from him in a recliner—but not reclining—Lisa told him what she'd done. "My problem is, I'm not feeling guilty about it. For days, I even felt proud of having pulled it off."

"Lisa, as you know, I'm not required to report a crime you have committed as long as I'm certain you are not a danger to yourself or anyone else." He paused and tented his fingertips together, touching the joined index fingers to his lips. "That said, I don't believe you are either of those things, but if at any point I feel differently, then I won't be able to retain your confidence."

"I understand."

"I don't have to give you the technical jargon I would another patient. You're aware of how this could affect you. I will remind you, though, that not everyone in your circumstances experiences PTSD. The fact you haven't, and possibly never will, does not make you a bad person."

Lisa winced.

"Do you feel you've become a bad person?"

"No, I believe what I did saved the lives of many more women."

"Yes, it very well might have. But that would lead us to a discussion of the pros and cons of vigilantism, wouldn't it?"

Lisa paused for a moment. "In the eyes of the law, vigilantism is never permissible. But we both know it's often overlooked—unprosecuted."

"That's true. But if you've come here for approval—or absolution—you're in the wrong place. Have you considered talking to a priest? Making a confession?"

"I've never found answers or taken comfort in organized religion. I believe God is forgiving—and understanding."

He studied her. "We aren't here for theological discussion or debate. I believe the fact that you aren't agonizing over this goes to your inner strength—your faith in your own morality.

"I'm not sure yet exactly why, but I believe part of your decision to eliminate Mr. Wilson goes back to your hatred for Lawrence— your plans for *him*. It's possible a part of you felt cheated when you didn't have to carry it out."

Lisa's mind drifted back in time. *Lawrence.*

He went on, "I believe the support of your friends has been essential to your peace of mind and will continue to be."

"But not all of them know about it. Only TJ." Lisa frowned. "It bothers me that I haven't been able to tell Eric."

"Is your reluctance to tell him based on wanting to protect him from this knowledge, or do you fear what you've done may hamper his feelings toward you?"

"Both, I'm afraid."

81

More than thirty days after the trip to Mellen, Detective Richard Conlin received the final report. All but two of the bodies had been on the group's list. Only one had yet to be identified. After he finished reading, he picked up the phone.

When Lisa answered, Richard said he wanted to see her. She pretended to check her schedule, trying to ignore her racing pulse. Was today the day she'd be arrested?

She said, "I'm busy today, but I have time from noon to one."

"That works for me. I'll bring lunch."

Lisa hung up the phone, her tension dissipated. He'd hardly be bringing lunch to someone he planned to arrest.

They ate the tacos he brought sitting across from each other in the conference room. Richard seemed amiable enough, and when they finished eating, he opened a battered leather briefcase and took out a file-folder. "This is the final report—I thought you'd like to see it. All the bodies except one have been identified." As he handed it to her, he said, "I've never apologized to you."

"For what?"

"That first day you came to my office—I didn't believe you."

"There wasn't anything substantial to convince you with at the time. The decision not to open a case based on the statistics hadn't been yours to make." It was easy to be gracious now, with everything settled, the bodies identified, their killer dead.

Lisa opened the folder, curious why he'd brought it to her rather than to all of them. She read through it, feeling a sense of satisfaction that their work had been the catalyst leading to the identification of the women. Her sense of accomplishment melted into disquietude as she realized whose name was missing—Jamie Denison. She looked up from the folder and saw sadness in Richard Conlin's eyes. She understood his visit. "You want me to tell TJ."

82

When Rollie called to tell her he'd found the perfect setting for her new business, TJ saw no harm in looking even though she was nowhere near ready to begin the endeavor. As soon as she saw it, though, she knew the large, two-story duplex off of State Street on the outskirts of Wauwatosa couldn't have been a better fit. An insurance office had been on the first floor, so it was equipped for a business. A spacious, four-bedroom flat made up the entire second floor. The place had been taken over by the bank when the insurance business didn't work out and was being auctioned off.

Eric had gone with her the day of the auction, acting as her advisor for the sale. She'd gotten a fantastic price and only used part of the money Jeff had left her.

She'd miss living downtown, but she'd only be minutes away. The view from the upper floor where she'd reside wasn't nearly as breathtaking as the one from her high-rise, but the historic riverscape of Milwaukee's Menomonee River Valley would be, nevertheless, an inspiring form of relaxation.

Her eyes welled with tears, remembering Jeff had made her dream possible, and vowed she would make him proud of her.

Busy organizing boxes in her apartment, getting ready for the move, TJ's cell phone buzzed. She looked down to see it was Lisa, but the doorbell rang before she could open the phone.

She wondered who'd gotten in without buzzing. Putting the phone back in her pocket, TJ opened the door to see Tommy Rennicke standing at her doorstep, looking uneasy.

"Some lady let me in. I hope it's okay." He shuffled his feet, shaking drops of rain from his shoes. "Uh, you said I could talk to you about the shooting. You know, when you came to my school."

She wanted to ask how he'd found her, but realized if Tommy had the computer skills of most teenagers, finding her wouldn't have been too difficult.

"Sure, come on in. How'd you get here?"

"I've got my dad's truck—I have my license now. Our school's in the playoffs today over in Shorewood, so he let me use it." He looked around. "Nice place. Must be really cool to live in the city."

She offered him a soda, wondering what he wanted, but knew she had to let him get there on his own.

He looked around as if making sure no one could overhear. "If I tell you something, will you have to tell the cops?"

"Depends. Did you commit a crime?"

"Dunno. Maybe."

"Talk to me."

Tommy swallowed. "I can't stop thinking about it. Sometimes it wakes me up at night . . . I have these nightmares. I guess I have to tell somebody it might be my fault that guy died. You know . . . James Wilson.

"*You* shot him." TJ couldn't imagine where this was coming from. Why would the kid think he'd shot Wilson or that he was in any way responsible?

"Um . . . no, I didn't shoot him. But I found him there. He might have been alive."

The kid looked about to faint. "Why don't you sit down and tell me about it."

She led him to the couch.

He told TJ about an incident with his dad's sled. Without permission, Tommy had taken his father's new snowmobile out for a spin. Wilson had run him off the trail and never looked back to see if Tommy was hurt. "He forced me off the trail and just left me there. I could have needed help. I hated him for that; used to think about killing him—even planned how I'd do it. So when I found him, I didn't do anything—just went back home and waited for someone else to find him—just like he did to me. That's what I never told anybody."

TJ sat next to him on the couch. Tommy had his face in his hands, obviously tortured with guilt. She put a hand on his back, waiting to see if he'd have anything more to say.

He looked up at her. "I saw another guy leaving the trail right after I heard the shots. I didn't tell the cops about that either."

"Why not?" she asked softly.

Tommy pulled off his hat, leaving his hair in stiff peaks. "There wasn't anything to tell. It was just a guy out sledding in the snow. I couldn't see much, couldn't even tell what his sled looked like. He was too far away." He swallowed. "And if he killed that guy? I wanted him to get away with it."

TJ sat back. The boy looked like he was fighting back tears. It would be self-serving, but she said, "If you're sure there's nothing you saw that could help the police, then it doesn't matter if you didn't tell them, does it?" The cop in her cringed at the blatant manipulation; the tiniest detail could be important in any investigation.

Tommy released a deep breath. "I guess not. But what if I could have saved him?"

"Tommy, whoever did it made a killin' shot, and two more to be positive he was dead. Guy probably was dead before he hit the ground, would have bled out in minutes. There was nothin' you could have done for him."

"Are you sure?"

Now for the big lie. "Yeah. I saw the autopsy report."

Tommy Rennicke walked out of her apartment a short time later, standing taller. TJ relieved him of his burden, but assumed one of her own. She hadn't done the right thing—but it was the right thing for the kid—and for Lisa.

83

Walking with Phanny along the streets next to Lake Oconomowoc, Lisa contemplated the direction her life had taken. She felt good about putting the families of the missing women at peace, assuring them the murderer wouldn't be terrorizing any more women. But personally, for her little had changed. Busier than ever with her practice, the publicity caused by the group's part in the discovery had made them all household names. In an attempt to smooth out the rough edges of her life, she continued seeing Bernstein. Their discussions had progressed from James Wilson to her ineffective relationships. She felt like they were making headway.

At Eric's request she'd stayed on in his house long after TJ and Shannon had left. It had been comfortable living with him, but little changed between them. They remained friends, nothing more. On the day of Kayla's memorial service, Kayla's sister Dawn had clung to Eric, apologizing over and over for not believing in him. Lisa knew all about Kayla's family, their rejection of Eric and their input to the police, spinning Eric as Kayla's murderer, even expanding on the most trivial details to cement his conviction.

She couldn't help but notice Eric and Dawn left the service together, or that he didn't come home until after midnight. Eric had apparently forgiven the woman. At length.

After a few days of quickly glossed-over phone calls when in Lisa's presence, she concluded Eric was spending time with Dawn. Not that she could blame him—the woman was striking, a tall, auburn-haired beauty like her sister.

Using Paige's possible return as an excuse, Lisa moved back home. It would have been awkward to stay with Eric under the circumstances, and she enjoyed being back in her own home.

Lisa and Phanny wound their way back to the house. Lisa looked at it affectionately. Despite her loneliness, her home was her sanctuary.

Later that night, Lisa sat in the screened porch overlooking the lake. A half moon lit the sky while Phanny snored softly at her feet. The trees were just starting to sprout, the cool air smelled of spring, newly mown grass, and fresh earth. She heard the ripples of the shoreline lapping at the rocks.

Lighting up the yard, the glare of headlights interrupted the tranquility of the night. Lisa no longer panicked at the sound of someone approaching and knew she'd come a long way since the days she'd been stalked by a murderer. She stood to see Eric climbing the stairs to the deck.

"Glad you're still up."

Dressed in a tuxedo, his tie loosened, his steps weary, Lisa couldn't imagine where he'd been or why he was here. She opened the door to him and sat back down. "I like to sit out here at night."

Eric lowered himself into a chair next to her. "I can see why."

Lisa's skin tingled at his nearness while she chastised herself for interpreting his arrival so late at night as something romantic. "Would you like something to drink?"

He leaned back in the chair with his legs stretched out in front of him, his dark eyes and hair ebony in the moonlight. "No, I've had enough to drink. I was at a banquet put on by the hospital where I used to work. They offered me my old job back. I turned them down and it felt great."

"Did you know before tonight you wouldn't accept if they offered?"

"Actually, I didn't. I thought it was what I wanted until it happened. It hit me that I'm satisfied with what I'm doing now. Along with my employees, I've turned a dying business around and made it profitable. I think your suggestion was a good one. I'll do some teaching instead of going back into practice."

Stunned by his decision, Lisa didn't know what to say. "Let me get you a cup of tea—I just had some heating up."

When she handed him the tea, he asked, "What's new with the case? I haven't heard anything about it for some time."

"Then you don't know about Jamie Denison?" When he raised his brows she said, "Jamie's body wasn't one of the women they found at Wilson's place in Mellen."

"I didn't see that one coming. How did TJ take the news?"

Lisa sighed. "Not well, I'm afraid. She's been trying to convince the Brookfield Police to change Jeff's cause of death to foul play. Now with this unexpected twist, the Brookfield police will never believe he didn't kill his wife—*and* commit suicide."

"I'll have to call her. See if there's anything I can do for her."

"She's at Janeen's."

Eric put his cup down and reached for Lisa's hand. The touch of his hand sparked her desire for him. She felt like a teenager—but he could be preparing to tell her about dating Dawn.

"I want you to come back."

Sure he'd felt the bolt of electricity that surged through her body at his words, Lisa asked, "Are you sure that's a good idea? It was starting to feel rather awkward for me to stay with you." There, she'd let it out.

"Because of Dawn?"

He apparently took her silence as an affirmation. "I did spend some time with her. I think I tried to convince myself that her family really hadn't thought I'd murdered Kayla, until it finally occurred to me what they thought didn't matter anymore. There's nothing between Dawn and me. When you moved out I thought you needed to have some time to yourself."

He'd twined his fingers with hers, his thumb caressing the palm of her hand. She was speechless with wanting him, but unsure if packing up and moving back at his whim was the right thing for her. And she still hadn't decided if getting involved with him made any sense without telling him the truth about James—that she'd been the one who'd shot him. The subject had been hashed over at length with Bernstein and TJ without resolution. Lisa remained torn; she wanted Eric to accept her despite what she'd done, but didn't want to burden him with the truth.

"I'm sorry, Lisa. I can't expect you to drop everything for me. Think it over. But no matter what you decide about the living arrangements, I want you in my life."

Filled with hope for a future with him, Lisa knew what she had to do. "Eric, there's something I have to tell you."

Eric placed his other hand on top of hers and turned to her. "Lisa, I know who you are. Nothing from the past matters; I want you to know that."

Lisa felt the first pangs of regret for her act. "It's something big, Eric. I've been struggling with telling you for months." She felt a lump forming in her throat.

"I know, Lisa. I figured it out a long time ago." He reached for her and held her as she sobbed.

Epilogue

"It's too late to say you're sorry . . ."
Dubai, July 4

An attractive blonde dealer slid the cards out of the shoe with rapid precision; the young woman had performed the task more times than could be counted. Her brown eyes flashed across the room. She saw him standing at the craps table—her husband—but it couldn't be. He was dead. Driven with guilt, she saw him everywhere.

Gathering up the cards, she paid the winners and swept out the next hands of blackjack by rote, her thoughts elsewhere. Not on Dubai, the most exciting place she'd ever lived, or the casino life that satisfied her constant craving for excitement, but on what she'd left behind.

When her shift ended, she stepped outside into the white brilliance of the early morning sunshine refracting off the endless, cerulean horizon. Its beauty failed to calm her. She needed a diversion—maybe a visit to the racetrack or a scuba dive could clear her head.

Then she saw him again. Or was it merely a phantom, an apport, a stalking specter of the man she'd been married to? She'd followed the story online: the police's suspicion her husband had killed her, the group he'd become a part of, the group who searched for a killer of abused women and had themselves been threatened. Followed by Jeff's suicide. He'd killed himself and it was her fault.

It was time to put it right—admit what she'd done.

352

Oconomowoc Lake, July 4

Lisa sat on the deck of her house watching Eric's speedboat fly across the water followed by a skier ensconced amid a frothy wake. Eric and TJ sat in the front while Shannon rode in the back watching as they towed Paige, who showed off with a fancy one-ski slalom. TJ, who'd refused to be left out, had climbed into the boat with the others, ignoring Lisa's cautions about her advanced pregnancy. There wasn't much she didn't do these days; being with child hadn't changed her lifestyle. Lisa envied her; the woman didn't seem to be cursed with swollen ankles, a blotchy complexion, or any of the other physical tortures that came with carrying a child. Lisa had had them all.

At about the same time TJ had discovered she was carrying Jeff Denison's child, she'd learned Jamie Denison's body hadn't been one of the women buried in Mellen. She'd accepted the baby into her life, but refused to believe Jeff had harmed his wife—or himself. She insisted Jamie must have run away, either with a lover or to escape what she considered a humdrum life. If anyone disagreed with TJ's speculations, no one spoke it aloud.

Richard Conlin stepped back into TJ's life, and surprisingly, became as excited as TJ about the baby. The couple appeared to have moved past the fact of Jeff Denison being the baby's father.

Lisa and Eric split their days between both of their residences. They'd been spending a lot of time at Lisa's lake house, weekends mostly, like today, then returning to Eric's during the week to give Paige, who was back for an undetermined amount of time, an opportunity for some privacy.

After they'd eaten grilled steaks and salmon, and played charades until they couldn't laugh anymore, the party prepared to take the pontoon out on the lake to watch the fireworks. They'd stocked it with a pitcher of margaritas, sodas, and assorted snacks, and been ready to leave the dock when Lisa remembered she'd forgotten to bring her CDs of patriotic music, a ritual every year during the show.

Lisa ran back into the house and was rifling through a corner cabinet when a phone rang, startling her. She realized it was her work number and couldn't imagine who'd be calling her at that number on a holiday—her clients called on her cell phone when they had emergencies.

She picked it up. "Lisa Rayburn, can I help you?"

Silence the other end. "Hello? Is someone there?"

It was probably a wrong number.

"Lisa?"

The voice sounded choked with emotion. It must be a patient. *There go the fireworks for me.* But someone needed her.

"Yes, this is Lisa Rayburn."

"Lisa . . . it's me, Jamie. Jamie Denison."

Unable to mask her shock, Lisa gasped.

"I know it's too late, but I'm sorry. I'm so, so sorry."

Also by Marla Madison

RELATIVE MALICE

If It is to Be Its up to ME
I can you can ToGetHer WE can!